The Fortune Catcher

For Haida,
I wish you good
fortune always.
Love,
Susanne

SUSANNE PARI

The Fortune Catcher

WARNER BOOKS

A Time Warner Company

This book is a work of fiction. Names, characters, places and incidents
are either the product of the author's imagination
or are used fictitiously, and any resemblance to actual persons,
living or dead, events, or locales is entirely coincidental.

Warner Books, Inc., 1271 Avenue of the Americas, New York, NY 10020

Visit our Web site at http://warnerbooks.com

 A Time Warner Company

Printed in the United States of America
First Printing: October 1997
10 9 8 7 6 5 4 3 2 1

Library of Congress Cataloging-in-Publication Data

Pari, Susanne.
    The fortune catcher / Susanne Pari.
        p.   cm.
    ISBN 0-446-52071-3
    I. Title.
PS3566.A649F67   1997
813'.54—dc21   97-12317
                                                        CIP

Book design by Giorgetta Bell McRee

This book is for my boys,
SHAHRAM and DARIAN

Acknowledgments

I am indebted to the following women for nursing me through the writing of this book, then shoving me out of the nest: Audrey Ferber, Molly Giles, Amy Hertz, and Amy Tan. It is my great fortune to have your friendship and guidance.

This book could not have found its way without my fearless, tireless agent Sandra Dijkstra. And it surely would have lost its way without the gentle, insightful attention of my editor Jamie Raab. I could not have hoped for better. Thank you both.

My everlasting appreciation to those who devoted their time over the years: Melba Beales, Linden Berry, Judy Breen, Asa DeMatteo, Chitra Divakaruni, Diana Fuller, Debra Ginsberg, Lisa Glatt, William Hamill, Danielle D'Octavio Harned, Jean B. Kelley, Gus Lee, Aaron and Nadine Matityahu, Timothy Truitt Mizelle, Blair Moser, Roxanne Dunbar Ortiz, Gretchen Schields, Roshanak S., Kelly Simon, the Squaw Valley Community of Writers, and Michael Strong.

Deep love and gratitude to my father for his patience with my questions, to my mother for her enthusiasm and belief in me, to my sister for unlimited ear time, and my brothers—uncles extraordinaire. Much thanks to Mahdad and Manaz N., for scouring the manuscript for flaws and to my sister-in-law Elham for excellent pep talks. Thank you to my dear friends Sara Bar Gadda, Sharareh Bijan, Carol Hodges, Alice Kleeman, and Laura Rich, for their warmth and support. And, of course, my love to Sara Levai who inspires me every day, despite the unbreachable distance between us.

Seeking a refuge from the cruel battering of Fortune
We have come.

Hafez, 14th century

The Fortune Catcher

One

Layla

We were married in secret on September 22, 1981. It was the thirtieth of *Mehr*, the Persian Month of Kindness, in the Iranian year 1360. I wore gray wool instead of white lace, and Dariush wore military fatigues. There was no satin wedding cloth spread before us to bear candles and a mirror and all the traditional Zoroastrian fertility symbols. And no one grating sugar cones or offering us honey to assure the sweetness of our union. Maybe I would regret the absence of these things later, but at that moment I was a bride, and everything sparkled like the Caspian Sea at midday.

The simple ceremony was performed by an old friend of my father's, a high priest, almost an *ayatollah*, a religious man who was not a religious fanatic—a thing as difficult to ferret out in post-revolutionary Tehran as a girl in a miniskirt. The witnesses were Dariush's father and their old cook's son, Jamsheed, who was the only trusted servant left in the house. The four of us stood stiffly, nervously, between the Louis XV chairs Dariush's mother had brought from Europe in the days when it wasn't a crime to import Western things.

After the ceremony, we packed only necessities and waited for dark. Dariush bundled his fatigues and told Jamsheed to burn them in the barbecue pit. His other clothes had been confiscated by the induction officers when we'd arrived at Mehrabad Airport a month before. He put on an old frayed suit that had belonged to one of the chauffeurs; it fit him badly—too wide and too short— but no one had the good humor to laugh at his appearance. In fact, Dariush's father, Hooshang, coughed quietly and turned away, tears in his eyes. I felt sorry for him and thought of Dariush's mother, Veeda, exiled to France because the insulin supply in Iran was now so unreliable. And I thought of my own father, also in France, and of my governess Banu—as close to me as my mother might have been—in New York, both of them ago- nizing over my safety and over their helplessness. A familiar pang of self-disgust washed over me. How could I have deserted them? How could I have ignored their warnings about the inhumanity I would face here? How could I have so ignorantly thought I could rescue my future from the hungry lion of the Revolution? I swal- lowed and touched Dariush's arm. It was time to go.

We said our solemn good-byes and rode a taxi to what had once been the Royal Tehran Hilton. We held hands on the sticky vinyl seat and tried to suppress giggles over the triumph of our marriage. Giggles were dangerous. They could raise suspicions. Who giggled nowadays? Certainly not the pious. Such a thing could get you arrested.

The bridal suite was sparsely furnished: just a sofa covered with a stained sheet in the sitting room; a king-size bed, straight-back chair, and a table with a broken lamp on it in the bedroom. The rest of the furniture had no doubt been stolen by laid-off hotel workers. It didn't matter. We wanted only the bed. It had been too long and there had been too many obstacles. I smiled to myself, victorious. I'd defied what the blind fortune catcher had predicted seven years ago. Dariush and I were together.

A sense that the bed was empty woke me. I bolted upright and wiped frantically at the sleep flakes in my eyes. But *there* were his clothes still puddled on the floor next to my own. And *there* was the water running in the bathroom. I fell back against the sheets and breathed deeply to calm myself. Beyond a slit in the drapes, the sky looked faintly silver with the approach of dawn. I imagined myself in Manhattan, walking in Central Park, autumn leaves falling around me like crisp orange feathers. It wouldn't be long now, I told myself. Thanks to Dariush's old friend Amir, Dariush wasn't going to fight in the war against Iraq, and I wasn't going to wait for him with the false hope that he could come back alive. We would be leaving the Islamic Republic of Iran. We'd been fools to come back.

I felt something sharp in the palm of my hand and remembered: Dariush's gold medallion inscribed with the word *Allah*, the word for God. His grandmother—*Maman Bozorg*, the Big Mother—had given it to him when he was born (as my grandmother had given me mine) and he'd worn it safety-pinned to his clothing until he was old enough to wear it on a chain. I'd slipped it over his head while we'd made love because I couldn't stand it dangling between us as if that wicked old woman were still dangling between us. It had been Maman Bozorg who had lured us—from thousands of miles away, with thousands of cultural dimensions between us—back to the country of our birth.

Dariush emerged from the bathroom, and I slid the medallion under the pillow so I wouldn't have to look at it anymore.

"Good morning, my beautiful wife," he said in Farsi, sliding on top of me, kissing me, tasting like toothpaste.

"Good morning, my gorgeous husband," I said in English, relishing the word I'd wanted to use for as long as I could remember.

"I've ordered us breakfast," he said.

"Good. I'm starving."

"Too much physical activity," he said, raising an eyebrow.

"Or not enough," I said, pressing my palms to his cheeks. His dark, arched eyebrows were so much more pronounced now that he had a soldier's haircut. He looked more like the Persian boy he was. His fair hair, golden in the summer, thick, wavy, and worn long, had caused him always to be mistaken for a foreigner. I slid my hands down his silky naked back, sensing the location of his faint tan line from the French sunshine we'd bathed in less than five weeks ago, but a lifetime ago, before all the trouble.

Someone knocked at the door and we froze, staring, anxiety passing like current between our eyes. Dariush tried a small smile. "Breakfast," he whispered.

"Right," I said. "But look through the peephole. Make sure."

"No one knows we're here."

I squeezed his arm gently. "Make sure," I repeated.

He kissed me quickly. The knock came again, urgently. "Don't worry," he said, vaulting from the bed. He pulled on his pants and disappeared into the sitting room, closing the door behind him. I reached for my long silk blouse and hastily put it on, buttoning two buttons. Quickly, I fished Dariush's fat Swiss army knife from the duffel and ran to stand behind the door. While I tried to hear what was going on—to detect disaster—I groped at the metal contraption in my hands. Shaking, I managed to pull out first a corkscrew, then a toothpick, three different nail files, a miniature spoon, and, finally, a wrench. By then, Dariush peeked around the door. "What are you doing there, *divaneh?*"

I leaned against the wall, my heart racing. "*You're* the crazy one, opening the door so innocently."

He pulled me to him. "Stop worrying so much. Nothing is going to happen to us now. Everything is arranged. You've got to get ahold of yourself." I breathed in the almondy smell of him, wanting to bury myself in the warmth of his neck. "Come on," he said. "Let's eat. Let's celebrate."

We sat on the floor, our backs against the sofa, and stuffed ourselves with bread and goat's cheese and honeycomb. We ate with our fingers, remembering aloud how, as children, we'd both often sneaked into the servants' rooms at mealtimes because we liked to watch them eat with their hands, folding rice and meat and greens into soft, dampened *lavash* bread and balancing it on their fingers before cramming it into their wide mouths. How much more tasty their food seemed than ours. Licking our fingers, we stretched out on the carpet as if we had all the time in the world. The sky had turned a pale pink. The dented aluminum tray that had held our food was empty except for two small oranges that I suggested we take for the ride to the airport.

This broke the spell, and Dariush looked at his watch. "It's time to get ready. The driver will be here at seven."

I sat up. "Whose driver?"

"Bijan, the driver from my father's clinic."

"But Amir said we should take a taxi to the airport."

He shook his head. "Bijan is totally trustworthy, Layla."

"But Amir said—"

He rolled over and silenced me with a kiss, then looked at my face, coiling wisps of my hair around his fingers. "Don't believe everything Amir tells you." It wasn't the first time since he'd come back from the training camp a week ago that I'd seen this caution and a hint of annoyance in his eyes about Amir.

"What is it with you two?" I said. "I thought you were friends. He didn't have to help us. He could've said no."

Dariush kissed me again. "As always, my love, you're right."

I pushed gently at his shoulder. "Don't patronize," I said.

He looked surprised. "I'm not."

"Seriously," I said. "What's the story with you and Amir?"

He rolled over onto his back and rubbed his eyes. "Nothing. We were friends a long time ago."

"That's it?" I asked, running the tips of my fingers over his chest.

"That's it," he said.

I leaned over him and let my long hair puddle onto his bare shoulder. "So you don't trust him?"

He nuzzled his face into the strands, breathing deeply. His voice husky, he said, "I don't want to talk about Amir, Laylee. Not now. There'll be plenty of time later, when this is all over."

We had only one small suitcase and two handbags—a far cry from the old days when luggage had to be sent to the airport in a separate car. Dariush went down to settle the bill while I finished dressing. This was no pleasant matter for a woman in the new Islamic Republic of Iran, a woman whose duty it was to repel men, a woman who would be expected to take the blame if a man were to become sexually aroused by her. So no makeup, no nail polish, no bright colors. I checked for runs in my thick stockings and slipped on my sensible pumps. On top of my gray skirt and blouse, I donned an ankle-length overcoat called a *roopoosh* or a *manteau*. Then I began the important job of folding my enormous opaque head scarf. I had learned to be glad for the *manteau* and scarf; they were a more modern Islamic uniform than a *chador*, which tended to billow and slide because it was nothing more than an oval length of fabric that a woman had to clasp—in the face of all kinds of weather and urban mishap— around her face or under her chin. Wearing a *chador* took prac- tice, something I didn't have.

I used the bathroom mirror to arrange my black scarf, careful to hide every strand of my hair beneath the cloth. I slid the scarf forward until the rim reached the tops of my eyebrows, then expertly tucked the fabric under itself at the corner of my eyes so it was flush against my forehead. There. Regulation Iranian woman: pale and hunched down as if peeking out of a small hole in the dirt. Perfect.

I took one last look out that window on the fifteenth floor. A strip of gray smog hung over the downtown area from too many old cars spewing smoke and burning oil. All across the imme- diate skyline stood unfinished high-rises, begun before the Revolution three years earlier and now looking like gutted buildings, haunted by cranes that hung rusty from abandon- ment. Business had been booming.

I took a deep breath and looked at my watch. Why hadn't Dariush called up for me yet? The driver was probably late. Dariush hated it when people were late. I imagined him pacing the lobby, scowling, his frown lines more prominent in that strange military crew cut. My stomach churned suddenly. Could something have gone wrong?

I crossed the vast marble-floored lobby and whispered the word "Calm" to myself with every echoing step. The male receptionist behind the desk shouted at someone over the telephone about a broken toilet. Three fat men in Arab dress sat across the room whispering in rugged sounds. No Dariush. Maybe he was wait- ing outside for the driver. I passed the cordoned-off stairway that had once led to a posh beauty salon; the hand railing, detached from the wall, hung like a loose tooth. I rounded the corner and the hotel's front entrance came into full view. I stopped in my tracks. Beyond the two sets of automatic glass doors, where there had always stood uniformed footmen, was Dariush, his back to me, flanked by several unshaven, sleepy-eyed but sneering *pasdaran*, the menacing revolutionary guards whose job it was to enforce ever-changing interpretations of the law. They pointed their Uzis lazily at him as a military jeep pulled up and deposited a grizzled officer in a heavy coat. The *pasdaran* stepped back a little. The man stared directly at Dariush, his lips set in an angry line. I knew who he was from Dariush's description: face scarred from smallpox and hair silver and wiry like steel wool. The general, the man who'd told Dariush that an angel from heaven had whispered to him the strategy by which to win the war with Iraq, the man who considered Dariush his favorite officer.

In one swift motion, the general slapped my husband's face with the back of his hand. I felt my body lurch forward, saw Dariush fall to the side against a *pasdar* who righted him roughly. I saw his blood spatter to the pavement. I'd begun to run toward them when I realized I was moving in the wrong direction. I couldn't save Dariush this way. If I went to him, they would arrest me, too. It didn't matter that I wasn't a deserter; I would be the *reason* for my husband's desertion. I had to get ahold of Amir. Quickly, I turned and retraced my steps, trying not to run, hoping that I hadn't already roused the hotel clerk's attention. I pushed the elevator button but soon realized that I couldn't go back to the suite because I didn't have a key. Where was the public telephone? The sour taste of bile covered my tongue. I rushed across the lobby again, looking at the floor to avoid what I sensed were the stares of the Arab men, and descended the spiral staircase that led to the restaurant. How many minutes had passed? How long did I have? The restaurant was closed, but there was a public phone and, luckily, no one around to hear me speak into it. I dialed the number I'd learned by heart. It rang ten times. My hand shook as I dialed it again to be sure. Still no answer. I dashed up the staircase, my shoulder bag bouncing wildly against my thigh. I would go to Dariush. What else could I do? Whatever happened, at least we would be together.

But I was too late. Just as I rounded the corner again, the military jeep pitched forward, and I glimpsed my husband's bloodied cheek through the back window as the vehicle sped off. I slowed and approached the doors, the pulse in my ears blocking out everything. The *pasdaran* lit cigarettes and let their guns hang loosely from their shoulders. I reached the glass door pane, not caring if they noticed me, and viewed the circular drive. Empty.

The fortune catcher had been right. I was alone.

Two

The Eve of Red Wednesday

March 1974
Esfand, The Month of Wild Rue, 1352

It is Dariush's Aunt Katayoon who hires the fortune catcher for a party she gives on the Eve of Red Wednesday. She tells him to come late, after dinner, after the Fire Jumping celebration, when everyone will be sated and pleasantly tired—and happy that the holiday has finally begun.

The blind man is the latest fashion in soothsaying. The previous summer, it was the Pakistani woman who read palms; she was rented for all the afternoon bridge parties. The winter before, it was a gypsy who interpreted Turkish coffee grains. And of course, there is always any number of card-reading clairvoyants for hire who say they can find and catch anyone's destiny in a matter of minutes. But these fortune catchers are not so fascinating to guests anymore. Katayoon is certain, however, that the blind man will make her party especially successful.

She finishes her makeup and looks at her face in the gilded mirror that was made for her marriage cloth nineteen years ago. She decides that she has aged well; perhaps she can wait another five years before a face-lift. Thirty-eight is a good age, she thinks. Not young, not old. But a widow must always strive to look younger, otherwise everyone wants her to become a woman who wears heavy brown shoes and never dyes her hair and does not need to visit the couture shows in Milano. Katayoon shivers at these thoughts. What would her life be like? She takes a sip of her vodka and tonic; the ice tinkles delicately in the silence of her bedroom. She looks at her watch and quickly gets up to dress in the wool trousers and argyle sweater her maid has laid out for her. Donning a fat row of stiff gold bracelets, she peers out the window onto the marble patio where the women servants rush about in their flip-flop shoes and *chador*s, putting cushions on the wrought-iron furniture and platters of mixed nuts and dried fruits on low tables. Her sharp eye takes in everything. She cracks the window open and yells down instructions for Habibeh to have the cook begin warming the *absh*; the guests will begin arriving soon.

Katayoon feels the crisp night air on her face. She smiles. It is as it should be in *Esfand*, the Month of Wild Rue, the last month before the Persian New Year. Not cold, not hot; a promise of warmth in the breeze. The mountains still gleam with snow, yet the air smells like hyacinth flowers and mint. She hears the doorbell. Who will be first? she wonders. She plays this game with herself every time. There are no foreigners invited tonight; they are always first, especially the Germans. And her sister-in-law Veeda is in Spain; she usually comes early to help pare the tomato skins into roses for the salad. If Katayoon's mother-in-law were coming, as she threatened to, she would have guessed her to be the first, but thank God the old woman had, once again, declined to join the living. But Maman Bozorg was no doubt sitting stiffly in her house across the family compound, beyond the apple and peach orchards, seething about something or other.

Katayoon notices her daughter, Mariam, in the garden beyond the patio. She stands under a poplar tree watching the houseboys lay out the *botteh*s for the fires. Katayoon grimaces; so Mariam did not wear the blue jeans she suggested, after all. Black gabardine slacks and that turtleneck sweater—so large it does not show anything of her fine figure. Katayoon wonders if she will always have to battle her mother-in-law's conservative influence over Mariam.

Beneath Katayoon's window, a girl with long, glistening hair the color of mink emerges from the house. Of course, Katayoon says to herself, I should have guessed Layla would be the first to arrive. She has not seen Mariam since the summer. Layla walks with the determined step Katayoon knows so well across the patio to the garden; she wears American-made blue jeans and fat brown boots that Katayoon remembers, with a smile, her friend Lisa from the Tehran American Club calls shit-kickers.

How tall Layla has grown, Katayoon thinks. She is as tall as most Iranian men. All that American milk, she chuckles to herself. And skinny; she is perfectly skinny. She watches Layla and her daughter embrace and kiss and giggle. She cannot believe they have grown so much; eighteen years old, both of them, and still best friends though an ocean has divided them for most of every year of their lives.

Katayoon sees the top of Ebrahim Bahari's bald head appear below her. She quickly slips on her shoes and makes her way through the house, eager to see her friend. Layla's father has always been special to her; she will never forget how he had comforted her after Mahmoud's death; how he had advised her to resist her mother-in-law's manipulations to move in with the old woman. Katayoon is always thrilled to see Ebrahim; she often wishes he had never moved to New York, but she knows how sorrow can propel a person to make unexpected decisions.

Layla and Mariam stand back and observe one another. They look for changes; they recognize even the most subtle ones: a few pounds, a new mole, a lighter shade of lipstick, the movement of a favorite bracelet from one wrist to another. And they look for deeper changes, changes that might have been too secret to put in any of their letters. But before they can begin to talk, the person they both love most in the world makes them forget one another.

"My favorite cousin," says Dariush, wrapping his arm around Mariam's shoulder and leaning down to kiss a blushing cheek. "And Layla," he says, reaching for her in the same way so that the three of them stand for a moment together, as if the love among them is symmetrical.

Layla slithers away, and Dariush feels his skin prickle beneath his sweater. She smiles at him carefully and says, "Aren't you supposed to be studying for midterms back in Boston?"

"*I* thought," says Mariam, resting her head on her cousin's shoulder, "you were supposed to be in Madrid with your parents."

He looks at Layla. "Yes, I should be studying for midterms." He looks down at Mariam. "The bullfighting was too much for my mother. Besides, we missed the celebrations back home."

"I knew you would," says Mariam. "No one should be away for the *Norooz* holiday. Now even Layla is here."

"Yes she is," says Dariush, looking, for the first time, directly into Layla's eyes. She looks back at him and he realizes, with relief, that nothing has changed. It does not matter that they have been apart for so many months, that he has not called her or visited her despite their physical proximity—he sees in her green eyes that she remembers everything that has ever happened between them. He watches her for as long as he dares in Mariam's presence. Her hair is longer, he thinks. She has lost weight. He wants to touch her cheek. But everything between them has always been secret.

Mariam is talking, her voice pitched high and excited. Now she holds Dariush's hand and looks from him to Layla. "Isn't it wonderful that we can all be together for *Norooz*? It's so much more sensible to begin the New Year on the first day of spring instead of in *Janvier*, isn't it?"

Mariam's legs feel syrupy; she is surprised that Dariush is here. She smiles up at her cousin, thinking of how best to have him to herself for a little while. She and Layla will have plenty of time to talk later. Having Dasha here is a treat; she has never become used to him living far away. And when he comes home for vacations, he is always rushing here and there; he has too many friends. She suddenly points to the patio. "Your father is calling to you, Layla. And there, my mother's looking this way, too. I think we have to go and say hello to everyone."

The patio is filled with guests now. Auntie This and Uncle That and Cousin So-and-So. Everyone has relatives here, yet not everyone is immediately related; perhaps their ancestors were related. And if not, their families have been friends for generations or at least as far back as the grandparents can remember.

Mariam leads her cousin through the crowd. Her cheeks become tired from smiling and kissing, and she is bored with all the same questions, about her studies in Switzerland and about the ski conditions in the Alps. Everyone jokes with Dariush, asking him if he needs money to bribe the Harvard president to graduate him; they want to know why he has grown his hair so long and if he is trying to imitate James Bond in his black turtleneck. Mariam bites the inside of her cheek; she is so angry she wants to spit at these people. He is beautiful, she thinks, with such long, wavy, fair hair and his sweet dimples and teasing smile. But he does not care about these things, does not pay attention to the guests' playful mocking. Mariam notices that he glances across the patio, and she follows his gaze.

Layla. There she is, blushing and bowing politely to the older matrons, who sit tightly wrapped in their tailored suits. Our chameleon, thinks Mariam; so perfectly behaved in all the places of the world—so American, so Iranian. Now she stands next to her father and smiles at all those people who kiss and pinch her cheeks and run their palms over her silky hair. They stand back to look at her as if she is some kind of unique doll sculpted from gold. Mariam's palms feel damp, and she closes her eyes briefly: I cannot think this way; I love her. She whispers in Dariush's ear, "Let's go rescue Layla."

Beneath the poplar tree, a servant offers them bowls of *ahsh* from a tray. "Don't forget to make a wish, Layla," says Mariam.

"I never forget," says Layla, shaking her head, sneering playfully. "I've eaten this lucky noodle soup every year for my whole life; it's the same lucky noodle soup if you eat it in New York or Tehran."

Dariush raises his spoon slightly. "Well said," he says. "And if the wishes don't come true, at least the soup will make us warm."

The three of them sip their thick *ahsh* and silently wish—a triangle of wishes, all secretly intersecting.

"So Layla," says Mariam, reaching up to remove a thread from Dariush's sweater. "Have you practiced the proper phrase for the Fire Jumping?"

Dariush sees Layla close her eyes in irritation for a second. "I know the phrase, Mimish," she says curtly.

"Of course she knows the phrase," says Dariush. "Her father told me that they always go out onto the rooftop terrace in Manhattan and he flicks his cigarette lighter on and they take little jumps over it."

They all laugh; Mariam laughs so hard she chokes a little on her soup. Layla pats her gently on the back. "That's right," says Layla. "My father says it's sort of like celebrating Christmas with a two-inch-tall tree."

Mariam calms down. "So let's hear you say it," she says, grinning at Layla.

Layla says, "*Sorkhieh toh as man, zardieh man as toh.*"

They pause. "Nice," says Dariush.

"*Très bien,*" says Mariam. "But the question is, do you know what it means?"

Dariush snorts, "Stop it, Mimish. What is this? The GREs on ancient Persian history?"

Layla puts a hand on Dariush's arm to silence him. "It's okay, Dariush," she says, grinning at Mariam. "Mimish and I have a pact that she makes sure I don't culturally embarrass myself." She pauses, looks at Mariam, and begins to recite. "The phrase means 'Your redness to me, my yellowness to you,' and it's a way of asking the fire to give you its healthy red color and to take away your sickly yellow color. It's a rite that was handed down from the Zoroastrians, who worshiped fire as a force of good."

Mariam nods with a playful look in her eye. "Excellent," she says. "You win two pieces of my mother's blackberry fruit roll."

"I think she deserves *three* pieces," says Dariush.

"Okay," says Mariam, flecks of teasing light bouncing off her black eyes. "But I get to share. Layla always shares with me. Right, Laylee?"

Suddenly, everything around them flashes an amber color. Fire reflects in Dariush's golden eyes, and Layla looks toward the gravel driveway, at the *bottehs*, the mounds of tumbleweed that have been placed at regular intervals, ready to be ignited. The first one is ablaze. The second is lit, and it whooshes and crackles bright yellow, then the next and the next: four in all. Mariam pulls Layla by the hand. *"Bereem!* Let's go!" she says urgently.

It is not as Layla had imagined it. The flames almost reach the top of her head. She pulls Mariam's hand back, slowing her progress. Mariam pivots to face Layla. "Don't worry, Laylee. The flames go down quickly."

People vie for turns to jump. Layla is jostled here and there in the excitement. Her muscles tremble. She looks around for Dariush, but he is lost in the crowd. A thrill hovers over the party while the guests queue up as if for a roller-coaster ride. Suddenly the crowd surges—*"Vaaaiii!"*—and there is Dariush now high above the second *botteh*, his calves breaking through the flames. When he lands, his shoes rattle the gravel and pebbles fly up as he takes off for the next hurdle. Each time he jumps, he pants out the proper phrase, and Layla hears the proud smile in his voice and sees it on Mariam's face next to her.

In a matter of seconds the flames are at ankle level, and some of the older women and children take their turns. When it is time for Mariam and Layla to jump, Mariam pulls her friend aside and says in her ear, "Let's wait until the servants put another *botteh* on them. The flames are too low."

Layla pulls her hand away from Mariam's tight grip. The servants feed the fires and leap back to avoid the flames. Despite the crisp air, Layla feels perspiration beading above her lip. She takes a small step away from her friend, and Mariam suddenly turns her back and flies into the fire. The flames reach above her head like yellow fingers grasping for the sky. The odor of burning hair wafts back to Layla, and she shivers. Then Mariam's trembling voice comes from beyond the crackling wall: *"Sorkhieh toh as man, zardieh man as toh!"* and a loud *hoorah!* rises up as she clears the next burning pile.

In just a few moments, Mariam comes around to stand beside Layla once again. Her chest is heaving, her face red and glistening. She challenges Layla with an unblinking look that says, *Well?* Another *botteh* is thrown on the embers. Layla turns and faces the violent fire. Now Mariam puts her hands on Layla's back and pushes. To Layla, this feels exactly like when they were children and Mariam would push her higher and higher in a swing Layla's father had hung from a tree in their garden. Layla would never tell Mariam how frightened she was of the height, and Mariam never knew that Layla closed her eyes and held on to the rope tightly, silently, until Mariam grew tired of pushing.

But Layla cannot close her eyes now. And she moves with her own shaking legs toward the flames. And then without thinking, without effort, she is up. Her legs straddle the blaze and she tries not to imagine her jeans catching fire. She takes a deep breath and lets the momentum carry her forward. Through chattering teeth, she says the ancient words in a gravelly whisper. And when she leaps for the last fire, she is not afraid anymore. She feels strong. Like she has conquered something. And there is Dariush watching her from the patio, smiling as if she has done a dance just for him.

Someone with a Polaroid camera insists on taking pictures of everyone. Flashbulbs go off sporadically while the driveway is cleaned and the dinner is laid. The photograph of the three of them comes into Layla's hand, and she stares at the black square. Slowly, colors and shapes begin to bleed through, and there they are, arms around one another, bundled in their coats, darkness behind them, feet firmly planted on the white marble patio. How different from one another they are: Layla with her olive skin and green eyes and scraggly hair to her waist, and Mariam so petite with frizzy, short hair and lips like quince marmalade, and Dariush, remarkably fair-haired with mischievous amber eyes, a half-moon scar above his lip, and skin the milky beige color of *halva*. She looks for her friends to show them the photograph, but they have disappeared into the increasingly festive party. She pockets the picture as if it is a jewel and goes inside to warm herself.

After dinner, while the aroma of basmati rice still floats through the house and the guests linger in overstuffed couches sipping glasses of tea or brandy and nibbling diamond-shaped chunks of *baghlava*, Katayoon announces that she has ordered a surprise for everyone's entertainment.

It is the *falgir*, the fortune catcher.

Katayoon places the blind man in the center of her large living room in a comfortable chair, artfully draped with a cloth so that his tattered clothing will not soil the silk slipcover. She has a servant bring him a glass of tea, which fogs up his sunglasses as he drinks. The guests are quiet now, subdued, waiting. Layla notices the blind man remove his cloth shoes and indulgently brush his callused toes along the silk carpet. She looks away and wonders if he has agreed to come to the party merely to get warm.

The blind man's fortune-catching method is extremely bewitching. He uses photographs. He holds them in his wrinkled palms and massages the glossy faces. He tilts his head toward the ceiling as if listening to an angel, and then he describes the people in the photograph. He does this perfectly, even down to the color and texture of their clothing. Everyone is mesmerized.

He has only a few teeth, so he speaks as if his tongue is fat. Everyone leans forward. He feels Katayoon's picture and tells her how much he likes the raised seed pearls on her sweater. He calls them jewels from the ocean. She asks him finally what he sees about her future, and he smiles broadly. "A trip to the West," he says. "To visit your daughter at school in the mountains of the West. It seems she is not making good numbers there." Katayoon's jaw drops, but she quickly recovers. So what if her friends know that Mariam is doing poorly in school? The point is that the fortune catcher has spoken the truth! And now the party will be a complete success. No matter that Mariam is mortified and has slipped hastily from the room. Layla notices this too, but she cannot go after her friend without weaving conspicuously through most of the guests. Without prompting, the blind man continues. "But unfortunately, lady, your visit will do no good. Your girl has much disgust for books." Everyone bursts out laughing, even Layla, who feels disloyal, but knows this is the truth about her friend. Her eyes meet Dariush's, across the room. He is laughing too and shaking his head as if to say that he, too, has tried to change this about his cousin without luck.

The fortune catcher moves to someone else's photograph. In this one he proclaims—to much laughter—that they suffer a mild illness, a fungus of the feet. And he congratulates them on the birth of a new grandson in fifteen months' time. More photographs. He predicts money and gifts and success. Layla notices that sometimes his face shows a glimmer of anxiety, but he always wipes it away with an amusing divulgence or prediction: that the guest in the photograph has a repugnance for spiders or an inclination to sip surreptitiously from the cherry *sharbat* pitcher in the refrigerator or a secret desire to poison a sister's pet cat. All these things are true, everyone proclaims!

And finally the fortune catcher is tired, and it is after midnight and the guests are yawning too. Yawning and satisfied with their fortunes. They slip carefully rolled-up *touman*s in the blind man's pocket, and Katayoon finally escorts him to the kitchen for a plate of food and the guests begin the long process of kissing good-bye and making tentative plans for more parties over the coming holiday weeks.

Layla fingers the photograph in her pocket. She loves the feel of the glossy surface and the idea that she can hold the past in her palm. She has always felt this way. Her first camera was a gift from her grandmother when she was ten years old. A Kodak Instamatic. She hung it around her neck every morning as if it were a part of her outfit, and she never left the house without an extra packet of film. Dariush and Mariam would tease her for the way she became preoccupied with lining people up, directing them into unusual poses, and ordering them to stay still while she took their pictures. By the end of that summer in Tehran, her father, Ebrahim, told her he would not spend another *rial* on film, and she heard him whisper to her grandmother that he would not mind the expense if only the pictures were any good, if only they were not mostly bodies without heads. She had run deep into the garden to hide beneath the drooping branches of an ancient tree, where she shed giant tears of heartbreak. Dariush had found her; he was fourteen then and already secretly in love with her. He had picked up her camera from where she had thrown it down, dusted the dirt from it, and placed it in her lap. "You love this, Layla," he had said. "You can't be bad at something you love. I think you just have to keep practicing." He spent a long time talking with her this way, and in the end convinced her not to give up what she loved. She always remembers how he had done this for her and often wishes she were not too embarrassed to tell him how much it had meant to her.

She wants so badly to know what the fortune catcher will say about this photograph in her pocket. She knows she should go upstairs to Mariam's room. Dariush stands in a group of men that includes her father; their expressions are grave as they listen to one man who looks to be telling a serious story. Layla itches to sneak to the kitchen. She has been there a thousand times; the servants all know her. She goes.

The blind man's beard is flecked with rice and lentils. He is alone in the vast kitchen. Layla hears the clatter of silverware as someone washes dishes in the nearby pantry. She is about to speak—"*Agha*, Sir," she will say softly so as not to frighten the blind man—but he suddenly stops chewing and cocks his head, hearing her presence, it seems. "*Hahn*," he says, nodding his head. "The lady girl from America." She gasps, steps back. "Don't be afraid," he says, wiping his oily hands on the front of his shirt and holding them out, palms up. "Give it here, lady girl." She steps forward and deposits the photograph on his wrinkled skin. She notices the sharpness of his Adam's apple as he crooks his neck farther back; the fluorescent ceiling light reflects sharply off his black lenses. He touches the photograph with his fingers, smudging oil across first Mariam's face, then Dariush's, then Layla's. He does not talk about their clothing, nor does he divulge any of their amusing obsessions. His smile melts away. Layla holds her breath as a stream of spittle streaks down the blind man's chin and drops onto the photograph. His fingers begin to move roughly, bending the thick paper, folding it in a sharp crease exactly between Layla and Dariush. He does this—folding and creasing, folding and creasing—until the image of Layla is bent behind the others'. Finished, he extends his arm, the paper dangling from his thumb and forefinger now merely a picture of two cousins. "Go back to America," he says, his mouth ajar, breath reeking of rotten lamb. She seizes the picture—careful not to touch him—and runs.

Three

Layla

I slipped through a back door into the hotel parking lot. For the first time in my life, I left the Tehran Hilton on foot. I maneuvered shakily over a rocky path along the beginnings of the autobahn until I reached the intersection of what had been Pahlavi Avenue but was now called Khomeini Avenue. I took a right down the hill and mingled with the passel of pedestrians moving along the uneven sidewalk toward the distant hub of the city. I tried to steady my trembling legs. There was nothing to do but roam the streets and keep trying to reach Amir from telephones along the way.

People passed me and I passed others; we were faceless, dark-clad figures. The anonymity comforted me, pulled me more deeply into my Persian consciousness and away from the horror of the present. So familiar. The sounds of vendors hawking their wares, the husky blare of motorbikes, housewives bargaining the price of food, the odors of diesel fuel, kerosene, barbecued kebab, bread. Like visiting an old friend.

I purposely averted my eyes from boarded-up shops and cafés, from buildings damaged by Iraqi bombs, from piles of garbage, from the remnants—broken bottles and burned, sooty walls—of Molotov cocktails used in the dark of night by counterrevolutionaries, from the mounds of sandbags for roadblocks, from the huge

banner spanning the avenue that read NEITHER EAST NOR WEST—
DEATH TO AMERICA, from the poster of a woman crying blood red
tears, and from an enormous color mural of the man from
Khomein. Three years since the shah had been deposed, almost a
year since the American embassy hostages had been freed, and still
the Revolution oozed like an infected wound. The theocracy clung
to power by a turban thread, fighting opponents with the shah's
confiscated guns and culling devotees with their misuse of religious
law. One thing was for sure: They had a knack for propaganda.

In the old days, I rarely walked in the street; girls like me
were usually driven everywhere. Walking in the street meant
enduring the *matalak*s from men: that elaborate though crude
Art of Flirtatious Remarks; the poems and puns and creative
slang, some replete with complicated metaphors and literary ref-
erences. Things like, "I am the carpet beneath your feet" or "Oh,
that I were a flea in your panties," to name the milder ones.
Mariam didn't mind the *matalak*s. She would look straight
ahead and pretend that she hadn't heard anything. Sometimes
she couldn't resist laughing at a well-said *matalak*. But I hated
them; they made me ball my hands up into fists.

There were no *matalak*s now. Not while I wore my *hejab*, my
Islamic clothing. And there were no cold looks from traditional
women who disapproved of my sandaled feet or bare arms. We
were all the same, covered in so much fabric that we barely noticed
one another. But this was good. The *hejab* was now a protection,
even a liberation, from scrutiny. Walking in the street calmed me
somewhat, helped me swallow the panic that seemed to scorch my
skin from the inside. I kept telling myself that I would find a way
out of this, that I couldn't let the fear take over because it would
take my logic with it. I fused with the others, matching their
rhythm as if we'd walked here together from an ancient time.

My eyes focused ahead on four women in black *chador*s, their
children straggling about them. One of the women was very old;
I could tell by the way she waddled from arthritis. She reminded
me of Zahra, the head maid at my grandmother's house when I
was little. Could it be she? How old would she be? In her seventies, eighties? Like so many of the servants, she'd drifted into the

turmoil of the Revolution. I quickened my pace. I remembered how Zahra had sweetened my tea with four spoons of sugar when I was a child; how she stirred and stirred until the granules were completely dissolved, then handed the glass to me and pinched my cheek gently. I tried to get a better view of her face. She held her *chador* between her teeth and peeled a banana, from which she broke off pieces and distributed them to the children. The other women gossiped, nodding and shaking their heads, looking, from behind, like crows on a high wire.

I looked at my watch. Eight forty-five. I swallowed. The flight Dariush and I should have been on would leave in less than an hour. I spotted a pay phone and dialed Amir's number again. It rang on and on. I chewed on my chapped lips and watched the space between me and the woman who looked like Zahra become wider and wider. She and her companions suddenly turned off the main avenue. I hung up the phone and hurried to follow them as if they were expecting me, as if I could pretend that I wasn't so utterly alone, that comfort and protection were within my reach.

The narrow lane twisted and curved; tall old buildings stretched up on both sides. The atmosphere was villagelike; the overcrowded city seemed like a memory. Turning a corner, I came upon a soccer game among some young boys. The ball bounced off my calf. The boys apologized and went back to their game. A woman in a small courtyard was hanging clothing up on a line while an infant slept against her back in a papoose made from a *chador*. The sounds of radio and television mingled like odors in the air, and my heels scraped along the cement street. Life went on as normal, of course. But not normal for me, for Dariush. Please God, I thought, don't let them hurt him too much, don't let them kill him. I imagined his face, the tone of his skin, the exact formation of the wrinkles on his palms, the veins along the insides of his arms, the scent of him. I imagined us in my father's duplex in Manhattan, sitting at the kitchen table eating doughnuts and reading the newspaper. I imagined this over and over as if the strength of my imagination could wipe away the impossibility of it. And I followed the women absentmindedly down the lane, around corners and over small hills as if I were tied to them by a slack string.

Without warning, we came to a large, bright clearing, a rocky, dusty, dirty plot of land where a building once must have stood, but that was now filled with discarded items like furniture and pots and torn pieces of fabric. People milled about; a growing crowd, which the women and children I'd been following joined. The old woman turned, and I saw that her face didn't resemble Zahra's at all. I felt a chill and I cursed my stupidity. Even if she had been Zahra, what had been the point of following her? She couldn't help me. Was I so desperate for any minuscule possibility of security? I had to focus. And I had to keep trying the telephone number. I looked back down the winding alley we'd emerged from and realized how confused my sense of direction had become. I'd trailed the women through a labyrinth that only a person born and bred to the area could have followed. There were no pay phones here.

My heart flopped around in my chest. How would I get back? And what was going on here anyway? Was this the beginnings of a counterrevolutionary demonstration? My stomach lurched. I expected a unit of *pasdaran* in their plain green uniforms and plastic revolutionary guard badges to begin sniping at us from the flat roofs of the surrounding concrete buildings. I knew enough not to turn and run, not to bring attention to myself. The people entering the clearing looked as if they came from the same neighborhood. They spoke to each other or remained silent, standing comfortably, as if in their own living rooms. Some of them glanced at me furtively. Clearly, I didn't belong.

The roar of a truck engine sounded from behind me and I moved quickly aside, twisting my ankle on a discarded pickle can. Pain shot through my leg, but I didn't reach down to soothe it. The dump truck, piled high with small stones, made its way past me into the center of the lot. People scattered away from the back of the truck as the stones were dumped out, clattering like thunder, onto the ground. The deafening noise was like a slap to my face. Suddenly, I understood what was going to happen.

I turned to walk back into the lane, to try and steadily retrace my steps. But I was almost thrown back by the arrival of a speeding revolutionary-guard jeep that stopped short at the entrance to the clearing, blocking my way back into the lane. I felt frozen to my spot, standing so close to the car that I could see the individual bullets in the magazine that the driver had wrapped around his torso like a guerrilla fighter.

A middle-aged woman, stout, with sallow skin and dark circles under her bugged-out eyes, sat in the back with two prisoners. She looked oddly familiar, but not in the nostalgic way I'd felt with the old woman I'd followed here. My scalp tingled, a warning from somewhere inside. The guard in the passenger seat jumped out and pulled the prisoners after him. They were dressed in long white shifts and had what looked like white pillowcases over their heads. I could tell they were women when I saw the low-heeled shoes on their small feet. The guards moved them roughly toward the center of the clearing. One of them stumbled and fell on her knee. The guard jerked her upright and roughly prodded her through the crowd. Everyone watched them. Except for the meek, questioning voices of the younger children, there was silence.

I saw the old woman I had followed, the one I'd thought was old Zahra. As the prisoners passed her, she clamped her lips tightly together and squinted her eyes: the look of an angry, scolding mother. She toyed with a fist-sized stone between her hands, passing it from one palm to the other like a juggler getting ready to perform.

They all had their stones. Even the children had collected pebbles and placed them in small piles at their feet. The heap of stones the truck had deposited had dwindled to nearly nothing. I tried to take a deep breath, but I couldn't gulp in enough air. I thought about reaching into my purse, slung across my shoulder, for a tissue to wipe the perspiration from my face. And as I contemplated this, I looked down at my purse and was struck by the appearance of my own attire. I may have convinced myself I blended in easily with my fellow Tehranis, but the fact was, even my Islamic dress was too fancy next to the used and threadbare clothing of these working-class people.

And what was about to happen would separate us in every sense. The punishment for adultery in Islamic Iran is stoning. We were here to do our Islamic duty.

I had to escape. I looked back toward the lane, determined to find a way around the jeep. My eyes met those of the woman guard sitting in the backseat. I could tell she'd been staring at me for a while, and I was so visible, being separated from the edge of the crowd by nearly fifteen feet. She frowned, and I knew immediately whom she reminded me of: Dariush's grandmother, Maman Bozorg, whose eyes never sparkled with a grandmother's unconditional love, only with a fanatic's desires. Intuition told me the woman guard was hard and unforgiving, like a child who calms her rage by punching and ripping at dolls. Suddenly, she leaned forward and called to me in a peppery voice: "Sister!" I turned away quickly, pretending I didn't hear. I realized there was only one way to avoid her.

I walked toward the pile of stones and chose a smooth one to fit snugly in my palm. It felt cool, and heavier than I expected. I stood on the edge of the restless crowd that had by now formed a tight circle around the prisoners. I couldn't bring myself to look up; I saw only the stone in my hand. I had to show that I was a loyal Iranian. Survival meant throwing that stone. Could I detach myself from them, the stone and the hand, when it was time to begin throwing? I expected to feel the woman guard grab my shoulder. She would ask me questions, arrest me for not giving her satisfying answers.

What was taking these people so long? Couldn't they start so it could be over? Out of habit and to my own amazement, I glanced at my watch. Nine-thirty. Dariush and I should have been in the air, far above this terrible event, so high that the whole city would look as small as the stone in my palm. Would Dariush be braver than I if he were here? Would he climb up on the top of the truck and persuade the crowd not to do this? Would he run fast enough to get away from the woman guard? My hands trembled.

Thwack! The human skull is also as hard as a stone. Stone against bone. *Thwack! Thwack!* Then everyone was moving and throwing, muffling the sounds their efforts caused. There were no screams from the prisoners; I thought I heard a grunt and maybe a sigh, but they could have come from anywhere. I had to concentrate on throwing my own stone. I would miss the target, of course. The guard wouldn't notice. Or would she? Maman Bozorg had noticed everything, all for the purpose of manipulating everything.

It was time. I had to look up. Look up, Layla!

I was closer to the victims than I thought. Maybe three yards. One of them must have fallen into the dust. The other one was standing, swaying drunkenly. Her hands must have been tied behind her back, but she managed to stay up—a final act of defiance. Voices cursed her: "Whore! Cunt-giver! Heathen!" Small patches of red stained the pillowcase over her head. A large stone, which must have had a point to it, struck her. Blood suffused into the cloth like ink from a fountain pen into rice paper. She stiffened at the blow, arching her back a little. Then she fell. I could hear her crying so clearly, sobbing, hardly catching her breath, saying over and over, "*Cherah, Khodah, cherah?*, Why, God, why?" People continued to throw their stones, determined to finish their ammunition, unmoved by the sound of this girl who cried like a child being raped. The stone I held slipped from my fingers and fell to the ground.

And then it was over. In minutes, people began leaving the clearing. The voice of the woman revolutionary guard, so close, said, as people passed by, "Remember the lesson, sisters and brothers, remember the lesson." She even sounded like Maman Bozorg, with a voice dry like smoke. The people shuffled away, many of them with heads bowed. And the clearing turned ghostly empty in moments. Before I could move, she grabbed my forearm. "So, sister," she said in my ear. "It seems that you are not willing to do your Islamic duty." I staggered. I couldn't take my eyes from the two crimson heaps, one still writhing, in the beige dirt.

She called gruffly to the male guards. "Take the shovels and finish them off," she said, pointing to the stoned women. The guards, matter-of-factly, smashed the heads of the victims, and they both became still. I stumbled and the woman steadied me. I felt her bosom against my arm and I wondered if she had given milk to a child from it. Was she human?

"Let's go, sister," she said, pulling me along toward the jeep.

"Where?" I managed to say, my voice a whisper.

"To the detention center, of course. Did you think I was taking you to a hotel?" And I felt the cold steel of the handcuffs.

Four

Maman Bozorg

April 1979
Ordibehesht, The Month Resembling Heaven, 1358

There is a story about my life that I have not told anyone, not even my grandson Dariush. When I was a young woman in the years between the Great World Wars, I went one day with my mother to the *hammam*. This was before everyone thought to build baths in their own homes. Pity. The *hammam* was a wonderful place. I can still smell the sandalwood oil and feel the warm steam settling on my skin.

I learned many things in the *hammam* by listening to the women talk. Even as a little girl, I listened. The other children in the *hammam* would play splashing and hiding games or they would pester and tease the washing-women, who finally ran after them and opened their *longhs* to frighten them with the sight of their dense, black pubic hair, telling them this was a hungry monster.

But I listened to the *khanooms*, the ladies. I learned how husbands can be cruel, but tamed, how servants must be disciplined and never trusted, how to handle the complexities of matchmaking. I cannot remember a moment in my childhood in which I felt like a child, in which I did not think of myself as a *khanoom*. I tolerated the way in which adults treated me and knew that when I grew to be tall and married, I could be a great *khanoom*, a great lady, because this was what I was in my *del*, in my heart.

It was my mother who taught me to value myself this way. It was she who always told me that *Allah* had given me a wise soul, had written an important destiny on my forehead. And it was she who held me up during the hardships of my marriage and my early widowhood.

I loved my mother more than anything on that day in the *hammam* while I sat and she braided my hair and whispered small kisses along the top of my head. Though I was twenty-five years old (a *khanoom* by then for certain), in my sweet mother's presence, I was content to feel, inside, like a pampered child.

After our baths, we walked out onto the sidewalk; it was only a few steps to our waiting carriage. I remember the gray sky—the color of an iron rice pot—and the chilly breeze that fluttered our *chador*s. I did not feel cold at all; my skin was warm from the water and my nostrils full with eucalyptus steam. My mother's round cheeks glowed pink as young pomegranates and her eyes smiled at me with the warmth of a bread oven. It was a moment so peaceful that I could have framed the rest of my life with it; I could have kept it in my thoughts, lacquered like the miniature paintings, so as to find comfort in it whenever I was troubled.

But the moment remains in my thoughts as a pin in a cushion, always puncturing, always painful.

It was one of Reza Shah's equestrian police who bounded his horse onto the sidewalk and reached down to yank my mother's *chador* from around her. My mother screamed and put her hands to her bare head. I looked up at this *paseban* atop his horse; the afternoon sun shone behind him, making him a shadow, hiding his features from me. He lifted his arm and I thought he would strike me, but instead he threw my mother's *chador* into the narrow *jube* and watched the rushing dirty water take it away. My mother clutched at her body, crossing her arms over her breasts as if she were naked in the cold. Not since her ninth birthday had she been without her *chador* in front of men outside her immediate family. Now her flowered shift fluttered in the wind. Her cheeks were pale and wet with tears of shame. The *paseban* spoke to her as if she could hear him, but I knew from her empty stare that she had taken herself somewhere else. He reminded her that the *chador* had been abolished, by order of Reza Shah, the new and modern king. He reached for me, but I stepped back. I would not let him take anything from me, not let him touch me. I believe it was the hatred in my eyes that gave him pause, for I have used that look many times since then and I have never lost a battle with it. I learned on that day how I must not let anyone force anything upon me. In the moment that it took the *paseban* to control his skittish horse, I drew my mother quickly toward our carriage and helped her in. The driver had been too scared to step out and help us. I held my *chador* tightly under my chin and ordered the driver to go while I continued to watch the *paseban* from the window. He did not follow.

I draped my *chador* over my mother, and she held it fast about her body and face. She sobbed into the cloth, and I felt a burning in my heart for her. Once at home in her bedroom, she began to pound at her chest, to pull at her braids, to cry at the terrible sin of her exposure. I held her against my bosom and tried to comfort her; she seemed so small now and so beautiful as the candlelight bounced upon her hennaed hair. She calmed and had me promise I would not tell anyone of this horrible incident, that it would shame her too much. I promised. Finally, she fell asleep, but only after I heard her vow to God that she would never leave the house again.

She became very devout. And very quiet. She was not like my old mother; she did not take interest in the same things, in cooking her special sugar-almond candy or in her embroidery or in tickling her grandsons' bellies or even in having her friends for lunch or tea as she always had. She took longer to say her prayers; she said them slowly, stretching out the Arabic words until they sounded like lyrics to a song. I found her taking *ghosl* more often until it seemed that she was always calling her maid to bring a bucket of water so she could purify herself. There she would be, out on her private balcony, sitting on a wooden bench in a thin shift, pouring water from a small porcelain dish onto first her head, then her right shoulder, then her left shoulder while she murmured the prayers that would purify her. The weather became colder, and I begged her not to wash so often, but she hardly answered. Her communication with me was no longer in words, but in kisses and caresses, as if I were an infant who could not understand. Helpless, I watched the hairs on her arms and neck stand straight up like goose flesh as she washed herself in a flurry of snowflakes. Even my father noticed my mother's excessive behavior; he scolded her mildly, but how harshly can you scold a woman for honoring God in this personal manner?

The doctor said it was the pneumonia that killed her, but I will always think of Reza Shah as her murderer and my mother's death as another casualty in his march away from the laws of God. And the British. They were responsible for my mother's death. It was their ideas that they sprinkled like seeds into our new king's mind, ideas that would grow into monstrous trees under which the whole country was made to sit and live. He wanted to be like them, was taken in by their pomposity, wanted Iran to mirror the West. Stupid man! And then the others came: the French, the Germans, the Russians, and, finally, the Americans. Occupying us. Telling us how to live. Telling us that bread and cheese and tea were unhealthy for breakfast, telling us to eat chickens' eggs and fried bread with a cloying syrup. Convincing us that our clothing was wrong, that the separation of girls and boys in school was wrong, that men should wear strips of cloth down the fronts of their shirts, that a woman's beauty belonged to everyone to see—her legs exposed, even her shoulders—so men could stare at her, violate her privacy.

Ah, the West. Not only did they steal our oil, they stole our traditions. And now, thanks to *Allah* and to the blessed Khomeini, they are gone.

Five

Layla

We rode bumpily through side streets, then down Khomeini Avenue. I couldn't focus. My breathing was too fast. I had a tremendous need to use the bathroom.

The position of the sun, dim behind clouds, told me it was close to eleven o'clock. I was afraid to move, even to look at my watch. I nearly gagged from the acrid odor of the woman guard on the seat next to me.

We came to a traffic jam. The scruffy guard in the front passenger seat ran a greasy rag over his gleaming Uzi. The driver chomped on roasted watermelon seeds and spit the shells out the window. I stared ahead through the windshield, afraid to look at the woman who had so shamelessly presided over the stoning.

It began to rain. Heavy drops smacked onto the windshield. Then the sun came out again; long slivers of yellow light shot through spaces between tree leaves. How could the sun come out after what had happened in the clearing? As the jeep had pulled away from the scene, I had watched the dump-truck driver heave the bodies—the smeary red sacks—into the back of his vehicle. He had done his job as if he were loading nothing more than old and useless furniture.

Suddenly, the woman guard leaned over me and grabbed my purse. The strap was still snug within the buttoned epaulet tie on my *manteau*, so the purse wouldn't go farther than my own lap. "You better not have a weapon in here, sister," she said, rummaging through the contents.

"Of course not," I said, lifting my hands to grab the purse and wrench it away from her. "I'm just an ordinary citizen."

She gaped at me, and for a second we sat motionless in a position of tug-of-war with our hands on my purse. What was I doing? Had I lost my mind? Had I forgotten where I was? This was no time to be thinking or reacting like my American half, like the half who could question authority, who had grown up hearing the echo of phrases like "life, liberty, and the pursuit of happiness." I had no rights here. I certainly didn't have any rights over my purse. No wonder the woman was gaping at me in surprise. I loosened my grip on the bag, and with a loud grunt she yanked the strap, popping the button on my shoulder, and brought the purse into her own lap. "Ordinary citizen, *hahn?* We'll find out who you really are, girl with the green eyes." The driver was wearing my Ray-Bans.

She began picking out items from my purse and looking at them. She opened my makeup powder, my blush, then rolled my mascara around in her dirty palm. She withdrew my lipstick— the color was called On the Town Red—and my hairbrush. My knuckles were white. My lips puckered with the urge to spit at her pitted cheek, only inches from my face.

But I had to think. I couldn't risk reacting improperly again. Could I escape from the jeep? Jump out and run? We were closer to the congested center of Tehran. I wouldn't know where I was. I hadn't been downtown here since I'd lived in my grandparents' old compound as a child. I would have to hire a cab to get me back north, where I could get my bearings and call Amir. I imagined cab drivers racing past me while I flagged them with my handcuffed arms.

I had to find a way to get the woman to release me.

"You have very expensive things, sister," the woman said, holding up a pair of leather gloves, shaking her head back and forth as if this were a crime in itself. "I knew you were a rich one as soon as I saw you. A fancy *manteau* from Europe." She pronounced it *Ooroopah*. "I have a good eye for expensive fabrics."

Then she pulled my wallet out of the bag, and suddenly it seemed clear that here was the answer to my escape. This was what Dariush would do; this was the correct way to get things done in Tehran. I looked at the woman's profile, willing her to look at me. When she did, I said quietly, slowly, "I have many *touman*s in there." She looked at me blankly. Then—Oh God—she was smiling. I calculated in my head that I had almost one hundred thousand *touman*s in that fat Louis Vuitton wallet—nearly a thousand dollars. She could have it all. Then she would give the boys in front an adequate excuse for letting me go. They wouldn't question her; she was so obviously in charge.

She opened the wallet and dug her hand into the billfold. Please God, please God, I said over and over in my head. She began counting the money—slowly—all the while keeping her hands within the purse in case the boys looked back. Her eyes widened and so did the smile. I dared not move. She whisked the wad of bills out of the bag and shoved them into a deep pocket in her faded brown *manteau* that looked more like a *mullah*'s robe than a coat. Then her hand came back; it held the handcuff key. She opened her fingers so I could see the dull metal item in her palm. Teasing me. Then she put the key between her gray teeth so she could finish her inspection of my wallet.

"There is no more money," I whispered.

She had already reached into the zippered compartment and was pulling out my small address book and some folded papers of lists and phone numbers. She shuffled through them.

"Don't you have any identification papers?" she asked. "I want to know who you are, girl."

What was this now? She should unlatch the cuffs and let me go.

"I am Layla Namdar," I said, using my new married name and trying to hide a quiver in my voice. "I don't have my papers because I just got married and they are being updated."

She stared at me obliquely, then continued to poke her fingers into the other compartments of my wallet. Her hand froze. Then I knew by her reaction—the line of her mouth, the whiteness of her fingernails—that I was in deeper trouble.

She held my old Barnard College ID card. I hadn't seen it in three years; as far as I could remember, I'd thrown it away. But there it had been, hiding like a piece of flypaper between the leather folds. And I'd been so careful to leave any trace of my Western-ness behind when I left Europe.

She spit the handcuff key out onto the floor. "You live in the land of the Great Satan, sister?"

"I used to a long time ago. Not anymore."

She slapped my face and my neck wrenched from the blow. "You are lying, whore!"

The guard on the passenger side turned around. "What's happening?"

She displayed the card to him with its faded picture and blocked lettering; I glimpsed the words NEW YORK. "Look at this. She thinks I am stupid." She turned to me. "I have been trained. This is an American document. You are a spy!"

My cheek stung and my vision was blurry on the side where she'd hit me. I wanted to claw at her face, and my lips trembled with my anger. The boy handed the small card back to the woman, nodding his head but obviously not knowing the first thing about what he'd looked at.

I tried to defend myself once more. "That is an identification card that I used when I visited America—"

Pap! She slapped me again. On the other side. The force pushed me over and my temple smashed into the door handle. I felt a strong pressure behind my eyes and my saliva tasted salty with blood. She pulled me upright. I tried to focus on something outside. We still moved slowly in traffic. People passed by on the sidewalk. Their faces became clear. They looked at me furtively, their eyes staring for a few seconds then shifting away, then back again. Help me, help me, help me, I said silently to each one who passed. But their faces only mirrored my own fear.

I felt stupid about the bribe. A bribe won't work unless you have some leverage. And I didn't. She had it all. She was Queen of the Jeep, Queen of My Life. Still, I had to take a chance. Making my voice loud so the guards up front—the ones she apparently didn't want to share my money with—could hear me, I said, "Excuse me, sister, but what about my money! You—" Her fist came into my throat with force and precision. There was pain, but in seconds the pain was nothing compared with the fear that I couldn't breathe. I moved my head forward and backward, side to side, frantically gasping, trying to get a breath past my broken throat. The woman leaned on my hands in my lap, and her face was inches from mine. "You shut up! Shut up!" she kept saying in the Farsi words that translate literally to "You choke! You choke!"

I passed out.

When I woke, my cheek was numb from pressing against the window. I stayed there, wanting to keep my wakefulness from the guards. My whole body hurt and I wondered if the woman had beaten me more in my unconsciousness. My thighs felt damp, and I realized, with shame, that I'd urinated. I swallowed and then winced from the searing pain.

It was noon. The Call to Prayer sounded on the radio. I expected the jeep to stop so everyone could pray, but we kept going. I wondered if Amir had learned that Dariush and I didn't get on the plane. Would he try to find Dariush first, or me? He would know how to find us, wouldn't he? He had so many connections. How many detention centers could there be in Tehran? Amir would find us.

The jeep radio blared revolutionary rhetoric. Something about loyalty to the Islamic cause; loyalty to the edicts of the *Emam* Khomeini. The government was trying to quell all the opposition, and there were more random arrests and executions now than there had been after the shah was overthrown. "A virus," Auntie Katayoon called it. "A virus of anger and power."

I pushed myself upright. The woman guard looked at me indifferently. She seemed sure that I was no longer a threat to her. Tears came to my eyes, but I was determined to keep her from seeing me in that kind of pain. So I looked outside.

We weren't on the main avenue anymore. We'd come to an old city street, a narrow and straight street whose asphalt had become so pounded down from time and use that its edges on either side sloped unevenly into the water ditch. Tall pine trees lined the street. Stone walls grew out of the narrow sidewalks on either side, but I couldn't see the tops of them because of the tree branches. The driver had his window open, and the smell of sheep drifted into the car. I remembered when I was a child, before we moved to the northern part of the city, how we often had to stop the car to let a shepherd and his flock cross. I had loved to watch the girlish faces of the lambs and the way their wool seemed to float about them like a cloud. My father had bought me a lamb as a pet when I was five and, until my grand-father discovered that the animal was really a billy goat whose favorite food was Kleenex (an expensive and rare item in those days), it had lived in the house and slept on the floor in my room.

I stared at the few people walking along the sidewalk. No women. Here and there a construction worker in his baggy pants and dusty blouse shuffled tiredly along, dodging pinecones. Where had I seen so many pine trees in Tehran before? Something familiar nagged at me. It was as if I'd just woken from a dream that I couldn't remember, a dream that had left me with only sensations and smells.

Suddenly I remembered. There was the Kashani Drug Store, a small corner shop with green neon tubes on either side of its low, arched door. Just next to it was the tiny mosque with its usual neat row of shoes along its outside wall. And before we reached it, I knew we were approaching the coffee shop, if it was still there. And it was, looking not much different than it had when I was a child. It was an ancient, filthy, one-room, unpainted place where working-class men came to drink tea or thick Turkish coffee; to smoke water pipes while they sat cross-legged on frayed rugs or rough-hewn benches. And there they were. They looked like the same men, in their tattered clothing and flip-flop shoes, that I had watched from the backseat of our car years ago. I sat up straighter and took in all the scenery of our old neighborhood. It was amazing. Almost nothing had changed.

Street vendors were cooking things on their wagons, and the smells were mingling in the air as they always had: sweet, simmering beets and chicken kebab.

The driver swung our vehicle into a driveway and honked at a deep green gate whose carvings were as familiar to me as the lines in my father's face. I couldn't blink. A mustached man opened the gate, and we drove in. I closed my eyes and felt the jeep move first to the left, then slowly to the right, turning fluidly and coming to a stop at exactly the moment I knew it would.

I opened my eyes and looked up at the building; at the tall French doors that led out onto the balcony where my father, grandparents, and I had eaten breakfast in the summer, at the wide entrance steps where I'd scraped my elbow twice, at the tiled roof where the garden kitty had gotten stuck, at the grand house where my father was born and where my grandparents had cuddled me during my childhood. To the house's left and right, and in what I could glimpse of the area behind it, stood the other, smaller buildings of the compound. They were dark and cold as monoliths. Back to the left was the old tree with drooping branches where Dariush had convinced me not to give up my passion for photography. And beyond the perimeter stone wall to the right were the tiled roofs of what had once been Dariush's family compound, where Mariam and I had played as children and where Maman Bozorg had been matriarch.

The guard woman came around the jeep and pulled me out. I noticed my purse on the floor, the dusty mark of her footprint on the leather. My legs were stiff, and I saw a spot of blood on one of my wrists after the woman yanked at my arm to make me stand.

"Wait here for me, brother," she told the driver.

I couldn't take my eyes off the house. The sunlight blazed at the windows, and I glimpsed the shadows of people moving about. For a moment, and even while I knew it was impossible, I thought maybe the government had gone to great lengths to interrogate me. Was this staged? Had they re-created my childhood? Would they have my favorite grape-leaf appetizer waiting on the table as my grandmother always had?

I shook my head, and the movement irritated my swollen throat. "Why—" I croaked, wanting to ask the guard woman where this place was, rationally certain now that the government would not go to such trouble to get information from *me*. What information, anyway?

"Don't talk, CIA whore," she snapped while she pulled me up the stairs. At the top, my question was answered.

Above the front door a long wooden plaque had been nailed. In large, handwritten script it said, *Central Komiteh Headquarters for Darvaz-e-Dolat District*. My grandparents' old house was merely an empty building to be used to benefit the Revolution.

The door opened, and out came an austere woman wearing a stained white scarf around her acned face. My captor handed her the small, square card that was my Barnard College ID. *"Jasoos,"* she said, spitting on my foot. I was officially a spy, I supposed. Then the new guard turned me around and fastened a blindfold over my eyes. My captor from the jeep whispered loudly in my ear, "So happy to have met you, bitch," and off she went down the steps, my money in her deep pocket.

The blindfold was tight against my eyelids. I allowed myself to be led. My new caretaker wasn't any less rough than the old woman. She smelled of garlic and said nothing while our shoes clicked on the marble floor. Noises came to me from above: footsteps, the scraping of chairs, muffled male voices. I somehow managed to keep my bearings. We passed the kitchen, the dining room, the downstairs servants' congregation room, from which I heard what sounded like a telex machine receiving a message. Then we were at the cellar door. The cellar had been forbidden to us when we were children. The servants went down there only to do the laundry. Once Mariam, Dariush, some cousins of mine, and I went down there to play hide-and-seek. But we soon scared ourselves out of that place: so dark, so many irregularly shaped rooms. We made up stories about the cellar after that: Immortal people lived there, were stuck there by some ancient spell; they ate bugs and bats and never changed their clothing; they were perpetually sad and pained. We stayed away, sometimes daring one another to go down there for timed intervals that never extended beyond a quivering five minutes.

The guard pushed me forward, still holding on to my upper arm. We began to descend the uneven stone steps. A woman's scream, followed by sobs, flew up from below. I shivered and swallowed painfully. Now I was going to be one of those invented immortals, there amongst the bugs and bats, filthy, perpetually sad and pained. It came to me then, clear as the polished mirrors in the Golestan Palace, it came to me that no one—not Dariush's father, with all his connections, nor Amir, with all his secret friends, nor Mariam, with all her Islamic faith—no one would know that I was here.

Six

Maman Bozorg

Oh God! My God! They have arrested my grandson Dariush! They say he left his post without permission. How can this be? He was not raised this way, to run away from his duty. *Allah* help us! As punishment, they are sending him to the war front to lead the weak and young into combat. That *mullah*, that lowly cleric at the war department, he promised me Dariush would never go into battle; after all, my grandson was too educated to waste on the warfield. He could have been a champion officer, a keen strategist in this war against the devil Saddam, a hero of the *jihad*. Instead, he is disgraced. And now I can do nothing for him.

I have always tried to keep my family pure, to honor *Allah* and the traditions of my country. I have always known what is best for my children and for my grandchildren. When my husband Teymoor died of the tetanus only five years after our marriage, I knew I had to learn how to read and write, despite the fact that this was not a woman's requirement. But doing such a thing was necessary for taking proper care of my family. Within one year, I no longer made my mark with my thumbprint, and I understood enough of my numbers to manage the household. I did not trust my husband's family to take care of me, yet I gave them the impression that I could not survive without them. This was the way my own mother taught me how to honor tradition.

I was lucky to have my two sons around me. My husband's parents believed in my abilities so they did not take the boys, as they had a right to. Anyway, they could not afford to. My father-in-law had gambled his fortune and lands away in sinful card games soon after my marriage to his son. What humiliation! Not only did I become the wife of a pauper, but the daughter-in-law of a sinner as well. My husband's whole family had turned its back on the laws of the Prophet: They gambled and drank liquor, their men and women mixed at parties, they no longer prayed their *namaz* to *Allah*. My father was stunned with shame; he had attended religious school with Teymoor's father, and he had known the family to be devout and traditional. What had happened?

I knew. Reza Shah had happened.

My father called for a divorce, but I was already with child, so we—Teymoor and I—moved into a small house in my father's compound. It was a joyous moment; I would be near my mother again. And when Teymoor died four years later, I mourned as a proper woman should, but I was not unhappy. The match had been wrong from the start. Much to my family's sorrow, Teymoor had tried to change me, had begged me to remove the veil, to visit the Western lands of infidels with him, to go to the cinema. My mother cried many tears for the loss of my honor. But I did not give in to Teymoor. I could never had led such an unholy life. Yes. His death was for the best. It was a relief to think that my children would not learn their father's promiscuous ways. Once Teymoor was gone, we happily moved into the grand house with my parents, where we belonged.

Still, my sons became a disappointment. First Mahmoud marrying that Katayoon, who insisted on buying her clothing in Europe and taking Mahmoud with her, exposing him to sins he was unable to resist. It took her only two months after their marriage to convince my son that he had no need for prayer or fasting or celebrating the Feast of the Sacrifice or respecting his mother. And because of her, he was killed in Europe, racing a boat on the sea, as if he understood the sea when he had spent his whole life in the desert. But the consolation was their daughter, Mariam. I swore to God I would not let Katayoon tarnish that girl. And then my other son, Hooshang, whose heart is too soft for the true world, who wanted to become a poet! Where would he be now if I had not insisted he study medicine? Still, he does not understand my points. We cannot communicate, do not think in the same way; we walk side by side like an elephant and a teacup: completely different.

But he gave me Dariush. He and Veeda, another misguided woman—yet a fair match for my pulpy Hooshang, who needed a willful woman to keep him moving in one direction.

When my grandson was born, I knew immediately that he was special. Even in infancy, I saw my own ambition in his eyes. He did not whine for his milk, he demanded it with a cry that pierced the household and made the servants jump. He had my energy, my conviction. He learned to do everything early: to walk before his first year, to speak in full sentences at eighteen months, to recite the Arabic prayers I taught him at two years old, and to look me straight in the eye as no one else could. He was so special that I did not mind when we learned that Veeda could not have any more children because of her sugar disease. In fact, I believed it was God's plan that I have only two grand-children; more than that would have been difficult for one devout grandmother to control.

I made up my mind to steer Dariush and Mariam in the proper direction. I would not allow them to fall into the dark-ness of immorality as my sons had. But I have had a great deal of trouble with both of them. Yet I never lost hope. God is Great!

I was forced to compromise—on the surface. When Katayoon insisted on sending Mariam to school in Switzerland, I almost struck her. But I reminded myself how pliable Mariam has always been; I did not worry that I would lose my influence over her. She would come back to Iran during her holidays, and I would tame her. But Dariush was a different matter. And with that stubborn mother of his, I won only small battles. Did not my Dariush stay in Iran for his primary schooling when Veeda wanted him to study in America? All right. So he did not go to the religious school as I wanted him to; instead, Veeda sent him to the International School, exposing him to *farangi*s and their bad habits, even to Jews, whom Reza Shah had of course liberated from their neighborhoods. I tried to sway the boy in my direction, but he was not like Mariam. I knew I could lose him. Still, I managed to have a religious tutor with him on Fridays. He learned his prayers and the laws of Islam. I was relieved and so I rested my mind. My two grandchildren would move toward their destiny, their *ghesmat*, with ease; I would be their guide. Soon they would realize what a perfect match they were for one another.

But as the fates always prove: If you do not pay attention and if you do not always appreciate your good fortune, the *jenn*s of darkness will sneak into your house.

And so came Layla.

It is because of that wicked girl that my Dariush is in trouble. That Layla. Daughter of an infidel! She is always where she should not be—a mirror to the truth that she should never have been born. Now they tell me that she has married my grandson without my permission—all with an innocent smile that convinced that stupid son of mine to arrange a secret ceremony, to exclude even me!—and now my Dariush must fight the vile Iraqis while *she* has probably found her way back to the unholy West where she sprang from.

I knew the first time I laid eyes on her mother almost thirty years ago, as she masqueraded through my parlor in a *chador*—thinking that she was showing me respect—I knew she did not belong with a good Moslem boy like Ebrahim Bahari. I tried to tell my friend Mina, Ebrahim's mother and the wife of our neighbor's son, that this was not a good match. But just as now, that marriage had already taken place, far away in that filthy New York. Done, done, done. Without any wise parents to arrange it. And then it seemed as if no one could *see* what I could see: that woman, that Rachel, she was not just a *farangi*, a foreigner, but a Jew as well! I saw the truth. I saw the long nose, the eyes so close together, the lips curled like the outline of a vulture high above the earth.

They told everyone that she had become a Moslem, that she had been a Christian before. No one questioned it. All of them were trying to pretend that it did not matter, trying to be modern, as if modern was the most delicious dish on the lunch table. But I knew that modern would lead only to pain.

And then Rachel was killed in her car, crushed and mangled by a school bus on Pahlavi Avenue. Layla was just two years old. Of course I pitied the child. Had I not been left motherless myself? I knew the heartache of a daughter's loneliness, how life can seem flat and long and barren like the desert when there is no moon. No question, the child would suffer. Then Ebrahim wanted to raise her in his wife's country, in America. He was such a weak one, that Ebrahim, sniveling and crying openly— like a woman—over his wife's death. He was an embarrassment to his mother, walking around with pieces of that woman's clothing, caressing the fabric as if he were some kind of homosexual. I could not wait until he and that child were gone.

The problem was my daughter-in-law Katayoon. She had begun to brew up a relationship between her daughter, Mariam, and the child Layla. Oh! how I cringed when I heard their gurgling laughter as they played in Mina's garden. I could not bear the image of those girls exchanging ideas as they grew older, of my Mariam sharing so much as a chickpea cookie with Layla. I did not want that child of infidels soiling her soul.

I can remember the day they left. I went to Mina's house to bid them farewell; those were the days when we were still speaking to one another. I had my housemaid hold the *Qoran* for Ebrahim so he could walk beneath it three times for safe journey. I am not hard-hearted; I did feel pity for the child and for my friend Mina as she wept. Still, it was difficult for me to hide my smile once the car disappeared beyond the gate.

It was that *naneh* of Layla's, that gnomish woman Banu, who ruined everything. She had gone with them to New York; she said she could not part with the poor child. Maybe she thought she could find a husband there, though she was well over thirty by then. The woman was a freak, she was no taller than 140 centimeters, and her voice sounded like a bleating lamb. But she was loyal, so loyal, especially to Mina, that she kept the memory of Iran alive in Ebrahim and Layla. And suddenly, they were back. Visiting, they said. Visiting summer after summer, sometimes even at the New Year or in the winter. Surprise! They were here! May dirt fall on their heads, I thought to myself.

I remember *Ashura*, one of our most holy days, the day on which Saint Hossein was murdered in Karbala by the traitorous Arabs. Mariam and Layla were eight years old. As usual, I was holding my famous annual Weeping Party.

Ashura is a healthy holy day. It is a day on which people also cry for their own lost loved ones. On *Ashura*, we must bring out all our sorrows and suffer over them as if they are medals of honor. On *Ashura*, I cry for my mother and for my husband, for my dead son and for all the saints and martyrs who died in the name of Islam. It is a most serious holiday, but most cleansing, as well.

I made the mistake of allowing Mariam to bring Layla.

The girls covered themselves with the tiny flowered *chador*s one of my maids had sewn for them, and I let them into my upstairs parlor. Layla's eyes grew immediately wide. I did not ever allow the children into that room; it was too magnificent. The golden furniture was upholstered in soft deep green, a color to honor Islam. An enormous carpet—a woven portrait of my husband—hung four meters down from the carved ceiling. On the coffee tables were my most unique possessions: silver ash-trays, porcelain figurines, bejeweled candy dishes, lamps that had once been water pipes, and the most exquisite ivory boxes filled with my favorite pink and blue Turkish cigarettes. Of course, I had had the servants furnish every empty space on the tables with platters of cookies and pastries for the twenty or so women—the city's most respected and devout women—who sat, each with a glass of perfectly tinted tea before them.

The *mullah* whom I had hired to recite Saint Hossein's story was not my first choice; the one I usually used was ill. I was already irritable over this issue, and I became especially upset when I noticed how he seemed unenthusiastic, almost matter-of-fact, when he came to the most passionate moment in the legend: when the poor *Emam* Hossein's severed head begins to chant for our people, giving them strength to endure their own deaths to come. That disrespectful *mullah* wallowed in his chair, fiddling with the prayer beads in his lap as if they were a toy, and looking bored, his eyes fixed on a plate of my delicious almond-paste sweets. So I was irritable, but I said nothing. The women were crying for the *Emam*, wailing in the most bloody places, sniffling when the story ebbed, and rocking their bodies when grief overtook them. All seemed to be going well enough.

Suddenly, I sensed something was wrong. The *mullah* was squinting with disapproval, his eyes on the girls. What were those children doing? Was that catlike whining coming from beneath those miniature *chadors*? This could not be! Did they think this was an adventure? Here I had permitted them to attend a most important adult event, trusted them to behave, and they were making a mockery of it all! To my shock, their artificial crying voices grew even louder until they were howling like wolves! And the room grew quiet. My humiliation hung in the air. I roughly lifted the tip of each of their *chadors* and out popped their dry faces. My granddaughter, who knew better, began to cry for real. But Layla, to my astonishment, looked me straight in the eye and smiled.

I wanted her away from my grandchildren.

Seven

Layla

The woman guard shoved me down into the cellar of my child-hood home and into a small, windowless place that had once been a storage room with shelves where my grandmother kept preserves and pickled vegetables. As a prison cell, it was infested with roaches and rats. In the corner was a rusty bucket, where I was told to relieve myself. When I used it, which was often because I soon came down with dysentery from what little they fed me, I was always careful to keep my skin from touching it, from the slime and bugs that rose from it.

When I became feverish I began to sense that Dariush was with me there in the cell, holding me, smelling like citrus, like the oranges we'd saved from our breakfast in the hotel room, pressing small kisses on my forehead with lips like a cool cloth. These were not dreams or hallucinations. I knew he wasn't actually there, but it seemed that his *thoughts* were there and I was wrapped in them for protection, to get me through those days of isolation and darkness.

After some time, maybe a week by my count of the *Azan*, the Call to Prayer, the guards dragged me out of that room and dumped me, weak and delirious, in a corner of what had once been the laundry room. I couldn't raise my head without becoming nauseated, but I knew there were other women around me, huddled on the floor and hostile because the guards kept calling me *khanoom taghoot*, lady royalist, in their cackling voices. After the guards left, I felt some of the women picking roughly at my *manteau* and my stockings, and one said, "I wonder what the princess paid for such material." And another replied, "More than it would take to feed my children for a month." Someone took off my shoe and said, "Oh-ho! From France!" I heard a snap and managed to open one eye; the woman had torn the heel off. I closed my eye. Burn the shoes, I thought. Tear them apart. Eat them, if you want. All I cared about right then was to be free of the nausea and the cramps and the tremors.

A young girl with a delicate voice told the woman with my shoe that *Allah* would punish her for being so wicked. I felt bony fingers slipping my shoe back onto my foot, then the girl's warmth came close and she rested her arm on my shoulder, claiming me, it seemed. I heard the other women slink back. For some days, the girl protected me, took care of me, helping me sip an occasional glass of rancid-tasting tea, whispering to me to stop dreaming in English because it was angering some of the others. Her name was Zeeba, which was a terrible joke because she was nothing like her name, not beautiful at all. She smelled as bad as a dirty diaper (or maybe that was my own odor), but she was as kind as a mother bird, feeding me and stroking my hair, and I remember thinking that I loved her.

Then they came and took her away, just as they took everyone away, eventually. This was a temporary prison, a kind of purgatory. All the people they suspected of being *Mojahedeen*—Islamic-Marxists, the most organized and hated counterrevolutionaries—they sentenced to death. But I could always tell when the judge had made a mistake about them because when the guards came to take them up to the roof to be executed, they would scream and wail and pray. When they took Zeeba, though, she went like a child going off to school: this was not something she liked, but it was something she had to do. As she was being guided out the door, she told me that she knew she'd see me soon. When I realized what she was actually saying, I knew my only chance was escape.

I forced myself to sit up and coaxed as much water and tea as I could from the guards. I'd become dehydrated, and I knew if I wanted to find a way to escape, I would have to be stronger.

As the days passed, women came and went—some to the roof, some to Evin, the big jail uptown that had been built by the shah to house all his political prisoners—until only one other woman had been there as long as I. In the mornings, when a sliver of light came through the one high window in the room, I would always first see her bugged-out eyes staring at me from the opposite wall. She sat next to the ancient washing machine that had been turned around so some incompetent mechanic could explore its motor. When she wasn't snoring, she would bark obscenities at me and fiddle her fingers over the big flaccid hose of the washing machine. "American spy, American whore, heathen, traitor, daughter of Satan." She never grew tired of cursing me.

I was the only woman there who might be considered a royalist, a *taghoot*. Auntie Katayoon would have laughed at that; she would have reminded me that the regime had gotten rid of most of the royalists by then. That was true, but it was still odd that I hadn't been summoned or whipped or murdered. I took it as a good sign. Maybe the officials were now only concerned with the *Mojahedeen*. Maybe they realized I had to be harmless.

So I put the idea of escape aside and began thinking about the possibility that I could convince whoever was in charge to release me.

Finally, the guards came to take the cursing woman to Evin. A five-year sentence for possession of alcohol. She wailed and kicked so much that the guard threatened her with eighty lashes if she didn't calm down. She quieted. But the last defiant thing she did before they dragged her off was point at me and ask the guard why, in the name of the great *Emam*, was "that daughter of a dog being taken care of like a princess"? That was when I realized, from the surprised look on the faces of the guards, that I'd been totally forgotten—not purposely reprieved, just forgotten, a shivering lump in the corner of the room. And now that I'd been remembered, I would have to pay, just like everyone else.

They took me upstairs. It was heart-wrenching to see all the familiar rooms with strange furniture in them. The carpet on the stairs and the wallpaper in the foyer had not been changed, and the staircase banister that I used to slide down was still as smooth as ever. All the rooms in the house had been made into offices, and men walked back and forth between them carrying papers and folders. After having been in the basement—the prison—it was difficult to imagine that these mild-mannered people were responsible for what was going on down there and up on the roof.

They brought me before a *mullah*, a cleric who was very young, twenty-five or so. His office was in what had been my parents' bedroom, and the emerald-and-gold drapes I remembered were still there. They were torn and dirty, hanging unevenly. Tears sprang to my eyes. The *mullah* asked me quietly, nicely, to sit down. He was behind his desk. I guess he pitied me. He watched me for a long time, pushed a box of tissues toward me, and waited until I blew my nose. The window was open, and a breeze wafted through the room. The air was so sweet with pine that I had to control myself from running out onto the balcony. I smelled myself then, my unwashed body—as if I'd been sprayed by a skunk.

The *mullah* then asked me the strangest question: "Who are you?" he said.

I thought, He's trying to trick me. I searched his face. No gleam in his eye, no sneer on his lips. Could it be that I'd become lost in the bureaucratic confusion of this place? Oh God, I thought. If I played the game right, could I talk my way out of here?

I gave the *mullah* a false name and quickly told him that my husband was at the war front. I had no idea then that this was indeed the truth. I just thought such a fact would win me some points. And it did. He was impressed. He smiled and nodded his head. He was trying to act like a benevolent, old, wise *mullah*. By then I sensed I could convince him to let me go.

"Why were you brought to the prison, *khanoom?*" he asked.

"I do not know," I said, opening my eyes widely, innocently. "I was merely plucked off the street and never given any explanation." Oh! It felt good to lie. "My husband, sir," I whined. "I am concerned that he might have tried to contact me and cannot find me." It wasn't difficult to bring tears to my eyes at this point; could I hope that Dariush was all right and trying to find me?

He nodded. "And your father's family name?"

"Kermani," I said, using another false last name. "My mother is dead, but my father owns a small pistachio farm in Kerman." What part of my brain had *this* outlandish story come from? "My father is very ill," I continued, golden lies pouring out of my mouth. "I had planned a trip to visit him. He is expecting me. But I was arrested. Just plucked off the street, sir, as I told you, for no reason. Excuse me, how many days have I been here?"

The *mullah* scanned his desk, piled high with papers and personal paraphernalia—wallets and cameras, cassette tapes and crinkled paper bags. Finally, he shrugged. "I have no information on you, *khanoom*. The guards tell me they think you have been here almost two weeks."

I made an exaggerated gasp even though it had seemed much longer than two weeks to me. "My father," I wailed. "I hope my father has survived. I must get the train to Kerman."

"Of course, *khanoom*. I will call a taxi for you."

I looked up, swallowing a gasp. "Thank you."

"May I apologize on behalf of the Islamic Republic of Iran. But you must understand that we are merely doing our best to make the country safe."

"Of course," I said, barely able to stand, shaking all over, ready to dance around the room.

Suddenly, a *pasdar* with a deep frown and a pointy nose came into the room. He wore fatigues and had a machine gun over his shoulder, the point of it buried in long hair that hung down below his neck. He crossed the room, went behind another desk, and shuffled through papers. I realized that he and the *mullah* shared the office. He might not have glanced up if the *mullah* hadn't sneezed loudly; it was just a natural reaction to the sharp sound. In the second—and it was just a second—that he looked at my face, I felt his recognition like a slap, even though I knew I'd never seem him before in my life.

Quickly, I spoke to the *mullah*. "I am grateful to you, sir. I am ready to go home now." He nodded and stepped toward the door with me, then the *pasdar* said "Wait!" and I knew the beautiful ruse was over.

Apparently the woman who'd arrested me had passed on the incriminating college ID card to the *pasdar*. He'd passed it on to the *mullah*, but the *mullah* hadn't gotten to it yet, what with his desk piled so high with evidence. The *pasdar* quickly dug through the mess and found my ID card. My fingers twitched with an urge to pounce on him before he could shove the evidence into the *mullah*'s hands. But then the *mullah* was pinching the card with his dirty fingernails, and I shivered as if my blood had turned into cold syrup. He peered at my picture, then at me. His cheeks turned red and he sucked his lips into his mouth. God help me now, I thought, not only am I considered a spy, but also a whore who has humiliated a pompous *mullah*. I swallowed. My tongue felt like an ice cube. This *mullah* would make me pay.

The *pasdar* gripped my arm and pulled me out of the room and along the hallway to the back stairs. I fell going up. My scarf slid off my head, and the *pasdar* grabbed a handful of my hair and dragged me up the rest of the way. Tears stung my eyes. We were in the attic. It was damp and dusty like the inside of an old adobe hut Dariush and I had ventured into long ago during a storm. A burly woman in a filthy gray *manteau* stood under a bare lightbulb that swung on a wire like in a spy movie. The *pasdar* thrust me at her. She smelled like wet wool. "On the table!" she ordered.

I took a chance—looked at the *pasdar*, then at the woman— and spoke, "Please wait. Please. I haven't done anything wrong. I swear to God." My voice was choked, desperate, like a hungry beggar. There was silence for a moment. They looked at one another. The woman had no expression; she reminded me of a doll I'd once had whose face was made of a malleable fabric that always returned to its original shape no matter how much punishment I gave it. Suddenly, the *pasdar* laughed loudly. "Have fun," he said to the woman. He turned his back and left.

"On the table!" she said again as if someone had pulled her dolly talk-cord. I climbed onto what was a gurney without a pad. "Face down!" she snapped. The cold metal stung the skin through my clothes. The woman yanked my arms above my head and strapped my wrists to a cold pipe that felt scaly, like a worn snakeskin bag. She removed my shoes. They thudded to the floor. She tore the feet off my thick stockings with her beefy fingers, and the scratchy ripping sound echoed off the rafters. I drew my legs under me, shivering. She grabbed my ankles and strapped them so tightly to the table that my toes began to tingle. My neck ached with the effort of twisting my head to watch her every move. She never once looked at my face. She reached behind her then and took something long and snaky and silvery off a nail in the wall. My intestines churned suddenly; sweat broke out around my eyes. "*Khanoom*, please," I begged, trying to lure her to look at me, to see the innocence in my eyes. "Shut up!" she said, stepping back, her eyes on my feet, lifting the wire cable slowly, then suddenly snapping her wrist forward and bringing the metal in contact with the soles of my feet. The pain went like a bolt of lightning through my body, forcing a cry I'd never heard come from my mouth. My cheek fell onto the table and I bit my tongue. She lashed again and again. The muscles in my legs convulsed and I smelled my own blood. She took a rest and massaged her arm, then lashed again: to the heel, *whack!*, to the arch, *whack!*, to the instep, *whack!* I banged my head against the metal table, trying to divert the pain. I cursed her. She beat harder. I tried desperately to find a way to shut my brain off, to keep it from receiving the terrible signal of pain. I tried to think of my father, of New York, of Banu, of my grandparents, of Dariush—why had he deserted me now? Where were his thoughts? Nothing worked. The pain came and came, boring deeper and deeper into me until I was one large bleeding ulcer. I begged them to kill me and finally, it seemed they were willing to give me what I wanted.

They demanded that I sign a piece of paper. Yes, I would sign. My voice was a whisper. They sat me up. I couldn't keep my head from rolling to the side. Will you sign? they kept asking. Yes, I'll sign, I said. I retched. Someone wiped my mouth with a rough cloth that smelled like garlic. "*Will you sign?!*" demanded the voice of the young *mullah*. Yes, yes, I thought I said. "Get her out of my sight," he said. "Teach her a lesson."

The shadow of another man who smelled strongly of cigar smoke and sweat came forward and lifted me off the table. My feet touched the icy floor and I heard myself yell. My knees buckled and I waited for my cheek to strike the floor, but the man held my arm and pulled me up. "Walk, whore! It is not far where you are going."

I was so cold. Shivering. A gust of wind swept over me. So here I was finally, on the roof of that old house. I thought suddenly how I'd been forbidden to come up here as a child. "We're not allowed up here," I said to the shadow. He didn't hear. I tasted blood in my mouth and felt it trickle down my chin as I spoke. The shadow still held me up. The cool air cleared the film of tears from my eyes. A pile of clothing was heaped at my feet. No, not a pile of clothing, but clothing on the pile of a person. The clothing was riddled with dark, round holes. "No," I said, knowing now that I was only speaking in my mind. "Don't . . . do . . . this. I'll sign. Tell me what to sign. I'll sign. Please." Only the "please" was audible. It seemed to act as a signal that made the shadow raise his arm and bring the pistol to my temple. He breathed heavily as if he were having sex. He slid the hard metal down my face and rested it against my lips. It tasted bitter like aspirin. He said slowly, "Say good-bye, pretty sister." I concentrated on the pain flooding through my body.

From a distance, as if beyond a cement wall, I heard Dariush's voice. "This will help," he said. And I felt a tingling kiss on my breast just as I heard the hollow click of the gun. And suddenly I was falling to the ground and away from the pain. The shadow sputtered with laughter, saying, "No bullets, foolish sister! No bullets."

Eight

Maman Bozorg

I have grown older looking in this one week since they arrested Dariush and took him to the war front. My silver hairs have turned white as cotton. I see this in the mirror when I remove my scarf. How long have I been covering my hair? How many youthful silken black strands have I left behind in all those beautiful fabrics? How many years is it? More than sixty? Nearly seventy? I do not know exactly; my birthdays have gone by without fanfare. But I remember perfectly the day I began to wear the veil.

The *Qoran* tells us that a girl becomes a woman when she is nine years old. This is when she must begin wearing the veil and saying her *namaz*, her Islamic prayers, five times each day. This is when it becomes dangerous for her to think she is still a child, for this is when men will begin to want her. She must protect herself. Of course my Mariam did not wear the *chador*, and I was not witless enough to insist that she do this. The schoolchildren did not wear *chador*; they were under the influence of their misguided parents, who had forgotten who they were, who would have drawn the map of Iran on the European continent if they could have. No. Only the truly pious and the poor veiled themselves. I knew if I insisted my granddaughter follow the ways of Islam, she would suffer ridicule and this might move her to rebellion. So I said nothing about the *chador*. And I was not regretful in the beginning; however, when she began to blossom, I became worried. She was changing too fast, changing like the city around us: growing tall like its buildings, cosmopolitan like its restaurants, and expectant like its naive citizens. Everything appeared new, yet the old remained; it was merely covered with a foolish grin. It was nearing the time when my granddaughter should marry, yet I knew it was too soon for Dariush—and too soon for Dariush to recognize that his cousin was his match. He was only four years older than her, after all, and he had his mind on other things, as boys do. Still, he was good and obedient to me. I knew he would follow the right path when the moment arrived.

It was around this time when I allowed my son Hooshang to convince me to sell my downtown property and move to Shemiran, an area in the foothills of the Alborz Mountains north of Tehran where, for generations, our family had owned a vast garden and several villages. We had passed the summers there above the city in the shadows of the tall peaks, where the air was fresh and cool.

But Shemiran had changed. It had become part of the city, a suburb. Well, of course it had; Tehran had become as bloated as oversoaked rice. So many people came from the countryside, believing that merely to come to Tehran would make them rich. Reza Shah's son, that boy who unashamedly called himself King of Kings, allied himself with the West, making Iran partners in oil and partners in the crimes against Palestine. That pompous boy and his family, they flaunted themselves and made everyone believe that wealth was within their grasp. And he pushed our *mullah*s aside, by force and in the name of the Devil's modernization.

Moving to Shemiran is a decision I will always regret. Hooshang had had sections of our garden cleared for three new houses—one for me, the other two for himself and Katayoon. Unlike our smaller compound in the downtown, however, the houses were far apart and walls of trees and hedges kept them hidden from one another. At my request, the small villa—only two rooms—that we had used during the summers was not demolished, but it was soon strangled by the growth of the garden, and eventually Hooshang ordered a tennis court built in its place.

I was unhappy from the moment I crossed the threshold into this plain box of white stone. The walls are so thin I cannot keep the growls of the street dogs from reaching my ears at night. And the evening breeze that sweeps off the mountains dries my bones. Shemiran is not a place where people should live the year round. I do not understand why everyone found it so alluring to move where only summer houses used to be built, where only the most beautiful gardens were tended. Now those gardens are blemished with marble monsters they call houses—buildings with flat lines and strangely placed windows and swimming pools and European balustrades and columns. It was true that the downtown had become noisy and polluted and congested, but it was our duty to stay and preserve the land our ancestors gave us. I realized the terrible weight of my decision only after everything was removed from the house of my father and I stood there in what I thought would be emptiness, but was in fact the opposite. When I left that house, I left the strength of our traditions behind. It would be the beginning of my troubles.

Of course the children—Dariush and Mariam—loved moving away from the downtown. Why should they not? They were no longer in the midst of religion and morality; Shemiran was a candy bazaar for them, a place filling up with Western imitations, luring them. And their parents were unaware of the hazards. They were too busy turning dollars into *touman*s and *touman*s into dollars. It was no longer good enough to have respectable lineage; they wanted to be splendidly rich as well. It is why Hooshang built all his clinics and why Katayoon's brothers built their carpet factories—Western carpets, can you imagine? Suddenly it was more elegant to have a gray or brown sheet of smelly fiber on the floor than it was to have one of our ancestors' hand-woven Kerman carpets.

And there was Mina's son Ebrahim, profiting at every turn because of his association with the Americans. They saw how thirsty our country was for all their so-called inventions: medicines and music and detergents and food and clothing. Suddenly, all the young people were wearing rough blue trousers and thin shirts that displayed words and pictures on their chests; even the girls whose parents insisted they remain pious would wear them beneath their billowing *chador*s. Yes, it was Ebrahim and those like him with their lust for Western things and their connections with the infidels who profited the most and who did the most damage to this country. But, thanks to the *Emam*, most of that is gone for them now.

I had thought the only good thing to come from our move was the separation of Layla from my grandchildren; the Baharis' new compound was no longer next door, but some fifteen minutes away. To my horror, however, Layla and Mariam, then twelve years old, were together more than ever. To compensate for their separation, that Katayoon let them spend nights together. And although Katayoon's house was only a walk away, I refused to set foot in it without invitation. It is the duty of children to visit their parents, not the opposite. I was frustrated. In my old house, I had merely to look out my window to see what things were going on at the homes of my sons. But now I had no such luxury. I was forced to rely on my servants as spies.

That first summer in Shemiran—the summer of 1346, fourteen years ago—was like a hell for me. They sent my Dariush away to a tennis camp in France; of all places, Europe for tennis, as if he could not play tennis at that ostentatious Club of the King of Kings that Pahlavi built in his own honor, appropriately in the middle of an ugly, barren piece of the desert. The children were always there anyway, mixing with one another, swimming in those garments as small as dolls' clothing, playing rummy and poker, forgetting the rules that would keep them pure and safe. And then there was that *boleeng* place. I never went there of course, but I heard from the *naneh*s who kept me informed. Suddenly everyone was playing this ludicrous American game of knocking down white sticks with a heavy ball. Why are Westerners so occupied with inventing games for balls? It is true that I believe that *takhteh* and *shatranje*—what the West calls backgammon and chess—are games that can pollute a chaste mind, but these two games that were invented by my ancestors are at least somewhat crafty and require the use of intelligence. The Western games are merely an excuse for men and women to congregate, drink alcohol, and forget their obligations. The children were exposed to such corruption more and more, because this *boleeng* place grew bigger and bigger. Soon it had a cinema where the children could see American movies, then a place for them to slide across a wide floor on shoes with wheels on the bottom, and then a place for something called Tea Dancing, because tea and sweets alone no longer fulfilled our children quite enough.

I will always believe the move to Shemiran was our family's most serious error. The children were set free like gypsies. My father, who had been an *arbab*, a man who owned many villages in the old days before the shah changed the laws, used to tell us how *all* people, like children, needed boundaries to make suitable decisions. I believed this. And I did not want my grandchildren to fall into that dark Western tunnel they think is filled with freedom but that will only crush them with too many choices. I had to take things into my own hands. And although I did not have the control I had before, I believed I could, in my own way, keep them on the correct road. I did this with my intelligence, my quick tongue, and with fear.

Children cannot be brought up properly without fear. How is it that no one understands this anymore? Perhaps it is for the same reason that, until the Revolution, no one understood the *Shari'at*, the regulations of religion, anymore. How could they? Even the *Qoran* was not taught in the schools. Instead, the children learned something called *ravan-shenasee*, mind-acquaintance. Veeda was especially fond of this new subject, only she gave it a showy French name; *peeseecology*, she called it. This was supposed to help our children learn to live in the modern world and to help their parents do away with the cloud of fear under which all children must live in order to attain righteousness. As Prophet Mohammad is my witness, I knew this kind of upbringing would only lead to sin. And while I watched these sickening foreign ways stream into the souls of my grandchildren, I saw our noble traditions leak out of their parents' spirits.

Even some of my own friends were lured by Western ideas. They allowed the world to weaken them. That Mina, I remember how we argued one day. She had an unusual notion that it was not her place to interfere in her son's life. What is a mother then? An ornament? And what is a grandmother? Merely bosoms for a grandchild to rest her head upon? Had she not seen what her leniency had done to her own Layla? The child had no reverence for her elders; she spoke to them about anything at will. And her camaraderie with other children was completely impudent. I forbade Dariush and Mariam to laugh at her practical jokes and her silly imitations of people, but I knew they did not obey. I heard about the device she brought from America that would make the rude noise of passing wind when unsuspecting persons sat on it, and I knew that she caused Veeda's cook to faint at the sight of plastic beetles floating in his yogurt-and-cucumber soup. I will never forget the time she sent Mariam a jar of a paste made from peanuts (the most inferior of nuts), telling her it was a delicacy in America. Such choking poison! The repulsive paste stuck to my tongue like an evil spirit and I cursed that tricky child until the vile flavor finally washed away. Much to my disappointment, Dariush claimed to like it and seemed to be choking only on his own laughter at my discomfort. I forgave him for this because I knew it was part of his teasing nature. As for Layla, what bothered me most about her was that picture-taking machine she used as an excuse to maneuver the children. Her fascination with it was the final element that led me to conclude she was surely power-thirsty and mentally unusual. No, I told Mina, I would not give up my influence over the members of my family. This would be like sending them into purgatory.

Even as the years passed and I had fewer and fewer opportunities to be with my family because they took their vacations in their villas and chalets in the West, even as I heard from the servants and friends about the immoral ways in which they led their lives, I continued to believe that my experience and plans were their best hopes. After all, I was their grandmother, and it was their duty to visit me every day that they were home. Thankfully, this was a tradition our people continued to respect. But I knew this was also changing.

That foolish Katayoon once told me she wanted Mariam to think of her as a friend. How ridiculous. Friends come and go. A daughter cannot come and go at will; a daughter must come and go by direction. And Veeda was worse. She refused to consider corporal punishment. And she convinced Hooshang to go along with such an idea. It seemed he did not remember the benefit of such a thing in his own life; he was such a disorganized child, never doing his lessons on time, always studying for examinations at the final hour. A few floggings and this was corrected. How could he have become a doctor without such discipline? He should have thanked me, but instead he discussed the right and the wrong of it. He had the disrespect to say he did not feel such punishment would be advantageous to his own son.

Four years after we moved to Shemiran, my Dariush left me to go to that university in America. This was the summer I felt as if I had lost my power to manage our family; I was failing my duty. It was also the summer in which Katayoon began making noises about enrolling Mariam in a Swiss boarding school. Forgive me, I thought *Allah* had abandoned me, and I was so angry I beat my favorite maid. I thought about my right as a paternal grandmother: I had the final word; I could insist that Katayoon give the child to me. One thing stopped me. This school in Europe was for girls only. Still, I did not give up my hold on Mariam. Although I never spoke another unnecessary word to my daughter-in-law, there were times in which I compelled her to send Mariam to me—the girl needed my way of straightening her out—but these times were few and then only when she was home from the West. In the end, my granddaughter came back to me of her own free will.

That summer of 1350, however, was painful and wicked for another reason. It was *Allah* who must have ordained that I attend Veeda and Hooshang's garden party at the *bagh* in Karadj; it is not my way to go out from my house, but this was a party in honor of my Dariush's journey, and he himself had asked me to come. Although I would rather have lost my eyes than to have seen what I saw in my grandson's face that day, I knew it was meant to be: that God wanted me to know the dangers of the evil Layla, not only to Mariam, but to my precious Dariush.

Nine

The Rules of Persian Etiquette

August 1971
Mordad, The Month of the Lion's Tower, 1350

They sit at opposite corners of the Cadillac's backseat, angry with one another. Layla, pressed against the door, focuses on the desert brush and asks the driver to turn the radio louder; Mick Jagger's voice fills the car with "Brown Sugar." Ebrahim, scanning financial reports scribbled in Farsi numerals, frowns at the loud music, but he does not look Layla's way. They had argued before leaving the house. He is infuriated at her clothing; he does not like this new fashion of hot pants; well, he likes it, but not on his daughter. For the first time, he had noticed that she wears a bra—well, of course she wears a bra, she is fourteen already—but he had noticed this specifically because she was *not* wearing one. Despite his disapproval, she had refused to change. She is so stubborn, he thinks. And she is so unreachable now that she has grown older. But what did he think? That she would be a malleable child forever? He steals a look at her, sitting with her chin in her hand, pouting, determined. He holds back a chuckle suddenly. If she is anything like her father, she will do what she wants.

They are on the road to Karadj, a dusty two-lane highway that first runs through the flat desert, then winds through mountains until it arrives at the city and the lush gardens—the *baghs*—that surround it. They have been invited to a garden party at the Namdar *bagh*; it is a going-away party for Dariush, who will be leaving for America, for Harvard, in a week's time.

Layla loves this drive, especially when she sees the roaring Karadj River that snakes through the mountains, sometimes entrenching itself so slyly between beige hills that she wouldn't know it was there unless she stood on the edge of its bank and looked down into the white water. She looks for village women with their *chador*s hiked up around their waists standing in the rushing stream washing pots and clothing, their bare legs blue from the cold mountain water. And then, rounding a turn on a part of the road that has been carved out of the side of a dusty, rocky mountain, they come to the Karadj Dam and the reservoir, like a glistening emerald between sand dunes, an oasis of aquamarine where Layla learned to water-ski.

Suddenly, a crimson roadster, low to the ground and moving fast, passes the Cadillac and narrowly misses an oncoming Benz truck. Everyone sits on their horns, including the driver of the roadster—as if this will make it look as if *he* is the one who has been wronged. Ebrahim gasps and tells their driver to slow down and watch out for such crazy people. Layla wonders if her father ever grew up in Iran; he seems always to expect the drivers to behave as if they are from prudent New Jersey suburbs. Layla slinks down farther in the seat and watches the back of the red roadster fishtailing slightly around the curves. She smiles, remembering Dariush and a little red go-cart his father had brought him from Germany.

She was nine that summer, Dariush thirteen. He would come next door to her grandparents' house to ride the little race car because their big driveway was perfect for it and because Maman Bozorg did not approve of the Western toy. All of them—the neighborhood children, she and Mariam, the servants' children— would watch him with awe every time. He would go so fast, pushing the flimsy machine to its deafening limits, zooming along the smooth asphalt like a red blur, forcing gardeners to leap into the wet flower beds and making the children scream with laughter.

Everyone wanted to drive it, but no one dared even ask. Auntie Veeda's cook's son, Jamsheed, Dariush's most loyal playmate, acted like a security guard and would not let the children within an arm's length of the machine. Dariush must have yanked the pull-starter on the go-cart more than twenty times that summer. And Layla remembers that they never grew tired of watching.

Then suddenly, shockingly, Dariush putt-putted to a stop one afternoon, his hair wet with perspiration and his cheeks tight with a frozen smile. He looked at Layla and said, "Come on, Laylee. I'll take you for a ride." And everyone became silent, standing completely still. She thought he was teasing her. She remembers the uneven snapping sound of the motor. He reached out and pulled her limp arm toward him. She was proud that he had picked her, even though she thought it must be because she was skinny enough to fit on the seat with him. She had to lean back against his chest and put her legs on top of his. She wrapped her arms around his thighs and he whispered in her ear, "Don't be afraid."

Her heart races every time she remembers that ride. The excitement, the vibration of the machine, Dariush's trembling arm around her waist, his white knuckles gripping the wheel. She could hardly breathe. The world jerked up and down like a film moving unevenly through a camera lens, and her bottom jiggled against the metal seat like corn in a popping machine. When they stopped, her whole body was vibrating. She had tried to get up, but Dariush held her against him for just a few seconds. She felt a strange thrill in her stomach. After Jamsheed helped her out, she turned around on shaking legs and saw that Dariush was staring at her, his chest moving in and out with a heavy breath. He looked puzzled, almost as if he did not recognize her. The children gathered around her, talking all at once. Mariam was gone.

Layla found her standing on the veranda outside her bedroom, leaning on the wrought-iron railing, staring into the garden trees. The strong afternoon sun rippled the air above the white stone patio. A forgotten Barbie doll, sheathed in a glittering crimson gown, lay against the wall. Layla picked it up, remembering how much fun they had had playing with it the day before. Suddenly, Mariam's hand slapped down onto Layla's arm, stinging the skin and sending Barbie to the stones. Her heel came down on the doll's head, smearing it with tar from the bottom of her shoe. "What're you doing?" Layla shouted, stooping to pick up the doll. Without a word, Mariam shoved Layla down onto the stones, then stomped through the bamboo shade into her bedroom.

Both of Layla's knees were bleeding, but she was more angry than hurt. She went into the bedroom, itching to pull at her friend's hair and punch her until she cried out. But Mariam suddenly appeared from the bathroom with a wad of gauze and a bottle of iodine, and she immediately crouched in front of Layla and began to tend to her wounds with exaggerated gentleness, as if she had had nothing to do with causing them at all. Layla stepped back. "Why did you do that?" she asked through clenched teeth.

"Let me clean it, Layla," Mariam said calmly, not looking up. "The blood is dripping down your legs."

"No!" Layla stepped back again. "Why did you do that to me? Tell me!"

Mariam stood up and threw the gauze on the bed. "I'm sorry I did it. It's just that sometimes you are bad mannered and that makes me very angry."

"I didn't do anything that was bad mannered." But Layla was never sure of this because Mariam was her mentor in the obsessive rules of Persian etiquette, the detective of all her American *faux pas.*

Mariam's upper lip quivered suddenly. "*I* should get the first ride," she blurted out. "He's *my* cousin, mine!" she said, using the Farsi words that could mean "he belongs to me."

Layla yelled back. "He *asked* me to go with him. I didn't have anything to do with it."

"Liar! I bet you asked him behind my back. You're always trying to get close to him; everyone is. Well don't ever forget that he has the most fun with me. You're just an outsider, Layla."

Mariam knew how to get to Layla, that it was Layla's wish not to be an outsider, to be accepted, even for the short three months that she spent with them every year. "You're mean, Mariam." Layla moved for the door; she did not want to cry there.

"Wait," Mariam called. "Your knees. They look terrible; everyone will see them."

"I'm going home."

"I'm sorry, Laylee. Don't go yet. I'll clean the scrapes for you." She grabbed Layla's forearm and started to sob. "Please don't be mad. Laylee, please, stay and we'll play with the Barbies."

"How can we? You ruined the one I gave you."

Mariam hesitated. "I know." She smiled suddenly. "Now she looks like Mirza's little sister." After a cautious pause, they both giggled because Mirza's sister had an ugly birthmark across her cheek that everyone made fun of.

Layla sat on the bed and let Mariam put Band-Aids on her knees. After that, they were playmates once more, and the summers flowed into one another so when Layla thinks about them now, they seem like one solid string of memory. But during all this time she has not forgotten the episode of Dariush and the go-cart, never forgotten its consequences. And even though he finds his way into her dreams, she has tried not to think about him. For Mariam's sake. And for her own sake. Mariam is her best friend, her ally in the Persian world. She does not want to lose her.

Layla watches the red roadster speed up and pass another car, then another; she wonders if the driver is someone they know, on his way to Dariush's going-away party too. The curves in the road are tight and close; the roadster is finally too far ahead to see anymore. All that remains is the dust it churned, now crackling on the windshield like rain. Layla wishes their driver would speed up and pass the cars ahead, but she knows he will never do this. Out of the corner of her eye, she sees her father craning his neck and shaking his head at the dangerous road.

They reach the outskirts of the city of Karadj, where there are tall stone walls that sometimes shadow ancient walls of *kahgel*, an adobe that makes them look molded from the same earth on which they stand, as do sand castles. Behind these walls are the *bagh*s where generations of gardeners have cultivated their masters' orchards and flowers, grapevines and berries, but mostly, they have cultivated the beauty of the *bagh*—defying the desert with their craft, making Eden from sand.

When Layla and Ebrahim arrive, the Namdar *bagh* is already filled with food and music and the usual guests, about two hundred family and close friends. Dariush's mother Veeda has hired a DJ from one of the discos in Tehran who has "Saturday in the Park" blaring from six enormous speakers. The patio has been turned into a dance floor. Layla does not see Mariam or Dariush. She is now even more angry with her father, who is embarrassing her by asking Veeda if she thinks it is proper for Layla to wear hot pants at her age. Fortunately, Veeda laughs at him. She pinches Layla's cheek with fingers as soft as warm bread and tells her she looks very fashionable. "I think Dariush and Mariam are behind the gazebo, Laylee," she says in a voice sweet and slow as cherry syrup.

But they are not there. Two old women sit within the latticed structure, talking in whispers. As Layla approaches, she recognizes Maman Bozorg and stops short before she comes into the old woman's view; she has never seen Maman Bozorg in any place other than her own home. Layla slowly turns and quietly retraces her steps. She thinks she sees a spot of color moving beyond the azalea bushes and wonders if this could be Mariam. She wanders into the density of the garden. The loud music and the sounds of conversation recede as the foliage closes behind her. The bright sunlight fades, making the leaves and flowers look richer in color, creating a cozy green maze of chambers. She strolls toward the orchards.

Dariush sits with his back against a peach tree, his legs stretched in front of him, crossed at the ankles. He does not like crowded parties very much; he has sneaked away for a short while. He sees Layla through the trees before she sees him. And he knows he should let her know he is watching her, but he does not. She is trying to reach a particular peach high up in a tree a few feet away. She jumps for it several times, and each time she lands giftless she whispers "Shit!" Dariush squelches his laughter and tries to steady his pulse. He cannot take his eyes from her long bronzed legs nor from the pink panties he glimpses beneath her shorts. Finally, he swallows and says quietly, so as not to startle her, "Would you like me to help you?" She flinches, and he regrets his silence when he sees the blush of embarrassment rise upon her face.

"What are you doing here?" she says in an angry voice that he expects; she has always covered her embarrassment with toughness.

"I'm listening to the soccer game between Tehran and Esfahan," he says, lazily unsticking a small transistor radio from his ear. He grins in hopes of softening her.

"Where's Mariam?" she says, looking around.

"I don't know," he says.

"Well, I should go and find her," she says, her voice catching.

"Wait," he says, trying to think of what he can say to make her stay. But he is not given the chance to think. A strange thing happens. A sudden powerful gust of wind rustles through the trees, twisting delicate leaves and forcing fruit to the ground around them. Their clothing flutters and sand blows into their eyes and mouths. Dariush drops the transistor, coughing, and scrambles to his feet. He steadies Layla, who staggers and rubs at her eyes.

"What *was* that?" she says, her voice frightened and confused as if she has seen a ghost.

But before he can answer, a clap of thunder explodes from above and heavy raindrops begin slapping onto their heads and onto the leaves, battering them, first slowly, as if each whack could be counted, then quickly, violently, a sound like pouring uncooked rice onto an aluminum tray.

Neither of them has known such winds in a Tehran summer; no such storms that, in an instant, rage with thunder and rain when the sky was so blue and the air so calm just minutes before.

"We've got to get out of here," Dariush says loudly. He searches through the trees for shelter, holding Layla's arms as if the storm might carry her away. He feels the gritty sand against her moist skin.

"Let's just run back to the main house," she shouts over more thunder. But he knows this is too far and is afraid that lightning could strike them. He suddenly remembers something and grabs Layla firmly by the wrist so she will follow him.

They run, dodging branches and tree trunks and bushes. Their clothing becomes wet and heavy from the rain. Their sandals fill with mud. Finally, they duck into a dark hut that smells like mildew and ashes. They stand there, panting.

"Where are we?" she says.

"An old shed the gardener and his wife used to live in."

She touches the adobe wall with her fingertips. "It's made of *kahgel*." Beyond a molded window that has no glass or shutters, the rain continues to fall with force, but the thunder seems to be moving farther away.

"Yeah," he says. "It looks barren now, but there used to be a rug on the dirt floor, and curtains and pillows. I came here a few times when I was a kid. Jamsheed brought me. He liked the woman; she made excellent *albaloo khoshkeh*." He can suddenly taste the dried sour cherries as if his mouth is filled with them, and he thinks he could feel perfectly anything he imagines; his senses are strangely keen. He looks at Layla. Rivulets of water stream down her cheeks. Her lips glisten with moisture. Her hair falls in heavy strands to the curve in her lower back. The rain has made her halter top a translucent sheath that clings to her breasts. His heart still races, though he knows it should have calmed by now. With difficulty, he moves his gaze to her face. She has been watching him watching her. He sees her breath quicken, chest rising. Slowly, she brings her arms across her as if she is cold. Her voice sounds thin when she says, "Should we try to get back to the house?"

He swallows, "I think we should wait until the storm is over." He wants to move closer to her, to feel the small hairs on her arm tickling his skin.

"Strange thing, the storm," she says, almost in a whisper, as if she is reciting someone else's words.

He hears a faint rumble of thunder. "It can happen in the mountains sometimes," he says.

Her eyes remind him of his mother's emerald earrings; she stares at him, unblinking, and the dim light bounces off her wide pupils. Suddenly, slowly, she reaches for his face, touches her fingers to his cheek; they feel like feathers. His heart pounds in his ears and he prays he can move slowly. He gently slides his hand around the back of her neck; her pulse beats against his palm. He sees the small vertical lines in her lips, smooth like a satin ribbon.

When he kisses her, he feels their bodies trembling. She tastes like cinnamon. He kisses her neck and she presses her hands against his back. He feels as if they have done this many times before, as if he does not have to think about what comes next, as if that also has already happened before. He feels her nipples against his chest and pulls back to look at her. She is perfect, he thinks. They stand there staring—breathless, expectant. He puts his hand over her breast. She closes her eyes. Opens them slowly. And suddenly, a streak of sunshine falls across her face. Startled, they look toward the window. The rain has stopped; drops of water fall from the trees arrhythmically onto the roof. Steam rises from the rain-pelted desert floor. And they hear the voices of Mariam and Ebrahim, calling to them.

Of course everyone has been so worried. The storm—so sudden, so dangerous. Layla says she was lucky to stumble upon Dariush; she scolds Mariam playfully, saying it is Mariam's fault that she was caught in the storm; she was looking for *her*. And Ebrahim is almost in tears, hugging his daughter, draping his cotton sweater around her shoulders and tugging it over her chest. Mariam holds Dariush's hand tightly, her knuckles white, until they reach the main bungalow.

The guests have taken shelter from the storm here, sitting on colorful carpets, eating fruit and drinking tea, telling jokes and playing simple games. Even Maman Bozorg sits, though uncomfortably, against thick pillows in a corner with several other older, pious women. Dariush sees her immediately—sees the relief flood her face—when he and Mariam emerge from the camellia bushes. Layla and Ebrahim come next, and everyone applauds when they all step into the bungalow. They are smiled upon, kissed and hugged and patted. This has been an eventful day.

Veeda reproaches Dariush playfully, and Hooshang teases him about looking like a cat who has fallen into the washing pool. Dariush gratefully accepts a pile of dry clothing from a servant, and Veeda leads Layla toward the cabanas to change. Mariam brings steaming tea for Dariush; she holds the tray before him, practically under his nose. "You must drink tea, Dasha," she says, her face rapt with worry. "You must drink or you will catch a bad cold." But he does not see or hear her. He nods to something his father is saying to him, but his eyes watch Layla as if she is the sun setting in a vermilion sky.

Dariush suddenly senses something from across the room. He feels a blush rise over his face and turns to meet his grandmother's granite stare. Between them are many people and a great deal of commotion, but their eyes lock. Maman Bozorg places her scented handkerchief to her nose. Dariush's smile fades as he realizes she has seen in his face what no one else has seen.

Ten

Layla

The morning after they pretended to execute me, I woke up next to the old washing machine. The laundry room was full of new faces by then. They weren't hostile faces; I guess I didn't look like a *taghoot* anymore, just like any other battered woman. Someone shredded a *chador* and wrapped my feet. I slept more. The laundry room grew cold and I shivered. Was I feverish? Were my wounds infected already? Would I die here of some insidious bacteria?

When I was a child, visiting Tehran in summer, everyone treated me like a delicate Shirley Temple; there was great concern about my Farsi comprehension (which was perfect, thanks to Banu), about my understanding of Persian customs, and about the state of my emotional health (I was not just a child to them, but a *motherless* child). People would gaze upon me sadly and admonish their children to take special care of me, to let me win the games we played and to let me have the best candies. Worst of all, they weren't embarrassed to ask me about the workings of my bowels; if I so much as reached for a piece of fresh fruit or raw vegetable, someone out of nowhere would slap my hand and warn me against the dreaded Tehran Tummy. And if I ran a small fever or took a nap in the afternoon, a doctor was called in immediately to check that I hadn't contracted cholera or typhoid or tuberculosis—diseases that fragile little girls from America could not battle so easily.

I hated the way they fussed. Maybe this was how they'd treated my mother, but I was no foreigner. Iran was the country I thought of as home; I belonged to it and I resented those who made me feel as if I didn't. But now I saw how unappreciative I'd been and I yearned for those doting adults.

I opened my eyes and saw the vapor of my breath. An old woman, face as wrinkled as dried apricot, lay inches away, eyes closed, scrunched in a ball, shivering too. I wondered if an early snowfall had come to the city. I was desperate to get warm. *Think warm*, I told myself. *Sleep. Unconsciousness. Think Dariush.*

And there he was. As a child. Muddied down the side of one leg, bleeding from a gash in his head, sweating through his clothing, smelling like skunk cabbage. Unreachable, ahead of everyone, leading the pack. Servants constantly chasing after him for stealing pastries or for hiding their *chador*s and stockings. Mariam following him everywhere ferociously, imploring, "Wait for me, Dasha. Please wait." His bedroom baffling and fascinating, cluttered with cardboard and wooden structures of all shapes, bookshelves filled with volumes containing complicated line drawings and photographs of incomplete artifacts. His obsession with buildings. Old mosques and shrines, European cathedrals, skyscrapers covered in glass. His sketches and models of ancient floor plans and buildings. Photos of him touching the cold marble at St. Peter's Church, the stones of the Colosseum, struggling to reach the stained glass at Chartres.

Banu's voice from my childhood whistled through my ears, telling me that Dariush's zeal was unhealthy, that it put him in the land of dreams. "What good would he be to his family?" she said. "Besides, that grandmother of his, she is a tower of snake poison!" It was just like Banu always to be thinking way ahead, I thought. She'd known what was coming; she'd known I was in love with him years before I could understand that kind of love. Still, she had spoken of Dariush as too *shaytoon*, too devilish, and too *por-roo*, too full of impertinence. In the winters, I would think of him, an ocean away, in his messy room that smelled of ink and glue and gym socks, then I'd remember the wall behind his bed and how he'd carefully covered it with beautiful posters of Van Gogh paintings. And I'd remember how he, unlike Mariam and others, accepted me the way I was and never tried to show me ways to fit in when all I really wanted was to be myself, even if it meant being a little different.

He was good to me and Mariam when we were small. He played soccer and basketball with us, took us on searches through Maman Bozorg's compound for stray kittens and smooth ancient stones, and even included us in his explorations of the old cisterns and secret tunnels left over from the old dynasties when all kinds of intrigue went on between the women's sections—the harems or the *andaruni*—and other buildings. We loved to watch Dariush and his friends go down into one of these tunnels. Mariam and I were the lookouts for Mashti the gardener, who would inevitably discover what was going on and order the boys up before they could get very far. But that didn't stop them from hinting at the skeletons and treasure chests they may have seen down there.

Suddenly a shiver rattled through me and my eyes flickered open. Of course! The tunnels! The tunnels! I was fully awake now and no longer so cold. I knew exactly what I had to do, even if I had to crawl doing it.

The entrance to the tunnel, concealed in the brick wall, had always been behind the washing machine. Since the machine had been moved for repairs, I figured I could get to the trapdoor. I lay there for a while, checking to make sure all the other prisoners were asleep. Then I crept behind the machine, lay on my side, and looked for the hidden latch in the mortar between the bricks. It wasn't hard to find. Slowly and quietly, an inch a minute, I pulled the door open. My heart pounded in my ears. I remembered how afraid I'd been to go down into the tunnel when I was a child.

But I wasn't afraid now. I was more afraid of staying in that prison.

I peered into the darkness and felt for the stone steps leading down. I crawled in and closed the door tightly behind me.

Blackness. Silence. Pulse beating against my temples. I closed my eyes and felt my way down each cold step. Then the steps ended and my feet felt nothing: empty space. Loose stones from the final crumbling step fell away, sounding like scurrying animals as they reached a bottom that I couldn't see. Suddenly, I thought I saw the back of Dariush's head, his fair hair—long and wavy as it used to be—swelling above him as he descended into the shaft. "Follow me, Layla. It's okay," he said. I allowed my body to fall.

The dirt floor met my inflamed feet sooner than I expected. I felt a wetness from fresh blood, but the pain was miraculously bearable. I fell to my knees and crawled. I heard the rasp of my quick breath. Soon my palms and knees began to ache from scraping them along the hard ground. Suddenly, the top of my head touched packed, cold earth, and I realized the tunnel was narrowing. Then a wall of that dirt was in front of me. I felt around for a way forward, but there was none. I knew that I hadn't gone far enough to reach beyond the compound wall. I was beginning to panic and to sob, sucking in dust from the floor with every breath. I rested my head on the ground and closed my eyes. I must have slept. I heard Banu's high voice in my ear. She was telling me the old story: *It was a cold day in the month of* Bahman *when your sweet Maman went to Paradise. You were two years old, and I had been your* naneh *from the beginning. You were my angel with a face like the moon. When your Baba-joon decided to take you away to America, my heart froze. What would become of you, I thought, a motherless child? I ran to my Armenian friend Emma. "Lay out the cards!" I ordered her. "Get my fortune!" Emma tried to calm me down. "For God's sake!" I yelled, frightening poor Emma. "I need to know what will become of that child." So she laid out the cards in her wheellike pattern, whispering Armenian incantations. A trance came over me and the cards began moving, floating, mixing their suits. They seemed to whisper, and I could not make out Emma's interpretation. She pointed to a six of clubs and said the word* journey. *And suddenly, clearly, I knew my destiny, my* ghesmat; *I had known it for a long while. I had not needed a fortune catcher to tell me, to lay out the cards and catch for me what I had already caught in my heart. I knew then that I would devote the rest of my life to you, Layla, that I would always be near to protect you as best I could. And I am here now, so you must save your-self and run, child! Your legs are long like your mother's! Run!*

I opened my eyes and saw the faint outline of my own hand next to my face. Light was coming from somewhere. From above! I felt around over my head and finally found the outline of another trapdoor. It seemed as if it hadn't been opened in a century. I clawed away the caked dirt from the wood and pushed over and over with all my strength, but it wouldn't budge; several times I grew so exhausted I fell asleep. Each time I woke and realized where I was, bile rose into my throat and I franti-cally went back to work on the trapdoor. Rational thought told me I wasn't strong enough to displace decades of packed soil; or maybe the door had been nailed shut. But I couldn't stop push-ing and clawing at it. I lay there in a coffin of earth, with worms and beetles and scorpions, all poised to chomp on my dead flesh; the thought of them kept me moving.

Suddenly, I heard the sound of a truck starting up, then the engine revving. I pushed at the trapdoor once more, and it burst open. Right there above me was the bottom side of a big truck and the tread of its back tire, moving slowly backward. It was night and the lights of the garden were what had seeped through the cracks and down to me. I was still in the compound. My neck felt as if a yoke were around it and my arms were nearly numb, but I managed to pull myself out quickly and slither along the ground toward the back of the truck, all the while expecting a rough hand to grab my leg or a bullet to pierce my head. The truck stopped rolling, and I took the chance to climb into the back of it, an open trailer. I burrowed in between sacks of rice. The truck lurched forward and crossed the compound toward the gate. I looked at the sky above me: pale dawn. We moved out into the street. I closed my eyes and pulled my scarf around my head tightly, as if the fabric could warm me.

Every now and then, I peered through the wooden slats around the back of the truck to see where we were in the city. That old part of town was unfamiliar to me, but I knew I had to get out before the truck reached its destination, even if it meant hiding in an alley until I could figure out what to do. Luckily, it was early morning, so there were fewer people who might take note of me, beaten and bleeding, sliding out of the back of a delivery truck. One thing I knew I'd have to do, regardless of the pain, was walk.

I recognized Lily Street immediately because of the honey vendor on the corner; I remembered Banu telling me that he'd been there since she was a young girl, and there he was, that rare thing untouched by the Revolution. No, I thought, lowering my gaze, I was hallucinating. Escape was not so easy—that was a disappointing truth I'd learned the hard way. I closed my eyes for a moment and thought about the time Banu had brought me to her friend Fereshteh's apartment on Lily Street to pick up some hairbrushes for my grandmother. Fereshteh owned a beauty parlor somewhere downtown. I knew her well because she often visited Banu at my grandmother's house. She would come and stay for days at a time, bringing gifts: pink barrettes for my hair, red nail polish, blue eye shadow. She brought bottles of henna for the maids, who lined up to have their hair dyed; she taught them how to apply makeup to please their husbands, and she waxed the hair from their legs and arms and stomachs.

The truck jerked as the driver lazily downshifted. I looked up again, expecting an unfamiliar alleyway or storefront, but the Lily Street of my weary imagination had not evaporated. It was real. And there! There was the old, dusty apartment building Banu had brought me to; inside was a narrow staircase spiraling up four floors. I pulled myself over the bags of rice and, as the truck inched along, I slid to the ground.

The honey vendor stared at me, but didn't move. I set my sights on Fereshteh's building and placed my feet as lightly on the pavement as possible and imagined that there was no pain and reminded myself that if I gave in to the pain, I would surely be dragged back to the prison. I walked.

I maneuvered, partly on my knees, the narrow, spiraling staircase up two flights. Strange how the first thing I noticed after Fereshteh opened the door were her gray roots; it was unlike her to neglect dying her hair, I thought.

Her face froze in shock. She reached out to steady me and I fainted into her arms.

Eleven

The Young Ones

When Fereshteh realizes that the stinking and tattered shape at her door is Layla Bahari, her first thought is of her friend Banu. Such a sight would kill her; she had cared more for this girl than Fereshteh thought was healthy. And she had worried over her every move. Fereshteh had warned Banu that attaching so strongly to a child who was not her own would only cause much pain later. Banu had asked her how it could be possible not to love a child so beautiful and kind and so unlucky. Fereshteh had thought Banu was talking about how the girl was motherless. Now she wonders if Banu's words and actions came from premonition.

The girl feels like heavy broken branches in Fereshteh's arms. Her face is bruised, her lips cracked, the skin around her eyes hollow and gray. She smells like muddy water boiling in the sun. And blood; Fereshteh smells blood. She reaches around Layla's knees and lifts her into her arms as if she were a small girl. She kicks the apartment door closed and, grunting, carries Layla into the bedroom. The girl may be taller than she, but certainly not too heavy. Despite the years, she thinks, I am still strong.

Layla feels her back against the softness of Fereshteh's quilt. She is so nauseated that she cannot open her eyes to show that she has come to. She feels the woman's solid arms around her and can picture her perfectly from long ago: big as the Cossacks she claimed were her ancestors, so large boned that touching her had been like touching a tree trunk; not fat, but massive and angular, with hands and feet that were enormous and hard, a big toenail so flat and wide she could balance a Turkish coffee cup and saucer on it.

It still amazes Layla how physically opposite Fereshteh is from Banu. Where Fereshteh is massive, Banu is minuscule. Where Fereshteh's voice bellows with assertion, Banu's is shrill or squeaky—yet still commanding. Where Fereshteh is firm and strong, Banu is reedy and diminutive. And Layla remembers how their friendship was like this, too. Full of disagreements and bickering, harmony and devotion. One minute they embraced and shed tears over the lost moments of their childhood near the Caspian Sea, the next minute they refused to speak over whether or not an eggplant stew required saffron. But there was no doubt that they loved one another and that they enjoyed this spicy kind of relationship. Even a child could see this.

Fereshteh touches Layla's forehead and feels the fever against her palm. Gently, she begins to remove the girl's filthy and torn clothing. Soon she notices the deep red blood seeping into her coverlet beneath Layla's feet. She takes a scissors from her sewing kit and cuts away the cloth, trying to ignore Layla's weak moans. Fereshteh has seen the *falak* once before in her life, when her brother's feet were beaten by the schoolmaster *mullah*; her brother had not walked for days after that. But the skin of Layla's feet is not merely blistered and blue; it is mangled and lacerated, gaping in places like the stomach of a slashed sturgeon, oozing blood and pus as the sturgeon oozes caviar. Fereshteh gags, then reaches under the bed for her mother's old chamber pot; it is filled with boxes of hair color and dying brushes and bottles of peroxide. She dumps these out and fills the pot with warm water and soap. She tries to dab at the wounds, but Layla cries out. So she gently wraps the feet with the soft muslin strips she uses for hair waxing. She must send for a doctor right away; the *Agha* Dr. Namdar. And she must be cautious. It is clear that the girl is running from those evil prayer-singers, she thinks. Quickly, she manages to dress Layla in a nightgown, though it is so large on her that she looks like a five-year-old child. Fereshteh shakes her head; a person would not have needed a fortune catcher to tell them such a girl would end up this way. What craziness had lured her away from the safety of America and of Banu's embrace? She pictures her own daughter and looks at her watch, wondering if this will be the time Asya's dangerous activities will prevent her from coming home safely. Young people are stupid as mules, she thinks, going to close the window and secure the blinds. She looks out on the windows of others who had once, not so long ago, waved or called to her, but who now close their curtains to eyes that have learned suspicion and betrayal. She looks at the gray sky and thinks of her friend Banu, who she knows sits with a heavy heart across the world. "I will do my best," she says under her breath. But she does not feel very hopeful. Hope is not something she has felt in a long while.

Layla dreams of Dariush running through the *bagh* with a child's sword, ordering the children to "Attack! Attack!" She dreams of him sketching a cone-shaped skyscraper that turns into a trembling, roaring missile. She dreams of Mariam, her frizzy hair blowing in the gusts of the Caspian seashore, lifting in clumps away from her head, finally ripping from her scalp and turning into an inky black cloth that falls across Layla's face, choking her. She dreams of Maman Bozorg with angry eyes and charcoal brows; Maman Bozorg growing a wide nose imbedded in cavernous cheeks and sprouting a stiff, elongated beard; Maman Bozorg with a turban atop her head.

The pain weaves through her dreams like a coarse string of wool through a silk carpet, ruining the texture, scarring the artistic pattern. Streaks of lightning spark up her legs—pain as if someone is pressing embers on the soles of her feet; pain that tells her to stop breathing.

She hears familiar voices but cannot concentrate on the words. Then a different pain, a stabbing pain in her buttock. And soon she dreams of Dariush bathing her feet in a warm pool of water, kissing her toes and turning the pain into air.

* * *

Fereshteh puts her easy chair next to the bed and watches Layla sleep. She has a pile of crossword puzzles from pre-Revolution magazines; she has erased the answers she put in before and does them over again to make the time pass. She does not flip through these magazines—called *Today's Woman*—anymore; they are filled with article after article about the shah and his benevolence, the Empress Farah Diba and her devotion to education, the Princess Ashraf and her commitment to the Red Lion and Sun. And always, the Royals are pictured in the opulent rooms of their opulent palaces wearing their opulent jewels. She files her nails and cuts her cuticles. She leaves the chair only to get a bowl of soup or some bread and cheese from the kitchen. Sometimes she stretches out on the floor for a short nap. When Layla moans or if a frown appears on her peaceful face, Fereshteh gives her another injection, as the doctor ordered.

And again Layla sleeps serenely, her head to one side, the quilt tucked under her chin. It is amazing, Fereshteh thinks, how her appearance has been unaffected. It is youth. Terrible things can happen to the young ones, yet they look unaffected. She remembers the beatings she suffered as a child, from her father and her brothers; she remembers the heartaches she endured because of her husbands and lovers. Yet her skin remained pink and smooth, her eyes clear, through everything. But now, it all affects her. The Revolution has put age spots on her hands and jowls on either side of her chin. Every time her daughter Asya leaves the apartment, walks out to the dangerous streets filled with her dangerous beliefs, Fereshteh looks in the mirror to find another line etched into her own face.

When Layla wakes up, she peers through the shadowy threads of her sticky eyelashes. Her body is a long tube beneath the covers that stretches toward a paint-chipped armoire against the wall. This is all she has the energy to see before her eyes close again. She knows someone is in the room with her; she hears the soft rustle of fabric and feels comforted as if Banu is there, watching over her as she did in her childhood when she was ill. Her feet throb, but the pain is no longer as sharp as knives.

Next when she opens her eyes she sees the steady drip-drip of solution into an IV bag hovering above her. She remembers the Namdar clinic, how she went there soon after she arrived in Tehran, frantic, looking for Dariush's father to tell him how the officials had inducted Dariush into the army and taken him away not fifteen minutes after they got off the plane at Mehrabad Airport.

The sights in the clinic had shaken her. Gone were the pastel-colored wallpaper and fresh flowers and white-capped French nurses. Instead, there had been the stench of salt and boiled alcohol, the maroon blotches of dried blood on the once shiny linoleum floors, the moaning boy soldiers draped in bloody bandages, the screaming amputees and their sobbing mothers. The sight of war. And her shame, shame because she had forgotten that the war was going on for everyone else too, that the Iraqis pushed forward and sent bombs; she was so preoccupied with saving Dariush that it seemed as if she had even forgotten that there had been a Revolution. She had found Dariush's father in his office, slumped behind his desk, asleep. When he woke, he mistook her for her mother, whispered "Rachel" incredulously, then turned angry and wide-eyed with fear when he came back to himself and realized it was Layla standing before him. How dare they come to Tehran against everyone's wishes?

She feels his anxiety now as if it is there in Fereshteh's room, clinging to the coverlet about her. And when she opens her eyes again, she does indeed see his silhouette against the bright window. His back is to her, yet she knows this is Dariush's father, the man who was her father's childhood friend, and who is now her father-in-law. He slouches, his head bent, his hands in the pockets of his flannel trousers. "Uncle," she says weakly, wishing with a stab of guilty longing that it was her own father who stood there. Hooshang turns and comes quickly to her bedside. He has a long and raggedy beard. The whites of his eyes are marked with red streaks and his shirt is rumpled. He is not the immaculate, cologned physician she remembers.

"How are you feeling?" he asks, sitting beside her, touching her forehead.

"Okay," she says in a slow whisper. She says something else, but he cannot understand. He puts his ear near her mouth. "Dariush?" she asks softly.

He shakes his head, looks into her eyes. "We do not know," he says. He does not tell her the truth; he does not think she can cope with it. Bad news is not good for the sick, not good for the healing. No, he will not tell her that Dariush has been sent to the war front. She is not stupid. She would know that soldiers in the infantry have little chance of survival. She must get better. Especially now.

She swallows; her throat feels sticky. "Water," she croaks. He helps her sip from a straw; lifting her head to do this seems to exhaust her. "My feet?" she asks, fighting to keep her eyes open.

"It will take some time, but they should be all right." He pauses, takes a deep breath. "Laylee," he says. "Did you know you were pregnant?"

She closes her eyes and he thinks she has not heard him, but then he sees the small tears emerge from beneath her lashes. He thinks he notices a faint smile on her lips. He blots at her wet cheeks with a tissue and holds her warm hand until her slow, rhythmic breath tells him she is asleep.

Twelve

Layla

It was appropriate that I learned of my pregnancy at Fereshteh's house because it was Fereshteh who had first taught me about sex. In fact, until I was old enough to have an interest in sex, Fereshteh was of no special interest to me. Her visits to our house meant nothing more to me than the haircut Banu insisted I sit still for.

Then it was the summer after Mariam's first year at the Swiss boarding school. We were fifteen, and suddenly sex was like a virus in our minds. We would walk for hours in the garden at my grandparents' house in Shemiran, whispering and giggling about boys and their anatomy, about girls and how their anatomy related to boys. We found a small carpet under a fig tree that the gardeners sometimes ate their lunch on. Despite the leftover crumbs and rice and tea stains, we would lie on that carpet and read one another the sexy parts from a book I'd found in the seat pocket of an airplane: *Forbidden Love at Glendale High*.

Mariam was happier than she'd ever been. Switzerland had changed her. She wore makeup and high heels and blew-dry her hair; her clothing was from Paris and her favorite singer was Charles Aznavour; she talked of drinking champagne with her roommate late at night and sneaking out to the nearby town to go dancing with the local boys. It seemed as if she'd completely dismissed the specter of Maman Bozorg. She was always talking about how grateful she was that her mother had sent her to Europe. I was happy about that too. And even then, it gave me a certain satisfaction that Mariam no longer said her *namaz* or read from the *Qoran*, that she didn't fast during *Ramazan* or cry for the dead-*Emam*s, that she chain-smoked Marlboro cigarettes and wore a purple French-cut bikini, that she'd learned some excellent curse words in French. And that she couldn't stop talking about love and sex.

This was how Banu talked about sex to me: "I realize that you already think you know about these things," she would say, in her birdish voice. "I have heard you talking about men's *dool*s with Mariam, but you have no idea how dangerous being with a man can be. You *must* keep your girlhood or no man will want to marry you. And if he does marry you and later finds out that you are not a virgin, he will think you are disgusting; he will think of other men touching you and he will never want to sleep with you again. Then you will be childless forever and he will divorce you and everyone will know that you were a bad girl and you will be a miserable, lonely woman for the rest of your life." Then Banu would stare at me as if I'd already been bad. She would narrow her eyes. "Boys only want to do *that thing*," she continued, her voice squeaky with emphasis. "They want to do it to every girl, even if she is not pretty—do it and go. Then they are crazy to find a virgin to marry. Be careful, Layla, or you will end up taking a capsule of chicken blood to your wedding bed; pity, starting off a marriage with lies."

When Fereshteh heard this speech, she said, "You are frightening the girl into her grave, Banu!" Feri had a deep voice when she was angry that frightened everyone except Banu.

"I am protecting her," Banu snapped back. "Do not interfere. It is my responsibility to her father."

That was the truth. I knew how my father felt about my exposure to sexual ideas. He didn't say much about it, but I knew. If we were watching television and suddenly the characters began passionately kissing, he would change the channel.

"This is not for you," he would say, his face red. Or if a boy called me on the telephone, he would interrogate me about him: his name, his age, his address, his parents' occupations, his cleanliness, his grades, and always with a glaring look as if I'd done some terrible thing to deserve a phone call from a predator of the opposite sex.

I knew my father had a hard time imagining me and romantic love in the same picture. In his heart, I think he wished he could choose my husband in the way his parents had hoped to choose a wife for him. And as I got older, there were plenty of opportunities for such a thing to happen; he was often approached by other Iranian parents who thought I was suitable for their sons. Usually he knew better than to mention any of these "inquiries" to me. But one night, out of the blue, he said, "You have a customer." I guess he was trying to be both serious and playful; he knew the proper word was "suitor." But I knew exactly what he was up to; he wanted to rile me, get me to argue the issue so he could explain the positive points of an arranged relationship. So I just laughed at him. "Oh Baba-*joon*, you're such a joker," I said, kissing his cheek and saying good night before he could go any further. I guess he got the message. We never talked about it again.

Banu understood how reluctant my father was to broach certain subjects with me. She told me she'd known many men like my father: "Forceful as kings in their work, but unsure as sheep in their home." So she would take care of my education in "these matters."

But Fereshteh was a problem. When she found out Mariam and I were finally thinking about love and sex, she wanted to teach us everything she knew. What a gift! we thought. There was no end to our questions. Banu's little face turned red as a pomegranate and she made us leave the room so she could talk to Feri, but I listened at the door and watched through the big keyhole. Feri's warning voice said, "You are cooking up a rebellious child, Banu. You cannot stop her from being curious. Better for her to learn about such things from someone who knows so much about it." She pointed to herself. "Someone who can give her excellent moral advice." She narrowed her eyes.

"Not someone whose only experience was a marriage that ended in the death of her wicked husband."

"Praise God," Banu said under her breath. Banu had often told me that the best thing about her mean husband had been his early death.

"You are too angry to teach Layla about such things," said Feri. "You speak about men as if your mouth is full of rotten food. She has no reason to feel this way. She must know how to manage their wily ways, not how to repel them."

"What about the other one?" said Banu. "Her grandmother would kill me if she knew I allowed her to hear such talk."

Fereshteh shrugged. "The other one is on the wrong path anyway. Do you not see it? And all because she has heard too many warnings in her life. That is the direction in which you will send Layla if you do not hold your tongue."

So Banu gave in. She would sit in a corner, usually sewing, while Fereshteh counseled us about love and sex. When Feri became particularly graphic, Banu would bark curses at her from this corner, but she didn't tell her to stop. She never admitted it, but I think she found Fereshteh's talk pretty interesting herself.

Feri had been married three times. Her husbands had gladly divorced her when she got tired of them; she was too large to argue with. She had a daughter, Asya, who studied at Tehran University, but who gave her mother a lot of "stomach sores" because she belonged to a student political group. Feri said Asya hadn't inherited any of her "feelings of the *romantique*." These feelings came from her Russian side; her parents had been exiles from Baku. She loved Pushkin and recited him with tears in her eyes. That summer and every summer after that, she told us the entire story of *Doctor Zhivago*, always interjecting some of her own amorous adventures. Sometimes she would check the hallway outside Banu's room to make sure none of the household servants were listening in. She didn't trust them, said she didn't trust anyone who couldn't read and wore a *chador* and trembled with fear if they missed one session of their *namaz*. "People like that will always look for ways to discredit me," she said. "Am I right, Banu?" Banu would nod; she didn't trust the servants either. "They think they are better," Feri continued. "I am a good Moslem. God knows this. Perhaps I do not follow all the rules, but in my heart, I am a good Moslem."

I would nod, then say something like, "Was your second husband a good Moslem?" This was to get her back on track. "Oh no," she would say. "He was an atheist. But he was irresistible, with black eyebrows that met in the middle and *kooneh koochooloo*, a cute little ass." Mariam and I would be lolling on the twin beds in Banu's room listening to her, drinking cherry *sharbat* and splitting sunflower seeds with our teeth. Once Feri got started she could talk about men for hours. She told us about the tricks of seducing younger men, men who were half her age, not much older than we were. She explained the importance of making the proper noises during love playing, and described a subtle exercise for enhancing vaginal grasping power. She made use of baby cucumbers to demonstrate both manual and oral fondling techniques. Then she would peel the cucumber with a small fruit knife and place the strips all over her wide face. "Keeps the skin young," she would say, lying back with her eyes closed. "Semen is also good for this reason. It must be refrigerated first, of course."

To Feri, grooming was a big part of the subject of men and sex and love. She thought Iranian women knew how to take care of themselves better than any women in the world. What did everyone think these women had been doing for all those centuries in the old harems? Why, preening themselves, of course. And inventing new ways of attracting their husbands—or husband. There was a great deal of competition, so much competition that it became part of the culture, and mothers passed it on to their daughters. "So," she would say, "I will help you girls look the best you can. It takes a great deal of experience and time."

She always came with a large sack full of paraphernalia from her beauty shop. She trimmed our hair in the layered seventies look, then curled our tresses with rollers the size of orange juice cans; this worked fine for me, but made Mariam look a little like Annette Funicello. She gave us manicures and pedicures and facials using odd mixtures of herbs like tarragon and chemicals like benzoin. She told us to cover our bodies with olive oil and rye whiskey if we wanted to get a golden tan. And she scolded us about using a razor to shave our legs; she said it would cause us to become hairier and in some cases, cause us to begin growing hair on our backs or even our chins. She insisted we wax. She did this for us. Sometimes she would try to convince us to do the *band andazi* instead; it lasted much longer. I always refused. But one day Mariam finally agreed to let Feri do it. I watched the whole thing, squinting with imaginary pain throughout.

"Come, Mariam-*joon*," said Feri, wrapping the string around the back of her own neck. "I will make your legs as smooth as a baby's cheek—and you will not have to wax for months." So Mariam agreed to be plucked. She lay down on her stomach on the floor where a towel had been spread. Fereshteh arranged the white string within her fingers so that when she pressed it against Mariam's skin, it formed a taut square. When she'd pull her upper body back, the string would tighten more and the square would become smaller and smaller until, with a jerk, the four corners would close around a hair and pluck it out. Of course, Fereshteh could do this very quickly—back and forth, forward and backward—looking like a psychotic in a mental hospital. After a few minutes, a thin layer of plucked hair shadowed Mariam's towel. "Give her a Kleenex, Banu-*joon*," Feri said. "This brings tears to anyone's eyes." Mariam had been sniffing occasionally. "You should see them when I do the underarms. *Vai Khodah!* Oh my God! And there was one last week who wanted the hair down there in the shape of a heart to surprise her husband. I did it, of course—what a perfect artistic heart—but she used a whole box of my Kleenex!" Then after it was all over, Fereshteh would rub her neck and complain about the pain in it and ask for a big glass of dark tea and some dates.

Eventually, Mariam and I would talk about our own experiences and Fereshteh dissected them, telling us what we'd done wrong, what we should do in the future. "Pull away if he sticks to you like that on the dance floor again. People will think you are an easy girl. Let him kiss you just once in a dark corner and do not forget to open your mouth."

Fereshteh thought a woman must know how to conjure up such passion in a man that he would cry for her. "Rashid would hold my feet in his hands and kiss them while his tears fell on my toenail polish. *Vai*," she would say, sighing. "Maybe I should not have sent him back to his wife."

She had advice about how to receive the most pleasure: "You must be on top, it is the only way." Banu would throw her an angry look. "Of course," she continued quickly. "This information is for later use, when you are married." She widened her eyes. "Oh, and you must not allow a boy to do it to you in the *koon*." Banu gasped and we cringed. "Some girls do this to satisfy the boy while remaining a virgin. Besides the pain, it is most unclean—such an orifice was not meant by God to have anything put into it, only unpleasant things coming out, eh?" she said with a painful look.

Mariam and I discussed everything Fereshteh told us. While many of our friends, especially the ones we went to school with in the West, looked forward to losing their virginities, we decided to keep our hymens intact. We didn't know it at the time, but our reasons were very different.

I think it was a matter of guilt for Mariam. Losing her virginity would have been the worst possible sin she could commit in her grandmother's eyes. And while I had the impression that Maman Bozorg had faded from the center of her life, I know now that that wasn't the case at all. As for me, well, when I dreamed of making love for the first time, when I listened to Feri's counsel, I thought only of Dariush. No one knew this. Not even Banu. I'd never told anyone about what had happened in the *bagh* during the storm. Nor did I tell about how Dariush reached for my hand under the table sometimes when our families were out to dinner nor how he often looked at me secretively and smiled. I knew we were too young for this kind of love; no one would have approved. My father would have been furious. So we hid our feelings for one another—for those reasons and, I assumed, for Mariam's sake. I was sure everything would change as we grew older.

But I was wrong. I had no idea of the power Maman Bozorg had over Dariush.

Thirteen

Maman Bozorg

Haji-Akbar is a *mullah* who works in the Ministry of War. He is the son of my husband's maternal aunt, a woman I always called *Haji-Khanoom Bozorg*, out of great respect. May she rest in peace. This woman was indeed the most agreeable and pious relative in my husband's family. Her husband had been a teacher of Islamic jurisprudence in the holy city of Qom, and *Haji-Khanoom Bozorg* had made the pilgrimage to Mecca on foot seven times. She had the blisters and calluses of devotion. She reminded me of my mother, looking as I imagined my mother would look in old age, like a radiant sunflower, ever touched by light. My most content moments as a young bride were during visits from the *Haji-Khanoom*; we often broke our fast together during the month of *Ramazan*; she appreciated my special rice cereal with cinnamon sugar, and I cherished the way her whispered prayers sounded like the lute my brother played for me when we were small children. Well, she finally died from heatstroke during one of her pilgrimages, but she left behind seven sons who all joined the ministry in Qom, who now hold much power in the government, which is as it should be.

It was *Haji*-Akbar who, at my request, arranged for Dariush's military commission. (An old pious woman like myself now has a certain power in this country.) Dariush was to be drafted upon his arrival at the airport, taken north to Ghazvin for military training, then returned after three weeks to Tehran as an officer and strategist. Despite my knowledge of this plan, I sent the driver with Mariam to collect Dariush and Layla from the airport, yet I knew she would return with only Layla and bring her to stay with Katayoon. I ached to see Dariush, but I was consoled by the knowledge that I had wrenched him from that girl's grasp. They were apart. And soon I would work toward accomplishing her deportation from the country. After all, *Haji-Khanoom Bozorg* had had seven sons; no doubt one of them would have influence in the Department of Foreign Citizens' Affairs.

It was not my fault that Dariush ended up at the front. I had been given clear and solid assurances that such a thing would never happen. Dariush was far too valuable to waste in combat. He was an officer, a strategist; he was to be a hero for his country and for Islam. It was Hooshang who ruined everything, Hooshang and Layla—*elahi bemeereh*, may God let her die! In fact, the military commission had not been my *original* plan for Dariush. Not at all.

I had merely wanted my grandson home. He had finished his studies in America. Why was he still there? Even before the Revolution, the shah's government offered him contracts to design two new office buildings in Esfahan. It did not matter that he was young and inexperienced; he was from a traditional, ruling class family and a graduate of that *Haarr-Vaarrd* Katayoon is always praising. His opportunities in Iran were enormous, his future determined. But he shocked us all. Why could he never do what we expected? Any boy would have jumped at such a chance to be above all others, but Dariush has never had an interest in impressing the world. I could not alter this in him; it was the one area in which he was not smart. He could not comprehend the importance of social position. This was obvious in his disinterest for fine fabrics and grand furnishings and the gossip about other families' fortunes. He was unbearably modest; this was the reason he would always let his hair grow too long— he rarely looked at himself in the mirror. His best friend was that cook's son, a humiliating matter for me to explain to my friends. Several times my houseboy caught him playing soccer with street boys and then my driver told me that he was riding the common autobus to school. There was no scolding him; he would smile and embrace me, squeezing out the anger. If I spoke to Veeda or Hooshang, their reactions were even more exasperating. They were so foolishly pleased with him.

So he shocked us all those two years before the Revolution when he wrote that he would be taking a job in New York after the summer. For experience, he said. So he would know exactly what he was doing when he returned to work in Iran, he said. Then after the next summer, he announced he would again go back to New York for more experience. I begged him to stay. Of course, my blood boiled that he lived in the same city as Layla, but I prayed to *Allah* and kept my faith strong. I told myself that I knew the deepest hopes of my own grandson and that in his heart he would never want a girl like Layla; perhaps he lusted after her, but what was lust? A sugar lump that melts away on your tongue? My Dariush loved Mariam. This was truth.

And after the Revolution and the glorious return of the *Emam*, it did not occur to me that Dariush would not come. There was no need for him to follow in the footsteps of the families who fled the new regime like sniveling children running away from home. Mariam was home; she showed no regrets about leaving Switzerland, but Dariush sent letter after letter filled with unacceptable excuses for not returning, excuses about the unsteadiness of Iran, the bad economy, and then the war. Once he even mentioned those American embassy captives, as if this should have any meaning to his situation. Why was the world so angry about those fifty-two insignificant people? What had they been doing in our country anyway? Telling us how to run things, spying on our government, scattering immoral ideas among our children? Which government would not have done the same to such intruders?

Well, I wanted nothing to do with *that*; my mission was to return my grandson to the bosom of Islam and to Iran. By then it was almost three years that I had not seen him. I determined to plan a course of action. I prayed and searched my mind, knowing that God had placed the answer there, that it would come to me as sure as the sun would rise over Mecca. In the end, the solution was so very simple; simplicity is God's gift.

When Dariush had turned eighteen some years before, I had taken the deeds to everything I had inherited from my father, from my husband, my brothers, all the homes and the land—thousands of hectares spread across all of Iran—and I had them placed in Dariush's name. Perhaps under normal circumstances, my son Hooshang would have protested. But Hooshang had just finished with one of his business debacles. He had decided to import from America packaged cotton pads for women to use during their monthly habits, but when the shipping container suffered water damage in transport, the hundreds of pads expanded and grew so heavy with water that they burst from their packages and fell into the Gulf, each one floating like a bloated white puddle of humiliation to our whole family.

So Hooshang was in no mood to protest my decision to deed our lands to Dariush. Veeda and Katayoon made their usual noises, but I ignored them. The simple fact was that Dariush was the most capable family member to manage such properties. Everyone knew this. So, suddenly, these actions from years before—*Allah* be praised!—became the tools by which I would bring my Dariush home. This was because the new government had issued an edict that all properties of the aristocracy would be confiscated unless they were claimed by their owners *in person*. So if Dariush did not come to Iran and claim his ownership of our properties, we would lose them. I knew that my Dariush would never want such guilt on his head: to be responsible for losing the family fortune, to disappoint and degrade his grandmother in this way. He would not allow it. He would come.

I wrote him a detailed letter regarding this matter and the need for his presence. I wanted him to feel a sense of responsibility tugging at him like a beggar in the bazaar. I also ordered Mariam to write him a letter. I directed her to hint that I was feeling ill and weak. This was a small lie, a bit of news to urge him forward, a necessary fib for which I am sure God has forgiven me.

In fact, the prospect of seeing my grandson gave me a sense of good health that I had not had in a long while.

Mariam, I must admit, was of great help. She had become truly devoted to me since the Revolution. I should have been grateful for this. And I was. *Allah* be praised. But her devotion had begun to annoy me. How completely eager she had become to do my bidding; she had given up all of her mettle to resist my regulations. She had become spineless, in fact. And her desire to have Dariush return had become far too ardent. She cried into her prayer cloth for him, embroidered slippers for him, ordered the cook to practice preparing his favorite foods, knitted blankets and sweaters for him, wondered over every item in her closet and in the house as to whether it would please him. Did she have no self-control? I tried to explain to her: A woman may have her passions, but she must regulate them prudently. She did not understand. I found myself hoping she would spend more time at Katayoon's, but this was not to be; I had done too well over the three years since the Revolution in drawing Mariam away from her mother.

It took several more letters and several cautious telephone calls, but some months later, Dariush made up his mind to return. Hooshang and Veeda tried to dissuade him—unsuccessfully. Dariush's mind is never easily changed. Much to my delight, Veeda had already fled Iran for France anyway. Hooshang, as I knew he would, finally accepted his son's decision and scrambled to bribe the correct official in order to keep Dariush from the draft. And in fact, he did bribe the correct official. Everything was arranged.

It was Katayoon who told us that Dariush was bringing Layla. And if that Katayoon knew, everyone must have known. She and her *doreh*, her circle of immoral friends, meeting every night for gambling and drinking and dancing as if nothing had changed in Iran, all of them thinking they could bribe the *komiteh* officials and draw their curtains to keep out the purity of Islam. I could imagine them talking, having news from their counterparts in Europe and America about the perfect pair: Dariush and Layla, so *romantique* (that meaningless French notion), returning together to Iran, to *marry*.

Why had I not allowed myself to consider that such a thing could happen? I was not a dim-witted person. I had used my wits to keep Layla and Dariush apart since that terrible day at the *bagh* when the two of them had gotten lost in the storm. It had been years since I had seen that girl in my nightmares, promising my Dariush sex with her green eyes, seducing him with a face like her mother's, a face that would wrench my boy away from all that is pure and decent, wrench him away from me. I had vowed not to allow it. So I had kept them apart. I did this with a gift from *Allah*, a skill that allows me to see—like a fortune catcher sees destiny—the weaknesses of others.

To reach Dariush, I had to be clever as a mother fox. Dariush was not pliable like Mariam. He did not feel fear very easily. With Dariush, I had to do a great deal of thinking and planning. They said I was different with him than with anyone else, that I was softer. Perhaps this was true. What could I do? He loved me. This I knew as well as I knew that my maidservant stole fruit from the pantry, as well as I knew there would be a Judgment Day. There were times when I may have given up his moral tutelage and found enough solace in knowing that he loved me. I could have been grateful for his visits for lunch and his gifts of soft cotton fabrics for my *chador*s and his quiet way of sitting by me for an hour or two on Friday afternoons. This is the way of many grandmothers. But I also am not pliable.

I knew one thing about Dariush: He worries about those he loves. He does this because he is so capable, because he can fix many things that other people cannot. Such capability makes him feel responsible. And Dariush feels he can take care of everyone. Even me. This is his weakness.

And this was how I kept him away from Layla. I could not reason with him; I knew if I spoke my opinion about the girl, I could drive him away. Dariush was not averse to rebellion, he was merely rebellious in an unusual manner; he would laugh things away, do what he wanted without remorse. He had his own mind. So I used irrationality to reach him. For the first time since my husband had died—except for the anniversary of the death of Saint Hossein—I wept. Almost every time I was able to see my grandson after that day at the *bagh* in which his lust was awakened, I found a way to weep and plead with him that he resist the temptation of that girl. And the more he asked for a reason, the less rational I became. I knew he merely had to see my pain and misery, not to understand it, and this would make his stomach burn for me. Such behavior was my only hope. And in my *del*, in my core, I knew my plan had been working.

But God will always challenge us. Even in the best of circumstances, he will challenge us. The Revolution, inevitable and inspiring as it was, broke my hold over Dariush. And in my heart, I must have known that he had developed an affiliation with that girl over the years that he was away from me and my persuasive influence. Now he wanted to marry her. But I would not even allow him the opportunity to *ask* for my blessing.

So I had telephoned *Haji*-Akbar at the Ministry of War.

Fourteen

Transparent Ice

Hooshang sits at his mother's lunch table with a plate of barberries and rice before him. It is his favorite dish, but he pushes the plate away. His mother's bowl of thick soup waits for her at the head of the long table. He hears her slow, uneven steps along the carpet behind him. Her maid has already told him that the arthritis is so bad today that the *khanoom* has said her *namaz* sitting in a chair. He knows he should rise and help her to the table, but he cannot even bring himself to turn around and greet her. His pity is gone.

She hooks her cane roughly over the back of her chair. "What in the name of Saint Ali are *you* doing here?" she says in a voice that is scratchier than usual. She leans over to peer at him. "Do you think I have forgiven you?"

"No, Mother," he says in his usual soft voice. "I am sure you have not forgiven me. You are not a forgiving person."

"Hmph," she says, pressing thick palms down onto her chair handles. Slowly, shakily, she lowers herself into the seat and leans back, exhausted from the short walk from her bedroom. Her face looks pasty, blending in with a cream-colored scarf whose bulky knot nestles within the folds under her chin. She is a stranger to me, Hooshang thinks. He cannot even remember the color of her hair; surely it has been gray for many years, yet he has never seen it that way.

"So?" she prods. "Why are you here?" Her smoke-gray irises dart impatiently, searching his face. As a child, he had tried so hard not to rouse her attention; those eyes threatened to reach inside him and steal all his thoughts, leaving him empty and hollow as the samovar at the end of the day. He had hidden from her a great deal; behind heavy dark drapes, beneath beds and in closets, in the peaceful garden—anywhere he could escape her pinched looks and scowling face. And her questions—accusations, really—were the only words she flung at him in her disapproving tone. He was not like Mahmoud, who could ignore their mother. When she spoke, he heard the real words that were hidden like slithery worms behind the words she spoke: "What *is* it that you are *doing*, Hooshang?" (How peculiar you are, she means. So humiliating.) "What *is* this you are *wearing*, Hooshang?" (How inappropriate, she means. How ugly.) "What *sort* of book is that you are *reading*, Hooshang?" (Garbage, she means. Western blasphemy.) "*Have* you washed, Hooshang? Had your breakfast? Visited your grandfather? Said thanks to God? Practiced your arithmatic, your religious lessons, prayers?" (And this means he is unclean, too thin, disrespectful, unappreciative, stupid, and—most hateful—an apostate.) And he would wonder, his skin prickling and his throat swollen with tears, why he was so incapable of pleasing her, of doing the things she wanted him to do. It became easier to hide from her. Even as a grown man, even after Veeda helped him understand that his shortcomings were only in his mother's perception, he hid from her, hoping she would change. But both are impossible now.

He sits up straight and turns toward her. He has remembered why he is here, and the anger wells up inside him. He has finally faced the truth that his mother is indeed a cruel woman. "I know what you did, Mother," he says, clenching his teeth. She frowns briefly, then sits forward and begins to sip her soup as if nothing he says could be of significance. "I know it was because of your influence that Dariush was drafted."

She grunts and slurps another spoonful. "What do *you* know?"

He swallows. "I had paid eight hundred thousand *touman*s for his exemption."

She shrugs. "Wasting money is your specialty."

He tries to keep his voice steady. "There was no reason for them to take him. Whom did you call, Mother? Which friend whose husband is a *mullah* or a *hojatolislam* or an *ayatollah*?"

She reaches for a piece of *lavash* bread from the warming basket, but says nothing.

He cannot sit anymore. He thrusts his chair behind him and paces to the end of the table. "I thought it was my fault," he says, "That I had not bribed the right official, that I had not paid enough." He rakes his fingers through his hair.

She wipes her mouth roughly, her knuckles white as she grasps the napkin but her voice is calm, as if they are talking about the weather. "So," she says. "It was your guilt that *forced* you to indulge my grandson's immoral desires and arrange for his military defection and his marriage to that girl? Are you apologizing, then?"

He is not completely aware that his hand has closed around a crystal vase on the table. It is filled with yellow roses from the garden. Before he can stop himself—for he has never done anything violent in his life—he flings the vase against the wall. It explodes and water streams down the green silk wallpaper like black tears. "Enough!" he shouts. A servant peeks her head into the dining room, then quickly retreats when her *khanoom* bellows "*Gomsho!* Get lost!" in a voice that makes Hooshang cringe with memory. The fury she showed for the maid evaporates from his mother's face as she turns her head slowly toward him. She picks up her spoon once again. It trembles ever so slightly. He is, as always, amazed at her self-control. She speaks calmly. "You still have not told me, boy, why you are here."

He places his palms on the table and leans in. A long expanse of white tablecloth separates them, yet he feels as if she could reach out and twist his ear as she had done so many times in his childhood. "I want you to tell me, Mother, *who* arranged for Dariush's military commission. Such a person could help return him from the front."

He waits while she takes two spoonfuls of soup. She chews the soft kidney beans and noodles, her dentures clicking like fingernails against wood. His stomach burns with impatience. Finally, she says, "My grandson is a deserter. We are lucky he was not shot to death for this crime. There is nothing anyone can do. He will return on his own. He is strong. And *Allah* will keep him safe." She rolls a piece of soft *lavash* into a cone and dips it into her soup.

"He is missing," says Hooshang, gnawing the inside of his lip.

"What do you mean, missing? My grandson is not missing. He is at the war front, thanks to you, leading soldiers against the demon Iraqis."

"No, Mother. I have had word that he has been lost in a battle."

She bites into her bread, and soup dribbles on to her chin. Reaching for her napkin, her hand now clearly trembles. "Well," she says, her voice a shade higher in tone. "Someone must find him." She stares at him finally, her eyes wider, less confident.

"Yes, Mother," he says. "I have calls in to the Ministry of War. They are trying to get word about prisoners."

"That is ridiculous," she says, pushing her plate away and spilling soup on the tablecloth. "My grandson would never allow himself to be taken prisoner."

"Well, then," he says, snorting sarcastically. "I suppose we must assume he is killed."

They stare at one another. He has always looked away. Not this time. Suddenly, she starts to cough and gasp as if she is choking. She clasps her throat. He begins to go to her, but stops. Is this real? And if it is real, does he want to help her? The indecision shames him, and he moves forward. She is still his mother. He pats her back and calls to the kitchen maid for water. Finally, he helps her to a chair in the parlor. The top of her head barely reaches his shoulder. She limps and groans from the pain in her joints, and he tries not to shiver as he holds her arm, the skin beneath the fabric loose like a dog's underbelly.

He sits on the green sofa opposite her. She seems smaller than ever. Her legs, where they fall out of her wide cotton shift from below the knee, are swathed in the Ace bandages he brings her from the clinic to ease her arthritis pain. She does not look at him. "Mother," he says. "Please, tell me the name of the person you spoke to about Dariush."

She looks his way, composed. "There is no one," she says. "I had nothing to do with it." She inhales sharply. "But you can be sure, Hooshang, that my grandson is not killed. I would feel such a thing in my bones. And I do not."

"Well, then," he snickers. "I suppose we can rest easy—since your bones have not told us otherwise. Perhaps we should hire a fortune catcher to tell us where we can find Dariush. Would that be your next step?"

She presses her lips together in anger. "Such sarcasm from a son to his mother is very ugly."

He suddenly remembers how she used to hurt him and Mahmoud when they were little, how her favorite punishments were subtle, as when she would weave a pencil between their fingers, then squeeze. He can feel the sparking pain caused by the hard pencil scouring against his bones. She was strong and quick back then, before the arthritis, and she twisted their ears and slapped their cheeks almost with glee. She truly believed that their boyhood transgressions (which never went beyond harmless mischief) were revealed to her by God: "See?" she would pronounce on an occasion when one of them had stolen a marzipan cookie from the pantry or the other had accidentally urinated in his bed. "God sees every bad thing you do and, in the end, He will let me know so I can punish you. This is part of being a good mother," she told them.

Hooshang stands up. His legs are trembling. He wants to leave and never come back to this house that smells of mothballs and dust. She still does not look at him. He pictures Dariush, as he used to sometimes sit, dutifully, right there on the carpet next to his grandmother's chair, talking softly to her, telling her stories and jokes—such that no one else had the courage to tell—that would make her giggle and pinch his cheek. He aches for his son.

"Oh, by the way, Mother," he says, knowing that he should be silent and just leave, but unable to resist the chance to shock her, to have, for once, a power over her. "Our Dariush is going to be a father." He had promised himself that he would not tell her this news, that no one, not even his mother, should know of Layla's flight from the *komiteh*. But he has been unable to control himself about the pregnancy and he wonders now what the harm can be. "Well, Mother," he continues, relishing his words as if they are fresh butter. "You are soon to be a great-grandmother."

She is staring at him, her eyes glossy as onyx. "A child?" Her voice, for once, is soft, meek, like someone searching for a friend in the dark. Her mouth is partly open, and he notices traces of white at the corners. He is suddenly taken aback. How can this small, old, ill woman be his enemy? Perhaps she once had the power to destroy them all, but her actions have been turned on her. Look, he tells himself. She is your mother. Has she really hidden her emotions from you? Yes, she is like a piece of ice, as she has always been to you and to everyone else. But now he sees that the ice is transparent and she is boiling beneath her skin with regret and anxiety. "A child," she says again.

"Yes," he says. "Dariush's Layla is pregnant with their child."

She clamps her hand over her mouth and leans forward slightly. "Layla?" she croaks, staring at the floor.

"Yes, Mother," he says. "Layla, the wife of your grandson." He slides his hands into his trouser pockets and looks down at the top of her head. "Haven't you grown tired of this unreasonable opposition? There is no longer a point in it—Dariush loves this girl; she is a part of our family now." His mother slumps even farther into her wing chair. Good, he thinks. Let her be shocked. Maybe the reality of a child will finally make her see reason and accept it all. Yes, he thinks, I do see some clarity on her face; she is gathering her strength after the shock. She always does.

"Well," she says, exhaling as if she has been holding her breath. "Is it not *Allah*'s kindness that allowed my grandson's wife to be in your care during such a time?"

Unsure for a fleeting second if he hears a sarcasm or a falseness in her voice, he says, "Thank you, Mother. I am doing my best for the girl. It has not been easy for her." He sees her eyebrow rise up slightly, but she says nothing. She still has not looked at him. She reaches for her glass of water and finishes it in one quiet swallow. Without thinking, he swiftly kneels next to her, resting his hands on the arm of her chair. She shifts slightly away from him. "Please, Mother. In this new government, surely you are more influential than I am. Please—the names of the officials who arranged for Dariush's commission?" She is as still as a statue, he thinks. Have I been wrong about her? Am I always to be wrong about her? He lowers his head on his hands and begins to quietly weep. The faint scent of rosewater perfume reminds him of lost moments in his childhood when he would search for loose buttons to play with in her undergarment drawer. Fleetingly, he thinks about reaching out to touch her.

"Hooshang," she says finally. "I have failed *Allah* and failed tradition. You still weep like a schoolgirl."

Fifteen

Layla

I lay in the dark, drunk from morphine, but awake with Hooshang's words in my ears: *Did you know you were pregnant, Laylee? Did you know? Did you know?* Fereshteh snored gently on the floor next to the bed, but this time her presence was of little comfort to me. I put my palms over my abdomen. How had I not known? Had my self-indulgence been so pervasive that I'd ignored the subtle changes of my body? All through my trip to Iran, all through the shock of losing Dariush, the stoning, the prison, all through the beatings and the escape—I'd been carrying this child. Was he—was she—all right? My chest tightened and I whispered to the walls. Where are you, Dariush? Hear me, Dasha. Please be okay; please come back. I have our child.

Tears flowed across my temples and into my hair. Fereshteh moved suddenly and I froze, but her snoring soon resumed. I wiped my nose on a corner of the sheet, took a deep breath, and began counting on my fingers the weeks since I'd become pregnant—I knew exactly when it had happened; there had only been one time when we hadn't been careful. Thirteen weeks ago. Fourth of July weekend. A little cottage on Montauk. It was the weekend I almost lost him.

We'd been lovers for a year already. Maybe we would have been married by then and living in Tehran, but the Revolution had put everything on hold. My father was trying his best to keep his export business afloat. He hardly noticed my comings and goings once the telex machines at his Fifty-fourth Street office stopped their usual frantic clacking, once he had to lay off most of his employees, once the factories in Iran had been taken over by the new regime, and once many of his European and American partners—people he'd been friends with for years— wouldn't even return his calls. Finally, in the spring, he'd gone to our villa in Cannes to rest, to escape. Dariush's father, on the other hand, had stayed behind in Iran to keep his badly needed clinic going and to take care of Maman Bozorg and find a way to secure their properties in Iran so he could at least visit the West without the regime confiscating them. But most of the people we knew had merely fled Iran, carrying more horror tales than belongings and less money than hope.

Being together kept us sane and gave us hope that the Revolution hadn't stolen that predictable future from us. I think we were superstitious; if we acknowledged that everything had fallen apart for good, then that would make it true. So, we decided, we would weather the storm. And Manhattan was not such a bad place to do this.

Dariush had a loft in Soho where I would have stayed all the time if I hadn't had to worry about Banu being alone in our duplex uptown. Making love surrounded by those tall frosted windows, I would imagine we were in the middle of anywhere: Paris, Johannesburg, Sydney, Tehran. The loft was filled with things Dariush had always been passionate about: blueprints and building models and renderings, art books and architectural magazines and Impressionist prints. Sometimes I would take pictures of him there, hunched over a drawing, bare-chested, pencil clutched between his teeth, or I would cook pasta and wait for him to come home from work. He'd grown bored with his job; he hadn't expected to stay there long, and he didn't have the proper visa to apply for another job.

We often went on binges to museum exhibits, to concerts in Central Park, to the theater, the ballet, the opera, Yankee Stadium,

Studio 54. We hid out in the public library one day, visited the Statue of Liberty another, and actually sailed on the Circle Line twice. I took photography classes at NYU and had lunch with my friends from Chapin or Barnard, all of whom had jobs with banks or publishing houses or retail companies. I tried not to think about what I was doing—what I was *not* doing—with my life. What I *did* think about was the lavish wedding Dariush and I would have in his family compound—two thousand guests, champagne cooling on mountains of ice by the pools, several orchestras. I refused to accept that fairy-tale weddings had been swept away by the Party of God or that I would never live with Dariush and our children in a glamorous white house in Shemiran where my grandparents and cousins and uncles and aunts and friends would come at all hours—not a house like the duplex, sandwiched between brick and mortar, filled more with silence than people. My father had always thought of me as an American child; I think it helped him keep something of my mother alive. But in my thoughts I snubbed America: its skimpy history, its unrefined people, its self-righteousness, its lack of passion. Iran was better, had been better. And Dariush and I, we truly believed that the Revolution would blow over, just as it had blown in, right there in front of our eyes, in that benignly two-dimensional way that tragedies do on the nightly news.

But by that weekend in Montauk, our shared fantasy was unraveling. The lease on Dariush's apartment was going to be up soon, my father had all but ordered me to join him in France for the rest of the summer, and Dariush's mother, who was now my father's guest at the villa, had kindly, but firmly, suggested that her son (whom she hadn't seen in a year) also come for a visit. Dariush's lawyer had informed him that if he didn't apply for political asylum soon or marry me, he would be deported. Either choice would mean giving up his freedom to leave the country until the U.S. bureaucracy verified everything and actually gave him his permanent residency. I know this thought frightened him; he wanted his father out of Iran before he gave up his right to go back, just in case his father needed him.

And money—that thing that had always been farthest from our thoughts, yet closest to our fingertips—it was slinking away like the surf at low tide. We weren't the only ones, nor the least fortunate. The Islamic government held almost everyone's *touman*s hostage in Iranian banks, and American banks wouldn't issue loans to Iranians for lack of firm collateral. For the first time in my life, I wished for the days not too long ago when people hadn't even heard of Iran and, if they had, thought I must have been born in a tent and that we traveled everywhere by camel. Since the American hostages were taken in Tehran, though, people knew exactly where Iran was and exactly where they'd like it to go.

The cottage Dariush and I rented on Montauk had hunter green walls and pine floors and a broken stove. A perfect place to forget the world outside. We spent the weekend strolling along the beach, reading *Middlemarch* out loud, playing backgammon, eating junk food, and boogie-boarding in the rough surf until we couldn't breath from laughing. On our last night, a sadness crept under our skin and we ate dinner in silence. Outside, it began to thunderstorm and a balmy breeze squeezed in through the cracks in the walls and flickered the candles. We moved to the overstuffed couch and faced each other, legs tangled, running our fingers through and over one another's hair and faces, and kissing.

"I love you," he said.

I smiled and ran my palm over his cheek. He was staring, unblinking, at me, his pupils small like dots in liquid amber. "What is it?" I asked.

"I've decided to go to Tehran." I gasped, and his hands tightened around my upper arms as if his words might whisk me away. A big hard candy seemed stuck in my throat. "Listen to me, Layla," he said, words rushing out. "My U.S. visa is valid for three more months; it's multiple entry so I can go abroad and come back before it expires."

"What are you talking about?" I croaked. "It's too dangerous to go back until things settle down."

He shook his head, candle-lit hair falling over his forehead. "Things are not going to settle down, Layla."

My bottom lip trembled and tears of anger and heartbreak welled up in my eyes. "So that's your argument for *going* there?" I asked, fighting for a steady voice.

"Maman Bozorg says it's safe for me, that everyone exaggerates the situation. I won't stay more than a few weeks, just until all this paperwork is done. Then when I come back, I want us to get married. I don't want to wait anymore."

"Oh. Is that my consolation prize for letting you go without a fight?"

"Come on, Laylee." He took my hands in his and kissed my fingers. "She's my grandmother. Mariam says she's not doing so well. I'll never forgive myself if I don't go, and I'm not sure I could get on with my life knowing that I hadn't been to see her."

I stretched my arms around his neck, put my lips to his ear, kissed him softly. He smelled of coconut oil. I whispered, "Please don't go, please." He pulled me closer, and I knew he was torn and hurt, but resolved. And when he began to kiss my neck, then lifted my shirt to press his lips and tongue to my breast, I clutched him to me and buried my face in his hair.

That was when it had happened. That night. I should have known. Everything was different about the way we made love that night. I felt almost bodiless, like a *pari*, a fairy, wrapping myself around us, hoping to fuse us. While I touched Dariush, his firm chest and honey-colored shoulders, and I felt his hands slide beneath my hips and lift me up, and while I felt him hard and warm against my palm, then inside me, our touching—the physical sensations—they were different, surreal, like an out-of-focus lens. The air in the cottage was thick with humidity, and flashes of lightning reflected off the wavy-paned windows. I watched Dariush's eyes, lashes glistening, lock onto mine and suddenly, I saw us as other people, different from ourselves—two lovers, passionate as Dariush and Layla, but nothing like them. It frightened me, and I clutched his arms. His eyes grew wide and he said my name in an anxious, searching way. Did he see it, too? "I'm here," I said in Farsi. "I'm here." Afterwards, we clung to one another, trembling and panting, awaiting the return, I think, of the Dariush and Layla who'd flown away with the *pari*.

I should have felt the creation of life in me, but I hadn't. Instead, I dreamed of the blind fortune catcher, folding and creasing that photograph of me and Dariush and Mariam so that I was separated from them. When I woke at dawn, tangled in the sheets of the bed we'd moved drowsily to during the night, I knew I was going with him to Tehran. "We're together or *not* together," I said. "Take your pick." He knew when not to argue with me. But over the next month while we rushed to get our documentation together, he tried tactfully to change my mind. I knew what concerned him most: He was afraid my father would kill him. And he was probably right. Nobody knew our plans, not even Banu. She thought we were going to Cannes to get officially engaged and that it was her job to begin making the candy favors for the wedding in October, when Dariush's father was expected to join Auntie Veeda in France. Her excitement kept her from snooping around in my shopping bags so she didn't find the dark, dreary clothing and scarves and stockings I'd purchased to pack in my suitcase.

I knew what she would say; there had been a time before when I'd toyed out loud about going to Iran. Banu had lost it and sat me down for a lecture (which she hadn't done since I was in junior high school). "You are the daughter of a millionaire," she said. "These *mullah*s think you are as bad as a whore, that you are rich because your family stole from the people, that you are filthy because you do not say *namaz* or use a *chador*, and you are a traitor because you are also American. They will come after you, Layla, one way or another. Listen to me; I know what I am saying. You do not know as much as you think." Well, *that* wasn't *my* fault, I'd thought. Banu and my father—their generation— had believed in keeping innocent rich girls in the dark for their own protection. We were discouraged from talking about Iranian politics—if not forbidden—the implication being that there were spies everywhere who could bring misfortune on the family if something improper were said (which was probably more true than not). I didn't know anything about Iranian politics that wasn't glossed over by the adults around me.

But that wasn't true anymore. The Revolution had forced Dariush and me to educate ourselves, and, despite the lack of input from our parents, we had come to know the true face of

Iran. Or so we believed. As the day drew closer, Dariush and I grew more excited. We were going home! The idea of it nearly erased the past three years from our memories and gave us the deadly ability to delude ourselves, to almost forget about the Revolution, Khomeini, the war.

We arranged to stay in Cannes only five days, enough time to tell my father and Dariush's mother our plans. They'd been ecstatic about our wanting to get married, but that was overshadowed by all the shouting and crying and pleading about our decision to go to Tehran. And my father, as always, forbidding me—absolutely *forrbeeding* me—in a frenzy until I finally just lied and said okay, I wouldn't go. There was no lying to Auntie Veeda, however. She was too sharp. She did her best to change our minds: begging, crying, threatening, even telling us horror stories about revolutionaries chopping people's heads off with dull kitchen knives and street children running wild with machine guns and about the threat of Iraqi bombs. Dariush and I had heard it all, and we weren't willing to give in to the exaggeration and melodrama of it. We remembered how Iranians would go back home from the States in the old days and tell everyone how New York City was filled with muggers and gangsters, boasting how they'd survived.

When Auntie Veeda finally realized she wasn't getting anywhere—that she'd (God forgive her) brought up the independent-thinking boy she'd always vowed to—she then accepted our decision and became her usual practical self. My father, on the other hand, was oblivious. He'd already started to make out the guest list for the engagement party. We were concerned Veeda would rat on us in the end, but she didn't.

The night before we left, Veeda came to my bedroom to give me advice. I'd been fretting over my clothing—whether my stockings were opaque enough, my *manteau* long enough; I was sitting at my dressing table vigorously removing all traces of nail polish when she knocked at the door. I felt like an actor getting ready for the first of many scenes. She handed me a cup of warm milk and sat on the bed. I remembered thinking how elegant she was, even in her robe—something simple and silk out of a Grace Kelly movie—she was truly a woman who reveled in her own style. A thrill tingled through me when I realized she was going to be my mother-in-law soon. We spoke for almost an hour; I mostly listened while she fed me doses of fear medicine to ensure my safety: "Before you go into the transit area in Paris," she'd started, "go to the ladies' room and put your *hejab* on. People will watch you without trying to seem like they are, but you must ignore them. Do not allow yourself to feel the degradation or discomfort of those clothes. You must stop thinking in a Western way—that you have rights and freedoms. Imagine you are a doll in the *mullah's* dollhouse. Think like a proper Islamic woman; think 'submission'; say the word over and over. At the departure gate, everyone will be very quiet because they are as frightened as you are. Keep your head down; look at the floor mostly and never make eye contact with anyone, especially not Dariush. You must absolutely not reveal that you know one another until you are safely out of Mehrabad Airport and with Hooshang. And Layla, once you are on the Iran Air plane, you are as good as being in the Islamic Republic. It is not too rare that the pilot is ordered by some traveling *mullah* or zealot to radio Tehran about a passenger who seems suspicious, or merely not religious enough, and this passenger is arrested as soon as he arrives. On the road from the airport, if you come to any roadblocks, you must remain silent and let Dariush and Hooshang talk; try to make yourself invisible. This is a rule for whenever you are in public. At home—in Katayoon's house and in my house—you will feel safer. But you must come back soon. Do not let that old woman convince Dariush to stay on and on. Promise me."

I'd promised. "I swear on the grave of my mother and the soul of my father," I said quite seriously, as if I believed I had any influence over Maman Bozorg.

Dariush and I left for Tehran on a Wednesday in September while my father was in Geneva on business. On the plane to Paris—the last time we would sit together, be able to touch, to talk, I finally asked him, "So does your grandmother know?"

"What? About us?"

"I should hope she knows about *us*," I said, frowning at him, feeling queasy suddenly. "Does she know I'm coming with you?"

He looked out the window, rubbed his palms on his thighs. "I thought we'd surprise her."

"If that's supposed to be funny, I'm not laughing." He was silent. "She's going to freak out."

"No," he said, trying to sound convincing. "She'll be happy for us."

I laughed. "Don't, Dasha. Don't patronize me. I'm your grandmother's last idea of an *aroos* for her only grandson."

"Not true," he said, lifting up the armrest between us and drawing me to him. "Besides, I know you'll make a perfect bride. You and Maman Bozorg, you'll be fine; she had a hard time with you when we were kids because you were so mischievous. I loved it when you did things that made her angry. Nobody else dared cross her, but you didn't care."

I shrugged. "She treated Mariam badly. And she hated me because my mother was Jewish."

"She didn't hate you," he said, shaking his head emphatically as if this could make it true. "She's a difficult woman with a lot of prejudices. She usually means well, Layla."

I didn't say anything after that. What was the point? He wouldn't allow himself to see it. Maman Bozorg was always on her best behavior when Dariush was around; I'd seen her with Mariam, and she ran a close second to the proverbial Wicked Stepmother. I wasn't looking forward to even *seeing* her, let alone being her granddaughter-in-law.

And now, I *was* her granddaughter-in-law. I wondered if she knew. The last time I'd seen her, she'd been picking stiff-winged bee carcasses out of her breakfast honeycomb and lecturing me about my life. It had been an obligatory visit that only Dariush could have convinced me to make. He'd written me from that boot camp saying he thought it might soften her up about our getting married if I visited her. Dariush was truly blind when it came to his grandmother. I couldn't think of anything that would soften her up. She was harder than a walnut shell.

So did she think I was dead? Would Uncle Hooshang tell her what I'd been through at the prison? About the child? I hoped not. The mere idea of her thinking about me made my skin crawl. My eyes filled again, blurring the shadows of Feri's bedroom until all I could see was the vision in my own mind, of my own grandmother, her hair in a silky chignon, the lavender aroma of her face powder in my nose as I kissed her cheek. I clenched my fists. How could God have taken my grandmother and left that wicked old witch behind to ruin our lives?

Sixteen

Maman Bozorg

A child! Surely not a child! From the seed of that daughter of a Jew! It cannot be.

And my grandson missing! It is all Hooshang's fault. Did he think his son could desert the military and leave the country so easily? There are officials with wide-open eyes everywhere. If only Hooshang had not disrupted my plan, Dariush would be safe in Tehran and Layla gone back to the land of the *Shayton-e-Bozorg*.

How free from worry I was during the time Dariush spent at the training camp. This despite that girl being so close at Katayoon's house. What could she do? Plan a wedding without her groom? Without his grandmother's blessing? To my amazement, she had come to visit me. It was very distressing.

I must admit that she had grown beautiful; she no longer looked like her mother, but more like her grandfather, Mina's husband, and he was a very good type in our younger days. Never mind. Beauty is easily challenged and crushed by wit. And I put the girl in her place easily. Of course I was polite—I have never been otherwise—and while I did not say exactly what I meant, I am sure she understood that her marriage to my grandson was not acceptable. When she left me, she smiled with false respect; I am certain she hated me. But there was something else in her eyes.

Some people might have mistaken such a look for repulsion or aversion, but I knew better: It was fear. I saw it first when she pulled back abruptly as I offered her a dish of vanilla cakes. And again, when she kissed my cheeks goodbye, I felt her lips, dry with fear, her breath, bitter and hot with fear. What good fortune, I had thought. Perhaps I would not need to convince Dariush of anything. How gratifying! It would be Layla who would see that they were mismatched and Layla who would leave him behind. Surely it would have happened this way if not for my errant son!

Layla had not visited again, though I could sense her closeness—almost smell her infidel odor, I often thought, as she passed the time with Katayoon just beyond the poplar trees. And then it had been time for my Dariush to return, and I was not thinking with my full mind. Mariam was, of course, almost too much to manage; she shouted at the servants even more than I did. Everything had to be perfect: his favorite saffron rice and my best golden-rimmed dishes and his old bed with a new green satin quilt that Mariam had sewn herself. Despite my hatred of the fresh air, I allowed the maids to open all the windows in the house; this also was Mariam's idea. And she pleaded that I allow her to be without her head scarf during his visit. I agreed to this. I am not completely unreasonable. Mariam had been a good girl about wearing *hejab* since the Revolution; I think she had even come to enjoy its protection and security. But the truth was that Dariush had never seen her as a veiled woman. It would seem awkward to him, and I wanted nothing to be awkward about his visit.

Then he was there. I heard the car door close, the front door creaking open, the sound of him clearing his throat—*aye!* how I always forgot that he had outgrown his boyhood voice, that he sounded like a man. In his usual way, he burst into the room saying *"Sal'm-aleykom!"* with that cheerful voice that makes it seem as if everything in the world has been fixed and will be perfect from now forward. He came swiftly to my chair and embraced me, kneeling by my side as if I were his queen. His breath smelled of basil leaves. He wore a Western perfume concoction that smelled unpleasantly like lemons dipped in sugar, but I did not mind. He held my cheek against his lips and kissed me many times. Silently, I told *Allah* he could take me to Paradise at that moment, that I thirsted for nothing more in my life. Then Mariam was circling us, tugging at her cousin. And my arms were empty once again; a grandmother's arms are never as full as she wishes.

How tall he seemed. The brown uniform fell in perfect pleats on his body. His boots were as shiny as onyx. They had shaved his head. No matter. I liked him better without the yellow hair he had inherited from Veeda's Russian side.

I do not remember everything we talked about. My head began to ache soon after we sat down to dinner. Mariam asked many questions—about the training camp and the strategies of the war. I had warned her not to talk about the West or Layla. But *he* brought these topics to the conversation—something about New York during the Christian holidays and then another thing about Layla's family house in Shemiran being confiscated. I could not easily focus on his words. I had a compulsion to remember him as a child of four, which was his most adorable period. But my imagination was sorely tested by the increasing pain in the back of my head and an unusual humming in my ears. He and Mariam chattered through the meal like two crows. When he used Layla's name, Mariam became silent as I had instructed. And I would stop eating. I knew my Dariush would understand our feelings in this way. And I believe he did. He understood our silences as disapproval of his desire to marry. But I also saw that he smiled at our faces and laughed at our opinions with his eyes.

Then I understood why my head ached and pounded with such force. *Allah* help me, I saw that he did not care about our opinions. He belonged to her. She had bought him with lust.

Mariam wept when he refused to spend the night. I nearly slapped the back of her neck for her lack of self-control. He claimed to have orders to return to his post in Tehran that evening, and he promised to visit the following week to discuss the matter of the properties. He embraced us warmly, as is his way, but left to visit Hooshang without any sense of obligation to us. Mariam wanted to walk with him through the garden to her uncle's house, but I pinched the back of her arm—that most tender spot where a bruise would remind her of her idiocy. I knew my grandson was eager to see his prostitute. She would be at Hooshang's. Or he would stop at Katayoon's to see her.

I am the boy's grandmother; I knew he was planning something. I told myself not to worry, that I had not lost my influence over him completely. But my limbs felt weak; my thoughts felt unfinished in my mind. I was so stunned by the evening that I retired to my bed without saying my *namaz*. My nightmares were filled with *jenn*s who wore the faces of my dead relatives and *div*s who chased my Dariush with their human legs and snapped at him with their dragonlike teeth.

Two days later, Layla and Dariush were gone. I learned of the secret marriage from Hooshang and of the desertion attempt from *Haji*-Akbar. My humiliation was great, but my fear that Dariush would receive the usual punishment, that he would be shot, was far greater. *Haji*-Akbar agreed to help me in this, but he could not guarantee that Dariush would not be sent to the war front. His voice was stern and arrogant; I wished I could have reminded him that I had donated many funds toward his brothers' and his education, but I could not do this. He had my grandson's life in his hands. He suggested that I pray to God as if such a thing was something I had never contemplated, as if I were one of his students.

And I have prayed. Despite the jabbing pain in my fingers, I have used the *tasbih* that belonged to my father until the circle of amber beads has become hot and sticky as warmed honey. I have used all my willpower to keep from dwelling on the possibility that my Dariush is killed, martyred—even such a revered word is like paste in my mouth. *Hazrat-e-Abbas!* Saint Abbas! Take me, instead! *Vai*, such a terrible sin, this request. I should be honored to have my grandson martyred, floating amongst the clouds, whispering his last words to me, on his way to Paradise. But I would rather have him by my side.

And now *Allah* is truly challenging me. Hooshang's news is unbearable. But I must calm myself. Hysterical women are always left in the dark tunnel of helplessness. I must use my resources to find Dariush. Certainly there are others besides *Haji*-Akbar who can help. I will swallow my old woman's pride and hold my humiliation behind my back while I beg for them to find my grandson. Hooshang was correct in one thing: Indeed, I am that boy's only hope.

Seventeen

Layla

When I was a child and we visited Tehran, it was my grandmother who I looked forward to seeing the most. I knew she would have everything waiting for me exactly as I'd left it: all my dolls seated on the bed atop the turquoise satin coverlet, my dresser still smelling like cedar, the same carpet woven with the almond-eyed deer that seemed to leap up at me in greeting. And when my grandmother dropped the mosquito netting back around my bed after tucking me in, I would feel—finally—safe and happy.

A lot of people have said that I'm very much like my grandmother. Not in looks. She was short and light-skinned. But in personality. I think I knew this instinctively when I was a child. She liked the kind of order in her life that I liked. She spoke to me in a quiet, concentrated way that she didn't with my cousins, whom she often sent off to play in the yard, each with a handful of butterscotch candies to last them the afternoon. Nobody, except maybe my grandmother, believed it, but I didn't like candy. So I often stayed inside and followed her around. She always had chores. Opening this closet and that closet using her wad of long-nosed keys; checking dinner linens and bed linens, counting silverware and crystal saltshakers, inspecting dishes and teacups. She would call to the servants in an even voice: "Sakineh, this needs better washing. Toori, this could use a hotter iron. And Habibeh, please set the table today with the British china."

Khanoom-jahn, which was what I called my grandmother, seemed always to be moving, in a very controlled and unruffled manner, ever forward. She wore colorful tailored dresses and lipsticks in reds and pinks to match. She wore her black hair in a silky chignon and smelled of Rive Gauche perfume. It was so natural to follow her around, and so comforting. The big old house downtown—the one the *komiteh* stole—with its molded ceilings and narrow hallways where a prince's wives had once lived, never seemed scary or daunting to me. My grandmother made sure the house was always full of visitors—cousins and aunts and uncles and neighbors and the servants. It was so wonderfully different from our home in Manhattan, where it was usually just the three of us. In the afternoon sometimes, when *Khanoom-jahn* took her nap and Banu occasionally visited her family in other parts of the city, my grandmother would urge me to go to the servants' congregation room. When I told Mariam about this, she was appalled; her grandmother never allowed her to mix with the servants. But then again, Mariam's grandmother was so unlike mine. It was hard to believe they were the same age. Maman Bozorg had such a droopy lined face and wide, rubbery nose; she looked like she was wearing one of those *Mission Impossible* masks.

So I would go to the servants' room, snuggle onto a *doshak* in the corner, and watch and listen to the women who sat cross-legged around the samovar drinking tea, their light-colored *chador*s relaxing about their waists. The sound of their steady gossip gave me a kind of serenity, a sense of belonging without having to actually participate. Occasionally they offered me a glass of tea or pinched my cheek with their callused fingers. They smelled of onions and bitter cigarette smoke, but I didn't mind. I loved them.

And I loved their stories, the way there was always an underdog who was either victimized by life—the will of *Allah*—or unlucky in life—also the will of *Allah*. Such a suffering person was highly respected for what they'd been through. Of course, such a person was also usually the storyteller herself. Sometimes the women would argue about who endured the most hardship: the woman who was beaten by her husband or the woman who was divorced by her husband, for example. I loved the way they argued. Stabbing their fingers toward one another, clattering their aluminum plates about, using words I'd never have the opportunity to learn from Banu, and finally turning from livid anger to belly-shaking laughter when someone made a joke out of it all. Sometimes, when they weren't too tired, the women would gather the pots and wooden spoons from the kitchen and play music on them. They taught me how to hold the pot between my knees and thump my palm and fingers against the metal, and I did this happily until my hand was red and sore. They sang for themselves; tunes no one knew the words to: *Na-nai-nai! na-nai-nai!* And everyone took turns in the center swinging their hips to the beat of the music.

My grandmother died in her sleep from an embolism about a year after the Revolution. I would have gone to Iran then, for the funeral, but those were the days before the hostages were released and the days before I'd begun to disobey my father.

People were right when they said my grandmother had an ear to the future; she hadn't overreacted about how far the *komiteh*s would go to enforce their idea of the law. She knew her history, knew that the face of one revolution is the same as another. She remembered the stories of the Russians, so close to the north, and how the properties of the rich were divvied up in the name of egalitarianism. Soviet or Islamic, socialist or theocratic or democratic, revolution was revolution. As soon as my grandmother was buried in our mausoleum in the Cemetery of Zahra's Heaven, leaving her properties unoccupied, the *komiteh* had taken our old house downtown where I would become a prisoner. And our house in Shemiran. They'd taken that, too.

Some weeks after Dariush and I arrived in Tehran, when I was trying to keep my hopes up that he would be released from the draft soon, I visited my grandparents' house in Shemiran. It had been officially confiscated by the government. Auntie Katayoon, with whom I was staying, pleaded with me not to go. She said it would only make me upset. She said there was nothing left inside anyway; what had not been stolen by disloyal servants had been impounded by the *komiteh*. She said my memories would be ruined.

She was right.

Jamsheed brought me the key. Uncle Hooshang had entrusted Jamsheed with all the keys to his houses, to his cars, to friends' houses, to everything. Jamsheed had turned out to be something far more than Uncle had ever dreamed. People had laughed when Uncle had sent Jamsheed to medical school in Germany about a year before the Revolution. They said it was crazy to think a cook's son would return to Tehran as loyal as he'd left (if he returned at all). But he had, and in the thick of the Revolution. Jamsheed thought of Hooshang as a father, of Dariush as a brother. His own father, the cook, had fled soon after the trouble started, taking all of Veeda's Wedgwood china with him.

So Jamsheed brought me the key to my grandparents' house. He apologized for not being able to take me there himself—too dangerous for him and me to travel in the same car without proof of marriage. He called me a taxi and dropped another, smaller key in my hand. "There is a tin trunk your grandmother left for you. I have it in my car. I'll leave it here with Katayoon-*khanoom*. And be careful at your grandmother's house. Some of the rooms have been sealed off by the officials."

I told myself to prepare for the worst. The house and the garden hadn't been maintained since my grandmother had died. When Jamsheed had discovered that the caretaker was stealing everything and renting the rooms out to strangers, he fired him and closed everything up. So I knew I shouldn't expect the house to feel much like the home I once knew.

After the taxi dropped me off and I walked toward my grandmother's garden, the aroma of the fruit trees and flowers playing in the air struck me. I couldn't resist closing my eyes and letting the past flood back. The smell of pomegranates stirred a vivid memory of my grandmother rolling the fruit around in her hands, pressing it, squeezing the seeds within, then poking a small hole in the skin so I could suck the juice. And the sound of Mariam's voice drifted on the jasmine-laced breeze from the pool where her ghost lay on a plastic float: "Layla, tell the houseboy to bring some melon-ball drinks."

But then I opened my eyes and faced the truth. The rusted gate, the overgrown grass, the unpruned rosebushes, the brittle leaves covering the pathways, the gazebo looking strangled by a dead bougainvillea. The pool water was green and thick, now a haven for the frogs who used to leap across our feet while we walked at night. And the house. Of course its walls and windows were filthy, the balconies and patios seeming yellowed as old paper. The carport was empty, looking as big as a school gymnasium. For three years, like a fool, I'd imagined my white MG parked on the marble squares just as I'd left it.

The house was freezing inside, and I remembered Jamsheed saying that there was no oil for the heater because he'd refused to bribe the oil man. But I would have been chilled anyway. Everything was gone. All the furniture my grandmother had imported from Europe, the carpets ordered especially made from Tabriz, even the counters in the kitchen were bare, the cupboard doors gaping to show only mice droppings inside.

The sound of my steps echoed off the cobwebbed ceilings and dusty moldings. Wires hung like lizard tongues out of the walls, the floors were spotted with dried mud, the bathroom mirrors were smeared with finger and water marks. In my grandmother's room, the wallpaper was less faded in the spot where her headboard had been. I remembered how she always slept with four pillows, practically sitting upright all night long, because of her asthma. Sometimes I would crawl in with her in the middle of the night and, without a word, she would rub my head until I nodded off and I never knew if she did that in her sleep or if she was awake. And now, all that was left of her was the faint scent of her Rive Gauche.

Upstairs, where my father and I'd had our suite of rooms, was also barren and hollow sounding. Even the frosted wall sconces were gone, the naked bulbs casting a harsh light. Our bedroom doors, mine and my father's, were officially sealed. A thin wire led from the door handle to a wax seal that was stuck like chewed gum to the door and marked with the government imprint. Did this mean there were things in there? Like Alice in Wonderland, I fell to my knees and looked through the keyhole into my bedroom. There was the bed, stripped. The bedside table, bare. The part of the closet I could see, empty. Whose daughters were now wearing my chiffon summer evening gowns and my flowered silk cocktail dresses to secret parties behind closed doors? I punched the door and the sound echoed through the hallway. The house so empty, so hollow, yet full of *them*, their seedy smell, their fanatic fingerprints.

I went into my bathroom and washed my face with cold water that smelled like metal. I dried with my scarf and looked in the mirror. A pale, red-eyed stranger looked back. I ran my wet fingers over the glass and blurred my image. There was nothing of my old self left in that house. Nothing.

And now, lying between Fereshteh's sheets, a fiery pain shooting up my legs, I felt there was nothing of my old self left at all. And I knew it was my own fault, that I had risked the destruction of my memories and I'd lost. It was true that there is no going back. Only forward. All right. Forward. I was going to be a mother and I was going to walk again and I would find a way to bring Dariush back.

I looked around Fereshteh's room for a telephone, but there was none. I hoped Uncle Hooshang had contacted Amir. I'd given him the telephone number, and he'd promised to call despite his reservations about Amir. *Amir was our best hope.* I stared at the cracks in the plaster ceiling and hoped for sleep. I didn't want to wake Feri up for another injection of morphine; I wanted to get a hold over my pain.

And what if Dariush was dead? I had to face that possibility; the odds were high that he'd been executed for desertion. I tasted salty tears in the back of my throat. No. I closed my eyes tightly to erase the vision of Dariush slumped against a wall, a bullet hole in his temple. I couldn't think the worst; I had to be strong. I shivered, and the slight movement brought the pain back to my feet. I bit my cheek against it. I thanked God for Fereshteh lying there next to me, and I knew things could have been much worse—that I could still be trapped in the prison or dead. But none of those realizations changed the loneliness that coated me like Fereshteh's heavy quilt. And a terrible regret nudged at me, tasting bitter as the orange rind Banu used to feed me when I had a cold: If only . . . if only Dariush and I hadn't waited so long; if only we hadn't taken the future for granted. We could have had a beautiful wedding that last summer in Tehran, the summer of 1978. That would have been the last perfect time.

Eighteen

Surface Kindness

August 1978

Tir, Month of the Arrow, 1357

Amir Hakim stands on the balcony of his twentieth-floor flat in Shemiran, his swarthy face raised toward mountaintops the color of ground cinnamon. A hot breeze flaps against his face and he grins. This time, he thinks, his visit to Iran will be different. This time, *he* is different.

Below him, fenced in from the parched earth, is an oasis of emerald grass, young trees, a swimming pool. The area is dotted with sunbathers, mostly foreigners drinking *café glacé*s and scheming up ways to stay in Iran, where money is as abundant as servants and Persian hospitality as sweet as a Khayyam poem. Beyond the oasis, Amir sees the masses, expanding the city as they rush in from the countryside and skitter about in hopes of seizing a piece of the wealth that seems to fall like rain. Rain that never hits the ground.

Last evening, as he rode to his apartment building from the embassy, he suddenly remembered how once there had been sheep and beggars in the streets, how there had never been autoroutes or working-class girls who let their *chador*s billow out behind them to show off their skin-tight blue jeans and T-shirts. The country has got its head stretching to the West, he decides, and its feet glued to the East.

Amir inhales deeply and leaves the balcony. His flat is decorated entirely in white; even white shag rugs cover the white marble floors. He likes it this way, distinct from his mother's cluttered Victorian taste that had so stifled him. He goes to the white marble bathroom, runs a comb through his black, wavy hair and carefully coils a few strands onto his forehead. He poses like a *GQ* model and is pleased with his rakish reflection—sort of the way his father had looked those ten years ago when it was *he* who worked Iran for Mossad.

Amir had been all of sixteen then, a slight, short teen with terrible acne and scant athletic skill. Cursed further with a high aptitude in history, science, and languages, he knew he stood no chance for popularity at the Tehran International School, known in Farsi as *Iran Zameen*—the Earth of Iran—where he would spend two years. He had been prepared. His new classmates did indeed scamper away from him like lizards from a scorpion. It had always been like that; in Israel, in England. And it was *nearly* the same at *Iran Zameen*—just *nearly*, if not for Dariush.

Dariush hangs up the phone and tries to remember how long it has been since he last heard that voice. Seven years? Yes. High school graduation. 1971. And yet Amir Hakim had greeted him as if they had spoken yesterday, refusing to give his name—as if Dariush could guess it. He hadn't.

"Who was that?" asks his mother, Veeda, as Dariush resumes his seat at the breakfast table.

"Blast from the past," he says in English, then switches back to Farsi. "Remember that shy, awkward Israeli guy Amir Hakim?"

"No," she says, spreading butter onto her *sangak* bread.

"His father was in the army or something. His mother was British, tiny, very white skin."

"Yes," she says, raising her face toward the crystal chandelier, whose prisms dance around her eyes. "I remember now. Judith

Hakim. She joined my bridge club for a while. And the husband—very stern man, always held Judith's arm like he would lift her off the ground any moment. They didn't stay in Tehran for long."

Dariush drinks the last of his grapefruit juice. "A couple of years. He wrote me letters for a long time."

"And you, my predictable son, did not write back, *hahn*?"

He pauses. "A little," he says, snatching a square of bread from the basket. "We didn't have much in common, Maman. He wrote me these long letters that were like dissertations—about politics and science projects and God knows—all in this tiny, precise script that made my eyes cross. After a while, I stopped trying to decipher them and threw them in a drawer."

"Dasha," she scolds, nibbling at her bread. "Did he stop writing?"

"Eventually. Past few years, we exchanged *Norooz* cards. But it seems not to have bothered him I didn't write back. He didn't mention it on the phone."

Veeda blots her mouth with a starched napkin. "Then he must be a loyal and forgiving friend, my son. Those are hard to come by."

Dariush has sent a black Mercedes to take Amir to the *Koloob-e-Shahanshahi*, Club of the King of Kings, known in English simply as the Imperial Club. It is where Amir has always longed to go, but never had because he spent his summers in Israel and because he was not part of the "in crowd." Now his longing is over. Outside the window, on either side of the smooth, asphalted road, is a scruffy, beige, flat field. They approach the entrance gate; the guard, familiar with the Namdar car and driver, waves them through. Amir feels his armpits begin to perspire despite the full-blast air-conditioning; he is perhaps a little nervous. His bowels grumble. What if Dariush has changed? What if he is no longer the kind and devoted friend? Had he not sounded rather distant on the telephone yesterday morning? Had Amir hoped for more surprise and enthusiasm? When he had told Dariush that he was in Iran to drum up business for his uncle's textile company back in Tel Aviv, he had bitten his lip almost to bleeding. He itched to tell Dariush the truth, to hear the surprise—the admiration—in his voice.

He suddenly pictures Dariush on that first day he saw him in the eleventh grade: a golden boy, tall and fair, dressed in a navy peacoat, corduroy trousers, and Top-Siders. American, Amir had assumed, turning his back, hating him instantly for all his football-star allure. But then Dariush had not been what he seemed. Farsi poured like a song from his mouth and there was nothing pretentious or arrogant about him. While the others had stared at him and whispered, sizing him up, Dariush had made no judgments, had immediately smiled and welcomed Amir using the few Hebrew words he knew.

No, he tells himself, friendship so unique does not evaporate, not with time nor with separation. Dariush drew friends to him the way the Wailing Wall drew the orthodox; it was a feat Amir found majestic. Dariush could have chosen (or not chosen) anyone as friend, yet he had let Amir walk at his side. Amir still recalls the ecstasy of climbing the winding stone steps to their classrooms—eager young voices echoing off curved walls, languages mixing and swirling like an orchestra tuning up, and girls with long hair parted down the middle in *Mod Squad* fashion, glancing furtively and with obvious longing at Dariush, perhaps wondering what special thing the new boy beside him possessed that would make Dariush take him as a friend.

Dariush waits on the steps outside the Imperial Club main building for Amir to arrive. It suddenly occurs to him that he has never played tennis with Amir Hakim, that Amir Hakim was a disastrous athlete whose only involvement in sports was to keep score for the school's basketball games. Well, he thinks, seven years is a long time. He must have picked up tennis. He must have changed a lot.

Will I know how he has changed? he wonders. I hardly remember him. What did we talk about? Which girls did he like? What was his favorite car? His favorite band? His combined SAT scores? Dariush swallows a slightly sour taste of guilt. On the phone, Amir had said, "I've missed you, old bugger. Can't wait to see you." That clipped British accent rings in Dariush's ears, and he struggles to remember just one particularly unique event that the two of them had experienced together.

It comes to him, like an old film. A Friday afternoon in the autumn, the only time Dariush had gone to Amir's house. It was not that Dariush disliked Amir—what had the American students called him? Poindexter? Dweeb? Four-eyes?—it was the fact that Dariush's schedule was always overflowing and, admittedly, Amir was a little dry on the humor side. Still, now Dariush remembers that he liked Amir for precisely those reasons the Americans hadn't: He was smart. That's right, Dariush thinks, they were in the same advanced science class, the two top students, and Amir had lured him to his house with the promise of a science experiment—involving fire.

They had rolled a barrel with no bottom out to the barren hills behind Amir's housing development, stood it upon a circle of bricks, and stuffed it with newspapers and dried brush and a few scraps of wood. It took only one match and several seconds; the fire was tall and violent. Its power awed them. Amir reached into a paper bag and brought out used aerosol cans he had collected from his household garbage: Taft hairspray and Bah-Bah air freshener and Piff Paff insecticide. Holding one can in each hand, clasping the cool metal surface, the boys had breathlessly nodded to one another and thrown the cans into the fire. Like frenzied monkeys, they ran like hell to the crest of the nearest hill and fell onto their stomachs just as the explosions lifted the barrel into the air like a rocket, making the earth tremble and shift. Their ears ringing, they had punched one another in the shoulders and laughed like hyenas.

It had been a dangerous thing to do, Dariush thinks. Not something I would have dreamed up. Amir had not seemed frightened by it at all, nor concerned about getting caught. He had seemed merely intent upon experiencing the danger and on culling Dariush's admiration. Remembering now, Dariush understands what he saw in Amir's eyes that day as the yellow flames reflected off the side of his face just before they threw the cans into the barrel; it had been a haunting, near-convulsive pleasure at his own inventiveness.

Amir emerges from the car and the boys embrace like brothers. "Congratulations, *pesar*, you've grown up!" says Dariush, squeezing his friend's shoulders. "I can't believe it. You look like a completely different person." These are words Amir has longed to hear, and his smile broadens.

"And you, Dariush, you look exactly as I remember you," says Amir, stretching to his full height, which is, to his disappointment, still some inches shorter than Dariush. The truth is, Dariush is more beautiful than Amir remembers. His hair is long and shaggy, almost blond from the summer sun and falling like a fringe onto his forehead. His eyebrows are dark and arched above amber eyes, and his lips are spread into his usual good-natured smile. Amir realizes that he had imagined that his own transformation into manhood would take him to Dariush's level, where he had always yearned to be, where he was meant to be, but he had stupidly forgotten that Dariush would change as well—that gold could become more golden.

They step inside the building, and Amir follows Dariush through a foyer and a posh bar. "I've reserved a court for five o'clock," says his old friend.

"Perfect." Amir grasps the handle of his racket, feeling the rubber stick to his palm. He notices how Dariush acts as if he has no memory of Amir's athletic inadequacies. It is his solicitude, Amir thinks; he does not want to embarrass me. Or perhaps he notices that the body of an athlete has replaced the body of a sissy.

They step outside onto a veranda facing a large swimming-pool area, and Dariush points to the far side, where a group of young people plays cards at a large table. They make their way past gaggles of trendy young sunbathers exquisite in their Italian bikinis, skin perfectly oiled, manners impeccably cultivated, and reading material exclusively European. Amir senses the admiring looks that follow him—the women's lustful eyes, the men's envious ones. He feels his thick, black hair grazing his nape and the fine cotton of his ellesse tennis shorts brushing against his muscular thighs. He cannot help noticing how he is dressed more stylishly than Dariush, whose tennis whites are dated and who wears a Fred Perry shirt rather than the more fashionable Lacoste. Still, walking side by side like this, Amir knows they are finally a striking pair, and the memory of Amir as a homely shadow by Dariush's side is covered in a thick haze.

As they get closer to the group of Dariush's friends, Amir's eyes are drawn to a tall, attractive girl who stands looking over someone's shoulder at their cards. She wears a bikini—red, white, and blue stripes—and the ends of her dark hair brush the curves of her buttocks. Her thighs are long and thin, and he imagines them wrapped around him. He feels a flame in his groin. What a prize, he thinks. She reaches up and gathers her hair atop her head, twisting it into a haphazard knot. He focuses his onyx eyes on her burnished lips, willing her to sense the electricity of his stare. But she does not turn toward him. No matter. He knows he now has a mask of charm, that his watery eyes and chiseled cheeks are assets that can make him wealthy with the trust of others.

Dariush introduces him around the table and he nods and smiles, lying that he remembers some of them from the International School. At last Dariush introduces the girl, who stands next to him, and Amir sees her full face for the first time. He is startled. Her eyes grab him—not the color, though they are a lovely green, but the way they effervesce with mischief and boldness. And her smile is not the usual demure smile of a Persian woman; it is playful and self-assured. He knows immediately that she cannot be full-blooded Iranian. Amir's smile is frozen against his teeth as he watches Dariush's long tapered artist's fingers glide over the girl's shoulder and rest gently on the back of her caramel-colored neck; she leans slightly into him. "This is Layla," he says, and Amir feels the magnetism between them push him aside as if he were a plastic chess piece.

The tennis match is vigorous, as if a current of electricity runs between the players. They grunt on every serve and smash of the ball. This, Amir thinks, is why he had worked his body so hard over the last three years.

People gather to see who will win or who will collapse from exhaustion first. The ball boy is changed four times. Two hours pass with the players always one point, one game, one set apart. Then suddenly, Dariush calls for a draw. Amir is stunned, frozen like a trophy statue. A draw?

Dariush leaps over the net and comes forward, looking at his watch. "I've got an invitation for dinner at Layla's grandparents' house."

Amir keeps his cool, even smiles. "Well, a good Persian knows how to be fashionably late."

"I already might be if I don't get out of here soon," he says, tapping Amir's rear with his racket. They walk side by side off the court, and Amir cannot resist another (seemingly) playful jab. "I guess old rekindled friendships don't rank very highly against beautiful women."

Dariush shakes his head and chuckles. "Not even close," he says teasingly.

"How cute," says Amir, his shoulders tightening like a drum.

Amir dismisses his servant and sits down to dinner. The meal before him gives off an exquisite aroma of basmati and saffron, but he does not lift his utensils. He stares at the sofa, where a small Impressionist painting of lovers embracing leans haphazardly amidst torn brown wrapping paper. It had arrived by courier today from Istanbul, from Josephina. It is another indication of her sudden, inexplicable, and annoying romanticism. They have been together on and off since they were teenagers, but not in love, not committed—that had been the unspoken rule. But Josephina had begun to bend the rule and Amir had been happy to get away.

But now, goddammit, he would not mind a taste of Josephina.

Amir scowls and abruptly pushes his plate away. Who *is* this Layla? Why had Dariush never mentioned her? Why had Amir never met her? Was it true that she had visited Tehran at exactly the times he had visited Israel during those years? And why had destiny put her in Tehran now? He gulps from his glass of water and rises from the table.

In the bathroom, he strips and stands naked before the mirror. He grabs his free weights and watches his pectorals ripple as he lifts and holds. He conjures up what Josephina might say to him now: that he is strong, powerful, beautiful—an agent of Israeli intelligence, hand-picked. He steps into the shower, where he leans against the tiles and masturbates. Josie had been his first. She knew how to fight for him, how to pinch and bite, to claw and clamp her legs around him until he could do nothing but give in to his orgasm.

"Amir Hakim is an *avazi* asshole," says Benjamin Schnur.

Dariush smiles and tucks the phone receiver under his chin. Although Benjamin Schnur has lived in Tehran since his father was posted at the Israeli embassy twenty years ago, his Farsi has never been as good as his English and, like most *Iran Zameen* kids, he speaks a mixture of both. "You think most people are *avazi* assholes," says Dariush.

"This guy is the real thing. I knew him when I was a kid in Tel Aviv. He's always been strange. A total outcast and really bitter about it. You remember him in high school?"

"That's the problem, I don't really, but he seems to think we're best buddies."

"It's your own fault, Dasha," says Benny almost scoldingly. "You were the only one who would talk to him. Everyone else knew he was trouble."

"Come on, Benny. I didn't talk to him any more than I talked with a lot of other kids."

"Like I told you. He's weird. He probably took it the wrong way. He's the kind to latch on and never let go, the kind you can never do or be enough for. Just dump him."

Dariush snorts. "I can't do that. He calls me every day. Wants to go to the cinema, to the bazaar, mountain climbing, whatever."

"Uh-huh. And he doesn't want anyone else around, just you and him, right?"

"Yeah."

"He's got an inferiority complex the size of an Arab's rectum. You know, his father was a militant fanatic who believed the best solution to the Palestinian problem was to kill all the Arabs. Genocide. And he really meant it."

"That doesn't mean Amir thinks the same way, Benny."

"Judge for yourself. Amir used to sit with a BB gun at his bedroom window in the apartment building in Tel Aviv where we used to live, and shoot at people in the street who had—quote, unquote—'betrayed' his trust."

Dariush laughs. *"Boro baba!* Get out of here! No way."

"It's true. People were wounded."

Dariush is glad Benjamin cannot see his still smiling face. "Look, Benny. I just wanna know how to deal with him—*without* hurting the guy's feelings."

"Look, man, he doesn't have the same kind of feelings we do. Dump him or you'll be sorry."

The sky is blue as sapphire against lofty peaks behind and above the Namdar house. Its tall frame, clean white stucco, and wrought-iron balconies are flooded with golden light from inside and outside. Bright pink bougainvillea flowers hang from the patio balustrades like the skirts of flamenco dancers. The servants bring candles to the tables along the patios, and the gardeners light the lamps that give the lush grounds a golden glow.

Amir arrives early, thinking he and Dariush can have some time alone, but of the family, Amir catches sight only of Dr. Namdar on one of the higher patios greeting guests. So he takes a stroll along the gravel pathways and comes upon a small, empty teahouse strewn with carpets; he pours himself a glass from the silver samovar, then moves on. He comes upon the lower level of the pool and learns something he has always wanted to know: There is indeed a gentle waterfall here, a cascade washing down a blue mosaic wall. It annoys him that he has any curiosity left about such a thing. While he remembers having a hot envy for his friend's cache of books and record albums and model airplanes and stereos and gadgets and European clothing, he has no such yearning now. Not one bit.

On a staircase platform overlooking a rose garden, Amir spots several Israelis, including the spoiled redhead Benjamin Schnur, who he remembers from the International School. Their fathers still push paper around at the embassy. Once Amir would have avoided them, but now he smooths his Ted Lapidus suit, saunters to the stairs, smiles broadly, and spreads his arms. "My old friends," he says in Hebrew.

Benjamin feels his jaw drop and he whispers incredulously, "Amir? Amir Hakim?"

Amir reaches the platform, touches Benjamin's shoulder, turns to the others—Lily, Moshe, Anat—and kisses their cheeks. He has pleasant words for each of them. His manners, Benjamin thinks, are polished and fluid; there is little trace of the diminutive weirdo. In fact, Amir is muscular and lean, masculine with black eyes and hollowed cheeks. Goddammit, Benjamin thinks, the bastard has turned into one good-looking son of a bitch. He takes a big swallow of his drink and snuffs out his cigarette in a clay sand-pot.

Amir is brimming with pleasure as Benjamin struggles to keep his expression bland, yet looks desperate to loosen his tie. The others are eager to know what Amir has been doing for the past years; they actually look at him when they speak, and smile. Josephina was right; appearance means everything to people. He looks around, across the garden, for Dariush, so they can nod to one another—a gesture between comrades—but there is no Dariush, and Amir feels suddenly irritated that his friend has not searched him out as yet. After all, the party is at *his* house.

A manservant in a white jacket appears and, in perfectly accented Farsi and with great aplomb, Amir orders a "vodka lime," asks the others if they want refills, and orders those, too. The servant bows and backs away, descending the stairs at a clip.

"How the hell did you remember your Farsi?" ask Moshe and Anat at the same time. Amir loves the admiration in their voices. He shrugs. "Good ear, I suppose."

"He studied it at Oxford," says Benjamin, staring at Amir. "Right?"

Amir nods, hating Benjamin's mocking tone. "You're smarter than I remember, Benny."

"Literature, too?" asks Lily with an adolescent smile.

"Of course," says Amir. "What's Farsi without Hafez?" It is a question not requiring a response. Even native Iranians have a hard time with Persian literature. For a moment, Amir feels the outcast, but then he reminds himself that he is standing at his full height, sleek and sinewy, artful in his French suit, dashing in his feathered haircut.

Many more guests arrive, and the garden and patios become spotted with small groups of people laughing and gesturing and craning their necks and shifting their eyes to see what is going on, who is here, how well everything is put together. The women's rubies, sapphires, aquamarines, opals, emeralds, and diamonds sparkle like fireflies in the garden light. Amir thinks about the strikes and protests and assassination attempts on the shah, the circulation of thousands of cassette tapes containing Khomeini's sermons, and the shifting of support from the bazaar away from the monarchy and toward the clergy—these are just rumors to these people of the aristocracy, rumors that bounce off their bejeweled ears and disappear into a fog of discarded gossip. They are oblivious, Amir thinks, to the storm that is coming.

The manservant brings them their drinks, then descends the steps to take orders from three young girls, one of whom Amir notices, is Layla. She wears a crimson halter dress in a thin silk that ripples against her breasts, her hips, her thighs, as if it is liquid; black thin-strapped sandals with four-inch heels make her taller than most everyone. Amir catches himself breathing with his mouth slightly open and looks away. "She's beautiful, isn't she?" says Benjamin in a muted voice, having noticed Amir's uncharacteristic reaction. Amir takes a sip of his drink and turns away slightly, but Benjamin comes next to him, their shoulders nearly touching. Amir continues to stare at Layla; he imagines his fingers caught in the strands of her voluminous hair, silky and soft as Persian cat's fur. Benjamin feels a shiver run up his spine and says, "She and Dariush make a perfect couple, don't you think?"

Slowly, Amir looks at Benjamin. Raising one corner of his mouth in a forced and ingenuine half-smile, he manages to say, "Nothing is perfect," astonishing himself as well as Benjamin, then looking toward Layla once again.

* * *

It is not dangerous to be an Israeli in the shah's Iran. The fact is, the aristocracy in Iran is well disposed toward Jews. Some say that is because Iranians are not Arabs; others say it is because they hide their prejudices well. Perhaps both are true, but Amir Hakim's theory has to do with economics: People who have more than they need of most everything are generally well disposed to anything.

But then there are the others, the working-class people, the rest of the country.

Amir was sixteen, only three months in Iran, when he overheard the school janitors' conversation.

"Again, you bring up the Jews?" said one to the other. "Complain about the Armenians for a change. At least the Jews don't strut around as if they fell from the sky."

"No sir," the other replied. "Instead, they hoard the money. They steal from us! We work like donkeys to earn a thumbnail of what they spend for their silk clothing. Infidels! How dare they rise up higher than True Believers? I wish I could shoot them all with a Kalashnikov so their dog mothers and dog fathers and dog sperm would perish forever!"

Amir's head had swelled with rage. He wanted to rush like a madman into the classroom and wrap his fingers around the janitor's pimply neck. He had thought about how his father Izaak was right; Iranians were not more well disposed toward Jews. His father had warned him about this "surface kindness," as he called it. "Don't forget your history, son. Not too long ago, these *Shiah* dogs forbade our people to go out of their houses when the rains came so the drinking water would not be contaminated. And Iranian Jews? They are traitors, weaklings, no better than the rest of Iranians who let the Arab conquest suck them into Islam. Their resilience to conquerors is abhorrent. They adapt too quickly to the winds of change—unlike Israel, unlike the Jews, who always fight for their identity. The Persians have lost their individuality by assimilating their conquerers' cultures. And Iranian Jews have taken on this terrible trait, forgetting their uniqueness, forgetting the importance of fighting the world, forgetting the significance of being Jews first and foremost."

The following day when Amir returned to school, he surreptitiously went into the janitors' changing room and used one of his mother's kitchen knives to split the soles from the bad janitor's shoes and to cut tiny holes into his trouser pockets and along the seams in his coat. It brought him great satisfaction to imagine the janitor slowly finding his clothing and shoes coming apart; it would cost the man many months' wages to replace those items, and it served him right.

This was Amir's kind of revenge. Secret and sweet. His mother had known about it; often, her white skin would turn blotchy red in shock and she would cry, begging him to tell her *Why, why do you destroy other people's treasures?* He could not help himself; it gave him something—a surge of power—that he could not deny himself. When he was a small boy, it was his playmates' toys that he broke; he did it subtly—a Matchbox car tire here, a G.I. Joe head there—and later he furtively pulled up the edge of a carpet or scratched the paint off a windowsill or loosened the buttons on a favorite coat. One time he'd gotten so angry with his mother over yet another one of her arguments with his father about her Arab friendships that he had methodically broken the heads off her collection of miniature glass animals. But his mother always forgave him his transgressions. After all, to her he was perfect.

Dariush and Amir do not debate far into the night about politics or history, as Amir had imagined. There are no discussions about Vietnam, OPEC, the international monetary crisis, apartheid, Egypt and Israel, communism, nuclear war, or even the future of Iran. Dariush's head does not burn with opinions the way Amir's does. It burns only with Layla. Amir has never given up his soul to a woman, and he wonders, with irritation, if Dariush has already sold himself. Wherever he sees them—at weddings and swimming parties and nightclubs—they have a visible hunger for one another. And not enough time for or interest in anyone else. Amir watches their every move; how they steal away into a garden or an empty bedroom or a dark corridor and emerge disheveled and red-faced. He pictures Layla running her long fingers over Dariush's back, pressing her pelvis against him, making him teeter on the edge of orgasm. He has dreams of Dariush watching him fuck Layla.

Out of guilt, Dariush phones Amir to invite him for a day of waterskiing at the Karadj Reservoir. It is late August, Dariush's last weekend before going back to the States, and he does not want to leave bad feelings behind to fester in the air.

Amir is inclined to say no, but Dariush's honey voice, filled with honesty, asking forgiveness, warms a sliver of hope in Amir's heart. "Come on, Amir. I won't take no for an answer, man. We've gotta see each other before I leave."

So he goes.

The air on the way to Karadj is hot like a stone bread-oven, and Amir is thirsty. Layla hands him a glass bottle of cool water as if she can read his mind. He thanks her with a profuse smile but feels crabby about her intuitive gesture. He has decided to feel indifferent toward her; she is nothing but a knot of hair that has come between a friendship. He looks at the others: There are about eight of them, not including the driver, in a VW minibus that belongs to one of the Bahari factories. Amir recognized the company name written on the side of the vehicle, and now he knows just how rich Dariush's girl is. He does not care.

Suddenly, they round a bend and come upon the immense white wall of the Karadj Dam. As always, Dariush is awed by the design, by the hidden steel and by the smooth concrete, and by the precise mechanics that make it a man-made god of electricity. Passing above it along the winding road, Amir, on the other hand, thrills to an image of the dam cracking and water spewing and tumbling through like a liquid demon.

The enormous reservoir beyond the dam is aqua and sits like a liquid gem between jagged stone cliffs and mountains. The winter waterline runs like a thick chalk mark along the canyon sides; they say the water is deeper than the mountains are tall. The resort is some kilometers beyond the dam. Steep stairs lead to a restaurant about halfway down the canyon; more stairs and a walkway lead to a row of bright-colored pontoons boats, called *eskeleh*s, that hug the canyon wall. That is where they go to meet the boats.

Amir has never water-skied, and he does not want to learn, certainly not while these elitist brats in their Rolex watches and couture sportswear look on. He sits in a director's chair on the *eskeleh* munching on baguette bologna sandwiches with corni-chon pickles and butter. He is not the only one. Dariush's cousin Mariam sits hunched against the changing-room wall, squinting against the sunlight, a floppy straw hat on her head. Despite the blazing heat, she wears a terry-cloth robe over her bathing suit. She is petite and could be pretty, he decides, but her expression is so sour, no man would be attracted to her. Sometimes he catches her looking at him, but she quickly glances away. Great, he thinks, me and the midget get to watch the show. He wishes he had never come.

The motorboats work continuously, dropping skiers off, taking skiers out. Some are better than others; the ones who fal-ter in the water, trying to keep their skis afloat while the boat pulls them forward, are laughed at and teased, and those who misjudge the distance to the pontoon when ending their turn are yelled at for splashing everyone. Others jump from the *eskeleh* into the water, skis on, holding the rope, and praying they can stay upright. This is the cool way to start, and most do not succeed at it. Except for Dariush, of course. *That* Amir could have predicted.

Finally, Amir agrees to ride in the boat with Dariush while Layla skis. They sit in the back, not on the seat cushions, but on the narrow lip of the deck so they are up high, facing one another, the powerful motor between them and to the side. The driver is the young cousin of Esau, who runs the waterskiing concession and who was a shepherd before the dam was built, before the rich people came and made him rich, too. "He's the best water-skier in Iran, but he's an arrogant son of a bitch," says Dariush to Amir. "There he is, in that other boat." Amir sees a man as dark as an African wearing a minuscule Speedo bathing suit and gesturing exasperatedly at a guy on the pontoon boat who is taking too long to get his life jacket on. Amir says,

"Maybe he's sick of catering to uncoordinated rich kids."
Dariush chuckles. "Maybe."

Layla calls to them. She bobs in the water, holding the rope,
her one ski sticking up in front of her like a fin. The driver guns
the motor and the boat jerks forward. Amir holds on to the edge
of his seat. They pick up speed quickly, and Layla rises gracefully
up on one ski, her thighs and arms taut as the tow rope; her long
hair flutters behind her like a flag. The motor rattles and
screams. The wind races at Dariush and Amir, whipping their
hair back. It is exhilarating, and Amir is suddenly glad that he
came. They travel across the reservoir until the pontoon boats
look like toys. Dramatic crags rise up before them like colossal
stalagmites. The spray against his skin is pure mountain water;
he can taste it.

Layla wends her way from left to right, gliding over the boat's
wash. Dariush does not take his eyes off her even when Amir
yells some comment or another to him. He is cordial enough,
tells Amir something about the rock formations, a story about
someone who had drowned in an accident the previous year, *but
he does not take his eyes off Layla.* Amir suddenly has a strong urge
to smack the sole of his foot into Dariush's stomach, pushing
him backwards into the water. He closes his eyes and searches his
mind for something to focus on that will calm him. Eventually,
he feels the boat beginning to slow down and hears the voices of
people on the *eskeleh.* Thank God it's over. Then, without warning, he feels a violent shove to his chest and he hits the cold
water on his back.

It is Esau's fault, what happens. Esau in the other boat, sick
and tired today of the haughty children of the big-headed elite
who keep losing their tow ropes so he must return the boat to the
eskeleh to throw it off to them. This is the last time, Esau swears,
driving his boat into position, perpendicular to the *eskeleh;* he
wants his afternoon *chai.* The boy holds the rope, the boat is perpendicular to the *eskeleh,* and *Khodayah!* God above! here comes
Esau's young cousin, driving the other boat toward the *eskeleh* to
drop the Bahari girl off. Aaah, shit, he thinks, now the fat boy
must drop the rope to allow the other boat to pass between them.

Impulsively, he gestures to the boy, who sits like a Buddha on the edge of the *eskeleh*, to raise the tow rope above his head. Esau knows it will clear his cousin's boat; he had done it before. But suddenly, he gasps and calls to God sincerely for the first time in years. How had he not noticed the Namdar boy and his friend sitting up high in the rear? Their heads will surely be broken off!

When Layla drops her tow rope and sinks toward the *eskeleh*, Dariush finally takes his eyes off her. He turns to tell the driver to pull up to the *eskeleh* so he and Amir can disembark. That is when he sees the tow rope from the other boat coming toward them. He lunges toward Amir, intending to dive into the water and shove his friend in at the same time. But Amir is more solid than Dariush anticipates, and his dive is broken. The tow rope from Esau's boat catches him under the arm, propelling and twisting his body so that his head cracks into the side of the boat before he goes in.

There is blood in the water, and Amir thinks it is his own. He reaches the surface and gasps for air. His ears are plugged with water, so he does not hear the screams from the pontoon boat; he only sees, through eyelashes beaded with water, the frayed remnants of a red-and-white rope. The water is freezing and, despite his strength and stamina, he is having a hard time treading. But he knows he is not hurt, not the one who is bleeding. He goes under and swims slowly toward an area where blood stains the water like a billowing cloud.

Dariush thinks he is drinking Maman Bozorg's special salty broth for healing. No. No, he tells himself, you must come to your senses. It is not Maman Bozorg; you are under the water, being sucked down and toward the dam by the current; *you are drowning*. The taste of salt is his own blood. His chest is bursting with pain. He tries to kick his feet. *Khodayah, help me; let them hurry*. But he sees no movement in the water around him, no one splashing in to save him. Is he too deep? Have they lost him? *Hurry, hurry. There! Amir! Coming toward him*. Struck with hope, Dariush manages to stretch his arm toward Amir.

Amir knows he can save Dariush, but something makes him hesitate. He is close enough to see his old friend's face: eyes open, somewhat focused, lips white, a red and swollen lump on his forehead. The blood, he realizes, comes from a gash under Dariush's arm that looks like a broken zipper. The thing to do is grab him around the waist and swim him up to the surface. Instead, Amir treads water just beyond Dariush's reach and imagines him sinking helplessly to the riverbed below. *Shall I forsake you as you have forsaken me, old friend? Shall I make you give up your golden-boy place in the world?* Dariush's eyes are wide with panic now; he stretches his arm minutely farther in hopes of grasping Amir. Amir's lungs have begun to ache; he reaches out and clutches Dariush against him as a child would do to a favorite doll. Still, he hesitates, relishing this moment of sovereignty. Suddenly, above him, on the surface, is Layla in her red, white, and blue bathing suit, swimming fast and strong toward them. Amir awakens his powerful leg muscles and propels them to the surface.

Amir and Dariush never speak of the incident. During his recovery, Dariush forces himself to consider that his own delirium and panic had led him to think Amir wanted to let him drown. But it is an empty consideration, he knows. When finally Amir comes to see him off at the airport, Dariush grits his teeth against Amir's embrace. He is a good actor, Dariush thinks, and would no doubt succeed in convincing everyone, including me, that such a horrific scene beneath the water never happened. Dariush is, therefore, silent. And while Layla and Mariam and the others say they will never forget how Dariush Namdar and Amir Hakim saved one another's lives on the Karadj Reservoir in that final summer of 1978, Dariush shivers and hopes never to see Amir Hakim again.

Nineteen

Layla

A sound came from the other room. A click. The lamp being turned on. A yellow glow. I heard Asya, Fereshteh's daughter, using the toilet, then her slight shadow crept toward the bedroom door. She stood here, blocking the light, leaning against the door frame. She watched me for almost a whole minute, unaware that I was awake and watching her, too. Her face was in shadow. She wasn't wearing her scarf, and some inches above her ear where the light shone, a wide cylindrical scar was carved into her scalp. Against her black hair, it looked bright white and mottled. I felt slightly nauseated but resisted the urge to look away. Finally, she turned and left. Soon the light in the other room was shut off. I heard Asya moving on her *doshak*; I thought I could hear her breathing.

I remembered Fereshteh's complaints about Asya in the old days. She would tell Banu how much trouble her daughter was—not the kind of problem daughter who defied her mother by wearing too much makeup or too-short skirts or by smoking cigarettes or drinking *aragh* with her friends. Asya had actually been a perfect student, making twenties—the highest marks— in her classes at Tehran University. Sure, she stayed out late, smoked Winstons, met with boys, and spent hours at her tiny desk with hardly a word for her mother. Fereshteh would tell Banu, "I would not mind if she did these things because she was crazy in love. Then maybe there would be some rosy outcome, like a marriage and the hope for grandchildren. But she has no interest in such things. She says she spends her best hours having discussions of philosophy. My daughter is a social invalid!" Banu would pat Feri's back and minister words of condolence and hope. Then one afternoon when I'd presumably fallen asleep on Banu's bed while she and Feri sat around the samovar and gossiped, I heard the real problem of Asya. "*Allah* help me," whispered Fereshteh to Banu. "My daughter is mixed up with political people. She meets them in dark basements and in the mountains. *Vai* Banu-*joon*, she writes articles for a forbidden newspaper that is against the shah. I think she is a Communist!" Banu had gasped.

I'd wondered why anyone would be against the shah; it was so obvious how much he'd done to bring Iran into the modern world. Everyone said so. I'd never heard a bad word against him. What a stupid girl Asya was, I'd thought, a silly girl who thought being a rebel was romantic. She'd probably read too many of her mother's Russian novels. I'd felt really sorry for Fereshteh, whose daughter was wasting her life on impossibilities.

But now I knew exactly which girls had been wasting their lives on impossibilities. And it hadn't been girls like Asya. I wondered if Asya condemned me for who I'd once been, if, as she'd stared at me from the doorway minutes earlier, she'd worn the look of loathing and anger that I'd so often seen from others who'd fought to free Iran from the monarchy and from families like my own: the aristocracy, the royalists, the *taghoot*s, the false gods of Iran.

I shivered even though the two quilts on me were heavy and warm. I suddenly wondered how Asya's loyalty to her political beliefs compared with her loyalty to Fereshteh. She was a revolutionary, after all. Would she keep my presence here secret? Or would she tip off the *komiteh* so they could come and take me back to the prison? I began to sweat. The noxious odors and pitiful sounds of the prison came back to me; the bloated face of the

woman who beat me loomed in the darkness above my bed. My
feet throbbed brutally now; stabbing pain shot up my legs. My
heart pounded and I gasped for air. I wriggled, tried to lift my legs.
The pain was so sharp the whole room seemed to turn bright
white. I knew what I was trying to do was crazy, but I also had
this thought that seemed very logical: that if I didn't try to get
out of there, away from Asya, I would die and so would my baby.

The commotion woke Feri. Comforting words tumbled out of
her mouth while her bear-strong arms held me firmly against the
mattress. She called for Asya. I yelled "No!" and saw the puzzled
look on her face. She directed Asya to get a morphine syringe
from the bedside drawer. I yelled "No!" again, but it was too late.

When I woke up, the room was flooded with daylight and Asya
sat in Feri's chair reading a beat-up, water-crinkled, English-
language copy of *Anna Karenina*. She saw my eyes open, splayed
the book on her lap, leaned over, and touched my arm. "*Chetori?*
How're you doing?" she whispered. She was frowning with what
looked like concern. I held my breath and watched her, hardly
blinking, though my eyes were dry from sleep. I waited for a
flicker of disingenuousness to pass across her features, a sign that
she was lying. "Do you have pain?" she asked. "Shall I get my
mother to give you another injection?" She gently massaged my
arm with her fingers while she waited for my answer.

"No," I said, barely loud enough for my own ears. "I feel better."

She smiled. It seemed genuine, and in the daylight my fears
from the night before seemed far-fetched. If Asya had wanted to
turn me in, she could've done it already. I'd been at Feri's almost
a week. Still, I was wary. Was she being just a little *too* nice?

"I'll tell my mother you're awake," she said. "She'll bring
some tea." She got up and I asked her if I could see the book she
was reading. Not that I could focus much, but I thought it
might feel good to touch a book; it seemed like years since I'd
done that. "Of course," she said. "It was your book, anyway."

"What?"

She smiled again. "Your grandmother, may she rest in peace,
gave it to me two years ago. She didn't think you would mind.

She knew the revolutionaries would eventually seize everyone's Western belongings." Asya shook her head. "We thought she was overreacting."

"Did you see my grandmother a lot?"

"My mother and I visited her several times after your grandfather passed on. Banu asked us to. And it was our pleasure. She was an interesting and kind woman. I have a few more of your books. My English is terrible, but if I read slowly, I learn many new words. Well, let me bring the tea and tell my mother you are awake." And she turned toward the other room, her scarf snugly bound around her head, covering the scar I'd seen during the night.

"Asya," I croaked, calling her back. She turned quickly and leaned over me; I must have sounded a little desperate when I said her name.

"What is it, Layla?" she asked. "Pain?"

I almost couldn't get the words out. Finally, I looked at her sincere brown eyes and said, "I thought you were a revolutionary, Asya." She stared at me a moment—no change in expression. My pulse quickened. Would she drop her sympathetic mask now? A fleeting image flashed through my mind of her slapping me; I think I may have even flinched. Instead, she dropped her gaze as if in shame and regret. "No, Layla," she said in a tired voice. "My kind of revolutionary disappeared soon after Revolution. Do not worry. I am not your enemy and you are not mine. Not anymore." She turned and left the room and I thought: So they stole her future too.

For the rest of that day, Asya and Fereshteh fluttered around me like worried hens. Are you all right? they kept asking, their faces coming close, searching mine. They seemed amazed that my pain could finally be manageable without morphine. They spooned sweet tea through my cracked lips and washed my face and arms with a warm sponge. Feri begged me to take the pills Uncle Hooshang had left for the pain; she promised they wouldn't make me comatose the way the morphine did. I agreed to take them because I remembered reading something in *Cosmopolitan* about how refusing pain medicine could slow down the healing process. And they did make me feel better—sleepy and weak, but not stoned. Feri told Asya they should go and let me rest, but I wouldn't let them. My arm felt like rubber, but I raised it and told them, in an airy voice, to stay. I didn't want to be alone.

Feri, on one side, held my arm and tickled my palm with her callused fingers. I felt hypnotized. Asya, on my other side, sat still and serene. I could hear her breathing, every inhale, exhale—long and calm. I imagined, perhaps I dreamed, that we were in a cave, its walls gold and warm to the touch, and that we could stay there, safe, forever.

I asked the women to talk; I wanted to hear the tenor of their voices, the words that sounded like everyday life. I wanted to make a little magic carpet out of their voices and transport myself to another world, away from my own thoughts. "Talk," I whispered.

"Talk about what?" asked Feri.

"Anything."

Both were silent. Finally, Asya spoke tentatively. "My mother and I—we don't talk to one another very much."

"Why not?"

"We have a—what is that English expression?" said Feri. "We have a 'generation hole' between us."

My stomach muscles fluttered with laughter, but I was too drugged to laugh out loud. Asya shook her head, smiling. "My mother does not approve of me," she said.

Feri frowned. "Approval is not an issue. I am afraid for you. If you were a mother, which you should be by now, you would know what I feel."

"Asya," I said, and they both leaned in to hear. "What happened to your head?" My words had come out automatically, as if my thoughts were inside my mouth and not commanded by my brain. Asya looked away. "I'm sorry," I said. She looked back and touched my arm. "Don't be worried. You have not insulted me. It is just the memory of it that hurts me."

"Never mind," I said. "I should not have asked." By now, I barely had enough energy to push each word off my tongue.

"It was the Black Friday," Feri said in a flat voice as if she were reading from a newspaper article. "The demonstration against the shah. I begged her not to go. But young girls with fantasy ideas do not listen to their mothers."

"I went with my best friend, Beheen," said Asya in a wispy voice.

"May God comfort poor Beheen," said Feri.

"Tell me what happened," I whispered, feeling my head spin a little as if soon I would become a character in their story.

"Pahlavi Avenue was a sea of people marching against the shah," said Asya. "I had put on a *chador* for the first time in my life because the leaders of the march said it would be a good symbol of protest. Even some women of the aristocracy who'd come to our side were marching in black *chadors*. Everyone looked so confident—smiling and raising fists as if our hopes had come true. No more oppression, no more forbidden political ideas, no more big salaries for—excuse me, Layla—for the few families like yours, no more poverty."

"False hopes," said Fereshteh. "Hopes to wipe your backside with."

"No, Mother," Asya said quietly. "Our hopes were real. The shah was blind to what his people wanted. Instead, he dressed up Iran in steel and concrete and military tanks and tennis courts and casinos and palaces filled with jeweled thrones and Western art. This was his skewed idea of a modern country. He was a corrupt king, a slave to Western ideas, ashamed of his own people."

"And so what?" Feri broke in. I felt her hand come down on the bed beside me. "Now we have a turbaned shah. Your hopes were absurd. Fantasy!"

Asya didn't respond. I forced my eyes open and saw Feri straightening out her shawl and Asya looking toward the window as if the bright light could remove the dark shadows of her memory. I put my hand, tingly from sedation, on her thigh. "So what happened?" I said.

She still stared, as if her story were written on the windowpanes. "I held Beheen's hand—she had always been much smaller than me, weaker—so I held her hand tightly even when the crowd thickened around us and she fell a bit behind me. I heard the *pap!pap!* of firecrackers and the crowd surged against us. *Pap!pap!*" she said again, her eyes blinking as if the sound had come from somewhere other than her own mouth. She looked at her lap, at my hand lying there; she took it lightly between her palms as if it were a delicate pastry. "But of course," she said. "There were no firecrackers, only the machine guns of the Imperial Guards firing into the crowd." She looked at me and blinked; tears spilled onto her cheeks.

"Were you hit?" I asked.

She touched the spot on her head scarf where I knew the scar was hidden. "The pain was like a hot coal. I fell to the ground and waited for the world to disappear from my eyes. But it did not."

"*Alhamdolellah*, Thanks to *Allah*," said Feri.

Asya turned to her mother so suddenly that my body jerked involuntarily. "No!" she snapped. "There is nothing to thank God for!" And she left the bed. I heard her slippers flop against the floor and recede. A door closed. I tried to lift my head, to focus, but everything beyond the milky light from the window was in a fog.

"What happened?" I asked Feri.

She bit her lower lip, then straightened up in the chair. "It was Beheen who died. The bullet grazed Asya's scalp and went then into Beheen's eye." The image of this was so vivid in my mind that I thought I would vomit. "Asya cannot forgive herself," concluded Feri.

"But it wasn't her fault," I said.

"She had always been the political one, the stronger one. Beheen followed her, just to be close, so their friendship would not fade. It was a harsh way to learn a lesson, but Asya now sees how none of the things she did in the resistance were worth the death of her dearest friend."

"Feri, you sound like you blame her."

She took a deep breath, stood up, and began smoothing the bedcovers around me. "I blame everyone who had false hopes. They ruined everything for all of us. And now we cannot go back." She stood up straight. "Someone is knocking at the door."

She looked at her watch. "That will be the *Agha*-Doctor Namdar." She smiled, but her lips seemed taut. "He will be happy to see that you are in less pain." She pinched my cheek, but I barely felt her fingers, and left the room. I tried to focus on what she'd just said, whether she blamed her daughter or not. My thoughts moved through my head like honey—slowly, not touching any nerves. Something wasn't right, I thought. Feri should have gone after Asya; they shouldn't be on opposite sides. Why was there so much pain between them? Poor Asya, losing her friend that way. I felt my eyelids droop and close. I dreamed of following Asya into an enormous ballroom strewn with colorful carpets. A crowd of people snapped their fingers to the beat of Arabic music while a small woman in a billowing crimson skirt danced round and round, whirling to the pulse of the drums. The people clapped their hands and threw coins at the woman. Asya suddenly yelled "No!" just as she'd done before she'd left the bedroom earlier. The people in the crowd stepped back; some of them touched their faces or looked away abruptly. The little woman kept dancing, her skirt flaring. Something wet hit my cheek. I touched my fingers to it and they came away bloody. The woman spun faster and her skirt seemed more liquid. Then I realized that the blood came from her skirt, splattering everyone as she turned. People began to scream. Asya lunged toward the little woman to stop her, but was instead sucked into the tornado of her whirling. I felt my forehead go wet and cold with more blood, then I opened my eyes with a start.

My vision wasn't sharp, but I could tell that the sunlight was gone; a yellow glow from Feri's porcelain bedside lamp cast a gentle radiance onto the uneven walls. A bulky shadow loomed over me; I thought it was Feri, but slowly the picture focused. "Amir?" I whispered, recognizing his eyes hovering above me; eyes that always looked like they were rimmed in kohl, like an Arab's eyes. His fingers were icy against my temple. "Your hand is cold," I croaked. Immediately, he took his palm off my forehead. I smiled, feeling the nightmare receding into my subconscious. I swallowed and tried to clear my throat. "You found me." The puttylike muscles in my face felt strained, but I couldn't stop smiling.

From somewhere behind Amir, Uncle Hooshang's voice said, "*I* brought him. Actually, he followed me here." Uncle sounded annoyed, but when his tired face appeared from behind Amir's broad shoulder, he was smiling and his eyes were watery with relief.

"I'm so glad," I said. I could hardly hear myself. Amir's mouth twitched trying, it seemed, to smile.

I'd run into Amir at one of the dinner parties Auntie Katayoon dragged me to during those anxious weeks before Dariush returned from the training camp. It was her way of trying to distract me from worrying about him. We'd put on stylish cocktail dresses, cover ourselves with *manteau* and scarf for the drive to So-and-So's house, then hang our cover-ups next to everyone else's, freshen up our makeup in the foyer mirror, and join a gathering that looked no different from any before the Revolution. The only difference was that the curtains were drawn, and someone had probably paid off the servants to keep their mouths shut. I'd heard of raids where the *pasdaran* would take the whole party to the local *komiteh* for whippings, but Katy waved it off, saying, "That will never happen to us."

I noticed Amir immediately across a crowded room, even though I hadn't seen him in three years and even though he looked very different, very Persian, not Semitic at all. I watched him for some time, trying to figure out how he'd transformed himself and how he'd managed to stay in Iran after the Revolution, seeing as how he was an "infidel murderer from Occupied Palestine." No doubt he was pretending to be Iranian. He'd ingeniously perfected his hand gestures and body language—things that can be more telling about a person's nationality than their accent. His required Islamic beard hid the cleft in his chin, and his inky hair was cropped close to his scalp; his eyes seemed mistier than ever, his skin paler without a tan. He wore a black turtleneck and black trousers and made me think of Sean Connery—which I knew wasn't far-fetched because Amir's only reasons for being in Iran at all (unless he was psychotic) had to be espionage-related.

I stared so hard and long that he finally felt my eyes on him and looked over. At first, a shadow of concern flashed across his face, but once he recognized me, it was gone. He didn't smile; he seemed frozen, then gestured toward a corner of the room where we could talk. "What are you doing here?" I asked under my breath.

"What are *you* doing here?" he responded.

"It's dangerous for you," I said.

"For you, too," he said, eyes teasing.

"You're a Jew," I said.

He paused, then looked pointedly into my eyes and slowly said, "Yes. I am an *Iranian* Jew from Hamadan, where Jews have lived for centuries. It is not a crime to be a Jew in the Islamic Republic. We are people of the Book; we are supposed to be tolerated."

He was right, but "tolerated" wasn't the same as being treated well. Most Iranian Jews had fled the country. What I hadn't known then was that Amir—as he pretended to be an Iranian Jew—had arranged most of those escapes.

After I told him my story, the first thing he said was, "Dariush should never have brought you here." He looked very angry, which I thought was inappropriate, and I said, "He didn't bring me, I came on my own; he couldn't have stopped me." Amir raised an eyebrow that said, *I don't believe that for a minute.* I didn't like that look. So judgmental, critical. I was sorry I'd told him about me and Dariush. And if it hadn't been for the next thing he said, I would've turned and left.

"I can help you." He paused. "Both of you."

I might not have believed him if he'd been someone else, but I remembered the terrible accident at Karadj and how he'd saved Dariush. His new air of self-confidence wasn't lost on me, either; such a thing is irresistible if you're in trouble. And I couldn't have been in more trouble.

Twenty

Maman Bozorg

My niece Monir was stolen for her blue eyes. This was many years ago, during the Second Great War, when the British and Americans and Russians divided and occupied Iran like hungry people sharing a loaf of bread.

Monir was just three years old. She was taken from the garden while her dull-witted *naneh* picked flowers behind the potting shed. Monir made no sound. She vanished as if a flying *jenn* had plucked her from beneath the olive trees.

The servants searched the grounds of the *bagh*, then the back hallways and cellar rooms of the house, for many hours. The family was called together. My sister rocked and beat her chest with her hands; her tears gathered in the hollows beneath her eyes. Imperial guards were sent from the palace of Reza Shah to search the neighborhoods house by house (my sister's husband was a so-called adviser to that crude king).

Two weeks passed. My father would not eat, would not speak. My sister and aunts began wearing black. Everyone lost hope but me. My faith is not so easily weakened; I believe in the benefi-cence of *Allah*. Monir would be found.

My son Mahmoud, just four years old, clung to me like a monkey, fearful of being stolen himself. One morning he asked me, "Maman, does Monir see everything in blue?" I was amused. I asked him if everything in the world seemed brown to him. This made him laugh. "But Yusef says he sees everything in blue," Mahmoud said. Yusef? My sister's houseboy? His mother had once been a servant in the house, a woman perpetually made pregnant by the animal needs of her gardener husband. Their brood was unusual: all blue-eyed, two with bright orange hair. Recently, a child had died of typhoid.

It came to me then like a vision! Of course! I nearly flung Mahmoud into the arms of his wet nurse and ran from the house, my *chador* tangled about my legs, and into the garden toward the poplar trees where the servant's shacks were. I found Monir in the first hovel, huddled beneath a scarred wooden table, playing with the dusty dolls of a dead child. A woman lay on the dirt floor next to her, her glazed eyes seeing only Monir, her filthy hand pawing my niece's hair. She called Monir by a different name, whispering it over and over. She did not notice me. I took Monir—took back what was mine—and left the woman shriek-ing with a despair that gave me great satisfaction; we must all accept our *ghesmat*.

This is an old story, forgotten for nearly forty years. Yet after Hooshang brought the news of Dariush's being lost, the story of Monir came to me often. Not once during that ordeal had I lost hope like the others. And it was my optimism and faith that had led to Monir's rescue. So I continued to believe that my Dariush was alive while Hooshang moped like a village farmer whose crops had gone dry and while Mariam washed her face over and over, thinking this would keep me from noticing the traces of her useless tears. They are fools. Yesterday morning, before dawn, I heard the hooting of an owl. It was a blessed omen.

Haji-Akbar called on me personally at lunchtime today; it is true that *mullah*s visit at times when they can be fed. He wore new robes, no doubt purchased with money from my bribe. The search for Dariush has indeed been costly.

At last, he finished his glass of weak tea and said, "Your grandson is in a hospital tent near the border. He is unconscious, but expected to recover."

Why was he unconscious? Who was tending to him? How was he wounded? Did this tent hospital have doctors and medications? Was it clean?

He had no answers for me. The men he had sent to the front would transport Dariush soon enough. He assumed they should take him to Hooshang's clinic. "What good fortune I have brought you, *khanoom*, no? Your family will have its boy back. I did not think we would find him alive. God has been at your back."

We sat for lunch then, but I could not eat a morsel. I was sorting my thoughts, trying to determine how best to manage the situation. It was truly a feat of will that helped me to remain calm; I could not wipe the image from my mind of Dariush wounded and in pain. *Haji*-Akbar ate like a bear, using his fat fingers more than the spoon and fork. My intuition told me he was a stupid man. But could I fool him? I would have to test him. Carefully. Finally, I spoke. "Your Excellency, I have been thinking that perhaps my grandson should not be moved to his father's clinic. In fact, it may be best to keep his location private."

My tongue immediately felt hot with remorse. *Haji*-Akbar squinted his eyes at me. His beard was spotted with rice and mulberries, red as blood. "What are you scheming, *khanoom*?"

"Nothing at all," I said, in my most confounded voice. "Whatever do you imply, *agha*? I merely thought to protect my grandson from too many visitors and perhaps to provide him with better care."

Haji-Akbar wiped his face with the napkin and belched. "This is not of my concern. I will have him delivered to the Namdar Clinic within a week's time."

"A week?"

"Yes, *khanoom*, this is not such a simple task, what I have done for you. There are formalities. It takes time." He rose from the table and bowed slightly. "Thank you for lunch."

I could not look at him. As he passed by my chair, I managed to say, "My regards to your family."

Indeed, I have a problem.

I do not want that whore and her unborn child to be here

when Dariush returns. He must start fresh. She must leave Iran so he will think that she left *him*, that she saved herself, that she betrayed him. Such a betrayal would surely dissolve their relationship. But how can I accomplish such a thing in a week's time? Should I inform the authorities of her whereabouts? I know where she is hiding. So simple. I had my driver follow Hooshang there.

No. I must not be so rash. Surely a judge would sentence her to Evin or even to death. And then she would become a martyr in my grandson's eyes; he would never recover from such a tragedy.

I must think of something! Oh, Saint Ali! Help me find a solution.

Twenty-One

The Black Jenn

Amir Hakim had wanted Layla from the moment he first met her at the Imperial Club pool in August of 1978. He had put thoughts of having her out of his mind. After all, Dariush was his dear friend. It was not until after the waterskiing accident that Amir began to daydream about stealing Layla from Dariush. And stealing her had not become a real possibility until they met at the party last month.

Now, he sits in the chair next to her sickbed and takes her hand; the bones are sharp against his palm, and he imagines her knuckles against his lips. His expression is unreadable.

"She has fallen asleep again," Hooshang says. "It is the pain medicine. You can wait in the other room while I change her dressings."

"I will stay," he mumbles over his shoulder.

Amir bites the inside of his lip when he sees the swollen and blackened skin of Layla's feet. A faint odor of raw beef and rubbing alcohol causes him to hold his breath. He has hardened himself against the sight of blood and torture in the last two years, but now he feels as heartbroken as a boy with his wounded dog. He wonders if Hooshang is being realistic when he says that Layla's wounds will heal. She groans and briefly opens her eyes;

their color has paled—apple green. She frowns and suddenly jerks in pain. Hooshang says, "There, there, my daughter. I am almost finished." The bed trembles as he applies new bandages. Layla's face contorts, and Amir takes her hand again, wet with perspiration. Her grip is tight, then loosens as Hooshang finishes.

Hooshang raises Layla's head and places two pills between her lips. She drinks from a glass of water he holds to her mouth, then falls back against the pillow, exhausted. "Let her rest," says Hooshang. "Fereshteh-*khanoom* has made us some tea."

"I'll be along in a minute," says Amir.

Once Hooshang is gone, Amir stands and watches her. He tucks the coverlet neatly beneath her chin and brushes a strand of hair from her forehead. Without opening her eyes, she says, "Amir? Can you find him?"

He knows who she means. "I don't know."

"Please," she says. "Please try."

He touches his palm to her warm cheek. "I will. Don't worry. Don't think. Just get better. We have to get you out of here."

She moves her head from side to side, dragging long strands of her hair across the white pillow. "Not without him," she mumbles—words that cut him like a razor. He sits there until her breathing is deep and steady. No, Layla, he says silently, you *will* leave this country without your precious Dariush. Clearly, he does not know how to take proper care of you. But I do.

Asya has heard about Amir from Jamsheed, but this is the first time she has laid eyes on him. He sits tall like a soldier at her mother's table and gulps tea. She knows immediately what Jamsheed could not explain; Amir is not right minded. It is so clear to her, an odd shadow behind his eyes, as if a black *jenn* moves around inside his brain. She has seen the black *jenn* before—behind the eyes of the fanatics.

Fereshteh, on the other hand, is impressed by a foreign boy who would risk so much for Layla and Dariush. And she is relieved that the problem is not entirely in her hands anymore; now she can concentrate on making Layla strong for giving birth and for motherhood. Let the men worry about keeping her safe from the *komiteh*.

Hooshang burns his tongue on Fereshteh's tea. It feels satisfying. He has an irrational notion that he can draw the pain away from his son and Layla by taking it on himself. He knows this is ludicrous, but he cannot help his thoughts and he cannot calm his emotions. He presses his fingers to the bridge of his nose, hoping to stave off the migraine he knows will strike him before the night is over. He blames the boy Amir. All this talk about what must be said to Fereshteh and her daughter, about what must be done for Layla, about how Dariush is at fault for what has happened—he has not forgotten that Dariush told him to beware of Amir's mercurial disposition. And he has heard enough of Amir's disrespectful tone. What does it matter that these trustworthy women know that Amir's job is to smuggle Iranian Jews to the West? This is not a terrible or strange thing. Does he think they will go to the *komiteh* about him? They hate the *komiteh*. And they know he is their hope for Dariush and Layla's safe future. And so do I, Hooshang reminds himself, so I must bear this insolent boy's attitude for the sake of my son.

Amir sizes up Fereshteh and Asya with little more than a glance. The old woman is stubborn, but her tenderness for Layla is genuine. He tells himself he should be relieved; the truth is, he has no safer place to take Layla. The daughter's eyes are dim with confusion, her shoulders slouched with weariness. Amir knows this look; it belongs to the counterrevolutionaries, the once idealistic youth who toppled the shah with Revolution, then saw their hopes crushed by a more ruthless foe, the Islamic fundamentalists. It serves them right, Amir thinks. They were shamelessly idealistic. They earned their disillusionment.

"You are an Israeli," the girl says, her chin raised. The older woman stands in the kitchen alcove studying him, her muscular arms folded. Son of a bitch told them, Amir thinks, glancing at Hooshang, who is writing instructions for Layla's medication dosages.

"No, I am American," says Amir, shrugging.

"But you are originally from Israel."

He looks at Fereshteh straight in the eye. "I was born in Occupied Palestine, but I live in America," he says.

"Yes," says Hooshang, sipping his tea loudly. "Amir-*agha* is a university professor in America." Amir shoots him a narrow-eyed look—how intelligent of you, simple man, to finally recall this agreed-upon information. Fereshteh's face immediately softens; her eyes glisten. She sucks in her breath with admiration. Ah, thinks Amir, the infatuation for all things American still flows as strongly as ever. Fereshteh swallows. "May I offer you some more tea?" she asks.

"Why are you in Iran?" interrupts Asya, her suspicious frown softening just a little.

Amir scratches his beard so he can watch her and gauge his answer. "I like it here," he says, dismissing her. "Yes, *khanoom*, I would like more tea."

"Your Farsi is perfect," says Asya, her tone questioning.

"I have a talent for imitation."

Asya says nothing, but looks away before he does. So he is an Israeli Jew, she thinks. For Layla, she knows this is good; he will help her. Still, Asya does not have a warm place in her heart for Israelis; their Mossad had trained the shah's SAVAK, the secret police, in all their gruesome ways of torture, and everyone knew that the Israeli government had encouraged the shah to amass all his military toys with money that could have been used to feed and house his people. "So you are American, but you live in Iran?" prods Asya.

"No." He pauses, inhales. "I am American," he says, sticking her with an angry look that does not make her flinch.

"Stop asking questions," says Fereshteh in a harsh tone to Asya. "This man has come to help Layla. Wherever he comes from, he is a friend. And a guest in our house." She sets a glass of tea before Amir and he warms his fingers on the steam that floats above it.

"Thank you, Fereshteh-*khanoom*," he says, watching Asya's frown.

"I'll go sit with Layla," the girl says. "In case she wakes up." And she leaves quickly, her gray shift flapping against her boots as she walks.

"So," says Amir to Hooshang. "How long until she can walk?"

"I cannot say for sure."

"Two weeks? Three?"

Hooshang shakes his head slowly. "Not that soon." He shrugs. "Well, maybe." He sighs. "It depends."

"No need to push her," says Fereshteh, looking at Amir.

He ignores her. "She must leave this country as soon as possible."

"Pardon me, *agha*," says Fereshteh. "But she is safe right here. I can take care of her."

Amir finishes his tea in one gulp. He feels the sting of the hot liquid in his throat and then his chest. He holds his breath and shuts his eyes for a moment. Still, he ignores Fereshteh's remark. The woman's opinions are useless to him; he has no intention of allowing Layla to stay in Iran. "Well, I must be going," he says to Hooshang. "I'll meet you again here tomorrow at the same time."

Hooshang nods. "If you hear anything about my son . . ." he says, looking up with hopeful eyes.

"I'll call you immediately." Amir finally looks at Fereshteh, at her offended expression. She will get over it, he thinks, as soon as she accepts that I am in charge. "Thank you for the tea, *khanoom*," he says, bowing politely before turning his back and leaving the apartment.

Twenty-Two

The Girl from U.N.C.L.E.

Mariam thinks it is ironic that Maman Bozorg is sending her to visit Layla when she had always tried to prevent such a thing. It is ironic also because Mariam does not want to see Layla now. She wants to forget about her.

"Kareem-*agha*," she says to the driver. "What's the problem? Why are we moving so slowly?"

"*Khanoom*," he says, turning his profile to her so Mariam can hear him better from the backseat. "There is a building ahead that fell into part of the street from a *Mojahedeen* bomb last night."

Despite the crisp air outside, Mariam's back feels moist with perspiration. They have reached the Tajrish Bridge and the square. As usual, it is jammed with bustling people and coughing vehicles. Sidewalk hawkers yell out the price of barbecued corn and soaked walnuts, dirty little boys in wide trousers try to sell sticks of gum to passengers, women cross the rotary clasping their *chador*s between their teeth and their children's arms in their hands, men nap on the grassy median with newspapers over their faces to block out the sunlight. Mariam cannot believe she used to like walking in the swarming streets before the Revolution, even without her *hejab*. Now she cannot bear it when so much is going on around her; she feels as if everyone is watching her. She secures her scarf over her forehead and stares at her hands for a while. She thinks about saying her prayers for serenity, but thoughts of Layla are too strong in her head.

It used to be that when Layla was not in Tehran, Mariam's life seemed as if it had no sound or color. When they were little, she yearned for the garden gate to creak open and Layla to step through, dressed in her crisp American blouses and colorful trousers, her skin so smooth and her smile so loyal. They had never tired of inventing games to play, of pretending they were mothers, diapering and feeding their babies; of pretending they were the Girls from U.N.C.L.E., spying on the servant boys who washed the cars in the garage; of talking about how much higher the Empire State Building would be than the old pine trees in the garden; and of dressing up in the chiffon dresses that belonged to Layla's grandmother—who was so entirely unlike Maman Bozorg.

Mariam also remembers the times when she felt as if she hated Layla, when she did not know why everyone thought Layla was so special: why that Banu was always fussing over Layla, why Mina-*khanoom* was always kissing and hugging Layla, why Layla always had to have so many pink dresses and white shoes and blond-haired dolls and English books. Then in the wintertime when the air was raw and dry as an old peach pit, Mariam had missed Layla with such fierceness she had wanted to scream. Yet it was also at those times that the thought of Layla filled Mariam with rage. She imagined Layla at her American school with all her American friends, wearing beautiful clothes, eating at restaurants, ice-skating in the park, shopping in the big department stores, taking piano lessons. They wrote constantly to one another about such things.

As Mariam grew toward adolescence, she began to lie in her letters to Layla. It was a lie that she saw school friends regularly; she did not even take their phone calls, did not wear the fashionable dresses her mother sent her from Paris, did not continue her flute lessons, did not go skiing with her cousins. She spent more and more time at Maman Bozorg's house while her mother was busy with charities or shopping in Europe. And Maman Bozorg had different ideas about what young girls should be doing. She wanted Mariam to be special, a pure, traditional woman. "Such a rare thing these days," she would say. Oh, how desperately Mariam wanted to please her grandmother; she sensed that Maman Bozorg had a plan for her. So she did her lessons, learned her Arabic prayers, fasted from sunrise to sundown during *Ramazan*, and learned the skills of embroidery and cooking and sewing. She tried to be the best for her grandmother. Still, at times, she had felt the rage—when she thought of Layla.

Now she feels nothing. No rage. No love. She will go and speak with Layla as her grandmother has ordered. Layla, the *kaufar*, as Maman Bozorg still calls her. *"Kaufar!"* Maman Bozorg had raged after the dreadful Weeping Party where Mariam and Layla had cried so overzealously. Pagan! Infidel! Atheist! Terrible words. "I forbid you to see that girl again!" Mariam had run into the garden to cry beneath the tall pine trees, her back pressed against the stone wall of the old water well. Maman Bozorg is wrong, she thought. Layla is a good Moslem. She *does* believe in God. Her family is just not so devout as ours. And Mariam was so sure of this—and so crazed about giving Layla up—that she decided to do something very brave, something she knew Layla would have the courage to do. She told Maman Bozorg that if she could not see Layla, she did not want to stay at Maman Bozorg's house anymore; she would go live with her mother all the time. This was a bluff. Her mother was rarely at home and their house was bare and lonely. But she took the risk. And it worked! Maman Bozorg was suddenly speechless, her lips pressed tightly together as if to keep her angry words from bursting out like a waterfall. Finally, she said, in a raspy voice like a handsaw on wood, that Mariam could play with Layla in Maman Bozorg's house, but she was not to visit the Bahari household, not ever.

And now, Mariam thinks, visiting Layla is Maman Bozorg's idea.

She takes a deep breath and looks out the window. A man sits on the curb eating roasted watermelon seeds; discarded shells have piled up like an anthill next to his foot. She feels the familiar emptiness in her stomach, the hunger. She imagines the crackle of the roasted seeds between her teeth, the dry salt on her lips. She peers through the windshield for the remnants of the old Kentucky Fried Chicken shop that had gleamed in red and white at the south end of the square before the Revolution. She sees the spot. Its windows are shattered and its large sign and Colonel's face blacked out. But she remembers perfectly, sensually, the crunchy batter, the fatty skin, the buttery potatoes; her mouth feels full for a moment. She scolds herself for not bringing a snack along. A bag of pistachio nuts or candied almonds. She thinks about asking Kareem to pull over and buy some snacks from the street vendors, but she does not want to be left alone in the car. (It amazes her that she once drove these streets herself.) Besides, she must try to eat less. Even Maman Bozorg has noticed her weight gain and begun to tease her, calling her "my granddaughter the Earth." Mariam winces and wonders how she was able to stay thin in the old days. All the dieting and exercising. Where had she found the willpower? Where had it gone? It had flowed out of her like so many other desires.

Kareem lights a cigarette and cracks his window. The sounds from the square stream into the car and rattle Mariam's nerves. She wishes she were a child again; she would close her eyes and press her hands hard over her ears and pretend she was deep inside the water well, protected by its walls and darkness. Instead, she coughs and tells Kareem the smoke bothers her. "And close the window," she orders. "It's too cold." She catches sight of herself in the rearview mirror. How soft and swollen her face has become, like a round pillow. Her once-plucked eyebrows are bushy and connect above her nose; her unbleached mustache contrasts sharply with the olive cast of her skin. Her appearance would have disappointed her once, but she feels indifferent now and slowly looks away and out the window. The traffic moves in a sudden burst, then slows again to a crawl. The crowd is thinner. Kareem struggles to inch the car forward; his fingers fiddle nervously on the steering wheel and he leans forward as if this will make the vehicle move faster. They are next to the public gallows.

Mariam tries to look away, but her eyes are frozen. Lifeless legs dangle; shoeless feet, bloody calves in tattered, loose, gray trousers. She looks up to see four mustached men hanging by distended necks, their tongues stretched and limp, their eyes popping. Drug sellers. A lesson for the people. They will hang for days. Mariam's stomach turns over in disgust and fear. The dead men remind her of Dariush and the bloody nightmare of his death that comes to her every night. Her lip trembles. She clenches her teeth. No. She must not think about that now. She must believe he is all right.

It was Dariush who had always calmed her when they were little, Dariush who had given her hope in the dreary house of Maman Bozorg. He came to the house often; Maman Bozorg would not go more than two days without the sight of him. She called him "my boy" as if she had given birth to him. He was a dutiful grandson, reciting his prayers, studying the *Qoran*, and learning the history of the Shiah Moslems without grumbling. But there was a lack of seriousness about him, a glimmer of amusement in his golden eyes. Everyone in the household sensed this, even the servants. Dariush had only to walk through the tall front door and everybody wanted to giggle for no reason. Mariam, up in her room, would suddenly think she could smell the basil leaves he loved to eat with his lunch. But no one felt the electricity of his presence more than Maman Bozorg; she would change into an angel.

Mariam loved Dariush because he took care of her. He defended her to Maman Bozorg when she forgot to follow the rules. He embraced her when no one else did. Sometimes she imagined them as twins, not merely cousins, but parts of one another, inseparable. He played games with her, taught her card tricks, let her win at Monopoly, and made her laugh even when she was so sad her stomach hurt. He often left funny drawings under her pillow, drawings of the servants making silly faces or of cartoonlike animals such as mules in turbans and camels in belly-dancer outfits. Twice, he had left a perfect sketch of her own face there. It made Mariam feel proud that he would be able to draw the curve of her cheek and the curls of her hair so well and that he was able to put a smile on her lips when she could not remember being very happy.

Then he went to America. And she was alone. Maman Bozorg's house was like a tomb. And without her precious grandson around, Maman Bozorg was very cranky; nothing Mariam did satisfied her. She constantly criticized: "Your hair is overstyled, your blouse is too thin, your prayers are too short, your fingernails are too long; stop mumbling, stop listening to that music, stop speaking on the telephone, stop reading that American book, and stop sniveling in your bed at night." Mariam's depression seeped from her heart out of her pores, her sadness and loneliness smelling like rotten eggs.

It was Dariush's mother, Veeda, who changed everything. She called Katayoon, who was on one of her shopping sprees in London, to remind her that she had a fifteen-year-old daughter who was miserable and needed her. Katayoon returned, taking on Mariam's unhappiness as if it were one of her International Women's Club projects. In a frenzy, she arranged for Mariam to be accepted at a chic school in Switzerland. America was out of the question because of Mariam's poor grades. To go there, to be near Dariush and Layla, was too lofty a dream.

Mariam still shivers when she recalls the day her mother told Maman Bozorg that she had enrolled her in the Swiss school. She had only heard that kind of satisfaction in her mother's voice when she admired a new and very expensive piece of jewelry. She remembers how Maman Bozorg's fingers twitched as if she were going to strike Katayoon. But to Mariam's amazement, her grandmother had given in and later called her to her bedside. "This venture to the West will be good for you," she said, smiling, but not with her small, round eyes. "It will be a test to see if you can resist temptation. *Allah* will be watching you. And so, in my dreams, will I. Do you understand, daughter?" Mariam had understood perfectly; she would be a good girl.

Katayoon first took Mariam to Paris, where they bought the latest fashions and went to beauty salons for retooling. Mariam actually began to like her mother a little, despite Katayoon's usual nervous chattering and constant movement. She referred to Mariam's father often when she spoke: "Mahmoud loved this restaurant." "Mahmoud used to carry you on his shoulders."

"Mahmoud was such a good driver." Mariam wondered if her mother whirled so quickly through her life merely to keep the pain of her husband's death from clinging to her. It was comforting to know that her parents had loved one another. When Katayoon dropped Mariam off at the school, she kissed her and said, "I wish I had taken you away from that old woman long ago. You endured too much. I am proud of you. Now you can start your life. And don't think about her at all. Promise?"

Oh, how free that promise had made her feel. She looked at the other schoolgirls and thought, I am not so different from them. She chose her best friends quickly. Carla and Maurizia and Anna. All Italians. Their warmth like Persian warmth. Their playful naughtiness like a candy Mariam could not resist. For the first time in her life, she wore jeans every day, smoked cigarettes, went braless, danced to disco, received phone calls from boys, and ate pork and shrimp. She bought a copy of *Our Bodies, Ourselves* in French and kept it under her mattress. She stopped saying her *namaz* and painted her fingernails and toenails bright red. She purchased makeup and perfume and lacy underthings with her extra francs. She masturbated.

Mariam knew she was a traitor to her grandmother. Even her compassion for Katayoon was a betrayal to Maman Bozorg, who considered Katayoon a buffoon led by the lures of Satan. Still, Mariam was able to erase the guilt from her mind as each day she woke up to a wonderful eagerness in her chest. But on many nights, when her mail packet would contain a letter from Maman Bozorg filled with reminders and admonishments that she maintain a pious life, Mariam was tormented. She would write back, reaching deep inside herself for the girl Maman Bozorg would love, but her stomach hurt with guilt. She cursed herself for deceiving her grandmother, and, sometimes in the blackness of the night, she would scratch at her arms and legs under the duvet as if by breaking the skin, she could eliminate unholy desires from her body.

Each summer vacation, she now stayed at her mother's house, even if Katayoon was away. It was Dariush who helped placate Maman Bozorg about this situation. Still, she visited her grandmother every day, dutifully donning conservative clothing and removing her makeup, spending an hour or two pretending she was the same girl her grandmother had molded. She knew Maman Bozorg was not completely fooled, and she endured the sour and mean comments her grandmother made. "What is this short hair? You look like a dirty lamb! I see the trace of polish around your nails! And the hairs above your lip. Yellow? Stupid! For who? To look good for some boy? You look like a *jendeh*. You better pray to *Allah* for guidance. He will not be as forgiving as me." Mariam's would tremble from the look of disgust on her grandmother's face, and she would swallow her tears when Maman Bozorg refused to kiss her, saying she had become impure.

But as soon as Mariam was beyond the gates of the old woman's house, she felt the electricity of freedom shudder through her body. Tehran was alive, an amusement park. Parties all day long! All night long! Swimming parties, horseback riding parties, tennis parties, disco parties, masquerade parties, waterskiing parties, weddings and birthdays and engagements. And when the summers ended, she and Layla would cry with frustration and regret. Until next year. And Mariam would embrace Dariush at the airport, clinging to his T-shirt while he rested his lips on the top of her head. The three of them whirled toward their separate lives. Boston, New York, Geneva. And Mariam promised herself she would study hard so she could go to college in America.

But that was not to be. By the end of her last year of high school—1975—she had decided to go to the university in Lugano. It was because of Roberto. Her roommate Carla's older brother. The most beautiful boy Mariam had ever seen. Tall and dark with eyelashes that you could feel tickling your skin when he looked at you. She fell in love with him the first time he drove up to the dormitory on his Vespa. Every weekend, he took her for picnics on velvety grasses in the shadow of the jagged peaks of the Alps. She never tired of listening to his dreams of going to Kenya to become a safari guide. She rode behind him on the Vespa, pressing herself against his back, feeling her nipples hardening and the vibration of the vehicle like bubbles bursting against her crotch.

She shudders with self-disgust now at these memories. "*Khanoom*, shall I turn the heat up?" asks the driver. She tells him no with an upthrust of her chin and slinks down into the seat, unable now to halt the painful retrospection.

Something had possessed her those two years. It was not only Roberto, but something more, something uncontrollable. Something that seemed, at the time, an epiphany to her, but later proved only to be, as her grandmother would say, the luring perfume of the devil. Sex. Lust. She wondered how something so pleasurable could be forbidden. Still, she controlled herself. She would not commit the ultimate sin; she would not lose her virginity.

Roberto did not complain; Mariam found creative ways of satisfying him—she had listened carefully to Fereshteh-*khanoom*'s advice. Oddly, she had no inhibition. Her nakedness somehow freed her from modesty. And Roberto's nakedness sparked everything inside her; and he was a generous, patient boy. She touched and inspected and kissed every part of him; she watched his reactions, learned to arouse him and to use his body to arouse herself. It was not easy to find places to be together, but they were not choosy and they were very creative. But finally, they rented a room in a pension several villages away because Mariam could not deny herself anymore. She wanted him inside her. And, God forgive her, she had never felt such pleasure in her life. There was no pain or blood as she had been told by so many that there would be. And she did not feel different. Only hungrier.

She wonders if things would have turned out differently if Roberto had not gone to Africa soon after. No. She knows now that Roberto was not her *ghesmat*. She was miserable after he left, physically sick with missing him. She skipped her exams, slept all day, could not eat anything but chicken broth. Maman Bozorg's letters still came three and four times a week. She stopped reading them when she realized she was pregnant.

Roberto was unreachable, chasing giraffes with his camera, not expected to return for another two months. And while Mariam knew Roberto loved her, she was not so naive as to think he was ready to marry her. Carla had already been through two abortions; she knew what to do. Mariam was scared. She called Dariush in America. He came to Lugano and went with her for the operation. Later, he lay beside her, smoothing her hair until she fell asleep, and comforting her when she woke up with nightmares. After he left, Layla came for a week. It was their spring break— already 1977—and they had planned to visit friends in Paris. Instead, Layla sat beside Mariam, never once complaining or showing disappointment about the canceled trip.

Mariam suffered from headaches and slept most of the time. Layla tried to distract her with stories of old times, but Mariam could not extricate herself from the horrors of the present. Layla begged her to talk, but Mariam could not tell Layla her dreams, the visions that came to her even as she lay awake with her eyes open. There! Such a terrible sight! A creature with such small arms and legs, struggling with jerky movements like a newborn foal trying to stand. A tiny mouth, open, seeking air. Little eyes, wide and unseeing, frightened by pain. A child—her child— drowned in her blood. She would turn to the wall, close her eyes, and try to stop the aching pulse in her head, to erase the vision of what she had done. Layla stayed beside her and read or played music on Roberto's guitar. When it was time for Layla to leave for America, Mariam made up her mind that she would go also, go to Tehran.

Reality had struck Mariam. She had learned the lesson of the West. Suddenly everything had become clear, and she knew she had to strip herself of the costume she had been wearing for two years.

Back to Iran, back to a homeland on the verge of revolution, a revolution that would take her even farther back to the lifestyle of her ancestors. And back to the dreary house of Maman Bozorg, to her room, which had not changed since she was a girl. Bare, cream-colored walls, narrow bed and white wooden desk and bookcase that held her prayer cloth and the *Qoran* that had belonged to her father, its cover painted beautifully in turquoises that reminded her of the inside dome of a mosque.

The room still looks the same today. There was a time, before Roberto, when she yearned to fill that room with down comforters and pillows, posters of The Beatles and David Cassidy, English and French books about romance and intrigue, bright yellow curtains, and a thick woolen carpet. Her room at her mother's house had some of those things, but there was no one there most of the time. Anyway, that was a long time ago. Now she does not think about changing her room at Maman Bozorg's. When she returned after the abortion, she in fact found satisfaction in the bareness of her room. Not comfort, but satisfaction, a sense that the spiritlessness of it was appropriate, that it fit her. She would never change it now. She belongs there.

Maman Bozorg does not know about the pregnancy. She never asked what made her granddaughter return to her, and Mariam understood that her grandmother cared only that she had come back into the bosom of piety. Maman Bozorg welcomed her granddaughter with more emotion than she had ever shown; she even told her she loved her, and her affection lasted over a year. Mariam had finally faced the truth: that she could not live as a Western woman without destroying herself. She had already destroyed one life. It was best that she stay where she belonged, where she really fit in, where she could protect herself, and where she could repent.

It was lonely. And lonelier after the Revolution, when Dariush and Layla stopped coming home. About a year ago, Dariush had written to Mariam in a careful letter that he was in love with Layla and that he was living near her in New York. The letter made her cry. She felt cast aside once more. It hurt her that they did not know how much she needed them. Months had turned into years and they had not come. Three years! They had left her adrift on the sea with no one to embrace her or talk to her or listen to her. Finally, she began to agree with what Maman Bozorg would say to her: that only Layla was to blame for this, Layla's attachment to the West, her selfishness, her disloyalty, her atheism. She had betrayed their friendship and taken from Mariam what she cherished most.

So Mariam has agreed to this mission her grandmother has sent her on. Maman Bozorg is right: Layla must leave Iran. And when Dariush comes home from the war, Layla cannot be here to lure him away. If she wants him, she will have to come back, share him. Mariam will never let him go again.

By the time they reach the place where Layla is staying, Mariam feels as if she will faint from hunger. She tells Kareem to wait in the car and climbs the four flights of stairs to the apartment number her grandmother gave her. The hallway is dim and vaporous with dust, but the unmistakable aroma of quince stew comes from the apartment. Mariam knocks. A familiar voice she cannot place asks who is there. "I am Mariam. I've come to see Layla. I am alone." Someone else tells her gruffly that she has the wrong place; there is no Layla there. She leans in close to the door; the quince aroma fills her nostrils like pure oxygen. "Please," she says in her most virtuous tone. "I swear to God, I mean no harm. I just wish to talk to my friend."

She waits for some minutes while muffled voices argue, then the door is thrown open. Mariam cannot hide her surprise. "Fereshteh-*khanoom?*" She has not seen this big old woman in years. They stand frozen and hesitant for a second or two. Then Fereshteh pulls Mariam against her in a bear hug and kisses the top of her head. Mariam smells cigarette smoke and onions in the folds of Fereshteh's sweater. She resists an urge to pull back; she does not like to be this close to people anymore. Finally, Fereshteh releases her and closes the door to the hallway, choking off the cold and dust. Mariam feels immediately warm. Golden light floods a room that doubles as kitchen and living room; it is in cozy disarray, scattered with half-empty tea glasses, blankets and pillows, clothing and toiletries. A woman several years older than Mariam sits stoically at a square table covered with a vinyl cloth. Fereshteh says, "You know Asya, my daughter."

Mariam bows slightly. "Happy to meet you."

The woman tilts her head slightly. "We met as children," she says.

"I'm sorry. I don't remember."

Asya says nothing, and the silence is awkward. Fereshteh offers to take Mariam's *manteau*, but Mariam claims to be cold.

She asks to see Layla. "She is sleeping," says Fereshteh. "Have some tea first." So Mariam agrees to sit for a glass of tea. The aroma of rice is so powerful that she finds herself trying to swallow it. When Fereshteh offers to make her a plate of lunch, Mariam thanks God that she is not so out of her mind with hunger that she does not remember her manners; she refuses politely several times until Fereshteh insists and places the dish of rice and quince *khoresh* before her. It takes all her willpower to raise the fork leisurely and to arrange the food daintily on the spoon.

"How did you know Layla was here?" asks Asya.

"My uncle told me." Mariam does not like the tone of Asya's voice—accusing, patronizing—but she is here to carry out her grandmother's orders. Besides, she is not as sensitive as she used to be to the way people treat her. What does it matter? She fills her mouth with quince and rice, bathes her tongue and gums in the salty-sweet and oil.

"Have you told anyone else that Layla is here?" asks Asya.

"Of course not. That would be too dangerous."

Fereshteh pokes her daughter's shoulder. "See? I told you she was trustworthy. They have been the closest of friends for years."

Twenty-Three

Layla

I opened my eyes and there was Mariam sitting beside the bed in Feri's chair. I felt the same cold shiver in my stomach as when I'd first seen her at the airport three months before when she came to pick me up. I remembered knowing immediately that I'd lost her, that our friendship was spent. In her eyes I saw a dullness, a vacuum of nonfeeling, a submissiveness she'd always possessed yet had never surrendered to. Until that moment, I hadn't wanted to face the fact that she'd truly become Maman Bozorg's possession. And the idea that I couldn't trust her seemed like a betrayal to me, but soon I realized I had no choice. She blamed me for all her sorrow; for keeping Dariush away from her, for letting him ignore his grandmother, for hoarding him, even for the terrible event of his being drafted and taken away at the airport. I hadn't argued with her; I knew when not to waste my energy. There was little opportunity, anyway. She hadn't even spent one night with me at her mother's house, and when she did come, sometimes for breakfast or afternoon tea, she was distant and haughty, eating everything in sight, hardly glancing in my direction. I told myself not to care, to let it go; the world had changed and some things would always be unrecoverable. But it was not easy to forget everything we'd shared, the games we'd played as children, the dreams we'd whispered to one another, the difficulties we'd endured. The truth was, I couldn't bury my tender feelings, and while I was often angry and sarcastic with Mariam, I was also sometimes overwhelmed by a compulsion to wrench the demons of guilt and self-hatred from her and take her into my arms.

But this—her visiting me at Feri's apartment—was not one of those times. No. This was not a good thing. Hideouts didn't usually have visiting hours.

"Hello, Laylee."

Her voice was soft and soothing. I'd always loved her French accent; I'd even begged my father at one time to let me attend the Tehran French Academy with her. I imagined myself saying *sherry blossom* and *Sharrlie's Angels*, or saying *Now leesten carefully*, while squeezing together my thumb and forefinger and stabbing the air for emphasis, to be able to look sidewise with a tilt of my head and a mischievous flirtatious smile—to be a *coquette*, as Mariam would say.

"Hello, Mimish," I croaked.

Her hand on my shoulder felt heavy and supple, like a leaden X-ray blanket. "Don't worry, Laylee. No one else knows you're here. I won't tell." She paused. Her frown of concern was a smidgen overdone. "How could this happen to you, Laylee?"

Well, *that* was a question. "A little thing called the Revolution," I said.

"Feri-*khanoom* says you're much better."

"I guess." I asked her to help me sit up; my back felt like warm dough. She stood up and adjusted the pillows under my feet as if they were the foundation pieces to a house of cards. She stepped back. "Are you in a great deal of pain?"

"Sometimes."

She stood there, staring at where my bandaged feet rested beneath the covers, and seemed confused about what to do next. She wore a *maghnaeh*, a cowl-like scarf that made her look like the Reverend Mother in *The Sound of Music*. Her *manteau* flared out from her ever more plump body. I told her to sit down, take off her *maghnaeh*. She sat down, but the *maghnaeh* stayed in place. I realized suddenly that her extra weight really suited her.

She'd always been too thin—curvaceous, but too thin—on the verge, it seemed, of drifting away. And her face. Her pores looked filled in; her complexion no longer blotchy and tainted with blemishes. She reminded me of a doll I'd once had whose skin was made of fabric.

She said, "We—Maman Bozorg and I—have been so worried about you."

My pulse sped up. "Your grandmother knows I'm here?"

"She was determined to find you."

I bet she was, I thought. "So now that you've found me," I said. "What does your grandmother want to do with me?" I couldn't control the sarcasm or the anxiety in my voice.

"What do you mean? We would never do anything to harm you, Laylee." She paused. "My grandmother has changed her mind about you."

"Really. How amazing. In what way?"

"I'm serious, Laylee. When Dasha came to visit her after he returned from the training camp, she realized how much he loved you. She knew it was time to accept you for his sake."

"How noble."

She leaned in over the bed and whispered, "My grandmother has arranged safe passage for you out of Iran."

"What?"

"A very trustworthy and capable Kurdish man to drive you across the border into Turkey."

"I'm not leaving Iran."

"What? Why not?" She sat back, her eyes wide. "The officials will find you eventually. They'll kill you. You have to leave."

"Not without Dariush."

"But this is what Dasha would want. Don't you see that?"

"I don't care. Besides, in my condition, I don't think the stress is a good idea."

"Come on, Laylee. Uncle Hooshang will bandage you up like a baby. We will make the backseat like a bed. You can take some pain pills and sleep the whole way."

Ah, so Uncle would wrap me up like a baby. And what about the real baby? She obviously didn't have a clue. I wanted to tell her, but I stopped myself. I couldn't predict her reaction. Would she be happy for me and Dariush or would she seethe with jealousy? I mean, I wasn't just riding Dariush's go-cart in this scene; I was going to have his child. I ruffled the covers over my stomach even though I knew I was hardly showing at all.

"Please, Laylee. You must consider my grandmother's escape plan. It is her gesture of peace to you. She was so hurt when you and Dasha got married secretly and then tried to leave the country without saying good-bye." Tears filled her eyes and she looked away. "So was I."

Oh, God. Please don't let me feel guilty. Not now. "I'm sorry, Mimish. But we had no other choice. Your grandmother had made it clear when I visited her that she didn't want the marriage to happen."

"She just thought you should postpone it until after the war, when it could be done properly."

I remembered what the old woman had said: *A wedding should not be put together like an overnight tent in the desert.*

Mariam sighed. She bent over and took an oversized envelope out of her purse. She put it on my lap. Inside was a red silk jewelry pouch, a packet of old airmail letters tied with a blue ribbon, and a black-and-white photograph of me as a baby with my mother. "When you disappeared," she quickly said, "we didn't know what had happened to you. We were looking for clues everywhere. My mother told me about the tin trunk in your room."

"It was my grandmother's," I said, my cheeks hot with anger. "I left it at your mother's for safekeeping. Jamsheed was supposed to come and take it away. He has the key. How did you get it open?"

She looked down. "We pried it open."

"Who, *we?*"

"My mother and me."

I didn't believe for a minute that Katayoon had been a part of that. "What did you think you'd find?"

She shrugged her shoulders in defense. "We didn't know. We were frantic."

I was mad. What a snoop. She'd probably gone through every-thing: the afghan blanket my grandmother had sewn for me, the picture albums of my father's childhood, the diaries I'd written when I was ten and eleven, the prayer cloth and antique prayer stone that had belonged to my grandmother's father. And my mother's things: the book of Shakespeare's plays inscribed from her uncle on her sixteenth birthday, the silver wristwatch that had her father's name—David Abramson—etched into the back, and the pink-and-white baby sweater and booties she'd knitted for me when she was pregnant. The rest of my mother's things were in the envelope Mariam had brought. "Why'd you bring these things?" I asked.

"I thought they might make you feel better. I couldn't fit any of the others in my purse." She reached over and took the jewelry pouch in her hand, opened it, and let my mother's Star of David necklace slide into her palm. "Here, put it on, Laylee."

"Why?"

"It will make you feel closer to her."

"What's going on, Mariam? What are you up to?" I was beginning to feel tired and sore.

"Nothing. Just . . . put it on and I'll tell you."

I fastened the chain around my neck. Mariam's eyes lit up as she watched the small star resting against my nightshirt. "It's very nice," she said. I tucked it inside my shirt. I thought about how fortune catchers sometimes said they could read a person's destiny by touching the jewelry they wore; maybe something of my mother could pass into me through the points of the star that tickled the skin between my breasts.

"You must go back, Laylee. Go back to where you belong."

"What are you talking about? Don't pull this Islamic xeno-phobia on me. That's your grandmother talking. I'm as much an Iranian as I am an American. And even if I *were* Jewish, there's no law that says I can't be Iranian. Jews have lived in this country for centuries."

"I am not talking about that. I am saying that no one can be two things—be East and West, be Moslem and Jewish, be Iranian and American—at the same time. We all have to choose."

"Bullshit."

She inhaled and pressed her lips into a thin line. She was losing her patience with me. "No one can live in two worlds at once. In my heart, I have always been a traditional Persian woman."

"Funny, I don't remember it that way. After your mother sent you to Switzerland, you turned into a regular Euro-freak." She closed her eyes for a second and I reached over to touch her hand, a gesture of peace. It was sticky warm. "You know, Mimish. When all this mess is over and Dariush finds his way back, you could go with us to the States. You don't have to stay here."

She stared at me, startled, recovering. "You know I have to stay here."

"I know you think you do. But you don't." Our eyes locked. She got up from the chair as if it were a hot coal. "Excuse me," she said. "I have to use the toilet."

Pity for her stuck in my throat. After the whole thing with Roberto—God, it was already four years ago—well, after that, I began losing her. I remembered when I'd gone to spend that week with her in Lugano, when she was recovering from the abortion. She barely spoke to me. No matter how hard I tried to reach her on the subject of her guilt, she was silent. The week before, Dariush had tried to get her to see a therapist or talk to her mother, but all she wanted was for him to be near her like a human security blanket. One morning I opened my eyes at dawn and saw her, in the dim light, completely shrouded in her white praying clothes. She looked like a ghost bending and straightening, bringing her palms—covered also in the *chador* fabric—up to her face as if she were holding a book. She then fell gracefully to the ground and touched her forehead to the prayer stone. I could hear the sibilant sounds of her whispered Arabic words and the inhale and exhale of her devoted voice. Then it was the end of the session and she kept her forehead on the stone, nose to the ground. She began to roll her head from side to side, choking down sobs and words I couldn't make out. She cried from deep in her heart, cried as if begging for a forgiveness no one could grant her. I'd finally gone to her, taken her in my arms, and held her, both of us crouched on the floor, rocking for a long time. I begged her to talk to me, but she said she couldn't. She said she just wanted to go home. I knew it was a bad idea, but I couldn't stop her. She'd gone back to Tehran and sentenced herself to Maman Bozorg's house. The friendship between us died slowly after that; I would say Maman Bozorg killed it, but a big part of me had grown angry with Mariam's complete submission to her grandmother.

And now she was really beyond my reach. She seemed totally comfortable in those Islamic clothes; she hadn't even taken off her scarf. Maybe she was right. Maybe I'd made some kind of choice about myself. Was it naive to think I'd somehow integrated all the fragments of myself into one? One what? One bunch of fragments?

She came back from the bathroom carrying a glass of sweet tea for me from Feri.

"Thanks," I said, reaching for the pain pills on the bedside table.

"Oh, poor Laylee," she said, smoothing her hand over my matted hair. She sat next to me on the bed. I tried not to wince as the movement pressed the coverlet down slightly onto my feet. "Listen to me, Laylee-*joonam*," she said as if we were children telling bedtime secrets. "Promise me you'll consider this escape plan my grandmother has arranged for you."

"I told you, Mimish. Not without—"

"Sssh," she said, putting her hand over my mouth; it smelled like marzipan. "Just think about it. For Dasha's sake, please. We want the best for you."

"How's your mother?" I asked.

"Getting along, I suppose. I don't see her often."

"You should. She's all alone in that big house with those wretched servants."

She shrugged. "She should get rid of them. Servants are not loyal anymore. One of these days, they will betray her to the *komiteh*."

"You know she hates to be alone. You saw how happy she was to have me as her guest for those weeks while we waited for Dariush to come back from the training camp."

"Then she should leave Iran and go be with her friends in Europe. So what if the house is taken over? She has money in *Geneve*." She tapped her thumb against the arm of the chair, annoyed.

"I think you're missing the point. She stays in Iran because of you."

"Don't be ridiculous, Layla. My mother has never stayed in Tehran because of me."

"She told me herself, while I was there, that she was worried about you, that she wanted you to come stay with her, that she didn't want you at your grandmother's house anymore."

"It's too late for what she wants. She has always been irresponsible and weak."

"Certainly not weak," I said. At the beginning of the Revolution, a street mob had tried to storm Auntie Katy's house; the mob had just ransacked the shah's cousin's house across the street and was obviously still riding the anarchical wave. The shah had already left the country, and by then the mobs were made up mostly of the poor and the hungry. Auntie Katy quickly dressed in *hejab* and ordered the gatekeeper to let the mob in; she went out and welcomed them to the "house of *Hojatolislam*-e-Golestani." Now this was an uncle of Katy's who lived in Mashhad, estranged from his family because he'd chosen religious study over the carpet business. Katy had never met him. But to the mob, she was the niece of an important religious man. She praised the Revolution and literally invited the mob to dinner. Over a hundred people climbed the walls and claimed spots in the garden to wait for their promised food. And they got it. Katy ordered the cooks to use every edible thing available in the pantries; she even served them the last of her caviar. Once sated, they grew calm and tired, and they left without damaging anything in the garden or the house.

"Weakness is not one of your mother's faults," I said to Mariam. "If it weren't for her strength and cleverness, the mob would have destroyed your house."

"That was dangerous what she did, Layla. Not brave. She does not *think* about consequences."

"Dariush is often like that too. I don't see you so ticked off at him."

"Dasha is different." Her lips clamped shut. Well, that was true, and I didn't want to get into a discussion with her about Dariush that might lead again to this issue of my leaving Iran. Finally, she said, "You know my mother drinks alcohol. Sometimes she drinks so much that she falls asleep at parties and someone has to take her home in the back of their car."

It was true. Katy wasn't an alcoholic, but she liked her whiskey. I'd often shared a shot with her from a bottle of Johnnie Walker Black that she hid under the sofa in her parlor. First we would have tea, then, while on the lookout for the servants, she'd fill our empty tea glasses and we would toast to the collapse of the evil Islamic Republic. I really didn't blame Katy for drinking; most women had husbands or sons who took care of their affairs, but she had only herself to rely on during the hard times. I said, "I don't think it's so terrible that she drinks sometimes. She has a tough life."

"So do we all. But we manage." She said this last phrase in Farsi and sounded exactly like her grandmother. I shivered. "Have you seen how my mother has deteriorated?" she continued. "It is from her sinful lifestyle."

"Blame the Revolution," I said. "She looked fine before that. And so did a lot of other women I know." But I did remember my shock at first seeing Katy when Mariam dropped me at her house after I arrived. She was so thin the sofa pillows nearly swallowed her up. In just three years, her skin, like porcelain before, looked wrinkled as linen. Her teeth and gums were stained from smoking so aggressively that she could finish an unfiltered cigarette in three drags. Her hair had thinned out, and although she'd made an attempt to comb it, she had only succeeded in teasing the top and flattening the ends so she looked like an unkempt Yorkshire terrier. She wore an outdated pleated skirt and brown sweater. Her legs, sheathed in nylons, were blotchy from lack of circulation. When she kissed me and told me I was more beautiful than ever, I replied, perhaps too enthusiastically, that she hadn't changed a bit.

"Well," said Mariam. "I don't like to see her. She is embarrassing and immoral."

I told myself to forget it, to tell Mariam I was tired—which I was—and in pain—which I really wasn't—and to slink down into the pillows and forget about Mariam's obstinacy about her mother. But the words wouldn't come out. I kept remembering Auntie Katy's kindness to me as a child and, more recently, as an adult. It was true that I'd rarely seen her back then, but when she would suddenly appear, she made a deep and genuine impression on me. For one thing, she never laughed at my Farsi mistakes, while Mariam and everyone else would be red-faced and holding their stomachs. She always kneeled down to my level and looked into my eyes, then embraced me, smelling like lilac perfume and whispering endearments in my ear. And she talked to me about my mother, as few others would, telling me about things she'd said or done, about how she dressed and spoke, about how I looked like her. I guess people wouldn't consider this much, but to me it had meant the world. And I pitied Mariam for not letting herself know this side of her mother and for thinking that the old witch Maman Bozorg could love her in the tender, unmalicious way that Katy could. But there was no reaching Mariam.

Twenty-Four

Water under Straw

When Mariam opens the door to leave Fereshteh's apartment, Amir is just about to knock, and they startle one another. Fereshteh tries to introduce them, but they remember one another perfectly. There is a lot of frowning and stumbling until Fereshteh gives Mariam a little push out and Amir a little tug in.

Amir stomps into the bedroom, furious. "How the hell did that girl know where to find you?" he says to Layla.

Fereshteh knows enough English to understand him. "She said Dr. Hooshang told her."

As if on cue, Hooshang appears in the bedroom doorway. "I haven't told anyone," he says in Farsi. "Am I a stupid donkey?" He is insulted by Amir's accusing tone.

"Then how did she know?" Amir paces the small room and rubs the back of his neck.

"I have no idea," says Hooshang.

"Can everyone stop yelling?" says Layla, pressing fingers to her temple. "Maman Bozorg probably had Uncle followed."

Amir looks at Layla, letting her words sink in. "Yes," he finally says. "You're probably right. If anyone else knew, they would have sent someone from the *komiteh* by now. But I still don't trust that old crone. We have to move you to another place."

Fereshteh gasps, not only because she wants to protest Layla being taken away, but because Amir has been so openly derogatory about Maman Bozorg in front of the mister doctor. After all, she is his mother. Layla, also aware of this blunder, feels her face turn hot with embarrassment and, for her father-in-law's sake, she says, "Maman Bozorg sent Mariam to offer me a way to escape Iran. She's found a Kurdish man to drive me out." Amir lifts an eyebrow slightly, but does not look toward Hooshang, who, tight-lipped, begins to remove clean dressings from his black bag. Amir finally says, "Forgive me, Doctor." But he does not sound as if he cares to be forgiven at all. "However," he continues, "you must realize the gravity of the situation. I am trying to save Layla."

Hooshang gently cuts away Layla's bandages. Was it only a week ago when this process brought tears to the poor girl's eyes? he thinks. Hooshang glances up at Amir with a tight expression. "We are grateful for your devotion to Layla . . . and to Dariush," says the doctor. "But I can assure you that my mother would never inform the authorities of Layla's whereabouts. My mother is not a murderer, boy."

"Well," says Amir, turning red at Hooshang's patronizing label. "I was just—"

"*Ai!*" Layla moans, thinking it is a good time to be in pain. Amir comes forward and squeezes her arm. She stares at his hand. She purposely does not look at her wounds; it had been too much of a shock when she had seen them the week before, looking like discolored, inflated surgical gloves. Finally, Hooshang is done, and he quickly dumps his instruments into his bag, snaps it shut, pecks Layla on the forehead, and says he will be back tomorrow. He does not even look at Amir, who now stands staring out the window, not seeming to care. Fereshteh shakes her head and sniffs disapprovingly. Then she is gone, too.

"You acted like a shit!" Layla snaps in a raspy whisper. Amir turns to her as if he has not heard and says in English, "I've decided you should go along with the grandmother's escape plan. Asya will take a note to her house saying you agree, but you need a few more weeks of convalescence. That'll keep her at bay."

"No," she says. "I'm not leaving without Dariush."

He sucks air in through his teeth. Irritated. "I didn't say you *had* to leave, I said you should merely *agree* to leave. In the meantime, we'll move you somewhere they can't find you. I truly think this old woman—from what I've heard about her—would turn you in to the authorities in a second."

"Mariam says she's changed her mind about me."

"Old fanatical grandmothers do not change their minds."

"Okay. Get me some paper. I'll write the note. But I want to tell you something first."

"What?" he asks impatiently.

"I don't want you to treat Dariush's father or Feri or Asya like that anymore."

"Layla, this is not the time to be worrying about manners."

"They're putting their lives on the line for me. And I care about them. I don't want them to be hurt . . . Just like I wouldn't want you to be hurt." As she expects, his expression softens.

"All right." He smiles and gives her a stiff little bow that looks strangely Gestapo-ish.

As soon as Amir is gone, Asya and Fereshteh take their usual positions, sitting one on either side of Layla. Fereshteh grasps Layla's arm nervously and says, "You're not going, *joonam*, are you? Not by that crazy old woman's plan? She is as sly as water under straw."

"It's a trick," says Asya. "No doubt." She crosses her arms stiffly. "She is trying to put a hat on your head."

"I am not that gullible," Layla says, sliding down and molding her back more comfortably against the pillows. "I'm not going. The note is just a way of placating her."

"Good," says Fereshteh, relaxing in her chair. "Are you hungry? I have some barley soup."

"One good thing about Dariush's egoistic friend," says Asya. "He gets good food from the black bazaar. I haven't had my mother's barley soup since before the war."

"Well," Layla says, smiling at Asya. "At least there's one thing you like about him."

Asya shrugs. "He seems too bossy for an American. I am sure everyone in America is less bossy. Power is better distributed."

"How do you know?" Fereshteh says, jabbing her hand at Asya, then looking at Layla. "She has a new idea. Now she wants to go to America."

Layla's smile broadens. "I think that's a great idea. You should go too, Feri. Banu would faint with happiness."

"I am not a fool. What would I do in America?"

"You would live with me and Jamsheed," says Asya. "We would take care of you."

"I do not need to be taken care of. I am not an old woman yet."

"Wait a minute," Layla interrupts. "Which Jamsheed? Dariush's Jamsheed?"

"Who else?" says Fereshteh, beaming suddenly. "Is there another Jamsheed worth mentioning?"

Asya says, "See, Layla? Jamsheed is the only thing about me of which my mother approves."

"I didn't know you two were together," Layla says. "What great news! You know, it was Jamsheed who helped to arrange for me and Dariush to get married secretly."

"Yes. I know that now. He did not tell me at the time. He is a loyal friend. Sometimes too loyal." Asya gets up and goes toward the window. It seems to Layla that the girl is trying to keep herself from crying, and she looks at Fereshteh for an explanation.

Fereshteh hesitates, looks away for a moment, uncomfortable. "Jamsheed has gone to the war front," she says finally. "To search for Dariush."

"What?"

She nods. "You cannot blame him. He wants to find the only friend who never treated him like a servant's son." She looks at Asya. "Yes, he is loyal, my daughter. Is this not the reason why you fell in love with him?"

"Yes," Asya says, pouring a glass of water from a pitcher on the windowsill.

Layla knows she should say something, but her tongue is frozen. She feels a burst of hope that Jamsheed has gone to find Dariush, but she cannot very well jump for joy while Asya is enduring the loss, though temporary, of her fiancé, and all for Layla's benefit. Finally, Layla swallows and says, in a trembling voice, "I'm so sorry, Asya. I feel terrible. I've put you all in such danger. I wish Dariush and I had never come to Iran."

"We will not hear such talk," says Fereshteh. "In these times, we must take risks for our friends. When I was a child, our family was forced to flee the Bolsheviks. Believe me, one revolution is the same as another. We came on the boat of a friend—a tiny boat, no bigger than this room—and we sailed across the Caspian from Baku through many raging *toofon*s until we reached safety in Iran. Do not apologize to us; this is friendship."

"Yes," says Asya, coming over to sit beside Layla again. "Please do not feel guilty about Jamsheed or anything else."

Impossible, Layla thinks, resisting an urge to sink down and bury her face in the pillows. She swears to herself that if she gets out of this mess, she will get Fereshteh and Asya and Jamsheed out too—if they want to go. And if not, she will do everything to make their lives easier, even if she has to beg Amir to smuggle money into Iran for them.

"However," says Fereshteh forcefully, "now that you are better, I will tell you that I think you and Dariush were stupid donkeys to come to Iran."

Layla bites her lip and stares at her knees under the coverlet. "You are right, Feri-*joon*, we were stupid. But we were also somehow wiser." Fereshteh lifts an eyebrow and Layla continues. "Perhaps the Revolution taught us a basic thing that most people who are not rich and do not have everything done for them learn early in their lives. We suddenly realized that the time we had was limited and unpredictable, that, in reality, we all stand on the edge of death. It made us take a chance—perhaps a stupid chance—but nevertheless . . ."

Fereshteh grunts, startling Layla. She has forgotten for a moment where she is, whom she is talking to. She feels exhausted, her body drained like a wrung-out sponge. "So," Fereshteh says, "the world is indeed magical; something valuable has come out of this stinky Revolution."

Twenty-Five

Tongue of the Invisible

Amir orders the taxi driver to take him downtown, to the Grand Bazaar. His palms feel sweaty and his neck stiff. His pulse pounds in his ears, and his hands tremble ever so slightly. After all these weeks, he is still furious that his scheme to have Dariush arrested for desertion had failed so badly.

The bastard had outsmarted him. All the while Dariush was agreeing to follow Amir's escape plan to a tee, he had been doing his own planning: the secret wedding ceremony, the night at the old Hilton, a car and driver to take them to the airport. If the moronic Namdar driver had not called Amir at the last moment to confirm that the couple should be collected from the hotel rather than the house, Amir would have never known enough to make corrections to his scheme.

Indeed, Amir had made the anonymous phone call to the military police with information about the deserter Dariush Namdar and where he could be found, then he had sped to the Hilton to "rescue" Layla, but she was gone by then, swallowed by the city.

That Dariush had been sent to the front brought Amir little gratification at the time. He was too humiliated, too furious, and too intent upon finding Layla. But now, he asks himself, is not everything resolved? Is there really any reason for his anxiety?

Layla is alive, in his care, so to speak. And Dariush, well, his old friend is getting what has been coming to him. Amir allows himself a small smile. For once in the Golden Boy's charmed life, he is immersed in reality, in hardship; for once he is alone, without his perfect family, his wealth; for once his good looks and university degrees and social position cannot help him. Amir wonders if Dariush will die at the war front; perhaps he is dead already, he thinks. His pulse quickens again and he catches himself frowning in the rearview mirror; no, Dariush's death does not, somehow, please him. After all, Dariush's death had once been in Amir's hands, but Amir had saved him from the cold waters of the Karadj Reservoir. And Dariush had never thanked him for that, not in the proper way. After that, Dariush had in fact shunned Amir, as if it were Amir who should have been grateful.

Once inside the bazaar, Amir feels immediately calmer. The stone walls and floor, the pointed arches that go on and on as if they are reflected in mirrors, comfort him. The crowd of hawkers and shoppers and merchants and porters seems to wrap around him like a well-worn robe. He has always preferred anonymity and the shadows of his aliases, the impostors of his imagination. He walks quickly, weaving his way through the crowd and turning indiscriminately down dimly lit corridors that smell of wild-rue incense and kerosene. He makes his way through various sections of the bazaar, each with its own odors and sounds and sights. The coppersmiths' section with its metallic smell and loud clanging as artisans flatten enormous trays, the mechanics' section with its oil smell and walls covered with ancient and rusted odd-shaped tools, the leather section where the odor is so intense it makes Amir's head ache, and the fabric section where women glide along in *chador*s, running their fingers over bolts of cotton and silk, and bargain relentlessly with shopkeepers for the best price. The women mesmerize him, as they always have. Even as a young boy visiting Jerusalem or other areas where there were many Arabs, he was drawn to these women who had no faces, no shapes. They made him tremble with curiosity. He would walk behind them, matching their paces, using even their most diminutive movements to draw a sketch of them in his mind. And he always imagined them favorably, with full breasts and rounded hips and skin like butter.

The other night he had bought himself a whore. His servant, who has no idea he is a Jew, sent for a *mullah*, who brought three teenaged girls with him. They wore *hejab*, but framed the cloth around their faces so he could see their young, pretty features. He told the *mullah* that he wanted a girl with very long hair. The one with peanut-butter skin stepped forward shyly, her white teeth biting nervously at full lips. The *mullah* married them in a ceremony that took only minutes, and Amir signed a paper saying the woman was his concubine for twenty-four hours. The *mullah* acted very seriously, as if he had no idea that he was breaking an Islamic law—that concubines must remain concubines for ninety days. But there were many things in the Islamic Republic of Iran that were not done by the holy book, that were interpreted in entirely new and different ways.

The girl's hair was long, but wavy, not silky and straight like Layla's. He was disappointed. Still, he closed his eyes and ran his fingers through the strands, willing his imagination to put him in a different place, imagining that everything had worked out as he had planned—that he had been at the hotel to rescue Layla after Dariush was taken into custody by the military police. If only he could have prevented her from slipping away.

Amir walks faster, seeking distraction, something calming. He follows the aroma of bread baking. It reminds him of his mother's flat in London. Sometimes the smell is irresistible and sometimes it is unbearable. He buys some *barbari* bread straight from the brick oven and burns his tongue biting into it. The doughy clump feels heavy in his mouth. A passing tea boy who balances the steaming liquid on a tray upon his head sells him a glass of strong tea. He sits on a bench outside the bread shop and leans his back against the warm wall that houses the oven.

He takes a final gulp from his tea and suddenly imagines fighting Dariush, beating at his face, twisting and cracking his limbs, tightening hands around his throat, squeezing, watching his eyes go dead. He gets up with a start and moves quickly away from the bread shop. Soon he is making his way through the perfume section. The predominant scent of rose water nauseates him. He walks faster. A thought suddenly strikes him: He must stop this nonsense about what has happened; he must think about what he will do about Dariush and Layla now. Is it not in his hands to decide? He slows his pace and a porter carrying a long, rolled-up carpet bumps him from behind. The porter apologizes and moves down the corridor quickly.

Amir stands still. A shaft of sunlight filled with dust motes strikes his face. He looks up: Tiny arched windows carved into ancient limestone; turquoise mosaics, pale with dust, form the veneer of a narrow cupola above him. He thinks of Dariush's love for architecture, of his incessant sketching and drawing, trying always to dream up buildings that combined modern lines and materials with these old Persian forms. Amir had not liked any of them.

He wants air and to see the sky, so he makes his way out a low door into a large courtyard where, on the opposite side from him, a small mosque welcomes the devout few through a pointed, arched door. It is midafternoon; rest time. The air is comfortably cool and still; the teal sky is brushed with diaphanous clouds. Several porters and shopkeepers lie on stone porches, their heads resting against flat and faded kilim pillows. Other men sit cross-legged in circles on thick carpets, picking at fruit, sipping tea, and discussing, no doubt, the new ways of doing business in the Islamic Republic of Iran, where even usury is against the law.

Amir shoves his hands into his jacket pockets and breathes the air laced with the aroma of grilling lamb kebab. The adobe and stone buildings that enclose the courtyard are centuries old; behind their small recessed second-story windows, the industry of the bazaar still buzzes in the ways of the ancient merchants. And there is power here, Amir knows. He is not fooled by the antiquated look of things; this place is the heart of commerce and therefore the lifeblood of politicians—old, new, and yet to be born—clerical, secular, or monarchical.

He decides to take a stroll around the courtyard; perhaps this will relax him. He passes several *falgirs*, who beckon to him. Each has his own method of augury: One uses the odd and even enumeration of prayer beads, another the interpretation of randomly selected sections of the *Qoran*. Peddlers of clairvoyance irritate Amir. They were rife in Israel when he was growing up; his father had warned him against them, had even forbidden his mother to visit an astrologer she was fond of. "These people tell addictive tales," he had often said to Amir. "They offer hope and take control like a narcotic. And you must never lose control in this world, my son." Remembering his father's rough voice makes Amir suddenly very tired, and he stops at a thick adobe ledge that juts out from a building wall and he sits down slowly, feeling like an old man. Memories of his father do this to him; they bring exhaustion, depression, loneliness. It is as if no time has passed since the news came that Izaak Hakim had been blown up by a Palestinian suicide bomber and Amir came face to face with the pitilessness of the world his father so wanted to triumph over.

"You mourn, *aghayeh aziz*, dear sir," says a thin voice below him to the right. Amir leans forward, surprised to see a blind man some feet away, sitting on a small kilim, his back against the wall.

"No, *agha*," says Amir coolly. "You are mistaken."

"Then your heart is tight with longing, *aghayeh aziz*."

Amir lights a cigarette and marvels at the blind man's acute senses. His eyes are shaded by sunglasses, and he holds his head in that particular way, back and cocked, that is the mark of the unseeing. How had the man known Amir was there, that he had been thinking of death? "I am merely resting my legs, *agha*."

"You are a traveler," he says, fiddling with the drab robes that cover him, arranging them by touch. "From Arabistan perhaps." His tongue tumbles over words. Amir guesses he has only a few teeth left in his mouth. "Am I not correct, *aghayeh aziz*?"

"As you wish," says Amir, annoyed that the man has detected his very slight accent. He gets up to leave, but a sudden breeze causes a fanfare of crisp autumn leaves to whirl through the air and sweep against buildings and trees and men like a swarm of locusts. The old man feels for his belongings beside him—a small burlap bag, a pile of books, and a folded prayer mat—and he slowly brushes leaves and dust from them.

"God sends the wind," he says.

"Yes," replies Amir.

"Do you wish me to do *estekhareh* for you, *ghorban*, my lord?"

"What?" Amir is astonished. His fortune? The blind man is a *falgir*? "No," he says, annoyed. "I am not looking for advice."

"Forgive me, *ghorban*," and he bows his head in apology. "But I sensed your indecision about a grave matter. And when a man questions—To do or not to do?—he may wish to consult higher powers for assistance." He lays his bony hand on a pile of books. "True advice is found in the great poetry of our Hafez—the Interpreter of Mysteries, the Tongue of the Invisible."

Indeed, thinks Amir. I know your Hafez better than you do. There was a time when, for amusement, he would consult Hafez's *Divan*; doing so was a fad at Oxford for a while: The seeker of advice poses a question in his mind—To do or not to do?—then closes his eyes and opens the book to a random page, where he sets his finger on the couplet that is Hafez's reply—as interpreted, of course, by the person himself or by a *falgir*.

A small tea boy appears and kneels next to the blind man, guiding his palm to receive the saucer on which the tea glass is balanced. "Leave another tea for my guest," he tells the boy.

"No, no," says Amir. "Thank you very much, but I must be on my way."

The boy leaves the extra tea glass on the kilim and runs back toward the interior of the Bazaar. "Please," says the *falgir*. "Share my kilim. You are thirsty."

It was the truth. The steaming maroon-colored liquid seemed irresistible. And what was the harm? Besides, something about the old man intrigued him. "All right, generous *agha*," he says. "I will sit and enjoy your cup of kindness, but please, I am not interested in doing *estekhareh*."

The *falgir* dips his head once again. "Of course not, *ghorban*."

Amir removes his shoes and sits on the kilim across from his host. He sips the perfect tea and immediately feels calmed. "Tell me, *agha*, if you do not mind my asking, how is it that a man who cannot see is able to do *estekhareh* using the poems of Hafez?"

"I have learned the *ghazals* by heart, *aghayeh aziz*." He opens one of his worn tomes. "And I have pasted paper symbols beside each couplet that tell my fingers to where I have come."

Amir leans forward and sees the unique form of Braille the man has concocted for himself. He is impressed and looks more closely at the *falgir*. Why, he is not an old man at all, not young either, maybe around fifty. His uneven beard is only streaked with gray, the hair that peaks out from his embroidered skull cap is black as coal; his hands and face are free of liver spots. Still, he is in worse shape than he should be for his age, Amir thinks. He smells putrid. His teeth are rotted. His cloth shoes are frayed and the wooden soles cracked. A consequence of poverty in the Third World. "You are very clever, *agha*," says Amir, referring to the *falgir*'s book of Hafez.

The man thrusts his chin up, refuting his guest's words. "It is nothing," he says.

They are silent for a moment, slurping their tea. The bare branches of a plane tree reflect in the blind man's dark lenses. A group of shopkeepers across the yard explodes into laughter, then begins to collect their things to go back to work. Amir watches a spider labor across the uneven stones. For the first time in weeks, his thoughts and worries are quiet.

Softly, the blind man speaks. "*Aghayeh aziz*, you desire a woman who belongs to someone else?"

Amir looks up, startled, squinting at the blind man's glasses, trying to see his eyes, what is behind them. "What are you talking about?" he finally says, his voice husky.

"Forgive me. I do not wish to invade your privacy. It is a gift given to me by God. I have no control over what I sense, over the visions in my head."

Amir is upset. He gulps the remainder of his tea and prepares to leave. Bloody insolent oracle. Bloody lucky, too. A woman who belongs to someone else indeed. Not an uncommon thing at all. Good guess, old chap.

"Please," implores the fortune catcher. "I did not mean to insult you. Please sit a while longer. I sense there is more I must tell you."

"How much do you want?" Amir asks gruffly. "*Touman*s I have; patience for auguries I have not."

The man hesitates. "I was once a much-coveted soothsayer. Can you imagine? I revealed the destiny of many by the mere touch of my fingers on their photographs. But I have lost much of my intuition since the prayer-singers took the country. My visions are gone and the photographs feel merely like squares of cardboard."

"I am sorry for your loss, fortune catcher," says Amir sarcastically. "But I cannot linger any longer. Thank you for the tea." He shoves a wad of *touman*s into the man's dirty hand and begins to rise.

The *falgir* grabs the sleeve of Amir's coat with an astonishing strength. "Rarely," he hisses, breath like pickled eggplant, "am I overcome with a premonition. Last night, I dreamt of you, though I have never met you." Amir yanks his arm away and stands up. The blind man continues. "You stood facing a man with light hair, amber eyes, and a half-moon scar above his mouth." Amir falters briefly as he steps into his shoes. The *falgir* has described Dariush. "This man was made of stone; he was a statue that you wished to move from sight, but could not. Suddenly, a metamorphosis occurred and this man was a soldier with shaved head and a long gun." Amir is frozen, staring down at the fortune catcher. "But then the man was also no longer a statue made of stone, but a statue made of sand. And when you touched him, he crumbled and was gone." The blind man wipes his dry lips with his fingers and shifts his weight. "Perhaps, *aghayeh aziz*, you will know what to make of such a dream."

Amir is quiet, frowning, arms limp at his sides, a breeze fluttering the collar of his jacket. He gazes out upon the courtyard to the mosque. His mind is full of images and ideas, yet he begins to count each pair of shoes that line the mosque's outside wall. When he is finished, he looks at the blind man and says in a slow, mystified voice. "Yes, fortune catcher. The interpretation of your dream comes to me quite clearly." He swallows and blinks. "You were right, clever man. I was in need of *estekhareh*, and your dream has been my poem of advice."

"I am your servant. It was my pleasure."

"I am indebted to you, *agha*," says Amir, kneeling now beside the *falgir*. "So. What is it you want most in the world, fortune catcher?"

The blind man smiles; his bottom lip glistens with spittle. "In this country run by godless, blood-lustful prayer-singers, anyone with wits wants the same thing."

"And what is that?"

"To go abroad, dear sir." Then he whispers, "Perhaps even to the shores of the Great Satan itself."

Amir throws back his head and laughs. "Well, fortune catcher, I am not a wizard like you, but this is something I can arrange." He is shocked by his own suggestion. All he need do is press a few *touman* notes into the man's wrinkled palm and go. But the man has given him clarity! His chest is filled with a pressing glee that bubbles up his throat and flaps his lips into these unplanned and uncharacteristic words of generosity. "I will send someone with the money and documents you need," he says. "But you must never speak of me to anyone."

"Upon my soul, I swear, *ghorban*. We have never met."

Amir can barely make it out of the bazaar fast enough. He takes long, bouncing strides that make him feel tall and light. A burden has been lifted from his shoulders, a burden that was unclear to him. And the solution? His lips twitch with a smile. The solution has already, quite providentially, been put in motion.

Yes. He is in love with a woman who belongs to someone else. But Dariush will never find his way out of the Iraqi minefields; Amir can make sure of this. He has lived in this bloody country for three years and he knows all the right people; he keeps their palms greased and keeps his ears sharp. His chest swells and prickles; he has the tools to succeed at almost any scheme he dreams up. Dariush will crumble into oblivion, trivial as a mound of sand. And Layla will not wait forever.

Twenty-Six

The Keys to Heaven

He cannot move. He smells boiling alcohol and iodine—odors that remind him of his father's clinic. His head feels like a smoldering ember. He wonders if he is dying. He imagines Layla, his parents, his sisters, Mariam, his grandmother—mourning by his grave. He wants to tell them he is sorry.

He smells oil from the wells nearby; the smell of Abadan, of crumbling buildings and sewage and unwashed men. The thunder of artillery suddenly rages in the distance, and the pallet he lies on trembles. He remembers the horror of what brought him here.

The minesweepers had come in buses. The young boys with their rag forehead bands on which they had scrawled prayers from the *Qoran* in red-as-blood paint. They hung out the windows as if they were going to a soccer game. They tried to touch the soldiers as the bus passed, tried to touch their heroes. The soldiers pretended not to hear or see, as if the boys were ghosts.

Dariush had heard about the plastic keys—keys to heaven given to the minesweepers by the recruiting *mullah*s. He had not believed it. But now he saw them, dangling from the boys' necks, worn by the old men with pride and faith. The profile of a boy, no more than ten years old, appeared in the last window.

He was crying. Too bad for you, boy, thought Dariush; too bad you are smart enough to know what is going on.

The general had not yet grown tired of punishing Dariush for his desertion. So he made him leader to the minesweepers. Get the job done quickly, was his order. The general itched for battle; the *jihad* must be won; the Arabs had occupied Iranian land too long. He wanted Iraqi blood to flow down the Karun River and into the Gulf—soup for the sharks.

Dariush thought about how he had always imagined his future, stretched in front of him like a field of emerald grass. He would watch the buildings and gardens he designed appear one by one, some made of stone, others of wood or brick or adobe— all blending peacefully with the grass and trees that grew from his watering until they bowed over the buildings as if sheltering and caressing them. And always Layla watched with him, holding his hand. And his parents stood behind him, smiling and proud.

But the future had changed. Not a field of emerald grass, but an expanse to the horizon of dry, cracking dirt, covered in the dust of shame, his shame. He glanced at the young boy who had been crying but now stood in a raggedy row of others like him biting nervously at his key to heaven, waiting for Dariush to kill him. He would not do it. Death would be better. Almost a relief. "I cannot follow your orders," he had said. The general came close to his face and bared his teeth as if he would bite Dariush. "You will be shot to death today," he said, offering, in his tone, a chance for Dariush to change his mind. Dariush said nothing, just stared at the general's yellow eyes as if he could see through them and beyond, as far as the Strait of Hormuz.

Two soldiers held him, one pointed a gun to his neck. The other soldiers were told to take their attack positions to the rear and wait for the field to be cleared. Dariush then followed the general's gaze to a point behind and to the left of them. A man on a horse approached the field. The minesweepers were bewildered and mesmerized by the sight that grew more clear as it came closer: a white horse, a man dressed in white robes, white turban, white beard, skin white as if powdered like a Japanese geisha. The man looked toward the horizon, never at them, and walked his horse ever closer to the minefield. The general suddenly shouted, "Again, the *Emam* comes to us! The spirit of Saint Ali!" The man on the horse lifted his arm and pointed ahead toward where the unseen enemy waited. "Go, my children," he said in a deep voice. "Go and win the *jihad* in the name of the prophet, and *Allah* will take you into the Kingdom of Paradise! You will be martyrs forever!"

And they went. Even the young boy who was the first to have his body cut in half by a land mine whose blast made Dariush's ears ring. The boy's parts lay on the ground, and for one second he lifted his head to see the horror of what God had done to him, then dropped back motionless.

There were mines everywhere. The sweepers ran forward, yelling like primitive hunters. War cries. Screams to keep the fear away, to keep sense away.

Then there was but one left. An old man, not running like the others, but limping gingerly over the desert brush and chunks of debris and human parts. He had lost control of his bowels, and he held out his trembling hands, palms down, as if to tell the mines to behave themselves. Dariush felt a knot in his throat, a fire in his chest that shot through his limbs. Death was his future. At least he could choose his own way.

He closed his eyes for a second. Forgive me, Layla, he thought.

Then he pulled away from the soldiers holding him and ran into the field. He heard a shot and felt the bullet sting his shoulder. Still he ran, his eyes watching the old man's stooped back. He stumbled and fell. A bloody foot, the sole smooth as only a child's can be, sat in the dirt next to his eye. Another bullet grazed his shoulder. He righted himself and continued his race to catch the old man. Why does the guy keep going? he thought. Does he think he can make it to the Iraqi lines without injury? They will kill him when he gets there anyway. And you, he said to himself, angry and disappointed at all his bad decisions, what will you do when you reach this stranger? Then he knows. He will grab him—he is almost there—he will grab his shirt and hold him against his chest. Neither of them will die alone.

But the mine blew. Blistering orange fire and hot smoke swallowed the old man. The blast threw Dariush into the air, and he dropped onto the hard ground like a stunt dummy, crushing his right arm. Dirt and shell fragments rained down on him. He tried to protect his face and head, but his left arm was useless because of the bullet lodged in his shoulder. Debris pelted him, denting his cheeks and lips. Something sharp stabbed his head behind the left temple; it lodged there like a skewer in kebab. Dariush opened his eyes and saw, in the distance, the general, his fists clenched at his sides. Behind him, the clown who had played the ghost of Saint Ali aimed his urine stream at the wheel of the bus. Blood trickled down Dariush's forehead and into his eyes. And just before he succumbed to unconsciousness, a strange image formed beneath his eyelids, a picture he had seen in a book his mother had shown him long ago: a translucent thing with tiny arms and legs floating in serene darkness, its eyes closed, its head meshed with veins as fine as silk thread. A fetus.

They left him for dead. The medics must have picked him up later, after the battle, after the general had retired to clean his guns and count the dead. Now he is somewhere on a scratchy mattress, half alive, his head sheathed in pain.

Suddenly he feels someone's touch, a warm hand on his arm, then puffs of breath at his ear. Muffled sounds. Someone is talking to him! He wills himself to concentrate, but his ears are filled with static and the pain in his head increases. He wonders if he is drowning at Karadj again, if Amir is holding him under and this time will not save him. He has no choice but to spin away from the pain. The sensations of touch and breath disappear. He is on the edge of dreams, visions, memories: in the garden of his grandmother's house, silky hair bounces in pigtails, eager green eyes dare him, a laugh that sounds like hiccups taunts him to chase between the trees and bushes. She is right there, and they are only children, and he feels the way he did then, not knowing his future. He talks to her about the pyramids, and she watches his eyes, his mouth, his cheeks, as if his words are made of candy. He loves the way she twists English into Farsi when she cannot remember the right words, the way she is patient with Mariam's moods, the way she stumbles in her American black-and-white saddle shoes and skins her knees and elbows without a whimper, the way she is not afraid to play soccer with the servant boys, the way her skin smells like vanilla cake, and the way she watches with such delight as he opens the gifts she brings every year from New York: Superman comic books and Hershey's chocolate bars and Wrigley's gum and a Yankees baseball cap. He imagines that all those things are still in his bedroom, in the bottom drawer of his desk, where he can touch them and feel them with his young boy's fingers. But he knows he is dreaming.

He hears a man's voice that he knows is part of the reality he cannot reach. "Yes, this is him, this is the boy we want." Callused fingers touch his hand, rough and cold like pumice stone. The fingers tug at his wedding ring. He tries to pull his hand away, but nothing happens. The fingers feel his wrists, take his watch, then flutter clumsily over his neck to find the chain, undo the clasp, and rob him of the medallion Maman Bozorg had given him to ward off the evil eye.

Twenty-Seven

Maman Bozorg

My husband Teymoor—may God give him mercy—was a lustful man. When we married, he was twenty-four and I thirteen. For me, our wedding night was a bad night. While my pain and blood were the cause for celebration by our families, they were my first taste of womanhood. I understood that I would often have to face degradation in order to obtain happiness. It was *Allah*'s way. A woman must prove her strength if she is to be rewarded. And so I prayed for a child.

Teymoor, though filled with lust, was not the type to take another wife for double pleasure. He wanted me. But I could not bear to have him devour me more than one time each week. So I learned to detect the beginnings of his lust, the manner in which his eyes smoldered when he looked at me over the dinner table or the way his voice thickened as if honey lined his throat or even by the musky odor from his skin, something like the odor of overripe figs. I became the mistress of excuses and, before his control was lost to him, before the *jenn* of passion who entered his body and caused his eyes to darken, his lips to tremble, his brow to sweat, his breath to come fast as a rabid street dog, I would retire to my rooms with some ailment or another.

Men are preoccupied with intercourse. It was for this reason that the Prophet Mohammad was forced to include *Allah*'s guidelines in the *Qoran* for men to follow. Still, how laborious it is for them to control themselves. It is therefore our duty as women to be aware of their urges and to be responsible for keeping their lust at bay. It has been many years since I have seen lust in a man's face. But the intuition is not lost to me. I saw it quite clearly in the face of the Jew called Amir.

What a bold man. He visited my house unannounced. He mentioned to the gatekeeper that he had news of Dariush, and I permitted him entrance. I ordered Firoozeh to spread a linen over an armchair so the foreigner's impurities could later be washed separately from our own. I covered myself as I would in the street: with a thick black *chador* and only one eye with which to examine him. It had been a long time since an outsider had come into my house.

I recognized him immediately as the man Mariam had described seeing as she left Layla the day before. His features were clearly Semitic and, though his Farsi was well pronounced, he was distinctly Jewish. "Who are you?" I asked him in my most authoritative voice. He told me his name. "I am a friend of your grandson's from high school," he said. His manners were irreproachable: He stood at a modest distance, never once letting his gaze rest on me and spoke to me respectfully while staring at the carpet. I was immediately pleased by him despite his infidel odor. I am not completely averse to Jews, especially if they are useful.

"What do you want? You say you have news of my grandson?"

"I have come to help."

"Yes?"

He hesitated and looked quickly behind him to make sure we were alone. "A grandson should be with the grandmother who loves him."

"This is true."

"My people have found your grandson."

I snorted. "So have my people." My throat swelled with anxiety. How would I keep Dariush from Layla now? "You have come here to tell me that you are taking my grandson to the girl who thinks she is his wife?" I felt the wetness of my spit on the *chador* fabric. "I know you are on her side, that you are her caretaker! But I will not allow him to be taken to her."

He put his hand up politely. "That is not why I am here, *haji-khanoom.*"

I barely heard him. "I have been benevolent until now. But perhaps it is time that the authorities know the girl's where-abouts. She is a criminal, a fugitive. I should—"

"Please, *khanoom*," he said, squirming in his loose clothing like a cat with fleas. "I do not want to take your grandson to Layla."

"What?"

"She . . . she would fare better without him." And there it was! On his face! The lust! A man who could not cool his own blood. "May I sit down?" he asked.

"Please," I said, pointing to the chair covered with linen. I could hardly contain my fascination. This Jew wanted one thing: to possess Layla. Dariush was in his way. Praise *Allah*! Hope had returned! "Firoozeh! Bring tea and cakes!"

The Jew's plan was to arrange for the charade of Dariush's death. Such genius! What better way to force that Layla out of Iran? She would be shattered and run back to her coward father.

The Jew was so resourceful. He knew people who could carry out subterfuge in a matter of hours. Dariush was already being transported to a house in Jamaran, not far from me, near to the *Emam*'s own residence. He would be hidden there, tended to by a nurse, until Layla was out of the country. The news of his death would come from that pompous lazy mule *Haji*-Akbar-*Agha*, who would think Dariush died of his injuries in the tent hospital.

"What of the body?" I wanted to know.

"A body will be tagged with the name of your grandson. It will be arranged for the servant boy Jamsheed to find it among the identified dead and to return it to Tehran."

"But that will not work. That boy knows Dariush like a brother. He will see that it is not Dariush."

"I assure you, *khanoom*, he will not. I would rather not explain the gruesome details."

"I am a strong woman, *agha*."

"I am aware of this and I have great respect for you. But your role in this situation is far more crucial than such details. I am merely trying not to waste time."

"All right. What must I do?"

"You must mourn. And you must trust no one to the secret. It will mean a great deal of deception, *khanoom*."

"Trickery is often necessary when one is trying to save a loved one. God praises such sacrifices."

The Jew nodded gravely, and I knew he understood my meaning completely.

I am planning an exceptional *khatm* for my grandson. Hundreds of people will come to mourn with me. How respectful they will look in their black clothing, the women wailing and the men fingering their prayer beads. I will hire the most eloquent *mullah* to chant the prayers. And on the seventh day, we will mourn again. I must plan a menu, hire extra servants. At least five types of stew must adorn the table. Rice enough for a village. The best Turkish coffee, homemade unsweetened *halvah*, the crispiest herb *kookoo*.

Funeral parties are my specialty.

Twenty-Eight

Layla

Amir didn't visit for a week. When he did, he seemed preoccupied—hardly animated at all even when I showed him that I could stand up for an agonizing sixty seconds. He hugged me, said he was happy, but our eyes barely met. He said he was working hard, that he couldn't come as often for a little while, but that I shouldn't be concerned. I knew what stress looked like, and I knew that what he was doing for me and Dariush was against the rules of his job. I wondered how I would ever thank him.

Another week went by. I was walking a little, but the pain of it made me sweat. I managed to get to the window seat in Feri's main room. It was snowing. I thought of Dariush, whether he had a warm enough jacket, whether the snow reminded him of skiing as it did me. I was trying to keep a positive attitude. If I could think about the things we'd done together that had brought us joy, then everything would turn out all right. But each day that passed without word from Jamsheed or Amir was, I knew, a bad sign.

Asya, Feri, and I played rummy. I won most of the time. What did they expect? What did they think I did during all those free hours as a *khanoom* of the aristocracy? We tried to keep one another smiling, and we mostly succeeded—during the day.

Nighttime was different. Feri moaned in her sleep, then got up to suck on cardamom seeds to settle her stomach. Asya kept the lamp on or lit a candle when the electricity failed (which was most of the time) and kept her room bright until dawn, as if the dark were an assassin. And me? Anxiety attacks. My hands shaking and my heart beating like a drum against my chest and in my ears. Stomach cramps and sweat all over. These were the times I asked myself those questions I could ignore in daylight: How long could I hide from the officials? What would happen to my baby? How would Dariush and I and the baby get out of Iran? And if we didn't go, could we stay hidden? I tried not to think about how I missed my father and Banu nor how miserable they undoubtedly were because of my absence.

I was dreaming of a beach I love in Aruba when I woke and saw Uncle Hooshang, the whites of his eyes marked with red streaks and his skin pale and slack as warm wax. I sat up. He kissed my cheeks, held me, and cried softly into my hair. I didn't speak. I didn't breathe. Jamsheed stood at the door, small, hard pupils sending me his painful message like a laser. I closed my eyes. One word spun like a funnel cloud in my head. *No, no, no.*

Uncle pulled back and brought something out of his coat pocket. With his lithe surgeon's fingers, he peeled back the leaves of a wad of tissues to reveal a gold wedding band, a gold-and-silver wristwatch, and a round gold medallion. My heart pounded. I picked up the ring as if it were some strange artifact. I saw the worst: mine and Dariush's initials and the date of our engagement inscribed on the inside. It dropped from my fingers back into Uncle's palm. Hand shaking now, teeth chattering, I picked up the watch. The strap was bent and twisted, the crystal cracked. The time said four-fifteen. A.M. or P.M.? I wondered. Had he last seen the blue sky or the flickering stars? I put the watch on my wrist and let it slide almost to my elbow; it left streaks of black soot along my arm. I didn't touch the medallion. I remembered how I'd removed it during our lovemaking, then how he'd slipped it back on before he'd gone down to the lobby. It was warped like a record album left in the sunlight. Let the old woman have it; let her see how well it protected him from evil. I snatched the ring, put it on my thumb, raised the pillow to my face, and began to scream.

"I want to see him," I said later to Jamsheed. We sat at Feri's kitchen table; the brown cats stamped onto her vinyl tablecloth swam before my eyes. Uncle had given me a Xanax before he left. It seemed that Amir had also used his connections to get medical supplies to the clinic.

Jamsheed said, "Even if it were physically possible, Layla, to arrange for you to see . . . his body, I would not do it." The frown lines between his brows were deeper than ever. Asya held his hand. Feri sobbed quietly into her handkerchief. I grabbed his arm, the muscle tight as a raw potato. "I want to know how it happened."

He pulled at his mustache nervously. "He stepped on a land mine. He died instantly."

"You can't know that. You're just saying that to comfort me."

"No, Layla-*joon*. I won't lie to you. There were many wounds and burns. I . . . I could hardly recognize him."

My lungs suddenly expanded. "So maybe it wasn't him," I said, hearing the desperation in my voice. "You saw his face, Jamsheed. Right?"

He hesitated and slowly twirled his empty tea glass. "I saw what was left . . . of his face. And I removed the wedding ring from his finger, the watch from his wrist, and the chain from around his neck."

"Do not go down this path, Layla," said Feri, now behind me, her large, warm hands squeezing my shoulders.

Tears burned my cheeks. "Where is he now?"

Jamsheed handed me a tissue. "We have already buried him."

I managed to nod, then I stood up and walked toward the bedroom; my feet didn't hurt at all. I felt like I was floating. The three of them watched me—wide-eyed and nodding—as if I were mentally ill.

I burrowed under the quilt, pulled it over my head. I thought: How could he be dead? I would have felt it. All the times he'd helped me through the worst, when he'd come to me in my thoughts, giving me strength and hope—at the stoning, in the tunnel of the prison, in my dreams of the baby, the three of us. I hadn't felt the connection between us break. If he were dead, I wouldn't be able to feel anything, just as I was never able to feel anything about my mother. Dead meant gone. But Dariush didn't feel gone. Feri's heavy weight pressed into the mattress beside me; she massaged my back. "It will take time, my daughter," she said. "But you must believe it is true and let your memories of him become a part of you. You must do this for your child."

Amir took me in his arms and whispered "I'm sorry" into my ear. He held my hands. "Forgive me," he said hoarsely.

"Forgive you? For what?"

"I could have saved him." He rubbed his forehead. "If I'd only worked harder, faster, used my connections more adequately. This never should have happened!" He stood up abruptly and strode toward the window. "Damn!" he rasped.

"You did the best you could, Amir. And I'm grateful. I think you should stop churning up guilt. You're not responsible for everyone, you know. Isn't that a bit arrogant of you?" I wondered how it had turned out that I was comforting him.

"Yes, arrogant," he said, turning around. "You're not the first who's accused me of that." We were silent for a moment, staring at the walls, listening to the clock tick. Feri's bedroom was getting on my nerves; I'd memorized every brown leak mark in her ceiling, every crack in the plaster walls, every cigarette burn on the edge of the night table.

"Layla," said Amir, "you have to leave Iran. I've come up with a way."

"I feel safe here with Feri."

He clenched his fists in frustration. "But you're not bloody safe here."

"The *komiteh* will forget about me eventually. I'm not some heavy-duty criminal. It would be more risky if I try to leave. Besides, how am I supposed to go anywhere with my feet like this?"

"Hooshang says you're healing quickly and that in two weeks you'll be able to walk all right as long as you're bandaged and wearing the proper shoes."

I looked at the floor, trying hard to stave off the anxiety creeping up on me. The idea of stepping out of Feri's apartment, into the street, into the world, turned my skin cold. "I just don't see the point in it."

He dropped into Feri's armchair and exhaled in frustration. "All right. Let's talk clear facts." He held up his thumb: "Number one: You're carrying Dariush Namdar's child." The next finger: "Number two: You're in the Islamic Republic of Iran, where children belong lock, stock, and barrel to their fathers. Let me finish"—he held up his third finger (which I felt like grabbing and twisting)—"Number three: The father of your child is dead. That means the child belongs to *his* family, not to you."

Oh my God. He was right. "But Veeda and Hooshang—"

"Veeda's in Nice and Hooshang is packing up to join her. He can't stand it here now that Dariush is dead." Funny, I thought, for me it was precisely Dariush's death that made me want to stay. Amir leaned forward and grabbed my shoulders, pulling me away from the propped-up pillows; his hands felt like cold sponges. "Don't you see, Layla? The old woman will want the baby. She didn't want you to have her grandson. Do you think she'll let you have his son? And she'll get him. By law. You can be sure of that." He brought his face so close to mine, I could see a small freckle on the bottom rim of his eye; his breath smelled of custard. "*Please* let me get you out of here."

Slowly, I struggled and pulled away from him. His expression was fierce, feverish, fervent, so different from the composed Amir I'd known. I wasn't frightened, but I didn't feel comfortable, either. I wished I hadn't let him close the bedroom door. "Why are you doing this for me?" My voice sounded like a little girl's.

"What?" He straightened and self-consciously brushed at a wrinkle in his jacket, then cleared his throat like a schoolboy about to recite a poem. "I am doing this for you because I cared about Dariush and because I care about you. We were such good friends."

We had been friends. That was true. But not tremendously close, not the way he seemed to think, not enough to risk one's life. And I'd only known him that one summer before the Revolution. I didn't see how we had suddenly become like blood relations. I must have missed something. I felt embarrassed suddenly. He stood there, his hands in his pockets, staring at me like a kindergartner nobody wants to play with.

I stammered. "It's just that I worry about the danger you've put yourself in on my behalf, Amir. I don't want you to get arrested or worse."

"Don't worry, luv," he said, looking away, no doubt hearing the falseness in my voice.

Was he angry? I sensed something like that. Anger. Maybe humiliation. Something ungovernable, stormy going on with him. Wait, I told myself. Stop this. I wasn't being fair to Amir. Was it so hard to believe that he cared about me and Dariush and our baby? Hadn't he cared enough about other Iranians to risk his life smuggling them out? Had I grown this hard-hearted?

"I'm sorry, Amir. I'm not thinking straight. You're right. I can't risk giving up my child." My throat swelled with fear. "I'll go. Tell me what to do."

Twenty-Nine

A Stairway to the Sky

It's crazy what he wants us to do," says Fereshteh to her daughter.

"Sssst! Keep your voice down. You'll wake her."

"I think we should refuse."

"We can't refuse. She has already agreed to his plan. We must help her."

Fereshteh crosses her arms beneath her wide breasts. "It will not work. She will be caught."

"She has no choice. She wants to save her child."

Fereshteh swats her daughter's shoulder. "We can hide them."

"Forever? Maman, be realistic."

Fereshteh sighs, lights a cigarette. "Poor child. She does not eat or drink. She walks on those butchered feet as if the pain is a comfort to her. I cannot bear this! I won't help her do this crazy escape."

Asya is silent in the wake of her mother's fury. Finally, in her calm, breathy voice, she says, "Do you remember when you took me to the Bahari house on one of your visits to Banu-*khanoom* one time?"

"Of course. You were ten years old; Layla was about four or five."

Asya smiled. "She was so straightforward. Not bashful, as was the proper way, with older people and strangers."

"Well, she was part American."

"Never in my life had I seen such toys: a full miniature kitchen, all in pink, with dishes and pots and utensils, all small enough for children. We stayed in her playroom all the day, do you remember?"

"I remember how it ended," she says, getting up to add water to the samovar. "That Mariam came along, then flew home with jealous wings to tell her grandmother that she had been replaced as Layla's playmate by a servant girl. She had a tantrum, apparently. So Banu told me it would be best if I did not bring you anymore. I was very angry. I did not speak to Banu for a year. How dare she allow my daughter to be so humiliated and hurt?"

Asya laughs and reaches for her cigarettes inside the pocket of her shift. "Banu had no choice. I was an Iranian child; I understood the look Mariam gave me when she saw me there in Layla's playroom. We were from different worlds. I was destined to stand one step below her on a stairway to the sky. And she was forever to be one step ahead. That is why when I grew up, it became my passion that such a thing be changed in our country. I thought the Revolution would do that, but it did not." These last words are almost a whisper.

"No. Finally, when it is too late, you see the truth. The aristocracy still exists. Only the players have been changed. Now they wear turbans."

Asya empties her tea glass and thinks about a summer night, just about a year before the Revolution, a time when she was still so passionate about politics. She was driving toward the mountains for a secret meeting when she began to pass a white palatial marble house held up by enormous Roman columns. Bright floodlights hidden in trees shone on the house and its garden. Mercedes-Benzes, Cadillacs, and Rolls-Royces spilled out blue-blooded passengers in expensive gowns and suits, wearing glimmering gems as big as fruits. Asya tried not to look, tried not to yearn for the fine fabrics and sophisticated lives. But at the last moment, passing the tall iron gate, she glanced over and saw Layla. It had been fifteen years since the day she had played with the miniature kitchen at the Bahari house, fifteen years since she had laid eyes on Layla. But she knew her immediately, and she can picture her now as if it is that evening in Shemiran. She wore a simple red gown with no sleeves and a scoop neck. Her long hair was loose, and she tossed it behind her with the back of her hand. She had a dark tan. Even from that distance and for just a fleeting moment, Asya saw in Layla's face the bold smile and the honest, glittering eyes she remembered with so much affection. Later that night, when Asya was returning from her meeting, the party at the big house was still going on. There was loud music, and the bulbs and lanterns in the trees beyond the walls lit up the whole neighborhood. Suddenly she saw a gathering of people in tattered clothing crouching before a portion of the wall. She slowed her car and realized they were beggars; it had been many years since the shah had banned them from the streets. She stopped the car across the street and watched them. Suddenly, several small dark things came soaring over the wall and the beggars dived onto the sidewalk to retrieve them. It was food. Leftovers. Meat and vegetables and bread—all covered in dust. Asya sat there, paralyzed, ashamed that this was her country.

"More tea, Asi?" asks Fereshteh. "Or are you asleep with your eyes open?"

Suddenly, Jamsheed bursts into the apartment. He stands there without the usual sparkle in his eye, his lips clamped together in rage. He points to his chest. "Look at what they did to me!"

Asya and Feri clasp their hands over their mouths; their bodies convulse with laughter. Asya shakes her head. "I've told you a thousand times not to wear a *keravat* in the street."

He strides to the table and drops his bag on the chair. "It's not funny. This was an Italian silk *keravat* that the *aghayeh*-doctor gave to me."

"It could be worse, *azizam*," Asya says, trying to calm him with her endearment. "They could have cut it off just below the knot. It seems they have left you enough material to perhaps make it into a bow tie." She turns and hides her face so he will not see her laughter. Feri snorts.

"You are both heartless women. Where will I ever get sympathy?" The sparkle has come back to his eyes. Asya rises and helps him remove his overcoat; she kisses his neck. "Poor thing," she whispers mockingly.

He sits and Fereshteh slides a glass of tea toward him. Her face is sober. "*Pesaram,*" she says. Asya likes it that her mother has begun calling Jamsheed "my boy" since he returned. "Be grateful that you are not a woman, that the fanatics do not shave the front of your head because a few hairs are showing, that they do not wipe the lipstick from your mouth with a cloth that hides a razor blade in its folds, that they do not consider your life worth half that of a man's."

Jamsheed gazes at the tea glass, glances at Asya, then nods his head. "You are right, Feri-*khanoom.* I will remember." She pinches his cheek, leaving a streak of red.

He sips his tea, then says, "How is Layla?"

"The same," says Asya. "In bed, in a sleep she gets from the pills."

"That's not good for the baby," he says.

Fereshteh says, "It is better than the agony of grief."

"She must face the grief sooner or later."

They are silent for a moment, hunched over the table, breathing out their pity.

"Hakim was here this morning," says Asya. A concerned look passes between mother and daughter. "He has come up with a plan to get Layla out of Iran. She has agreed to it. He wants us to help—"

Fereshteh interrupts: "I am completely against it. Why risk her life? She is safe here."

Jamsheed rubs his eyes, massages his temples. "He's right. She has to leave."

"But—" says Fereshteh.

"I thought you didn't trust him?" says Asya.

"I don't. But Dariush did and Layla does. We must not judge." He puts his dark, long fingers over Fereshteh's pink knuckles. "I know," he says. "He is odd. What is he doing risking his job and his life to save Layla? I can tell you that his friendship with Dariush was not so loyal to make him go this far to rescue her."

Asya speaks softly. "Because he desires her."

"That is disgusting!" says Jamsheed. "She is Dariush's wife."

Asya puts her hand on his arm. "She *was* his wife."

"Besides," says Fereshteh. "It is not your duty to be jealous and possessive for Dariush's sake. Layla will take care of herself in this matter. The point is, should we go along with this escape Hakim has planned?"

Jamsheed sighs. "She has agreed to it, you say?"

"She said she knew it was dangerous, but it was the only chance for her baby," says Asya.

"I know her," he says, gulping his tea and pushing the empty glass aside. "She cannot be swayed easily. And Dariush would have wanted me to stand behind her. So what is Hakim's plan?"

Fereshteh leans back and cracks her knuckles. Jamsheed looks at Asya, her elbows on the table, palms held against her cheeks. Without looking at him, she says, "He wants to disguise her as a man and send her out on a flight to Istanbul."

Jamsheed drops his forehead onto the sticky tablecloth and says, "*Khodaya komakemoon kon!*"

And Layla, standing at the bedroom door, having heard these last remarks, says to herself, "Yes indeed Jamsheed-*joon*, God help us. God help my baby."

Amir is proud of himself. His plan is brilliant. Too bad Dariush will never be privy to this new act of ingenuity. And Amir is certain the plan will work. With Layla's height and features, it is the most logical way. As a woman, even in *hejab*, she would stand out; the *komiteh* has circulated a description of her. But as a man! They will never guess! And she can be a good actress, Amir thinks. He has seen that. That summer when she and Dariush were not officially together—her flirtatious yet unassuming airs. Like a ripe red apple, too high to reach. But now he will save her, and her airs will be for him. He thinks of her all the time now; it is as if he holds her essence in the palms of his hands. Warm and glowing. He daydreams. Their future. He marvels at how everything has changed, how gracefully destiny worked to push Dariush aside and bring them together.

What a shame, he thinks, that my old friend cannot see how I have made Layla my own. The dishonorable asshole never understood the value of friendship. Now I possess his most prized treasure. In the end, every man gets his due. The world is carefully balanced. And so it should be.

But he must concentrate. There is so much to do. He must call in some favors, pay off various officials and forgers, obtain the proper immigration papers and the essential tools for her costume. He will need to communicate with Josephina in Istanbul. He grimaces; their last meeting some weeks ago had ended, not for the first time, in her tears and his angry exit. She is becoming more difficult to handle, especially since Layla occupies his thoughts most often, giving Josephina more fuel for her argument that he is noncommunicative. (She has not been bold enough yet to mention his impotence with her, and that is just fine with him.) But dropping Josephina is out of the question. Her role is essential for the success of Layla's escape, though she will not be aware that Layla is any different from the hundreds of other refugees Amir has sent her in the past. Josie is the least of his worries.

He must keep a watch on those three in the apartment, especially the boy Jamsheed; he is sharp, and his suspicions are street keen. He still wonders if he should have involved them in the plan; he could have called on local Jews to help. There were still plenty left—the *sayanim*, people who would help without asking questions and all the while think they were aiding in the protection of Jews in the diaspora. But it was risky, so he must trust those three. No matter. He will make sure Jamsheed and the women know only what he wants them to know. And there will be no mistakes this time; they will do exactly what he tells them to do or have Layla's death on their heads.

In all of this, he continues to do the job he has been sent here to do. But that has grown easy, even boring. The regime is filled with idiots, each one trying to be more powerful than the other; they are completely and chaotically involved in keeping down the counterrevolutionaries and rambling on with all their pent-

up rhetoric. Anyone else who can be of use is on the take, and
Amir has a smooth flow of funds with which to bribe them. He
is not smuggling people out of the country as much as he used
to; many of the Jews who wanted to leave have already gone. The
others—Persians before Jews—can rot here, Amir thinks.
Anyway, he prefers smuggling wealth and valuables. He relishes
using his mind in the cunning way necessary to put schemes
together, whether they involve duping bank officials or arranging for antique carpets to be wrapped in plastic and smuggled
across the Turkish border buried in trucks of manure.

Until Layla came, he had been looking forward to his tour in
Iran ending. But now intriguing things are happening, and it
seems as if he could be involved in some very stimulating and
prestigious assignments. Last week, Jacob Steinman showed up
in Tehran dressed convincingly in Arab costume: checkered *kaf-
fiyeh* cascading around his head and a scruffy Islamic beard. Amir
knew immediately that Jacob had been sent to replace Aaron
Sowan, a mediocre agent whose only asset was his ability to
speak Arabic like a Saudi; beyond that, he was of low intelligence and even lower cunning. Amir had offered Sowan his services, hoping he could become involved in the more intriguing
aspects of Mossad's operation in Iran, but he was rebuffed. And
finally, because of Sowan's incompetence, the entire Iranian operation was nearly blown when a planeload of arms from Israel to
Iran crashed into a Soviet jet. Amir knows Jacob will do a better
job; he also knows Jacob will throw him some bones, grace him
with some new experiences. After all, Jacob is a seasoned agent
and an old friend, not to mention Josephina's brother.

So tonight Amir is going with Jacob, aka Tarek al-Nasser, to
a secret meeting with an Islamic government official from the
war department.

They dress as Arabs—Jacob, Amir, and Jacob's driver. How
delicious it is, Amir thinks as they sit in the limousine, to live in
the skin of his enemy in order to dupe him. The meeting will be
conducted in Arabic, which Jacob speaks like a Palestinian; he
wants Amir to eavesdrop on the Farsi spoken between their
counterparts.

Pedestrians and other motorists throw them looks of disdain. It still amazes Amir that Iranians dislike Arabs so much and use every opportunity to remind people they are not an Arab race. There are a thousand contemptuous jokes about dumb, dirty, stubborn, and oversexed Arabs—all this, and still Iranians believe diligently in the religion that was forced on them by those same Arabs thirteen hundred years ago. Izaak Hakim had been right: The Persians had paid a high price for assimilation.

They drive up north past the suburbs and into the hills, where small villages thrive as if oblivious to the encroaching city. They stop at one of the many ornate homes in the Mahmoudieh District and are ushered into a large room covered wall to wall with an antique carpet. Dim light. In the center of the room, two *mullah*s from the war department and one *hojatolislam* with an enormous belly sit on the floor. Strong, dark tea is brought by a manservant, and Jacob begins to negotiate the price for millions of dollars' worth of armaments, most of which are manufactured either in Israel or in the United States.

Amir is fascinated, but he soon learns there is little reason for his presence. The *hojatolislam* speaks Arabic to Jacob; the others say nothing, not in Farsi or any other language. He gets the sense that, while they all play this charade, everyone knows who everyone else really is. Neither side cares. The objective is to provide and obtain armaments. To the world, Israel pretends to satisfy the U.S. embargo against selling arms to Iran, but Mossad continues to do so. And the fighting will go on. The arms will be massive, but limited. No need for anyone to win. Sell the Iranians enough to survive; keep Saddam Hossein occupied. The war can go on for years. And Israel will be protected from one side, at least. And in the best of outcomes, Iran and Iraq will destroy one another.

During the drive back, Amir feels powerful and proud. He sits in the back with Jacob, watches his own face in the rearview mirror, admires his eyes and ruddy skin. Finally, his superiors have noticed his extraordinary abilities; he is truly involved now with the most refined and clever organization in the world.

"Did you enjoy yourself?" asks Jacob in a deadpan tone.

"I found it extremely interesting."

"You would like to do it again?"

"I would." Amir's pulse quickens with exhilaration.

"I can arrange it," says Jacob. "But you must not disappoint me."

Amir shifts in his seat as he detects the edge in Jacob's voice. "I don't disappoint," he says, insulted.

Jacob looks over and smiles crookedly. "Really?" Amir says nothing. "But I'm certain I heard disappointment in Josephina's voice when she said she had not seen or heard from you in several weeks."

Amir grits his teeth and looks out the window; they pass slowly by a huddle of scrawny dogs fighting over the scraps of a small rodent. Without looking at Jacob, he says, "We communicate; she is my contact in Istanbul and—"

"I am not talking about work," Jacob interrupts.

"I have been busy," says Amir.

"I see. Then perhaps attending more meetings such as the one tonight would be too much for you—since you are so busy."

Amir understands completely. So this is a bribe. He feels his face growing hot. How dare that bitch try to control him this way. He musters a neutral voice and says, "I will make plans to visit her."

"Good," says Jacob.

Yes, thinks Amir, I will visit her. And she will be sorry I did. But first there is another matter. News came this morning that Dariush had arrived at the safe house in Jamaran. Amir wants to see him with his own eyes, but he will not risk it yet. The old Jewish couple he is paying to keep him have said he is still unconscious, hooked up to an IV. Their son, a doctor, has said if he recovers, it will take months, maybe a year. How fortunate, Amir thinks. The grandmother will have plenty to do once Dariush is moved to her house. But this will not happen until Layla is gone.

Fereshteh feels sorrier for Layla because she will not cry openly. She hides in the bathroom or under the quilt or waits until everyone is asleep. This is something very Western about Layla. Fereshteh does not like it. She does not believe that suffering should be done alone; it is not healthy. Suffering must be shared, divided among friends and family. Otherwise, how can it be used for survival?

Banu did not teach Layla this, Fereshteh thinks, wishing, with tears in her eyes, that her friend were here—even if just so she could scold her. Or perhaps it is not Banu's fault; a child who loses her mother so young and lives far from her family cannot help but turn out this way. The poor girl hides her grief, thinking this will protect herself and us.

But a Persian woman learns early that personal suffering, more than anything else, brings attention and admiration. It is the foundation of her culture: it is what is supposed to bring a woman her spirituality, give her wisdom, prepare her for motherhood, permit her to know happiness, protect her from worse pain. The stories of suffering come to Persian women early and are repeated and reconstituted and refined until they are their dictionary of life.

But Layla has not often been in the circle of Persian women.

Fereshteh goes to the bedroom and sits on the bed. She caresses Layla's forehead with her palm. Layla opens her eyes and frowns, then her pupils contract and she closes them again. Fereshteh knows this feeling of waking up to tragedy; God gives you less than a moment to think that the world is as it should be—sweet and hopeful—then He reminds you that the world has fallen apart for you. And the pain is fresh and stabbing like ice hitting your cheek.

"Laylee, it is time to leave the bed. You must build your strength if you want to do this thing. Do you still want to?"

Layla swipes at a tear on her cheek and says, "Yes. What is today, Feri-*joon?*"

"It is Wednesday, the twenty-fifth of *Aban*, Month of Iron."

"So November is almost over."

"Yes. Turkey holiday must have been last week. Banu always wrote to me about this."

"Really?"

"Yes. And one year Katayoon-*khanoom* visited you and took pictures of the party. Banu asked her to have a few delivered to me. Such a big turkey on the table! Impossible! Of course, I told Banu, the bird was clearly a lamb disguised as a turkey. And this would make her so angry."

Layla laughs halfheartedly. Slowly she presses her arms into the mattress and rises up, sluggishly and shakily as an old woman. Fereshteh props the pillows against the wall and Layla sinks back into them. "This will not do," says Fereshteh. "You are too weak. You must eat more. I will fix you a big dinner. And you must get out of bed. Hakim has brought extra bandages and men's socks and an old pair of Dr. Namdar's shoes for you to wear. He says you must get used to walking in them. Before the doctor left, he told me he thought you would actually feel more comfortable in such shoes with so much padding than you would without. Okay, Laylee? If you truly want to do this escape, it is time to begin strengthening yourself."

"All right, Feri-*joon*," she says with hardly any expression in her voice.

Fereshteh rises from the bed. "I will get some *ob-goosht* for you to eat and also bring the shoes."

"Feri-*joon?*"

"Yes, child."

"So Uncle Hooshang has gone to France already?"

"Yes, yesterday. Remember? He came to say good-bye the day before."

She hesitates. "Yes, I remember." She looks toward the window, her eyelids heavy. "I remember everything now." And Fereshteh wishes she had never had to wake her.

Thirty

Layla

I knew I had to get out of bed. I remembered the decision I'd made to escape and the reason why I'd made it. Still, part of me felt dead without Dariush. It was difficult to care what happened to me. Sleep seemed like the best escape.

Then I felt it. Lying on my stomach, pillow over my head, my body molded to the pliant mattress, feeling as fluffy as the sheets. It was an almost imperceptible sensation that I'd been ignoring as just another internal, involuntary gastrointestinal function. A light, feathery, fluttery tapping from inside. Like my heartbeat, only farther down and unsteady. It made me throw the pillow off, raise my head, and gasp loud enough to bring Feri running in. "What! What is it! What has happened!"

"The baby! I feel the baby!" I was crying and smiling. Crying mostly. Crying for my husband, buried deep beneath the marble tiles of the mausoleum, and smiling for the life of our child, buried deep within me. I let Feri embrace me and I held on to her strong arms. No more sleep, I told myself. This child will see the sky and the mountains and the clouds his father once saw.

Uncle Hooshang was right. His size-nine men's shoes, stuffed with cotton and thick gauze, were easy to walk in—certainly more comfortable than bare feet. Each day I could put down more weight. Still, I wasn't confident that I could walk or stand for more than fifteen minutes at a time. And I knew that soon I would surely have to.

Amir wouldn't tell me exactly when I was supposed to leave. He had turned very serious, businesslike, almost detached. I followed his lead. He was the expert. Every day he came with more "essential tools" for the escape. "Here," he said one day. "Study this." He handed me a brand-new Iranian passport with the *Allah* logo stamped in gold on the front. Peering inside, I saw that my name was to be Javad Mahmoudi, a cook by profession who was of medium height with black hair and green eyes. "We'll have to take a picture soon," said Amir. He turned to Feri who was, as usual, preparing some delicious meal. "It is time to cut her hair, *khanoom*." Feri nodded and I felt queasy. I'd never had short hair.

"I don't know much about cooking," I said to Amir.

He chuckled. "I doubt they'll ask you to give a demonstration. As far as I know, there aren't any kitchens at airport security checkpoints."

"You don't have to patronize," I said, staring at his eyes until he looked away.

"Very sorry," he finally said in that stiff British way.

I closed my eyes while Feri cut my hair. I imagined Dariush braiding it—he used to do that—gathering the tresses together with such gentleness, as if they were made of silk thread.

When Feri was done, she handed me her old salon mirror. I opened my eyes and saw the floor and my lap littered with discarded strands. I rubbed some of them between my fingers; they felt inorganic, like a fabric sample. My head felt light, like a helium balloon. My neck and ears were cold. I looked in the mirror; the hair was half an inch long. I saw tears well up in my eyes; now I was as different on the outside as I felt on the inside.

Asya couldn't hide her shock when she came in later. "Talk so I know it is you," she said. Then she smiled. "I think you look cute. And short hair is fashionable in Europe now."

I rolled my eyes and said, "Thank God!" The three of us burst out laughing.

Asya took a small red bottle from her pocket and placed it on the table. "Jamsheed finally found the right color."

"*Alhamdolellah!*" said Feri, gazing upward as she praised God.

None of us, except Feri, had realized that in a country where ninety-nine percent of the people had black hair, and where Western fashion was exalted among those who'd dye their hair in the first place, that the color black would not be in demand at all. In fact, it was almost nonexistent. There was plenty of moonlit brown, sunlit brown, toasty brown, and chestnut brown, but absolutely no black.

"Where did he find it?" I asked.

"The Swiss embassy. He has a friend who works there."

Feri began mixing the dye with peroxide, and the strong odor filled the room. Images of beauty salons ran through my mind: ones that my grandmother had taken me to when I was a child; the sticky sensation of my thighs against the booster chairs, the red scratches on my neck from the plastic capes. I loved the salons in Tehran, where gossip was more abundant than shades of nail color. I always preferred them over the salons that various aunties took me to in Paris, London, and Vienna with their flamboyant hairdressers who sulked when you asked for just a trim.

I stood naked in Feri's bathroom, toweled off and warm from a long shower, marveling at the simplicity of drying my short hair. I combed it away from my face as I thought a man might do. My skin looked bright white against the darker shade. Even my eyes seemed to have a different depth, a larger pupil. I looked at my belly, which seemed rounder even than two days before. I couldn't see down to my pubic hair unless I leaned forward. I whispered to the baby, "We have to leave soon, sweetie. You're getting too big."

I pulled Feri's massive maroon robe around myself and reached for her terry-cloth slippers. My feet were feather light without the bandages, the soles both caressed and scuffed by the bath mat. They still looked terrible. Still swollen, as if they had grown bunions in all the wrong places, the skin like white plastic in some areas and then black in others; thick scabs had formed on the soles, and all my toenails had fallen off. I reminded myself that Uncle had said that the skin would heal, that I would have some scarring, but that a plastic surgeon could fix them if I wanted. Maybe I would. If I lived.

"We have to take the passport picture now," said Amir, already setting up the camera and clearing a space by a bare part of the wall. "Your ticket is set for three days from now. That's how long the immigration officials require for passport processing."

I was frozen in my chair. It's really happening, I thought. I can't do it; I would have better odds going rock climbing in my ninth month. I tried to speak, but nothing came out. Suddenly, Feri was smudging dark foundation on my face and Asya was stuffing my arms into a yellowed man's shirt that we'd chosen from the pile of old clothing Amir had brought some days before. Feri slipped a cotton beard over my face and stepped back to examine me. She put her hands over her puffy cheeks and closed her eyes. "Oh God," she whined. "She looks like *Haji Firooz*." *Haji Firooz* is a minstrel-like clown that dances through the streets during the *Norooz* celebrations. *Haji Firooz* is so over-made-up he would put a drag queen to shame.

I shot up out of the chair and reached for the hand mirror. Amir grabbed it from me. "No! It's fine. You look fine for the picture."

Asya snatched the mirror from him and gave it to me. She stepped between us and turned her face toward Amir. Her bangs fell forward onto her forehead, and the scar on her scalp shimmered with perspiration. I waited for her to punch him, but they stood in silent rage. I looked in the mirror. Feri was right. My voice trembled and I growled at Amir, "Are you living in a fantasy world? Are you trying to kill me?"

"Listen to me, Layla," he said in Farsi so the other two could understand perfectly. "This is not your costume. This is just for a fuzzy black-and-white picture. In fact, the heavier the makeup, the more exaggerated the costume, the more realistic the picture will seem. We're not going to use that fake beard in the real costume, and the foundation will blend in better and you'll have an eye patch."

"An eye patch?" I said, my hands shaking. "Like Captain Hook?"

"Who?" said Feri.

"A bad sailor from a fairy tale." I couldn't remember the word for pirate.

"Never mind," said Asya. "Why now are you talking about eye patches, Amir?" She'd never before used his first name and addressed him in the informal second person.

"It will draw away from her eye color," he said. "I tried to get the new colored contact lenses to make them brown, but I was unable to."

"It's not like there aren't any Iranians with light eyes," I said.

"True. But your other features are so Western. And the eye patch will also explain why you aren't fighting at the front at your age."

"No," I said, sitting down. "It's over." Asya stepped back and Feri folded her arms.

"What do you mean?" he said.

"I mean I'm not going. This isn't going to work. I don't look like a man at all!"

"But you will! I promise you. I've done this before." He knelt on one knee in front of me, his warm hands on my arms. I shivered. "All right," he said. "Let's make a deal. If after we're done making you up for the escape, we *all* don't agree that you can pass as a man, then you won't go and we'll find a place to hide you in Iran." He peered up at me; I felt like a sulking child. "Please," he pleaded in English. "Just give it a try. For the baby."

We all stood silently, but I could hear everyone breathing. Out of the corner of my eye, I saw Asya's chest heaving out and in. An ambulance siren blared outside, and I listened until it faded completely. Then slowly, my joints feeling like rubber, I walked to the wall and stood solemnly against it while he took my picture.

Thirty-One

Measuring the Worth

Amir must get a grip on the details of Layla's escape. He had allowed Josephina to distract him, but not anymore. Yesterday as she was leaving, he threatened to break off their relationship entirely if she showed up in Tehran unannounced again. He pretended his reasoning had to do with her safety: Iran had become too dangerous now. He tried to be nice to her, thinking of his relationship with Jacob. Still, she irritated him so much with her complaints—even once saying that she missed the homely boy he used to be—that he struck her and she flipped him, nearly dislocating his shoulder.

He remembers her first visit. Almost three years ago. Just after the waterskiing accident. No sooner had Dariush and Layla gone back to the States than Iran had begun to show signs of revolution. For Amir, it was perfect timing; he had desperately needed to throw himself into his intelligence work. Josephina's visit was a nuisance. Seven hundred people had just burned to death in a movie theater whose doors had been locked from the outside. It had been the first clear terrorist act from the fundamentalists. The unrest in Iran was blooming like a smoke bomb. But Josie wanted to fuck. All right. Then she wanted to talk. "No talking," he said. "I want to listen to the BBC."

"What's the big deal, Amir? We've known for years this would happen. Let's have some fun before the hard work starts. Come on." She had nuzzled his neck, an act that annoyed him because of her nose; it was not a big nose, not anymore, but he could not forget how big it had once been. He pulled away and she dropped back on the sheets, swiping at tears he pretended not to notice.

What had amazed Amir most about the terrorist incident in the movie theater was the nonreaction of the aristocracy. At first they were properly horrified and solemn, but not for long. After all, it had happened in a southern city, to lower-class people, nobody *they* knew. As for the political intrigue that surrounded the incident—the accusations that the arson was the work of religious insurgents—they seemed ridiculous. None of them remembered that the *mullah*s had always called for a ban on the cinema, that they had warned believers that the images on the screen would rob their souls. And those people who *did* remember, like the parents and grandparents, they dismissed the idea: *The mullahs have no power; the shah is in power.*

"Well," Josephina had said, sliding beneath the sheets, "you can't blame them for their confidence in King and Country. Why, the *mullah*s have even lost their Islamic calendar." She was right about that. As ordered by the shah, the Persian year had become 2536, a commemoration to the continuity of the Persian monarchy beginning with Cyrus the Great and culminating in the reign of Shah Mohammad Reza Pahlavi, King of Kings (no matter that this had little to do with bloodlines). All right, the aristocrats sometimes admitted, perhaps the shah *had* become a little megalomaniacal, but such prosperity was certainly worth a minorly eccentric king. Nobody, they sneered—especially not some doom-preaching and exiled *ayatollah* called Khomeini— was going to put a damper on *this* party.

But the party, thought Amir, had indeed been over, and so would begin the most exciting and intriguing part of his life. He had craved the hard work that was ahead, not only because he believed in glory for himself, but because he would think less about Dariush and Layla. As for Josephina . . .

Back and forth they went over the years; Istanbul, Tehran, Ankara, Shiraz. Stolen weekends. As Amir hardened, Josephina softened. As Amir became embroiled in the machinations of his job, Josephina became haunted by the hope of them moving back to Israel and settling down.

He would say, *What do you want from me, Josie? Let me do my work; let me make a name for myself in the organization. You are dragging me down. This was not the deal.*

What deal? she would say. *We were two awkward ugly kids who found and made each other what we are today. We were not making deals then. We were lonely and thirsty for hope. I love you.*

He would tell her he loved her too; he still tells her this. What he does not tell her is that when he looks at her, he sees the repulsive girl she used to be. And as long as she comes to him and he sees her this way, he cannot be who he wants to be. She is forbidding him to shed his old skin, and he has begun to hate her for it.

For now, he must tolerate her; his career—and Layla's escape—demands it. So he copes with her ardor and her whining—and her questions, which seem to be what is left of their relationship. *What has happened to you? Why are you so distant? So angry? So condescending? Are you trying to be harsh like your father? Why can't you accept my love? Why do you only want to capture the love of people who don't care about you? And who is this Layla you whisper to in your sleep?*

But he does not hear.

Patiently, Amir works with mother and daughter, with Layla. They practice a man's walk, a man's gaze, a man's voice, a man's gestures. He teaches her to take longer, wider steps, to force a slight frown on her eyebrows to make her face seem less delicate. He teaches her to hold her cigarette farther down between her fingers and to inhale roughly so the smoke flips up into her nostrils. Tirelessly, he helps her rehearse her voice into a passable baritone.

He had not wanted to do this. He had hoped the girl and her mother would have done it; he had given them instructions earlier. But after the terrible outburst over the passport photo, he knew he had to stay. It is almost unbearable for him. His desire for Layla has heightened since she agreed to the escape. She is so vulnerable, looking almost feeble in her short hair and pale skin. He thought he would have been uncomfortable when her belly began to show, but he is not. In fact, he wants to touch the round softness of it, have his hands fully on the whole of it. He can stand to be with her only for an hour or so at a time. He makes excuses to leave the apartment for breaks. He goes into the cold air and walks quickly, looking down at the pavement and thinking thoughts to make his erection go away, telling himself that he will have her in time.

He is also afraid that the escape will go wrong. Nothing is certain, and tragedy is always around the corner. He knows this. But this is the path he has chosen and there is no turning back. Even if he *could* turn back, that old witch grandmother of Dariush's would surely not allow it. She has been pushing him. Stupid arthritic crone treats him like a servant; she had it in her mind that her grandson would be delivered to her immediately. She has made the last weeks miserable for him, calling him constantly, jeopardizing his life with her intrusions. Well, it will be over in three days, he thinks. Over, one way or another.

He must focus on preparing Layla.

Candlelight flickers over their faces. The electricity goes out every night now. Amir and Layla sit at the table and drink tea from the kerosene samovar. Fereshteh and Asya are asleep in the bedroom.

"All right," says Amir. "Let's talk about things that could go wrong."

"Okay."

"What will you do if they don't have the passport waiting?"

"Turn around and walk out of the airport. Everything canceled."

"Not so fast."

"You want me to make a stink to an official of the Islamic Republic?"

"Remember, you're a cook, not a quivering aristocrat. You still believe that the Revolution liberated people like you. And you deserve this first trip on an airplane, just as surely as you deserved the valuables you took from your absent employers so you could pay for the first vacation abroad in your life."

"Okay."

"You have to think like someone who has spent his entire life feeding people who hardly paid him enough to feed his own family. And now—imagine—he's doing something that never would have been possible before. He's going to ride in an airplane to Istanbul. He wouldn't want to give that up so easily."

"So if my passport isn't there, I should ask why. Maybe I should make them check again or insist that they call someone more important to look into it."

"Exactly. Good."

"But I won't make a big stink. I'll protest a little, then leave the airport." She hesitates. "God, Amir, what are the chances of them withholding my passport?"

"We can't find a pattern to whose passports are liberated and whose aren't. The customs agency is disorganized and driven by people whose personal biases determine who can leave the county and who cannot. So, if your name's on a list—and there are a lot of lists coming out of *komiteh* buildings and mosques and God knows where else—then your passport gets held up and you're stuck."

"Or arrested," she says.

"But Layla, your alias is not on any list. Besides, a mere cook isn't going to arouse any interest. If your passport is held back it's because some guy in the customs agency was in a bad mood when he reviewed it. Maybe your name reminded him of a schoolmate who beat him up or maybe your picture resembled his father-in-law, who cheated him on his wife's dowry. Or maybe he was constipated or impotent and he took his frustration out on your passport."

She is laughing by now, holding the noise in with a hand over her mouth. Finally, she says, "Thank you, Amir, for trying to amuse me."

He smiles and suddenly pictures himself sucking on her middle finger. He clears his throat; his voice sounds animal-like, feral. He imagines grabbing her, having sex with her on the table, his penis wet with her juices. Perhaps he once would have felt ashamed by such a thought, but not anymore. She is his now. He has done so much for her already that she can never walk away from him.

"All right," he says. "Let's move on to another question. Ready? What will you do if the flight is delayed for, say, twenty hours?"

"I stay put. I shouldn't risk leaving, especially if I've already gone through the checkpoints and I'm waiting in the transit lounge."

"Right. Also, you never know if the officials will change their minds and give permission for the flight to leave earlier. Now, imagine this: You get past the first two checkpoints and you're waiting in line to be searched. A *pasdar* points to your eye patch and says, 'How did you get that, brother?' "

"I know the answer is that I fell on a kebab skewer when I was six. But in a case like that, wouldn't it be better if I said it happened in the war? Wouldn't it make the *pasdar* less suspicious?"

Amir shakes his head. "No, no, Layla. Don't change the story. And don't assume that the *pasdaran* are suspicious of you at all. If you tell him you got wounded, he'll ask you all kinds of questions about what it was like at the front lines. Can you answer them?"

She cringes a little. "No. Of course not."

"Okay," he says, pinching her cheek lightly. "You're doing well. Now, what if the official with the medical bracelet isn't at the body-search checkpoint?"

Her head snaps up. "You said that couldn't happen, that he would definitely be there. Maybe I can *look* like a man, but this pregnant belly will never pass a body search."

"He *will* be there. I promise. I asked you the question because I know this is the part that worries you the most. If you have a plan of action in your mind in case the worst happens, you'll be less nervous going into the whole thing. That's all."

"Okay. What do I do?"

"Fall down and be sick. Maybe you have food poisoning or a bleeding ulcer, something that wouldn't make you pass out completely but would require that you retreat to the men's room and miss your flight. Whatever happens, don't get behind the curtain with someone who isn't wearing a visible medical bracelet for diabetes. That's not our man."

"Are you sure I can trust this guy?"

"Absolutely. He's helped many other people out. Jews especially, letting a lot of them pass with money and jewels in their bras and panties. Secretly, he's a *Bahai*."

"But *Bahai*s are never secretive about their religion. It's part of their belief system not to deny what they are."

"Well, *this Bahai* wants to stay alive for his wife and children, who are already living in Watertown, Massachusetts, and I've given him the monetary incentive to save himself for their benefit. He also seems to get immense satisfaction out of duping the regime. Wouldn't you? Hundreds of *Bahai*s have been executed since the Revolution began. And, Layla, he has never betrayed me. I trust him and so should you."

But Layla does not look convinced.

Amir pours more tea without using the strainer; tea leaves swirl chaotically in the glass as he stirs. Layla watches them in a weary daze. "Tired?" he asks.

She blinks and peers at Dariush's watch hanging loose on her arm. "Yeah, it's past midnight."

"You'll have to leave that behind, Layla."

"Why? It's a man's watch."

"It's a Rolex watch that customs wouldn't allow out of the country under the best of circumstances. Besides, where does a cook get that kind of jewelry?"

"He steals it just like all the other servants did."

"Okay. That's a possible argument. But it's not worth adding another risk to your situation."

"Who's measuring the worth?" She watches his eyes, her lips trembling slightly with anger or grief, he cannot tell which. Slowly, he reaches across the table and lets his fingers rest on her neck. She flinches. Gently, he pinches the gold chain around her neck and draws it up out of her shirt. He imagines the chain moving along her breast, hardening a nipple. She does not move, but he feels her swallow against his fingers. Finally the chain is out, and the two charms at the end of it slide out of Amir's hand and bounce lightly against her T-shirt, plinking against one another.

It is Amir's turn to be surprised. He had expected Dariush's wedding band and his *Allah* medallion to be hanging from the chain. The wedding band is there, but in place of the other is a Star of David. His chest swells with emotion. Finally, he says, "You wear a Star of David?" He cannot hide his smile.

"It was my mother's."

"Of course it was. But you wear it. This is important."

"I wear it because it was my mother's."

"You wear it because your mother was a Jew. And so, then, are you, Layla. I am so pleased that you have finally understood this."

She looks away. "I guess I have to leave these behind, too."

"Yes, but I'll find a way to get the pieces out to you later."

Thirty-Two

Layla

I was on the verge of canning the whole plan the night Amir told me I couldn't take Dariush's watch and ring with me. He was so wrapped up in the fact that I was wearing my mother's Star of David. He suddenly turned orthodox on me. Almost like he'd been waiting and preparing for this moment of my epiphany so we could join hands and float up to heaven. It occurred to me that the reason he was risking so much to help me was because he considered me a Jew. The truth was, I would have been wearing my own *Allah* medallion on that chain as well if it hadn't been stolen from me at the prison. I wondered what he would have said about that. Sorry, escape aborted? Stop it, I told myself. That's idiotic. Amir had tried to save Dariush, too. Still, I wasn't a stranger to fanaticism, and while it didn't seem to be oozing out of Amir's pores the way it did from Maman Bozorg's, the hint of it was there.

After he left, I poured myself a strong tea and held before me the envelope filled with my mother's things that Mariam had brought me. I emptied the contents onto the table. The candle-light flickered over the photo of my mother and me. I have other pictures of my mother, one that once sat in a crystal frame on my dresser in New York. I used to study it, looking for a trace of the mother I'd never known. One time it slipped out of my hands and I remembered watching, astonished, as the heavy frame shattered on the parquet floor. Tiny crystal pieces skidded frantically in all directions, some traveling as far as the bathroom, where they had skipped along the tiles. Banu said she thought I dropped the picture because I was angry with my mother for dying. I hadn't felt angry, just frustrated.

I peered at the photograph that was fairly new to me: a picture of my mother, not alone, but with me, caressing me, smiling at the feel of my kiss on her cheek. I did what I always do. I struggled to recall the memory of my mother. How could I have grown inside this woman for nine months, been stroked, kissed, and fed by her for two years, and yet not have any visual or sensual remembrance of her? I touched my stomach. Doesn't my baby know me? Feel me? Feel my love? I traced my fingers over the grainy paper. My mother's face was unlined, unblemished, smooth as a sand sculpture, with just a trace of grayness under oval eyes and a subtle cleft in her chin that I inherited. Her hair fell down one side of her forehead and then waved around her cheek and onto her jaw, where it touched my little cheek as I kissed her. I pressed the photo against my face and closed my eyes. For maybe a millisecond, I was back there, and the paper felt like warm skin.

I'd been angry with Mariam for bringing me these things. Now I was grateful. She was right; they made me feel closer to my mother, closer than I'd ever felt. I put the picture aside and unwrapped the blue ribbon over the packet of five airmail letters. They were letters my mother had written to her mother in Manhattan when I was a baby. They'd all been returned to her unopened. When I'd found them in the tin trunk, they were all sealed, but I'd carefully slit open the envelopes that folded up like a puzzle and were addressed to Mrs. Margaret Abramson. Now I opened them, flattened them with my palm, and stacked them chronologically, beginning with the one postmarked 1336, which was the Western year 1957.

Reading the letters again was going to give me strength, I decided. My mother was going to give me strength.

February 4th

Dear Mother,

Forgive me for writing when you requested that I not. I think, however, that it is my duty to give you some information about your granddaughter. I felt you would want that.

She is six months old now and she has definitely inherited your and Grandma Muller's eye-color: green as can be. She is pudgy as I know I was as a baby and her cheeks are big and round like soft balloons. Everyone wants to kiss them. I am sure you would be pleased to hold her, especially since she is your first grandchild.

I am hoping to arrange a visit to New York before the next year rings in. I would want you to meet Layla.

Love,
Rachel

March 15th

Dear Mother,

I was surprised to receive my last letter to you unopened. I'm assuming a postal error has been made.

Your granddaughter has begun crawling, not rapidly or for great distances, but enough that I or the nurse are forced to bring her back to the center of her playing blanket every few moments. She also has quite a pleasant voice, babbling rather like those pleasantly cooing babies in motion pictures. She repeats the syllable DaDa over and over. I am trying to teach her MaMa, but I think she knows that she has no need to call me since I am there for her every need.

I am also trying to teach her NaNa, the name I have chosen for her to call you. I hope you approve.

Love,
Rachel

April 2nd

Dear Mother,

I have decided to write again. Perhaps you will open this letter. I am not trying to change your mind about any of those things we talked about before my marriage. These letters serve

only one purpose. To give you information about your grand-
daughter. It would be unfair to make her pay for my decisions.

She is quite beautiful now and changing every day. I find that
she is also very bright because she recognizes everyone in the house-
hold now and that is an awful lot for a baby to remember. She
has conjured sounds of her own as names for everyone. There are
quite a lot of servants and relatives who come in and out. Her
gleaming smile, reminding me of Papa's, pulls everyone to her.

I am arranging to come for a short visit to New York. But I
will wait to hear from you before I make any specific dates.

Your Rachel

May 24th

Dear Mom,

I wonder why I am writing again. Perhaps I just cannot
believe that you would shun me so blatantly over and over. I am
not asking you to forgive me. I am merely trying to prevent
Layla from a rejection she should not have to bear. When she
gets older, how will I explain to her that her grandmother does
not want to know her? That her grandmother considers me
dead. Think about this, Mother. I am doing this for a small
helpless child who also carries your blood in her veins.

You should see how much she looks like you. She is standing
now and sometimes she attempts to take a step away from what-
ever she is holding onto. I have shown her your picture frequently
and she points to it and says NaNa. Doesn't this break your
heart? You are depriving yourself too. Please, Mother, I pray
that you will open this letter and respond. It is for her, not for
me. I know and accept that I cannot be your daughter anymore,
but this should not have anything to do with my darling Layla.

Rachel

June 16th

I do not expect you to open this one, Mother. But, for my own
sake, I am writing it.

I want you to know that you have finally had a great impression on me. This is what you have always wanted, isn't it? I have learned an important lesson from a mother like you. I have learned never to treat my daughter as you have treated me, not in the name of morality or common sense, or even love. And certainly not in the name of any religion. I will always be here for Layla and nothing, nothing, will change my mind on that, certainly not something as petty as whom she decides to marry.

It has always been your way or no way, hasn't it, Mother? Run things or run away from things is your motto. It is my turn to tell you I will never forgive you for sitting shiva for me and then for shunning your beautiful granddaughter. I can promise you that when she grows, she will know the kind of woman her grandmother is not: one with a mind of her own and not a mind that was given to her by an ideology interpreted from a book written thousands of years ago.

You love your god and your religion so much. You can have them. Have them for the rest of your life and see what comfort and joy they give you. I promise you it will never match the comfort and the joy that my Layla could have given you.

Goodbye.

R.

I'd never met my grandmother—Margaret Abramson—or any other members of my mother's family. I'd yearned to. I found out about them when I was ten, while snooping through some documents my father kept in his study. I'd thought my mother's parents were the Hobsons and that they'd died long before my parents met. My mother had supposedly grown up an only child in Ohio, which was where all her distant relatives had scattered, unreachable.

I remembered my father's expression—greenish, guilty—and his voice—hoarse, quiet: "My Layla, do you think you are grown-up enough to keep a big secret?" When I grew older, I learned that it wasn't really a secret; it just wasn't something anyone found proper to talk about. So I learned to be silent, but the fact that the truth was hidden made the union of my parents somehow shameful. And I never forgot that I was a direct result of that union.

Until I'd read the letters, I hadn't considered my mother's decision to marry my father as brave. I'd always viewed the situation from my point of view—which was the hurtful one of knowing that half of my family refused to acknowledge that I existed, that they found me offensive, and that the other half ignored the issue completely.

The letters now made me proud of my mother. The confusion I'd always had about her decision to give up her family was gone. I thought about what my mother would do if she were me, right then. Would she risk her life and the life of her unborn child to get out of Iran? Yes. Hadn't she risked everything to come to Iran all those years ago? She'd married my father, gone after the kind of freedom she believed in, and resisted the same kind of fanaticism that I was forced to escape from now. As I folded the letters neatly and placed my mother's Star of David, Dariush's wedding band, and his watch in the envelope, it struck me that the world had not changed all that much.

The following night—the eve of my departure—I took a couple of Valium Uncle had left and went to sleep early. The next thing I knew, Asya was shaking me awake. It was three A.M. Three hours left. I had to be at the airport at six. We had a lot of work to do.

Feri was ready. She'd spread all the bottles of foundation and powder and liner pencils and brushes neatly on the table. I sat in the chair, shivering. The electricity was still out, and the apartment was freezing. I slid my feet close to the warm, ancient brazier that was under the table. Feri draped one of her old plastic beauty-salon capes around my neck and handed me a cup of tea. Asya stood by the table too, assistant to her mother. I almost laughed. This felt like an operating room.

Feri and Amir had discussed my makeup extensively after the passport picture. He'd brought in an array of theatrical supplies that I couldn't imagine how he got his hands on. Suddenly Feri was pressing putty to my nose, molding, standing back to assess her work, consulting Asya with a look, molding again. Once satisfied, she began smearing foundation cream from my neck up; she must have used five different colors and just as many powders. Soon I felt like I was wearing one of those stifling rubber Halloween masks.

"All right," Feri said. "Now we must put on the glue for the beard. Keep very still, Layla." She rubbed a waxy-smelling glue on my jaw and cheek. Her face was only inches from my own. Her warm breath smelled like cardamom. She had a round pock-mark on the side of her nose. In a few hours, I thought, I would be alone. Feri would only be with me in my memories.

She began brushing cut hairs from Jamsheed's beard onto my face where she'd spread the adhesive. The idea was to make me look like a law-abiding Islamic man who clipped his beard rather than shaved it. "Don't scratch," she said. "The glue will come unstuck. Then you will have a splotchy beard and you will not look like a man at all. Besides, think of all my work."

"This is worse than poison oak," I said in English.

She stepped back, frowned. "Do you think I would put poison on your face?"

"No, Maman," said Asya. "It is a kind of rash she is talking about."

I smiled at Asya. "You'll do well in America."

"No smiling!" scolded Feri. "Your face must be still. And she is not going to America."

Finally, when I thought my back would crack in half from sitting in that hard chair, Feri was done. She exhaled and sat down, observing her work. A smile came slowly to her wide face. "Amazing," she said. "You *do* look masculine."

Asya handed me the mirror. It was true. I looked like a boy with a manly bit of stubble. My lips looked larger as they pro-truded from the black shadow, and my eyes looked bigger too. My nose popped out from my face like a soft beak, a nose that could definitely use some rhinoplasty by Western standards. I touched my jaw. It felt real, like Dariush's cheek when he didn't shave—like a Persian carpet when you brush your hand over it against the weave. I wished he could see me. What would he say? Would he want me to risk our baby this way? Stop it, I told myself. Don't think about him now at all. Don't be sad or unsure or preoccupied. Don't cry or sweat or lose your concentration.

Amir's knock rapped at the door, which meant it was after five; curfew was over. Amir saw me and his jaw dropped. "Unbelievable!" he said.

"I know," I said. I tried to smile, but my cheeks felt like they would peel away from the bones. "Ow!"

Feri quickly pressed her palms against my cheeks. "You must not make any sudden facial expressions."

"That's my fault," said Amir. "Sorry I couldn't find any spirit gum. This kind of glue won't make the beard come apart, but it will pull at the skin underneath. You'll find a special adhesive remover in the hotel room in Istanbul."

He looked at his watch. "Jamsheed should be here any moment. Time to get dressed, Layla."

In the bedroom, Feri and Asya bound my breasts with Ace bandages, making them ache and throb more than usual; they'd become startlingly full from my four-month pregnancy. Mariam had always teased me about how small they were, calling them mosquito bites. My belly looked enormous below the flattened breasts. "Oh no!" I said. "The clothing will never hide this stomach."

"Of course it will," said Asya, bending and holding open trousers for me to step into. "See? There." She fastened the waist. "The shirt and the loose jacket will hide everything. And you will be wearing a coat, too." She asked me to bend down so she could slip the eye patch over my head. It was awful, pressing against my eyeball like the tight blindfold I wore at the prison. I adjusted the strap and it loosened. Better. But I wished I'd worn the patch earlier, gotten used to the difference in depth perception.

Finally, I looked in the full-length mirror on the back of Feri's closet door. The costume worked. I was a simple servant in a hand-me-down polyester suit, a shirt with a pointy collar, and scuffed brown shoes that had been worn down by the master who'd once owned them. I turned to look at my profile. No pregnant belly; Feri had let the jacket out in the back just in case. I looked right. I felt terrible. Everything itched and throbbed; I felt like I was walking around in a full-body paper bag. Ironically, the only parts of me where there was any comfort were my plushly bandaged feet. Then came a faint flutter in my belly and I whispered, "Okay, sweetie. We're going."

They waited for me at the door. I'd planned many things I wanted to say to Feri, but all I was able to do was press her against me hard, inhaling the minty smell of her. There couldn't be any tears. Finally, Asya pulled me away from her mother and hugged me too; I whispered in her ear, "I'll see you in America," and she squeezed me as if this were a promise. Then Amir's hand was on the back of my neck. His touch felt like a caress, and my skin tingled. I looked at him and saw that sincere smile, the friendly grin that a teacher gives a troubled student before he slaps the final exam down on the desk. "I'll contact you at your father's in Cannes in a few weeks. I know you're going to make it." I nodded, my throat so swollen I couldn't speak. He turned to Jamsheed, whose thick brows were furrowed with seriousness and concern, and said, "Wait five minutes before you leave." Then Amir was gone, leaving behind a hole of loneliness and fear burning its way through my chest.

Thirty-Three

The Favor

The old couple and their son have been good to him, Dariush thinks. He does not know how long he has been here or why he is here, but they have been gentle and attentive. He knows they are Jewish; he has heard them praying. He wants to talk to them, but he is somehow disconnected from his body. His head spins and throbs when he is awake, which is not too often. He has tried to open his eyes, but nothing will come into focus and the vertigo worsens. The bandages around his head feel tight and moist.

They think he is in a coma. Perhaps he is. He often hears them talking about his injuries, how his brain has swelled, how he needs surgery. The son brings medicines and nutrients for the IV that Dariush feels taped onto his arm.

It seems that he has been here for some time because the noises from the street and the routine of the family have become familiar to him. He has a sense of the times of day, though the light in the room seems never to change. When he smells bread and cheese, he knows it is morning. When he smells rice, he knows it is midday, and the evenings smell like fruit. He often finds himself smelling morning, then morning again or evening, then midday. He assumes that he sleeps but he is not sure. He does not remember dreams. Perhaps his mind goes somewhere else where there are no memories or senses.

He knows he is in an old part of the city. Wooden wagons rattle along the street outside his window; mules bray and kitchen utensils clang against one another as they are being washed on the sidewalk. The smell of incense and candle wax is strong. It reminds him of the *madraseh* his grandmother made him attend on Fridays for religious instruction. He had hated it; the *mullah*s were cruel, always looking for reasons to beat the students' palms and knuckles with wooden sticks. One of those smelly *mullah*s was fond of sitting the young students on his lap and having them recite *suras* from the *Qoran* while he took his pleasure in a subtle manner. Dariush was only seven when it was his turn to do this, and after a few minutes, he asked the master why he was moving and breathing in such a way—was he sick? And the *mullah* scolded him, told him he was bad mannered and too inquisitive, told him if he mentioned their private lesson to anyone, he would be flogged. But Dariush had never been a timid child and certainly not one to keep quiet about anything that caught his interest or his suspicion. So he had gone straight home and told his parents everything, concluding with a question: "Tell me, Maman, what kind of prayer was *that*?" It was a story that they had recalled often over the years with much amusement. But it was also an event that marked Dariush's conscious distaste for the clergy. And now, in his semiconsciousness, he senses that he is in the midst of the men who hide their sins beneath the turbans and robes of religion.

He moans. His head burns again. Footsteps hurry toward him, and he hears things being moved around next to him, then a tug on his IV cord. Minutes later, the pain is gone. When he wakes again, he smells the crisp coolness of falling snow.

Sometimes he hears the family arguing in whispers, the woman trying to convince the others that having the soldier here is too dangerous and they must figure something else out. But the men tell her to be quiet, that they have no choice, that this is their duty to their people, to the diaspora. Dariush does not understand this at all, and he wants to tell them the woman is right. Some mistake has been made.

Then it all becomes clear. He hears Amir's voice. "Pleasure to meet you," it says to the family after another voice introduces them. "You have no idea how your help has truly benefited the security of Israel. The soldier will be leaving today. I thank you for this immense favor."

And before Dariush loses his link with the physicality of the apartment and slides into the empty space of sleep, he realizes that *he* is the favor Amir is talking about.

Amir edges closer to the sickbed. "He has not spoken at all, you say?"

"No, *agha*," says the old man. "Nor have we seen him open his eyes. His brain may be dead, my son says."

Amir is sure this is not true. He can *feel* Dariush thinking. Still, to look at him, one would not imagine he could recover. The grandmother will have a stroke when she sees his wasted body and translucent, grayish skin. Too bad for the old crone, Amir thinks with pleasure. The bandage around Dariush's head is bloody, though the family claims to change it twice a day. His crew cut has grown, and spikes of hair stick up like wheat around the bandage. Amir has an urge to touch him; maybe he is really not alive, he fancies. His neck suddenly feels hot, and he turns away. "All right," he tells the old man. "The car will be here to take him soon. If you do not mind, I will wait in your salon until it arrives."

"Of course." He bows slightly and ushers Amir through old French doors into the salon. "I will have my wife bring tea. Please sit down."

Amir can still see the sickbed from here. Everywhere he looks, it is in his peripheral vision. He wishes he had not come here. The men he has hired will transport Dariush to the grandmother's; there is no reason for his presence. He feels as if the limp body in the sickbed can hear his thoughts, and he tries to erase them from his mind. But he is unsuccessful.

A gaudy alarm clock on the table next to him ticks loudly; it begins to annoy him and he rubs his temples, clenches his jaw, and finally grabs the clock and stuffs it beneath a seat cushion. He still hears it.

He is tired. He will go home to sleep after this is done. Maybe he will go home now. Yes, that is a good idea. No. He must stay and make sure the deed is done, no loose ends. Suddenly, he sees movement out of the corner of his eye, from the sickbed! He is on his feet, pulse pounding, staring at his friend's body. Still as a corpse. He swallows, sits down. The chap is in a coma, he reminds himself.

"Damn you for being in a coma," he whispers, eyeing Dariush's chest as it inhales and exhales. "Die, you fucking bastard." The woman stands at his elbow with a tray bearing tea and lump sugar; she looks puzzled, and Amir feels dizzy as he looks up at her. "Are you all right, *agha?*"

"Of course, it's obvious. I'm fine. Leave the tray." Her lips tighten at his rudeness, and he feels like telling her that he has enough problems without having her spring an attitude on him; is this her thanks for the one hundred thousand dollars he smuggled out to her daughter in London? His hand itches to slap her until she cries bloody tears; he sweats in an effort to control himself. She leaves the room in a huff, and he gulps her bitter tea, then promptly breaks the gold-rimmed tea glass into two neat pieces.

He feels dizzy again. He leans his head back against the wall and closes his eyes. He hears snatches of the woman's tirade against him to her husband: "Insolent . . . arrogant . . . rude . . . unbearable . . . cruel . . ." They are not such bad words, he thinks. Honest, at least. There. His head feels better. The noon call to prayer swims to his ears and a breeze flutters his hair, which is strange, he thinks, because there is no window in this room. He opens his eyes and there, standing beside Dariush's bed, is the blind fortune catcher. His skin turns cold. He stands up and demands, "What are you doing here?" The blind man cocks his head, stretches his arm toward Amir, and beckons him to the bedside. Without thinking, Amir finds himself standing over Dariush, holding on to the fortune catcher's arm to steady himself; his head whirls and his stomach hurts. The blind man whispers in his ear, "*Aghayeh aziz*, you must not forget the dream, how you must obey your destiny. Look," he says, sweeping his hand over Dariush's body. "He is yours." Amir looks, then grips the bed's iron safety bar with his other hand—it is not Dariush there, but himself, lying comatose, his skin tinged with the blue of the near-dead. He hears his own voice in his ears: *So, Dasha, you are awake and you know what I have done to you and what I have won from you and still you want me gone.* His head spins, and he grips the fortune catcher's arm more tightly. "Do it," the blind man whispers. Suddenly, a crackling voice shouts, "What!" Amir looks to his left and blinks; it is the old woman, her mouth open, staring at him in horror. He turns to the fortune catcher but he has vanished, and Amir is gripping the IV pole instead of the blind man's arm. He is not dizzy anymore; everything is crystal clear. He feels the softness of the pillow against his other hand and slowly, he lifts it away from Dariush's face. He inhales deeply, suddenly, startling the old woman to take a little jump back. "You were killing him!" she says in a choked voice. Amir drops the pillow and shoves his shaking hands into his pockets and glares at her. "No, madam, I was not." She puts her hand to her chest; her expression is filled with loathing and fear. He returns to his seat on the sofa, stares at the sickbed. He hears the woman move quickly out of the room, but he is too distraught to worry about it. What can she do anyway? Call the *komiteh*? He begins to chuckle, then stops abruptly, his throat suddenly dry. What is the matter with him? He tries to swallow and wipes the sweat from above his lip. It is all right, he tells himself, I am just tired. Too much going on. Until the men arrive to remove Dariush, Amir avoids looking at the sickbed. He focuses on a scuff on the tip of his shoe and tries to remember exactly how this scuff occurred.

Thirty-Four

Layla

The boulevard near Feri's apartment was deserted. The sound of the dawn *Azan* swirled in the cold December air. Jamsheed opened the passenger door and I stepped over the gurgling water ditch into his Paykan. How wide the narrow street looked; how spacious the tiny car seemed. I'd grown so used to small spaces; I felt like a mouse in a cartoon. I slid down into the seat and rested my head against the seat back, so anxious now that my eyelids wouldn't stop fluttering.

Jamsheed drove slowly, sleepily. We didn't speak. I thought about nothing, about everything; my mind raced. When I focused on our whereabouts, we always seemed less close to the airport than I expected. I took slow breaths.

Finally, the Shahyad Monument loomed before us like an alien spaceship made of white marble, a massive carved structure that looked like an arch with bell-bottomed legs and a top hat. *Shahyad.* "In Memory of the King." Built by the shah himself to mark the entrance to Tehran. I thought of Mariam, how she'd scolded me for calling it that after I'd arrived this last time. "*Meydan-e-Azadi*," she'd said as we entered the rotary that surrounded the monument, and I pressed my cheek against the window to look to the top of it.

"What?" I'd said.

"Freedom Square, Layla," she'd said in English. "Don't call it Shahyad. You could get arrested."

These words and Dariush's swift military conscription at the airport had been my welcome to the new Iran. Hopefully, my leaving would be less unfortunate. I sat up in my seat. Jamsheed looked over and smiled. "Dariush used to talk to me about you. Did you know this?" I shook my head. "He said you made him *geej*."

"That's not good. No one likes to be dizzy."

"No!" Jamsheed said, his eyes bugging out with concern. "He loved this about you, how you could dance from place to place, people to people, America to Iran, so easily like that lizard who changes color. He was dizzy with your differences. He said you were a good actress who played parts of yourself depending on the scenery."

"Well," I said, having difficulty concentrating on Jamsheed's words. "I definitely have to be a good actress now." The airport was in sight. My stomach burned with fear. Okay, I thought. Fear is good. Dariush used to say that. About taking exams and playing tennis matches. Fear keeps you alert, the adrenaline moving.

Jamsheed pulled up to the curb behind a row of orange taxis regurgitating passengers and suitcases. He jumped out and emptied the trunk of my bags. Nausea washed over me as I opened the door and let myself out. Jamsheed handed me my carry-on, and I slung the strap over my shoulder. He put my small, beat-up Samsonite next to me. We shook hands and kissed cheeks. "Good trip," he said, looking at me with glistening, bloodshot eyes, then turning away sooner than I wanted.

It was only after he sped away from the curb that my hands, miraculously, stopped shaking and my heart slowed down. I inhaled deeply and composed myself. Now I was completely on my own. It reminded me of when my father would drop me off at school the first day—how, while he still held my hand and I could smell his cologne, I felt I couldn't bear it if he left me there alone, then suddenly when he was finally gone, I wasn't nervous anymore. Something inside me—maybe some kind of survival instinct—took charge. Or maybe it was just that I had no choice but to rely only on myself.

The airport terminal stretched out before me. There were three entrance doors: a middle one through which suitcases were sent to be searched for weapons, and the other two, one marked SISTERS for the women, the other marked BROTHERS for the men. I gave my bag to the official at the middle door and moved on to the BROTHERS line. The crowd had thickened. The eye patch skewed my vision, and I had trouble focusing. Pale faces reflected in the fluorescent lighting from inside the terminal. People were subdued, serious, whispering good-byes at the curb, inspecting their tickets. I glanced around to see if anyone watched me, if anyone noticed that I looked strange. Perspiration collected in my armpits despite the steel-cold air. There were too many people. I felt dizzy. I took a deep breath and remembered what Amir had said: that the crowd would frighten me; I hadn't been around so many people since the stoning. *Calm, Layla. Concentrate on the plan. Picture the checkpoints: weapons search, contraband search, ticket counter, luggage weighing and transfer, passport pick-up, passport stamping, body search, transit. Edge forward in line. Each step is closer to freedom.*

Finally, I was inside. My bags were searched by stern officials who barely looked up, then waved me on. Whispers echoed off the two-story-high ceiling. Outside, the sky was tinged with pink: the sun coming up. Would I be on my way to France when the sun came up again?

I edged forward behind a short man on crutches; a leg lost in the war. *Komiteh* officials, customs and immigration officials, and armed *pasdaran* bustled everywhere, their heels clicking sharply on the vast marble floor. They moved with exaggerated self-importance like extras in a slapstick movie, lethal little Chaplinesque officials. I remembered how, before the Revolution, I would arrive at Mehrabad with three or four large suitcases filled with expensive gowns and dresses, jeans and shorts. Someone was always sent to meet me at the plane. Armed with a large wad of *touman*s for bribes, my escort would whisk me through immigration and customs, where my bags were marked in chalk with a big **X** that said they'd been checked when, in fact, they hadn't been at all.

I shoved my hands inside the pockets of my rumpled wool coat. Feri had brushed hair along my knuckles, but my fingers were too tapered to look convincingly masculine. I placed my feet wider apart in a manly stance and set my jaw in what I thought was a bold, arrogant look.

I was getting the hang of it when I noticed a young woman watching me from the roped-off well-wishers' corner. She threw me quick, frightened glances, then fiddled frantically with her *chador* until only a portion of her right eye peeked furtively out of a triangle made by the cloth. She seemed terrified. Did I know her? Worse: Did she know me? Recognize me? I tensed, ready to run. I looked behind me to map out a quick course to the exit doors. Glancing back, I saw that the woman wasn't there anymore. Oh God, I thought, she's gone to get some official. A faint rattle of chains came to my ears, and I whipped my head around, expecting to see handcuffs coming toward me, but it was just the man behind me fingering his key ring. I swallowed dryly and looked again to where the woman had been. There she was, a little to the right, standing close to an older woman with angry gray eyes and wisps of brittle white hair that fell out at the peak of her *chador*. Her mouth moved in conversation with the younger woman, but she kept her eyes on me. Then she raised her thin hand and shook it in my direction, wrinkling her lips and mouthing curses at me. My eyes met the younger woman's again; she gathered her *chador* even more tightly around her face and turned her back to me. That movement and the way she edged nearer to the old woman woke me up. My God. What an ass I was. I'd been concentrating so intently on projecting the correct masculine image and I'd forgotten the most crucial thing: that a man must never look squarely at any woman who isn't his mother, his wife, his sister, his niece, his daughter. It was worse than just bad manners; it was sexual harassment, it was sinful. I could get arrested for it.

I stared at the floor, disgusted with myself. I had to *think* like a man, not just pose as one. I had to imagine that women didn't exist, to let my gaze drift and jump over them as if they were invisible or I was partially blind. I'd learned to do this with men. So now I just had to switch—look at men instead of women. That's all. Easy. I tried. There was a guy, about my age, a few paces in front of me, flipping through his passport. He felt my gaze and looked up. Our eyes met. It was uncomfortable for me, sort of like keeping an ice cube on my tongue, but I did it and he looked away first. From then on, I kept my back to the well-wishers' corner.

I edged closer to the three customs officials searching our suitcases. They looked bitter about their jobs but hungry to catch someone smuggling contraband: gold, gems, carpets, antiques, dollars. The Revolution had messed up the economy so badly that anything was worth more *outside* Iran than inside.

An old man with trembling hands blushed badly while one of the searchers emptied the contents of his faded Adidas bag onto the table. The old man was apparently incontinent; the table overflowed with large cloth diapers and plastic panties. All that cloth must have made the searcher suspicious. What better place to hide things?

Then it was my turn. I'd memorized everything in my suitcase: another brown suit and yellowed shirt with a tiny hole in the elbow, a gray sweater with a red stripe across the chest (left over from some aristocratic ski buff), two pairs of brown socks, a pair of rubber slippers, a muslin prayer mat folded in triangular fashion with a chipped prayer stone in the middle, a cracked vinyl trouser belt, and two shoe boxes wrapped in brown paper, one containing roasted watermelon seeds and the other, golden raisins. The official sized me up, then gave the bag a cursory search. After all, I was one of many poor young illiterates in a too-big hand-me-down suit whose idea of contraband was probably a pound of precious sugar. I was a member of the masses. Feri had even made me eat onions for dinner and puff on a few Tir cigarettes so I'd have an authentically "city odor," an acrid, pungent scent that reminded me of the bazaar and the gardener's shed in the late afternoon when the gardener took off his shoes to rest.

It was working.

The searcher waved me on to the ticket counter.

A bored man weighed my suitcase and transferred it to a conveyer belt. Bloodshot eyes scanned my ticket.

Now to the passport counter.

As I walked, I looked upward to the balcony. The *pasdaran* stood at regular intervals, automatic rifles poised, mouthing into walkie-talkies, eyes darting, taking in everything. How many potential bullets? How many could reach me?

Shivers scuttled over my scalp.

The line moved more quickly here. I cleared my throat and gave my name in the raspy voice I'd practiced. The immigration official reached behind him to a rack of pigeonholes. "Here it is," he said politely, dropping a passport on the counter. I took it and opened it, flipping quickly to the picture just to make sure. There I was, Javad Mahmoudi, a cook. I couldn't help it; I smiled, stretching the sore skin around my mouth. "Thank you, *agha*," I said in formal Farsi. He even flashed me a small smile.

Relief.

But I warned myself: *Stay alert. It's not over.*

When I joined the next line, a familiar voice floated to my ear. It was just the snatch of a word, an intonation, maybe even only a whispered vowel, but it was so familiar. It came from the luggage search table. I scanned the distant faces. Then I saw her, a navy silk scarf draped over her small head, her long, manicured nails bare of polish, nervously scratching the side of her nose every few seconds. Katayoon.

I pivoted quickly, putting my back to her. This was terrible. I'd never thought of the possibility that someone who was practically family might appear at the airport. Auntie Katy would recognize me—man *or* woman. I had to make it upstairs to the transit area before she got any closer to me. I was sure she would depart from a different gate—on her way to Europe, visa for France or England probably in perfect order.

So she'd finally given up on Mariam and on keeping her property from the fanatics. I was glad. It was for the best.

The strap of my carry-on was slippery against my perspiring palm. I inched forward in the line and glanced back at Katy again. She'd irritated the search official. Her face was pale. He rummaged furiously through one of her two matching suitcases, pulling out clothing, the worst kind of clothing: short-sleeved silk pastel dresses and flowered peignoirs. He crumpled these with his rough hands, feeling every inch of them, looking disgusted. He knew what kind of woman he was dealing with; he would have known even before he'd opened her bag and seen the Western clothing. Even Katy's *manteau* was expensive and personalized, with flared sleeves, massive shoulder pads, and expert pleats down the back.

Soon Katy's suitcase looked like a disemboweled animal. The official, whose greasy mop of hair hung over his forehead, opened all her cosmetics—compacts, tubes of cream, a shampoo container, nail polish bottles—and smelled each one, snorting and smirking at them all. I wanted to tear his eyes out.

Katy had licked and bitten at her lips so much, they looked blotchy even at my distance. She brought her hand up to her temple and rubbed in tiny circles; it was something she did before one of her headaches. She probably could have gone for a drink right then. I hoped she hadn't been foolish enough to hide liquor in one of those suitcases. I could just see her filling a nail-polish-remover bottle with scotch and complimenting herself on her ingenuity.

The official asked her a question. She thrust her chin up emphatically in the Persian gesture for no. She was responding in as few words as possible. That was odd. Talking herself in and out of situations was Katy's specialty. My stomach filled with butterflies. She was terrified; I saw it in her face. God help her, she was up to something.

The searcher emptied Katy's second suitcase, which contained, among more clothing (bright sweaters mostly), a maroon leather-bound photo album that I knew contained pictures of Mariam growing up. I was in some of those pictures, and so was Dariush. I longed to look at them: the one of a bare-bottomed infant Mariam on a cream-colored satin pillow, the one of Dariush cross-legged on the hood of his father's Porsche, the one of me and Mariam ready to dive off the pontoon at the Karadj Dam. The official flipped resentfully, disapprovingly, through the album, inspecting our pre-Revolution lives, probably smudging our young, happy faces with his oily fingers.

My line moved forward. Only two more people left in front of me. I tried to concentrate on my role, shoving my hands in my pockets and clearing my throat gruffly. But only about half a minute later, I turned to glance subtly over at Katy again. The official was taking out her shoes now; he inspected each one, looking inside the toe and then banging the heel against his table. I choked down a laugh. I'd heard about them doing this, tapping the heels of everyone's shoes, as if a James Bond transmitter could be hidden there. I was beginning to feel a little better about Katy's situation. The searcher had obviously reached the bottom of her bag. Soon he'd send her off to the passport counter. It would take her a while to put her things back, and I would be gone to the next checkpoint by then.

Suddenly, she was paler than ever. She cupped her hand over her mouth as if she were gagging. The searcher was tapping a pair of scarlet sandals, ones even I remembered from a few years back when platform shoes were so popular. He put one of the shoes aside, but began prying the heel off the other one. Twisting and pulling, his face turning red. With a snap that reached my ears, the heel came off. I clenched my jaw, heard my teeth scrape together. Out of the hollowed appendage poured a stream of gold and two sparkling droplets: her diamond rings, no doubt.

It seemed like everyone noticed. The airport became even more hushed. An armed guard stepped forward in two large strides. Katy cringed, putting her hands up as if to protect her throat. The *pasdar* used the point of his gun to fiddle with the gold chains on the table, examining them. The searcher scooped the jewelry into a plastic bag. If I remembered correctly, each of those diamonds was eight carats and "D" color rated; Katy could buy a nice house in New York with the proceeds from those stones. The searcher looked at Katy with disgust. She was crying now. She looked so much like Mariam when she cried, her eyes becoming small and dark. Her lips moved: Forgive me, forgive me, she said. I looked at the floor, embarrassed. Then I started praying. When I finally had the courage to look up, a female customs official was leading Katy away. The guard with the machine gun was close behind. I was breathing hard.

"Your passport, *agha*." I spun around. My God, I'd fallen completely out of my role. I searched the clerk's face, but he looked bored. I wrinkled my brow and slid my passport across the high counter. Looking it over, the clerk said, "They got that woman good, *hahn*?"

"Yes," I said, trying to sound delighted, like a good revolutionary. I rolled my tongue around in my mouth to coax up some saliva. I dared to speak again. "What'll they do with her?"

He snorted. "It's up to them," he said, shrugging and waving me on.

I made my way to the escalator and looked for Katy surreptitiously. There she was. Still gripped tightly by the woman guard, deep in conversation with a turbaned man behind a counter near the well-wishers' corner. The *mullah* listened, with a smug expression, to what looked like an effusive explanation— interspersed with pleas—from Katy. I wished she would stop that. The *mullah* put his hand up to silence her, and the woman guard shook her jerkily to shut up. The *mullah* then began what looked like preaching. Listen, Katy, just listen, I begged silently. Let him do his speech and maybe he'll let you go.

As I climbed the escalator, I could see what was going on better. The plastic bag containing the jewelry lay on the counter between Katy and the *mullah*; he kept stabbing it with his fingers as if he were testing a rodent for signs of life. Katy nodded her head a few times, wiped her tears, and moved, taking little worried steps like Edith Bunker toward the well-wishers' area. She raised her hand to signal someone. The woman guard followed at a distance. *Agha* Sayrafi, a cousin of Katy's, emerged from the crowd.

I reached the balcony. Instead of going straight back to the next line, I dared to linger. I lit a cigarette and held it close to my palm, like a cool guy. I glanced at the stationed guards; they ignored me. Katy spoke to *Agha* Sayrafi frantically, gesturing with her hands. He reached into his breast pocket, pulled out a long envelope, and handed it to her; she walked quickly back to the *mullah* with it. Out of the envelope came a stack of bills, 10,000-*touman* notes, judging by the size. She counted them: twenty—200,000 *toumans*. At the pre-Revolution exchange rate (when *toumans* were worth something), it was almost $30,000. The *mullah* stashed the notes beneath the counter, but he wasn't smiling. He shook his head slowly and clasped his hands in front of him. Katy spoke rapidly, emphatically, obsequiously: a hand on her chest, head bent, a small bow. What was she trying to convince him to do now? Tentatively, while she continued to speak, she reached for the plastic bag containing her jewelry, but the *mullah* nonchalantly pulled the bag away. He was talking now, explaining something, rolling back on his heels like a lecturing professor. I got it! The money had been a fine (the amount probably determined indiscriminately by the *mullah*) for trying to smuggle the contraband. Apparently, however, the fine didn't also cover the *return* of her jewelry. They were negotiating. Katy kept gesturing to where *Agha* Sayrafi still stood, his face ashen. I was becoming annoyed with her. Was she going to get *him* in trouble now? Why didn't she just give up?

Finally, and to my surprise, the *mullah* reached into the bag and took out the diamonds. He gave them to the woman guard. Katy thanked him profusely, her hand on her heart, bending her head so her nose almost touched the top of the counter. She wiped tears again. The *mullah* waved her away like he was telling a dog to go lie down. The woman guard took Katy's arm again and led her over to *Agha* Sayrafi. She dropped the rings into his hand, then let the guard lead her back toward her suitcases. She'd made it—though a lot poorer. I stepped on my cigarette butt and moved shakily on, now with nothing to think of but myself again.

Long line. Too far away to spot the official with the medical bracelet. Perspiration under my chest bandages tickled like slow-moving bugs. I craned my neck to see ahead. Once in a while, the official's arm emerged from behind a curtain and beckoned to the next passenger. Shirt cuffs covered his wrists. The man who'd been behind me in the passport line was now in front of me. We looked at each other but said nothing. His eyes blinked and winked spasmodically; his jaw muscle throbbed inside his cheek. No one spoke at all. We shuffled forward like homeless on a bread line. I smoked from my package of Tir cigarettes, lighting the next from the last, careful not to inhale, thinking of the baby. The man behind me cleared his throat over and over, kept spitting into a trash can next to the wall. Everyone had heard stories about the body search, the worst ones about the officials who poked gloved fingers into body cavities, searching for contraband. They'd heard, just as I had, that desperate people had taken to swallowing gold coins and gems in Iran that could be retrieved later, safely in some European bidet.

It took five cigarettes, smoked down to the last string of bitter tobacco, to reach the curtain. When the body searcher beckoned to the man in front of me, who farted loudly as he stepped into what looked like a long dressing room, I was finally able to see clearly both of the official's wrists.

No medical bracelet.

I knew what I had to do. Fall down, Amir had said. Pretend you're sick.

I couldn't do it. My knees wouldn't buckle. The baby fluttered against my belly as if urging me to make the move, but I just stood there, my heart hammering against my chest, pulse roaring in my ears, blinding me. I was frozen in panic. Waiting for a miracle.

"Brother, it is Hassan," said a deep voice in front of me. I focused as a newly arrived official poked his head inside the dressing room. "Sorry I am late. My lousy car wouldn't start." He leaned against the door frame, scratched his nose. His eyes locked on mine briefly, wide eyes full of alarm. His chest heaved as if he'd been running. His wrist gleamed silver; the medical bracelet.

Now I felt like I could faint.

The curtain jerked open. The body searcher smiled mockingly into his friend's face. "You should buy an Iranian car, then you won't have so much trouble." The searcher named Hassan—my searcher—chuckled at the joke.

Hassan slapped his crony on the shoulder. "Go on home, brother. You look tired. I'll take this one," he said, gesturing to me. The body searcher pulled Hassan close and whispered into his ear for almost a minute. Hassan nodded a few times; it seemed they were talking about some procedural thing. Finally the body searcher left, and Hassan and I went behind the curtain.

In a rapid motion, Hassan grasped my upper arms. Our faces were close. Mint on his breath. Forefinger to his lips in a sign to remain silent. He pointed to the wall on his left and cupped his ear in a listening motion. Loudly, theatrically, he said, "Take off your coat, brother." Muffled women's voices came from beyond the wall, one saying something about expensive perfume and the other whining softly in response. I understood we were adjacent to the women's body-search room and that we had to be careful about what we said; we had to pretend that everything in our dressing room was proceeding normally.

So I took off my coat. Hassan took a step back and appraised me, nodding his head, impressed with my disguise. "Put your bag on the table," he said gruffly, the voice not matching his sympathetic eyes. He pretended to rummage through my bag, saying, "What's this?" and "What's in here?" every so often. It was funny to watch him, his hands skittering over and diving into my bag randomly, without any purpose. It reminded me of the old radio dramas in which sound effects were created in the studio to enhance the story. I wanted to burst out laughing. Amir had been right: This guy was on our side!

"Put your arms out," he said. I didn't comply, thinking there was no reason to; no one could see us. He said, a bit louder, "I said put your arms out." His eyes glanced off the curtain behind me. I guessed he thought a *pasdar* might step into the dressing room to tell him something. It was possible. I'd seen it happen while waiting in line. Hassan was being careful, taking no chances. I knew the pose; I put my arms out like a child playing airplane. "Turn around, brother," he said. I began to do so, but he stopped me suddenly, hands gripping my upper arms, bringing them to my sides. I'd been staring beyond his shoulder (I was a bit taller than he) to the exit curtain, beyond which I assumed was the transit area. But now I looked at his face; he was staring, stunned, at my midsection. Slowly, his eyes mesmerized, he eased his hand from my arm to my swollen abdomen. He looked at me, his eyes suddenly red and glassy. He whispered, "May God take care of you." And he used the Farsi word for God, not the Arabic one, not the Islamic one, not *Allah*. The word from ancient times.

I managed to nod slightly. I felt tremendous pity for him, for the fact that he'd been forced to play a despicable role in order to survive, for the fact that his family was far away, for his loneliness. I hoped the money Amir had promised him would free him, too.

"All right, brother," he said hoarsely. "Have a good journey."

I closed my eyes briefly in relief. It was almost over.

As luck had it, our wait in the transit lounge was short. Soon we were inching along the aircraft aisle, looking for our seats. I had a window seat, and the space next to me was empty, so far. I had to urinate badly; this, despite the fact that I'd made sure not to drink any liquids since dinner the night before because I knew I couldn't fake peeing into a urinal. I quickly went to the bathroom. In the mirror, I still looked unrecognizable and masculine. I'd worried that my beard had become patchy, but it hadn't. Unbuttoning my shirt, I found that the skin on my chest where the binding ended had become chafed. My feet throbbed and felt swollen, but I was afraid to remove my shoes in case I couldn't get them back on. Since Hassan had so easily become aware of my pregnancy, I decided it would be prudent to wear my coat or keep it on my lap at all times.

As I returned from the bathroom, I noticed that the seat next to me had been filled by a man with sparse black hair. I hoped to God he wasn't the talkative type and prepared at least to pretend to sleep the entire five and a half hours just in case. When I came around and saw the man's face, I was so stunned I actually swung my body away as if I could run off the plane. Instead, I bumped one of the veiled flight attendants so roughly that she fell shoulder first into the opposite seat. It was a stupid, involuntary reaction on my part. "I'm sorry, very sorry," I said in my deep voice; I almost took her arm to help her up, but realized at the last minute that it was inappropriate to touch her. She was mad, sweating, tense. "Get in you seat, *agha*! We are almost leaving." So I bit my tongue, turned around, and climbed over the very

same blind fortune catcher whose foreboding predictions I had
fled on the night of the Fire Jumping so long ago. I sat in my seat
and waited for him to discover—with those supernatural senses of
his—who I was. But he said nothing, just stared into the blackness of his lenses, resting his palms neatly on his thighs. I pressed
myself against the wall and window of the cabin, making sure not
a thread of my clothing touched him. After a moment, he leaned
slightly toward me and said, "Excuse me, sir. Have you been on
an airplane before?"

"Yes," I said.

He smiled. "This is my first time. I am a little nervous."

I wanted to say, Well, if the plane was going to go down,
wouldn't you know it already? Instead, I said, "No need to be
nervous." I told myself to shut up, but I had to know. "To where
are you traveling, sir?"

He sat up straight, smiled broadly, showing the rotten teeth I
remembered so well, and whispered with the glee of a child, "I
am going to America."

"Congratulations," I said, still so stunned that I felt like a
wooden ventriloquist's puppet. I finally turned my head to get a
good look at him. He was a little thinner than I remembered.
His beard was still spotted with old food, and he smelled like
mutton. His clothing was different; instead of tattered, baggy
garments, he wore a forties-style moth-eaten pin-striped suit. I
leaned over and looked at his feet, remembering the cloth shoes
he'd worn so long ago; someone had fitted him with square-toed
half-boots. He looked ridiculous and pathetic. Had I conjured
up an unrealistic fear of this man?

Then he spoke again. "I apologize for taking your head away
with my talking, but something extraordinary has happened to
me this morning—I must tell someone."

"Please, go ahead."

"I have been blind since a young age, but suddenly, by the
grace of *Allah*, I am seeing very slightly the light of day from the
corners of my eyes. I feel, in my *del*, that my sight is returning."

"Wonderful news," I said, though not as enthusiastically as I'd
planned. "I will pray for you, *agha*."

He bowed slightly. "Thank you very much."

As Amir had warned me, a team of *pasdaran* made a final security-check walk-through of the cabin, harassing passengers with their glaring stares and loaded Uzis. I explained to the blind man what was going on, that we should be quiet. He didn't look like the dreaded fortune catcher to me at all anymore, just one of the many overexcited, idealistic immigrants on his way to the golden country. I looked out the window, bit the inside of my cheek, and concentrated on the tarmac, where I spotted Auntie Katy, some distance away, climbing the steps to another plane. I smiled, then cursed myself for causing the skin on my face to pinch painfully.

We took off. It was the tenth of *Azar*, the Month of Fire, 1360. December the third, 1981. Tehran faded slowly from sight. I'd watched this scene through wistful tears almost every year of my life. Now my eyes were dry. I peered toward the south of the city, toward the cemetery where Dariush lay in a white shroud beneath the ground near the others I'd lost, even my mother. My eyes were still dry. I was not leaving them all behind, I told myself; they were with me, somewhere in the air I breathed, in the breezes that would caress me, in the cells that multiplied in my womb.

The Shahyad Monument became smaller and smaller, became finally a toy marking the entrance to a toy city. Mount Damavand, ancient and dormant, poked up through a cluster of clouds; a snow-covered cone, a funnel of pearly silk, a pyramid veiled in a white *chador*.

I closed my eyes and felt the plane climb and bank and climb. And I didn't open them until the pilot announced we had cleared Iranian airspace.

Thirty-Five

Maman Bozorg

When my granddaughter Mariam was ten years old, she willfully disfigured herself. A terrible burn from the steam of a samovar; the large, dappled scar remains on her thigh to this day. She claimed it was an accident, that the urn had been improperly placed in a servants' congregation room where she had gone to retrieve something from a closet. But I knew better.

Still, we thanked *Allah* that the misfortune had not been worse. The servants were punished for their negligence and a nurse hired to sit beside Mariam. She received a great deal of attention and sympathy from everyone—daily visits from Katayoon and Layla and Dariush, visitors all during the Friday Sabbath, and flowers and gifts arriving at the house every day. The wound was quite serious, blistered and oozing yellow liquid. She was unable to walk for the better part of the summer months. I have no doubt she was in great pain, much more than she had foreseen. I found myself amazed and somewhat admiring of the feat she had endured; for once, she had risen above her own meekness.

But I wondered at her sanity. My family had not been free of mental illness, though its occurrence had been carefully guarded, since knowledge of such a thing could jeopardize the marital opportunities for all the women in the family. I remember my cousin Bahram and his hallucinations of *div*s chasing him. So often, the night watchmen were made to search the gardens for hours to find Bahram huddled against a wall or beneath a bush, motionless as a frightened animal, hushing everyone so as not to alert the *div*s to his whereabouts. Finally, the *div*s apparently captured him and mangled him with their monster teeth, though no one was witness to this. Bahram was found bleeding in the dirt. The wounds were superficial—scratches to his face and leg. But he never recovered. He walked crookedly, as if his bones had been broken, and kept one eye closed, claiming the *div* had eaten it. The doctors assured his parents that the eyeball was in excellent condition and that no bones or muscles had been affected. Bahram was finally sent away to the mental hospital south of the city. It was our duty not to speak of him.

But Mariam did indeed recover from her wound, and I put my concerns aside.

Until the news of Dariush's death.

I had never seen such lunatic grief in a person. And I had seen a great deal of mourning in my life. A certain measure of wailing and sobbing and chest-beating is beneficial. How else can one release the pain? I have known several widows who took to pounding their heads against a wall and some women who screamed like gypsies and others who wore black for the remainder of their lives. All of these acts seemed eventually to comfort. But Mariam was not comforted. Her grief for the death of her cousin was endless and extreme.

She whined, she wept, she wailed. She scratched herself, tore her clothing, refused to bathe. She ate and ate, using her hands like a servant and allowing her tears and mucus to drip into her food. She conversed with herself in childish voices and would not look anyone in the eye. I tried everything to reach her. I called for her old *naneh* to come; perhaps the child needed some physical comfort. But Mariam would not allow the *naneh* to touch her. I called that mother of hers. She came, but without any hope in her heart. "I have been trying to reach her for years," she said, sipping tea with trembling hands. "Ever since she returned so suddenly from Switzerland. But, *Haji-khanoom*, she does not think much of me. Perhaps she has heard too many slurs against me for too long." She dared to squint at me. But I remained composed. I would not waste my energy on her. I wanted her to speak to her daughter. That was all. "She will refuse, I assure you," she said.

Indeed, Mariam bolted the door and remained silent as an invisible *jenn*.

I contemplated revealing the truth to my granddaughter. I could not endure two weeks or more of such behavior. But I stopped myself. Nothing could go wrong if I wanted my grandson home. And Mariam was too unstable to trust with information; there was no telling what she might do in her ignorance. The Jew would have to confirm that Layla was gone, first.

Finally, the news came. They were bringing him! Within the hour. I dismissed all the servants except for my trusted Firoozeh, who knows her livelihood is in my hands and will go along with everything. She prepared my grandson's bedroom while I went to tell Mariam.

She fainted to the floor. I had no choice but to watch until she recovered. What was I to do? An old woman with such terrible aching joints? It was not long before she opened her eyes. Still she did not grasp my meaning. I spoke slowly. "Our Dariush has been found," I said rather loudly. She rose from the floor, and I gave her a sugar cube for energy. "Such wonderful news," I continued. "We buried the wrong person. He has been in a tent hospital this whole time." She seemed to comprehend me, so I told her everything as I wanted her to know it. "We must hide him. He is still a deserter. We cannot tell anyone that he is here. It seems he is wounded badly, unconscious. We must take care of him ourselves. If he wakes, I do not want you to talk to him of Layla or anyone else. You know how he is; I do not want him to do anything that might jeopardize his life again. Mariam, are you hearing me?"

Well, of course she was. And there! She seemed quite her normal meek self again.

They brought my grandson into my house, those filthy, rough men, as if he were a slaughtered lamb with all the blood drained out and feeling nothing. I swear I will have the Jew flogged if I ever see him again. My Dariush! He looked like a corpse! The two men who brought him claimed merely to have been paid to transport him, and they took no responsibility for his condition. For once, thank *Allah* for Mariam. She was an excellent nurse to her cousin. Without a word, she brought sponge and soapy water and cleaned his body and face. She was calmer than I have ever seen her. There was not one wrinkle of dissatisfaction on her face, while I was quivering inside with worry. She removed the bandage—such a wide-mouthed wound! I realized I would have to find a doctor who could be bribed to stay quiet.

I cannot imagine that my grandson will ever wake up.

Thirty-Six

Layla

The Istanbul Hilton was more low-key than I'd expected. I was worried that a bellhop or the concierge would stop me as I walked down the long corridor toward the rooms. What was a raggedy young man with a sinister-looking eye patch doing in a place like this? After all, the cab driver had raised his eyebrows when I'd told him where to take me. "Hilton?" he'd questioned, pronouncing it *Heeltawn*. But at the hotel no one gave me a second look except for the shoe shiner, who offered me a seat in his high chair. I smiled a little and waved my hand in polite denial. By now, my feet felt like carved roasts. I made my way to the room number I'd memorized. Two-four-one. I knocked three times, paused, knocked twice. A woman opened the door and gently pulled me in. She was tall, dressed in an elegant houndstooth suit, high heels, and noisy jewelry. Without looking directly at me, she grabbed my bags and ushered me to a chair. "Are you all right? Are you in pain? Do you need a doctor?" Her English was perfect, British intonations, slight Arab accent. She spoke softly but directly. She didn't seem nervous, just very serious. It was clear that we were not going to strike up even the most superficial of friendships.

"No, I don't need a doctor. But some aspirin might help."

She walked to the bathroom, her pointy heels wiggling slightly in the plush carpet. The room was otherwise drearily furnished—dark, heavy furniture, maroon and brown paisley bedspread and drapes. I heard the water running in the bathroom. She brought me two aspirin and said, "The bathroom contains toiletries and medical supplies." She slid open the closet door. "Blue jeans, a heavy sweater, and an overcoat. Forgive me if the sizes are incorrect. I was told you were large."

"No," I said. "Just pregnant."

She had no reaction or, rather, her nonreaction was a clear reaction. She didn't seem surprised or horrified or even joyful. She seemed frozen, without expression, like a mannequin. Slowly, the way an epileptic returns from a trance, life came back into her eyes, and she said, in the same humdrum voice, "Underthings are in the duffel bag on the bed. I was not directed to purchase shoes." I was sure I heard a slight tremble in her voice.

"That's right," I said, sticking my legs out in front of me. "These are the only ones that'll fit." I'd tried to make my voice a little light; maybe we could at least share a smile. She looked at my enormous shoes, then up at my face again. No smile. I noticed that she'd drawn her lipstick line a bit beyond her lips to give the impression that they were fuller. "Now," she said, walking over to a desk, where she picked up a small leather pouch. "These are your documents. Your passport, your visa for France, your airplane tickets, and some francs." She dropped the pouch on the bed next to a medium-sized duffel bag. "You must leave the bags you brought from Tehran in this room and take only essentials in the duffel. Do you understand? Am I speaking too fast? Is my accent difficult to make out?"

"No, no. I'm clear on everything." I was dying to ask her why my pregnancy had thrown her off. Hadn't Amir told her? Obviously not. Was it against "secret agent policy" to transport women with fetuses? Well, Amir had made me promise that I wouldn't ask her anything, nor reveal anything about myself to her.

"I suggest you order room service this evening and for breakfast. You do not have the proper clothing for dining downstairs."

"I'll probably sleep through dinner."

"You must eat. Energy is important at this point. Your flight leaves tomorrow morning at eleven. Please leave the hotel no later than nine o'clock. Do not check out; I will do that later. Do you have enough Turkish lira for the cab fare?"

"Yes," I said, now wanting her to leave and take her iciness with her.

She reached into her Chanel bag and handed me a small piece of paper. "This is a number you may call only in an emergency. Please memorize and flush."

"Okay," I said, feeling like a drug dealer.

"Do you have any questions?"

"Yes. But none that you would answer," I said, smiling even though it hurt like hell.

Still no change of expression. Maybe the Mossad was already manufacturing androids, I thought.

"Good luck," she said just before she hung the DO NOT DIS-TURB sign on the door handle and left.

The bathroom was indeed stocked with anything I could possibly need. Bandages and cotton swabs, scissors and tweezers, shampoo and conditioner, blow dryer and round hairbrushes for styling, makeup and bath gel, perfume and body cream.

It took two hours to peel off my clothing, remove the fake hair, the putty nose, the three-inch-thick foundation, and to soak in a warm bath then rinse in a hot shower. I made myself concentrate on the grooming, and whenever thoughts of Dariush or Feri or Asya and Jamsheed—even Mariam—came to me, I pushed them away. My throat often swelled with tears, but I swallowed them. There would be plenty of time for that.

I should have known better, but I ordered a hamburger from the room service menu. The patty was lamb meat and the ketchup was clumpy. The chips were homemade; I ate them all and flipped through the items in the leather pouch. Everything she said was there. The American passport was in my name. I was Layla Bahari, the American, again. The picture was one Amir had taken of me without any theatrical makeup. The plane ticket would take me first to Paris, then to Nice.

It had just grown dark when I took two Valium and climbed under the bedcovers. I fell asleep imagining Feri and my father standing on either side of me; I stretched my arms toward them, but my fingers wouldn't reach. I woke in the night to sounds of laughter in the hallway; I didn't know where I was at first and I yelled out, "All right. I will sign!" I must have been dreaming of the prison. I cried softly into my pillow for some moments, then drifted off again until the sun woke me.

I dressed in the blue jeans, which fit around my waist, but were clearly too baggy everywhere else. The sweater reached down to the middle of my thighs and the sleeves to the tips of my fingers. I'd rebandaged my feet the night before, and I slid them into the brown shoes, which now, below the jeans, looked enormous. I looked in the full-length mirror and saw a tall, dumpy pin-headed woman. But it didn't matter. I was free. Best of all, I didn't have to wear *anything* on my head!

The flight to Paris was long. A woman from Kansas sat next to me, told me minute details about every one of her eighteen grandchildren while she knitted booties for a new one. When she insisted I learn her special purl stitch, I was ready to tear her hair out, but I persevered and held the needles between my fingers and managed, finally, an entire row. Well, I thought, this was better than thinking about how I'd just spent three months of my life in hell and about how I was going to explain it all to my father, who'd probably suffered a nervous breakdown since I'd disappeared. Knitting was just fine. "I'm going to have a baby," I suddenly said to the old woman. Her face lit up. "Oh dear! That's wonderful news. Now you can make him some booties."

"Her," I said. "I'm sure it's a girl."

"A mother knows," she said, nodding, making her jowls jiggle.

It was true. I believed my child was a girl. Feri had agreed when I told her. "No pimples around your mouth," she said. "Of course you will have a girl." I'd decided she would be a strong girl who would grow up without any of the illusions I'd been brought up with. A little friend who, small as she was, understood the real reasons why things happened in the world. I imagined her with a deep honey complexion and amber eyes like her father's. I would tell her the truth and she would confront the world sensibly, never afraid, never in danger, because she would be able to take care of herself. I would call her Rachel, of course.

In Paris, I stood on line at passport control and sweated. Amir had told me not to worry, but it was tough to do, standing there with a forged passport burning the tips of my fingers. Then suddenly, a customs official came alongside the line and addressed us in English, "Passengers with American passports, this way please," and she pointed to an opened gate to customs. I went to hand her my passport, but all she wanted was to see the cover. There were about fifteen of us; we were waved through.

In Nice, I really began to sweat.

I was going to see my father.

Thirty-Seven

The Many Gods

Jacob pulls on his cigarette. "Your audacity amazes me, Amir," he says, sitting back into Amir's sofa and crossing his legs. He is not wearing his Arab disguise, and his driver stands quietly near the apartment door. Amir's throat feels dry; he knows Jacob well enough to be wary of that quiet voice and overrelaxed body language. Jacob shakes his head slowly now, even smiles, though Amir sees the lack of amusement in his eyes. "Do you know that my sister has an IQ of 160?"

Amir frowns. "So do I," he finally says.

Jacob's face turns red; his cheeks swell and tremble slightly. When he speaks, his voice rattles, startling Amir. "Do you *always* manage to bring the conversation back to yourself?"

Amir clenches his fists, feels the veins in his neck popping out. Without warning, Jacob is up and lunging at him. He hears the crack of his cheekbone before he feels the daggerlike pain. He is on the floor and Jacob is kicking him, bruising his kidneys. His neck tightens as Jacob pulls his head up by the hair so he can break his nose against the edge of the marble coffee table. With every blow, Jacob insults him: "Piece of shit. Asshole. Sociopath. Traitor." Amir closes his eyes, blocks everything out, focuses on the corkscrew on the table nearby. If he can reach it, he can hold the cold metal in his palm, he can plunge the sharp point into Jacob's eye and twist and twist until Jacob's brain is a bloody soup. His meditation is so deep that when Jacob, exhausted and panting, finally stops the beating, Amir lies still, breathing regularly, expression almost peaceful.

Jacob's driver pulls a straight-back chair over and Jacob falls into it. The driver lights a cigarette and hands it to him, then moves back to his station at the door. Jacob drags deeply on his cigarette, leans over Amir's sprawled body, and exhales a shaft of smoke toward the bloodstained shag carpet. "You dared use my sister to transport a Moslem whore across the border. You dared use Mossad money and contacts for your personal obsessions." He reaches for the glass of scotch Amir had poured for him when he arrived; he empties it roughly onto Amir's face. "I know you can hear me, moron. You're not unconscious. It's always amazed me, Hakim, that you really believe yourself to be smarter than everyone else. I thought you'd grow out of it. But you're like your father. King of his own Psychotic World. There. See? I knew you were awake. What are you going to do with that fist you've made, Mr. Powerful?" Jacob sneaks his foot beneath Amir's stomach to roll him over onto his back. Amir squints in pain, but does not make any sound. "Pity," continues Jacob in a suddenly relaxed, almost chatty voice. "The girls won't be looking at you for a while, pretty boy. And as for my sister? Do so much as *think* about her and I'll serve your dick to the Syrians for breakfast."

Amir opens his eyes, blinking back the sting of the scotch. Jacob rises, hikes his trousers, and turns to leave, then stops with an afterthought. "By the way, Hakim, you're out of the organization. Pack your bags and go to hell. And don't show your face in Tel Aviv or I'll tell the right people a good enough story to get you hanged. If it was my choice I would put a bullet through your putrid brain, but my sister begged me not to. As you know, I'm partial to my sister's desires."

It takes Amir an hour to clean himself up, then he drops onto his bed and falls into a deep sleep where he dreams of Josephina, legs clamped around Dariush's hips, long red fingernails reaching for his testicles, and calling him Amir. He wakes up as stunned as he was when he fell asleep. He knows he must think about what to do next, but instead he rambles about the apartment without any purpose. His face feels like it is on fire; he cannot breathe through his nose, and his cheek is swollen and discolored. He does not have pain medication; he would not use it anyway—he is stronger than that. So he sits on the sofa and closes his eyes; this time his meditation is for strength. He focuses on his pain, finds the most tender parts with his mind, and lets the pain grow larger and larger, all the while refusing to cry out. He imagines more blows to his face, a searing iron laid on his cheek, slaps of a wooden paddle to his sore kidneys. And he fights. Sweat rises onto his skin, pooling, stinging, filled with the odor of fear and loathing. And after a long struggle, the flames become smaller, the fear evaporates, and in its place is a rising anger that Amir knows will rush like molten gold through his veins and blanket everything else so he can think about what he must do.

Indeed, how had Josephina figured out that Layla was of any significance to him? Amir sent many people over the border to Josephina; how had she realized that Layla was different? Damn. It was his own mistake; he should never underestimate Josephina. He had gambled on her and lost. Well, her loss.

Finally, he opens his eyes to the pale light of dawn and thinks of his father. He, too, had faced difficulties with the organization; the Office, as he had called it. Izaak had often complained that his superiors did not understand him, that they were not truly loyal to the struggle and responsibility of protecting Israel, that they had forgotten the atrocities done to Jews over the centuries, that they had grown numb to the danger of the Arabs swallowing them up. Amir knew people called his father a fanatic, a zealot, too militant. While Izaak had always followed orders, he often added his own twist to assignments and sometimes stepped over the line. (Amir remembers a certain shipment of M-16s to the Kurds.) But Izaak had been a master at the bureaucratic game. He had a certain charisma that seemed to release an invisible electricity from his pores, an electricity that surrounded people and drew them to his strange, soft voice and luring smile. Izaak Hakim could talk himself out of anything. But Amir has not inherited such a trait. Charisma has always been Amir's unfulfilled hope. And so, he thinks, I will resign from Mossad—why not? He is tired of it, tired of bullies like Jacob and tired of Josephina's strangling desires. Dabbing at the blood dripping from his nose, he realizes that he wants only one thing: Layla. Only Layla makes him feel like the man he was meant to be.

He steps out onto the balcony. Despite the stinging wind, he raises his face to the sky, to gaze at the tops of the massive mountains, their glaciers covered with new snow, looming like giants made of ancient earth; mountains that had witnessed the invasions of the Mongols and the Arabs and the British, mountains that had heard prayers to the many Gods and to the Sun God and to the One God, mountains that knew the treachery of kings and of clergy, mountains that would stand quiet and lofty when all was said and done. He remembers Layla telling him how, before the Revolution, before all the pollution, the mountains at dawn looked purple as grapes.

He inhales deeply and thrusts his chin up. Well, so what if he never sees Iran again.

Thirty-Eight

Layla

It was raining and chilly. I'd only ever been to the Côte d'Azur in the summer, a tourist, like everyone else. Now it was winter. The airport was relatively empty and didn't smell like coconut oil and flowers; it smelled like mildew and seaweed.

The cab drivers waiting at the curb didn't exactly jump to be of service; I must have looked shabbier than I thought. I told the first cabby where I wanted to go, and he quickly took my bag and opened the door for me. I ignored him the rest of the way. I looked out the window, bit my lips, and read license plates until we exited the autoroute and reached the main thoroughfare in Cannes, La Croisette. The designer boutiques were all there, the famous Carlton Hotel, the median that bloomed with flowers in warm weather, the Café Festivale where all the snobs would go to show off their tans or their clothing or their jewelry. But the whole place looked different, like a black-and-white picture of itself. I knew it was the emptiness that made it seem this way—the emptiness, the rain, the chill—it reopened the hole of loneliness in my chest.

All these months, I hadn't wanted to imagine what my leaving had done to my father; deep down, I knew he'd been terribly hurt, not to mention frantic and frightened. I wrote to him from Tehran several times to assure him I was fine, that there was no danger, that I would be back before he knew it. He hadn't replied. I'd disobeyed him in the way a Persian daughter who respects and loves her father would never disobey.

The cab stopped at a traffic light. My mouth was dry, jaw stiff. I placed my palms over my belly and looked away from the buildings and out onto the Mediterranean. The water was gray, not cobalt, and dotted with boats and skiers skimming one another's wakes. Beyond the palm trees along the roadside, a few feet below, was a small beach that was blanketed with imported white sand. Down the coast in Nice, the beach was rocky, and hardly anyone would sunbathe on it when the weather was warm; sometimes naive tourists would venture into the water there, but once they spotted the floating dollops of excrement from the sewage system, they stayed close to their hotel pools. After Nice, there were Monaco's cliffs, carved like Aztec pyramids with winding roads. From up there, when the sun shone, the sea looked like a thousand sparkling sapphires—a shimmering blue that the Italians in San Remo just over the border called *azzurro*.

The cabby slowed the car, looking for my turnoff. I directed him and he swung onto the narrow lane. I remembered how Dariush used to drive my Alfa up this hill, screeching the tires around every turn just to infuriate me, tease me. The memory seemed impossible, a made-up story; Dariush had mellowed so much after he'd come back from the training camp.

The cab turned slowly into the circular drive, tires kicking up gravel. The villa was unchanged: tall and whitewashed, ivy climbing along the walls to the red-tiled roof. I paid the driver and stood there watching him go, stalling. I ruffled my hair as if this would make the lack of it less of a shock to my father. I took a deep breath, climbed the three slate steps, and let myself in the front door.

It was very quiet, except for the usual ticking of my mother's Seth Thomas clock on top of the mantel in the salon. Everything seemed the same: all the dark, heavy furniture atop the Tabriz carpets and everywhere the odor of my father's cigarette smoke and the lavender perfume worn by the housekeeper. I walked slowly, trying to minimize the sound of my heels clicking on the terrazzo tiles—a circus clown in oversized clothing, long shoes, and sad face. I passed beneath the curved staircase and by the two ficus plants. I stopped at the arched teak door of my father's study and paused a moment to collect myself. As a child, I'd learned how to open this door without a sound so I could slip into the room, spread out on the sofa, and read a book while my father worked at his desk.

He sat there now, whispering and copying numbers from his adding-machine tape. He looked small and slumped behind the unusually messy desk, wearing a rumpled white dress shirt, sleeves rolled up sloppily, two yellow stains down the front. His beard was scruffy and the skin on his neck wrinkled and loose. His bald head shone in the light from the desk lamp. When I was little, I would rub suntan lotion over his smooth head, marveling at how it felt solid and soft at the same time.

I leaned against the door and it clicked closed, making him look up. He stared as if he didn't recognize me and I wondered if it was just the short hair or if he could see the differences in my soul. He stood up. His hands shook. Tears welled up in my eyes. He came forward and embraced me with such strength and trembling love that my knees nearly buckled with relief. I stretched my arms around his neck and sobbed like a child.

People said that my father had lost face. His daughter had run away to Tehran against his orders and had now returned pregnant with her dead husband's child. Everyone on the Riviera was talking about it. "Everyone" was all the Iranians who'd been stranded in their summer flats and villas for three years waiting for the Revolution to "blow over." But the scandal didn't affect my father; at least he didn't show me that it did. He had changed. I'd given him no choice.

Much to my disappointment, Dariush's parents were no longer in France. Veeda had taken Dariush's death very badly, and the stress had affected her diabetes. They'd gone to London to visit her doctors there and also to get away from the Iranian community with its constant pity that never gave them a moment of peace. Katy had also gone to London. I spoke to them all by phone, telling Katy how I'd seen her at the airport and listening to her sobs of relief that I was all right and her sobs of grief over leaving Mariam behind. Uncle Hooshang asked me questions about my feet, told me which doctors to see in Cannes; he was trying to be stoic for the others. When Veeda came on the line, words were difficult for the both of us. I knew her pain had to be at least as deep as my own. She said she would try to be with me when her grandchild was born.

My father had a maternity shop in town deliver some black dresses for me to try on. People wanted to visit me; it was the way. No one endured loss alone, even if they wanted to. I had a cobbler come to the house and take measurements for special shoes with soft inserts. He was an old French guy with a goatee and wax-stained hands; he tried not to react to the condition of my feet, but I saw him flinch. I refused to show the wounds to my father.

The people came, a string of black-clad visitors holding crisp white handkerchiefs and carrying homemade edibles made with no sugar out of respect for the mournful occasion. They came forward, the women especially, their arms out, their faces creased with pity, and embraced me, calling me *dokhtaram*, my daughter, and whispering sympathies in my ear. There were no children, but then, it was not customary. Still, I thought about them, how they were attending their French schools, ashamed of their alien status, angry with their parents for moaning and groaning about a Revolution that, for them, was in the past.

The young visitors—mostly my age but seeming much younger to me now—watched from a distance with hooded, anxious eyes, as if I had a plague they could catch or as if I were a Hollywood femme fatale. I think they would've liked to know all the details. I remembered the terrible photographs of executed royalists that people were passing around before Dariush and I left for Iran. The photographs had conveniently found their way into my hands at Jimmy'z, the discotheque at the casino in Monte Carlo. "Bette Davis Eyes" blasted from the speakers. I held five color glossies, all of men I knew—friends of my father or fathers of my friends. The first one was of the shah's former Prime Minister Hoveyda lying faceup with a black-rimmed, gum-red bullet hole in his forehead. All the dead men's faces were discolored from beatings, and some of them looked as if their eyes were open, staring at me. No, not open. Gouged out. I jerked my thumbs over the wounds, covering sockets with red-painted fingernails. I handed them to Dariush and watched as his face turned ashen.

But the photographs of the executed men hadn't had any impact on our plans to go to Tehran, just as a graphic news report of a fatal crash on the George Washington Bridge wouldn't have kept us from driving to New Jersey. I know my father never saw those pictures; it would have devastated him. But we young people found them horrifying and fascinating. And that was what *I* was to them now as they congregated in the corner of my father's living room. I was the accident, and they were rubbernecking.

The stream of visitors coming and going went on for two days. People wept and sometimes laughed with tears in their eyes as they remembered Dariush. "He was overwhelming, a little devil," said Mrs. Hadipour, wiping her cheek and thus displaying her eight-carat diamond that overlapped her wrinkled knuckle. "He could not sit still as a child. So quick, so smart. My Kaveh used to play war games with him. They were such close friends." Then she covered her nose with the ever-present hanky.

"Yes," said Mr. Bijan, looking at the floor. "Everyone wanted him as playmate for their children. He was something. A perfect child. A genius in mathematics."

"And in science," said Dr. Khalili. "He could build anything."

"He was an artistic prodigy," said my father.

"And such a devoted and respectful son," said Mr. Majidian.

"*Haif*, what a shame," said Mrs. Alizadeh, offering a bowl of nuts around the room.

This went on and on. Words that only served to remind me how my life would be monotonous and empty and endless without him.

Each woman who visited gave me the name of her favorite obstetrician. They smoothed their palms over my belly and told me to eat a lot of yogurt soup and suck on rock candy for the morning sickness. Their advice was incessant; their stories about their own either unbearable or incredible pregnancies never-ending in detail. The gathering was, as usual, turning into somewhat of a party.

After dark on the second day, I said to hell with my Persian manners and nestled into the corner of the down sofa. By then, most of the visitors were close friends, probably related in one way or another. Someone took my slippers off and drew a blanket over me. I floated in and out of sleep. The conversation had turned to politics and the state of Iran. This wasn't so bad, I thought. Not so lonely as my wide bed upstairs, not so lonely as listening to the echo of my own sorrowful thoughts.

"The children are being taught to spy on their parents," my father was saying. "The schoolteachers tell them to reveal if there is alcohol at home or if there are parties with modern music and card playing."

"But there are parties all the time," said Auntie Jahan. "Have you ever known an Iranian to give up their social life?"

Uncle Mehdi was saying, "Did you hear about Akbarzadeh's son? He has several shops that sell cassette tapes of Khomeini's sermons and other allowable things, but in the back he has a secret stock of the latest Western films that he rents at very high prices. He has become a millionaire since the Revolution."

"No other way to know what is going on in the modern world," said Auntie Minoo. "It is like a prison, our country. We used to listen to the BBC on our shortwave every night just to learn what was really happening in the world."

It doesn't matter what's happening in the world, I thought. Who cares? You're wasting your time.

"What has become of Sepehr Levai?" asked my father. "Has anyone heard?"

"Nothing," said Auntie Jahan. "We hid him in our basement for some time, then smuggled him to Morteza's house. He himself didn't know why he was blacklisted. We thought he got out, but we have not heard a thing since we came back to France."

There was silence for a while, and I opened one eye, hoping they weren't going to stop their chattering. My father told me to go up to bed, and everyone agreed. But I said no, I liked it better in the salon with everyone around me. Someone called for the housekeeper to bring more tea, and Auntie Minoo began making up little plates of fruits for everyone.

Mr. Teymouri, an old man who'd escaped Iran with nothing but luckily owned an apartment in London he sold for cash to live on, spoke up in his raspy smoker's voice. "The masses will pay," he said bitterly. "They already are." Mr. Teymouri had been a Communist in his youth, but had done a one-eighty by the time he was thirty-five and inherited his family's textile fortune. "All revolutions are about economics," he continued. "They thought we had too much and they had too little. Now what do they have? Still too little, and even less, because we are not there to make jobs for them anymore. They will not take it much longer. A coup will happen."

"Or Khomeini will die, God willing," said Auntie Jahan.

"God willing," everyone said.

"Let me tell you," said Uncle Mehdi. "Nothing will change unless the Americans and the British want them to. We all know that."

"That's right," said Auntie Minoo. "Lift Khomeini's beard and it says 'Made in Britain.'"

I laughed quietly. I hadn't heard that one. They all believed in these conspiracy theories, that the British and the Americans and sometimes the Russians planned all major world events and controlled heads of states like puppets. If only Ronald Reagan and Margaret Thatcher (and their secret high-powered cronies) wanted to, they could have Khomeini overthrown and the Iran-Iraq War halted. The consensus was that the superpowers allowed the shah to be overthrown because he had become too powerful with all his weapons and his influence with OPEC, driving up oil prices despite America's wishes. Conspiracy theories was one of their favorite topics; strangely, it gave them hope. Someone ran their velvety palm over my cheek and I heard myself sigh. I could keep my eyes closed forever.

About a year after the Revolution, when the American hostages were in their two-hundredth-something day in captivity, I'd asked my father for the umpteenth time if his business was in trouble. As usual, he became irritable and withdrawn. "Don't worry, Layla."

"I know you don't like to talk to me about it. . . ," I'd said.

"It's not of your concern."

"Please, Baba-*joon*. I'm not a child anymore."

"That has nothing to do with it."

"Well," I said, fed up. "If I were your son instead of your daughter, would you talk to me about it?"

"Naturally," he'd said, his expression puzzled.

But this was not a conversation we would have had after my return from Iran. First of all, there was no hiding the truth about our financial troubles. Second, what I'd been through, or was going through, forced him to stop seeing me as a little girl whom he could protect *and* intimidate. I'm not saying that his puritanism had vanished; I'm saying that he didn't have the strength or the solid reasoning to hold on to it. And I was a different person; he knew that much.

We didn't talk openly about finances or the particulars of how the regime in Iran had nationalized our businesses one by one until only our names remained as shareholders on documents that were useless. Profits now went into *bonyad*s or foundations that were meant to benefit the masses, but mostly funded luxuries for the ruling class, the clergy. I knew this because I'd listened to the talk in Tehran, not because my father confided in me. I think it was too painful, maybe even shameful for him, to explain the details. The truth was, I didn't care if we had fifty million dollars in the bank or fifty thousand. After everything, being rich seemed valueless to me. But *he* cared. It was a matter of pride and duty.

So I asked him nothing. And when a realtor appeared one afternoon to discuss putting the villa on the market, I acted unsurprised. Later, he called me into his study and haltingly tried to apologize for having to do such a thing.

"I think it's a good idea," I said.

"Yes," he said, looking away. "A small apartment in Paris would be more practical."

So he still didn't want to go back to the States. I didn't remember him liking Paris much. Well, it would take a while for the villa to sell; he could change his mind. He wasn't really himself. Look at the condition of his study, I thought. My father had always been orderly, with only a few papers neatly stacked on his desk at one time, staplers and paper clips and pencils all in their specific places. He was forever straightening pictures, picking lint from fabrics, and blowing speckles of dust off books and tabletops. Now his study was a mess. Papers and manila folders piled on the leather sofa, on the coffee table, on the liquor cabinet, on the mantel, all over the floor so you had to maneuver around and over them. Heaping ashtrays and the smell of stale smoke. Dust on the tables, cobwebs in the ceiling corners.

My bedroom, however, still smelled of peaches. I'd always thought this was because of the peach trees in the garden, but it was winter now. Maybe the smell was some kind of mental association and it only existed in my brain. I leaned against the window frame and looked down to the pool below; raindrops pelted the water, but I closed my eyes and pictured it glistening in the August sun. I swam as I used to. Lap after lap, my strokes effortless. I was like a current in the water, part of the water. My shadow moved along the even blueness of the pool bottom, a wriggling silhouette dragging tendrils of hair behind it. Then suddenly, Dariush was there, swimming underwater toward me like a missile, his bathing trunks waving against his thighs. Our heads bobbed up and every feature of his face was so real, even the drops of water that fell from the tip of his nose and the stubble of his beard and the gleaming wetness of his lips.

I opened my eyes and hugged my shoulders. Was this the way it was going to be? Would he always seem alive to me? Or would the years make his face fade like the colors in an antique carpet? And which did I want? To have him living in my thoughts or in my memories?

Baba-*joon* convinced me to go with him into town. He had some errands to run. It was a beautiful sunny day, windy but not too cold. I said okay. We ran into Iranians we knew in the bakery, at the *tabac* stand, and at Benetton. They looked at me, at my belly, at my big shoes, with a kind of pity that shriveled their faces. I told Baba-*joon* to finish his errands alone; I would wait for him on the stone wall above the Carlton beach. He almost objected, as he would have in the old days, then caught himself and instead pulled up the collar of my coat. "Don't catch cold," he said softly.

I sat on the wall, my legs dangling above the sand and my feet feeling good for once. There was no one else around. The breeze whipped at my hair, which had grown a little; the ends tickled my ears. Little Rachel was stronger now, like a little drum inside me. I liked to talk to her sometimes, mostly in Farsi. "The last time your daddy and I walked on this beach," I said, "we took our shoes off and sank our feet into the smooth sand. The most beautiful fireworks covered the sky and all the colors in the world rained down like wedding confetti. We were so happy, so hopeful."

I looked down the long sidewalk at two elderly men strolling toward me. I could tell by their hand gestures and facial features that they were Iranian, no doubt discussing politics. I pulled my collar up higher to hide most of my face and stared out to the sea until they passed. Back in August, while Dariush stayed behind one night, I strolled along this very same area on the Croisette with some twenty of us who'd just had dinner at a small Italian bistro down the way. We strolled in groups of two and three, dressed in silk and suits, inhaling the warm sea breeze, telling jokes; Auntie Veeda's arm hooked on mine, my father's cherry pipe tobacco drifting back to me, and the children in our group playing tag around our skirts. Next thing I knew, someone had discovered a row of folding chairs propped up against the seawall, perhaps left over from a hotel event, and they began handing them out, setting them up. Soon our group was seated in a wide circle, as wide as the sidewalk.

The women sat with their legs delicately crossed, their Chanel purses resting on their silk laps, their diamond-studded ears alert to kind and cruel gossip. And the men fingered their ties, patting their smooth hair lightly and laughing deeply at jokes about *mullah*s. It was proof that the Persian social circle could go anywhere, that it could move over continents and oceans and countries, from tent palaces to desert high-rises to a European sidewalk. And all the nuances of Persian etiquette were right there in that circle: the overpoliteness, the age hierarchy, the sportive rivalry. A whole culture—its properties of parochialism, imperiousness, pride, its endurance, resourcefulness, and heart—

all in a circle that could easily have been picked up and transported from an Iranian living room or garden, flown across the earth, and set down there on the French Riviera.

Pedestrians had to step into the street to walk around our circle, and some threw us angry looks or shook their heads disapprovingly as they continued down the promenade. It seemed I was the only one who noticed this. I wasn't sitting; I'd receded to the shadows near the sea wall, uncomfortable. I couldn't help myself; I was embarrassed. This wasn't right; we couldn't just pull chairs up streetside and have an ethnic get-together. It was tacky.

Now suddenly, sitting on that wall three months later, I knew that what had really made me feel uncomfortable then was a striking glimpse of the Persian tomorrow, as if the future were a whole pie and I'd been presented with a small slice on a plate in front of me. There was the ethnic circle, no longer vacationers, jet-setting globe-trotters, doing something travelers don't do, especially not travelers from the Third World who know the importance of conforming in the "civilized" First World. They were behaving as they would at home. They couldn't help it; they missed it, they hated the exile, and it felt good to be themselves.

But these were people who would never go back to Iran, people whose lives had vaporized with the raising of a revolutionary fist. They were going to have to start over even if it was the last thing they wanted to do.

Yet for years to come, I knew their voices would carry the near-panic and denial of this truth: that they had become not just visitors, but immigrants. Even as I heard about them, so many of them, moving their lives to Los Angeles, where the weather is more like Tehran, where the odor of smog is familiar and the dust of the desert feels not too far off, and where already the elders complained that their children had forgotten the Farsi words and that they didn't roll their *r*'s as easily as they used to, even as I heard about this, I knew that they still trusted that we would all go back and everything would be as it once was.

I couldn't be a part of that.

I wanted to go home.

To America.

Thirty-Nine

Grandmothers

Mariam sits by Dasha's bed and sings to him. Her voice has never been strong, and the tones are wrapped in whispery air; still, she thinks the music may comfort him. She sings songs from their childhood: Russian lullabies his mother used to sing, silly ditties their *naneh*s taught them, melancholy lyrics in minor keys, and Western songs, because these are the ones he loves most. Simon and Garfunkel, Stevie Wonder, Chicago, Elton John, James Taylor. She does not remember most of the words to these songs; she had erased them from her mind long ago, but the melodies are clear. So she sings the words she knows and hums the rest, allowing the memories of her teenage summers and the years in Europe to come freely. Her chest feels heavy with regret and nostalgia. She thinks of the servant boy Jamsheed who, though he could not speak English, listened to American Air Force Radio constantly and taught himself to imitate the rock-and-roll songs perfectly.

She decides to speak her thoughts to Dasha. First she gingerly wipes a glistening line of drool from his jaw, then sits back. "Dasha, remember how Jamsheed would sing the American songs? 'I am just a poor boy . . . Lai lai lai,' and that other one by that handsome boy from the bird family. 'I think I love you . . .

I think I love you!' Layla said Jamsheed was so good, he sounded like a boy from New Jersey or that faraway state . . . Vinsconsin, something like that."

The door behind her bursts open. "Who are you talking to? Is my grandson awake!"

Mariam looks over the back of her chair at her sallow-faced grandmother. "No, Maman Bozorg, he is not awake. I was talking because I think he might be able to hear me."

"*Ahmagh!* Stupid girl!" she spits. "Only prayer will rouse him—and then only if *Allah* wishes it. Instead of singing sinful songs and talking to the walls, you should count your prayer beads, plead with your God. Even the doctor advised this."

Mariam turns away and folds her hands. "Yes, Maman Bozorg," she says.

After a short silence, the old woman asks, in a more tentative voice, "How is his pallor? Has he moved at all?"

"He is the same," says Mariam.

"*Allah Akbar!*" Maman Bozorg says, shuffling away, moaning with each step.

Mariam is disappointed in her grandmother. This is an odd inversion of the way things have always been. And in some way, her disappointment has freed her, calmed her, given her a power all her own. She no longer feels compelled to do everything her grandmother tells her to do. Sometimes, she even feels it is *she* who should give advice to the woman she has always looked to for approval and guidance.

How is it that Maman Bozorg barely comes into Dasha's room? She cannot bear to see him sick, immobile, undignified. Is this the way a grandmother should be? Mariam remembers all the times she wished for Maman Bozorg's caress or concern. Neither was ever given.

Every night since his daughter returned to Cannes, Ebrahim dreams of Iran. This night is no different. He is sitting in the darkness, sweating and gasping from the nightmare that still swims before his eyes. He was in a vast garden where sunlight streaked through the trees like klieg lights on a stage. Rachel lay in the dirt beside him, her head resting on her shoulder, severed from her body as it had been after the accident. He covered his eyes and wept. But when he looked again, it was Layla lying dead in the dirt.

He walks quietly down the hallway to check on her, but finds the door closed and locked. This had never been her way. But now she retreats like a cornered mouse, into a hole of darkness where perhaps she hopes the demons cannot reach her.

He is to blame for what has happened to her. He raised her badly. Had he been too lenient? Too harsh? Too inquisitive? Too uninvolved? Where had she developed the daring to slip through his protective arms? He had not given her a good life; he had given her a mirror of his own life. Widowhood and a child. Anguish and anxiety. Loneliness and love.

What will become of her?

It is now, most of all, that he wishes she had more family to console her. He misses his brothers, who are in London and Dusseldorf, trying to salvage what is left of their business. He remembers when Layla learned the truth about Rachel's family, that it was the religion that had kept them from being in her life. He told her the grandfather had died long before he and Rachel had married, then he lied and told her that the grandmother had died soon after Layla's birth, and this was the reason she had never seen Layla. But it had not been like that. She had died just a year before, two days after Layla's ninth birthday. He had read it on the obituary page: MARGARET ABRAMSON—a grainy photo of a silver-haired woman wearing a circle of fat pearls. Phrases jumped out at him: "society hostess" . . . "contributions to the Jewish Women's Art League" . . . "devoted wife and mother." It had enraged him. Every year on the anniversary of Rachel's death, he had written to her, imploring her to establish a relationship with Layla, but all his letters were returned unopened. When he had initially come back to New York after Rachel's death, he actually went to see Margaret Abramson—she lived only blocks away from them, for God's sake!—but she ordered the doorman to send him away. He had thought about contacting the two brothers Rachel had spoken of, but by then his pride could not stand for more rejection. Now, when he sees the grief in Layla's eyes, he wishes he had tried harder.

What can he do for her? She wants to return to New York; she begs him to let her go. It had always been his wish that she think of America as her home; this, for the sake of Rachel's memory. But Layla had always wanted Iran, and when he would point out to her that she was American in many more ways than she was Iranian, it was visibly painful to her. Now it is she who wants America and he who wants oblivion. Well, what does he expect? These days, their existence is marked only by the immutable changes that have befallen them.

Forty

Maman Bozorg

It has been a month! It has been too long! He will never wake up. The arrogant and immoral Armenians are already celebrating the birth of their Jesus. The snows have come. Oh, God, why do you challenge me so? I have wrested him from the Great Satan and from the arms of the infidel. Why must you keep him from me? If you want him as your martyr, take him. But this dormant ghost that lies in my house is too much for me.

I must calm down. "Firoozeh! Bring me my pills!" My voice has grown weak as an old hen's. And Firoozeh has grown slightly—perhaps conveniently—deaf. Who knows if I will get my pills? The half-witted doctor gave them to me last week when he came to see Dariush. "I am sorry, madame," he always says. Does he think I appreciate being called madame? Has he missed the Revolution? "I do not know why your grandson has not woken," he says, as if these are not the exact words he spoke the week before and before that. "Without the proper equipment to analyze his brain, I can give you no specific prognosis. We must be patient." Idiot man! Patience does not come so easily when the future is so unknown, so unmanageable. My patience has turned into smoke. Anyway, this was when the doctor gave me the pills. I must admit, they are good pills; they soak up my grief and anger for a few hours.

"Mariam!" *Bah! She* will not hear me. *She* is always by his side. Dasha this and Dasha that. Where did she find this ridiculous name for him? He is not some kind of Russian Cossack. He is like the great Persian king he was named after. *Vai!* He must wake up; I am dying from this agony! I have done everything I can: pledged thousands of *touman*s to five different orphanages, promised *Allah* I would visit the tomb of *Emam* Reza in Mashhad if he would only spare my Dariush, and sent for the old Tabrizi *naneh* to minister against the evil eye. Besides this, Firoozeh burns wild-rue incense over Dariush three times a day. But nothing has worked!

"Firoozeh!" How itchy these sheets are against my skin. "Mariam!"

Last evening—miraculously—my granddaughter did in fact appear without a sound at my bedroom door. "Why are you in bed, Maman Bozorg?" she asked, her voice empty of any concern over my obvious ill health.

"*Hahn!* Now you suddenly remember your old grandmother. My joints ache, girl! What else?"

"Shall I bring you some aspirin?"

"How kind of you," I said, but she ignored the sarcasm in my tone and calmly went to retrieve the medicine from my cabinet in the hall. When she returned, I snatched the aspirin and glass of water from her hands; still she did not seem concerned by my gruffness.

"I hope you sleep well, Maman Bozorg," she said, continuing in this annoying soft voice, then turning to go. How could this be? I was having no effect on her at all.

"My room is cold," I told her. "Tell Firoozeh to raise the heat."

"All right," she said, turning at the door, her shadow dark and long on my ceiling. "Is there anything else, Maman Bozorg?"

"Where are you going?"

"To tell Firoozeh to raise the heat."

"After that."

"Back to Dasha's room."

"You are pale. You have lost weight." She said nothing, and I could not read her expression. At one time, I would have thought this behavior rebellious and I would have punished her. But there was no sign of disrespect on her face; there was no sign of anything I had seen before. Where was my agitated and obedient granddaughter? "Your hair is unkempt," I said. "Where is your scarf?"

She brought her hands slowly to her twisty hair, patting it down. "Wear my scarf? For whom, Maman Bozorg?"

"A pious woman feels comfortable in her coverings." She frowned at me, puzzled like a child. "What is the matter with you, girl?"

"Nothing is the matter. But there is one thing I have wanted to mention."

"Yes?"

"It has been a month since we found out that Dasha is alive. Is it right for us to keep this from Auntie Veeda and Uncle Hooshang for so long?"

My hand shook and water spilled on my most valuable coverlet. "Why must you always disappoint me, girl? You know very well why we cannot contact them. Do you want the officials to learn that Dariush is alive?"

"I can send Auntie and Uncle a letter."

"The letters are opened."

"I would say nothing revealing in the letter. I would tell them they must return for reasons having to do with property, as we did with Dariush."

I squinted my eyes at her. "And what will you do when Hooshang or Veeda telephones here to speak with you about the letter you sent? They like to question everything. And you never know who is listening in. There are spies of the government everywhere. And so there should be. No. I will not hear any more of this stupid talk. Go away. I want to relax my joints."

I rested back on my pillows and closed my eyes, expecting to hear her whimpering down the corridor as is her way. But I heard not a sound. Finally, I opened my eyes to see if she still stood like a simpleton at the door. But she was gone.

I did not sleep at all during the night. I am still shaken by my granddaughter's transformation. Not only must I cope with the nearly hopeless condition of my grandson, now I must worry about his cousin's frivolous ideas, perilous ideas. My blood boils like a stew through my veins; my neck is swollen with the lumps of fear. *Vai!* "Firoozeh! My pills!" Where is that useless woman! I must collect my thoughts. Mariam must not become a threat to my plan, to her own future. I must have a serious talk with her.

How did this happen? I never had difficulty taming that child. She was afraid of me, respected me. They are the same thing, you know. And such fear and respect always produce the best children. It is true that Mariam was for a while living a sinful life. Everyone thought I did not know this. Sometimes it is best to allow people to think you are not aware of things. But I was certain she would eventually stumble and fall. And so she did, back to the home that could offer her the most protection and guidance and discipline. God's subtle ways gave her the vision to make a choice and return to me.

I must straighten her out.

Forty-One

Broken Eggshells

Mariam is sure that Dasha will wake up; she has never doubted it. She knows it will take time. She does not mind. In fact, she is content in a way she has not been since they were children together. She thanks *Allah* whenever she says her *namaz* for bringing her cousin back to her. She changes his dressings the way the doctor showed her; she fills his IV sack, empties his urine bag, and washes his body every day with perfumed soaps from her mother's house (where she must go stealthily so as not to raise Jamsheed's suspicions; even Maman Bozorg does not know that Jamsheed is caring for Katayoon's house). She massages Dariush's limbs and shoulders and back with jasmine and sandalwood oils. She does all this slowly and with great concentration. Her arms and hands grow strong from carrying pots of bathing water, from turning his thin body, and from kneading his atrophied muscles. She does everything for him. Firoozeh is forbidden to do anything. She washes his sheets, vacuums his floor, dusts the dark, heavy Russian furniture that once belonged to her grandfather. She cannot wait for spring when she will fetch fresh-cut flowers from the garden. In the evening, she undoes his head bandages in order to feed air to the wound that covers his left forehead and temple; she thinks it is improving, though not very quickly. She slides Dasha slightly down on the bed and sits above his head to comb his hair. She does this for almost an hour, alternating with a soft brush and sometimes running her fingers through the long, thick strands. She talks to him then, memories of their childhood. Sometimes it is impossible not to include Layla, and Mariam hesitates, thinking of Maman Bozorg's instructions, but eventually she forgets what Maman Bozorg wants and thinks only about what Dasha needs.

She tolerates the old *naneh* from Tabriz who comes to minister against the evil eye. Mariam remembers her from her own childhood, her scabby, scaly, cold skin and her rotted teeth and gums that smell like moldy fava beans. She had come when Mariam was ill with cholera, bearing her raw eggs, black charcoal, fake gold coins, long narrow cushions, and a bag of wild rue. The agony for Mariam had been lying still and waiting for *Naneh Baji, Naneh* Sister, to finish her ritual of superstition so she could rush to the toilet. She had chewed on her tongue to distract herself from the stomach cramps while *Naneh Baji* drew small squares on the outside of an egg, then wrote the names of those closest to her in each square. She talked the whole time in her Azarbaijani dialect to the maidservants who stood around watching. The egg was held above Mariam's head, the coins placed at its ends, and a towel wrapped around the whole thing. *Naneh Baji* held the wad and called out the names of those written inside, bearing down on the egg with every name. Finally, when Mariam felt she would burst and embarrass herself, the egg broke. "*Kee bood? Kee bood?* Who was it? Who was it?" everyone wanted to know. "Who is Katayoon?" asked *Naneh Baji,* opening the towel to reveal a yolky mess.

Mariam had run to the bathroom. So it was her mother who had given her the evil eye. Well, that is not so bad, she had thought. My mother has bragged about me to someone and forgotten to protect me by knocking on wood. Mariam returned to her bed and fell asleep smiling. *Naneh Baji* took the broken eggshell and put it in the *jube* for the water to take the evil eye away. Mariam had improved quickly. No one said anything about the tetracycline Uncle Hooshang gave her that evening; *Naneh Baji's* medicine was far more fascinating.

When *Naneh Baji* comes to see Dariush, she uses her narrow pillow, wrapping it around his neck, then his arm, then his leg, all the time telling Mariam to wave the smoke from the burning wild rue over the pillow. She mumbles phrases from the *Qoran* and rocks back and forth in the chair by Dasha's bed, placing her prayer beads on his chest. Mariam has no faith in this. The old *naneh* seems as foolish now as she had long ago; even the old woman herself seems aware of this. In the face of someone so gravely ill, her hands and lips tremble with an urge to escape. So Mariam lets her go, giving her one of her own *chador*s as she leaves, seeing that hers is torn on the bottom. The *touman*s Maman Bozorg had left for her come to almost nothing, so Mariam adds to this and sends her away quickly, before the *khanoom* can see that she is leaving early.

Mariam thinks Dasha needs to know that the people he loves are around him. This is why she wants Veeda and Hooshang to come. Maman Bozorg has her reasons—her excuses—why this cannot happen. But Mariam has seen Maman Bozorg achieve many things by using her contacts in the regime to cajole and bribe and bully. Is there no one who can carry a letter out of the country? No way to dream up a tale to get Dasha's parents here? How is it that suddenly her grandmother has lost her ability to take risks for Dasha's sake?

Maman Bozorg is *ghahr* with Mariam. Not talking to her, not looking at her, not hearing her. Mariam has been through this many times. She can do nothing but wait it out. The pain of it is not deep anymore. It only bothers her now because she has wanted to continue discussing the issue of Veeda and Hooshang; she also wants to convince her grandmother that Dasha needs a modern hospital. She does not believe it is reasonable to leave his fate so entirely in the hands of *Allah*; what if *Allah* is busy doing something else? But she cannot say these things to her grandmother. At mealtimes, they share nothing but the food Firoozeh has cooked; the sounds of silverware against china, of chewing and swallowing and sipping, of a cough, a sneeze, maybe a belch, are the only things they experience together. When Maman

Bozorg comes to Dasha's room, Mariam leaves and stands outside the door until her grandmother is done with her visit.

She sighs and wonders when this will be over.

It takes a month. An earthquake shakes the house during the night. Mariam jumps from her cot and shields Dasha's head from falling plaster dust. It is over in seconds. Mariam is amazed to hear Maman Bozorg's voice yelling for Firoozeh from all the way across the house. She pities her grandmother suddenly. She cannot remember her ever behaving with such agitation. Mariam shakes Dasha's quilts to rid them of plaster dust, then she covers him carefully, tucking the duvet around his body as if he were her baby. Perhaps, she thinks, Maman Bozorg has grown too old for self-control.

Firoozeh appears at the door. "Mariam-*khanoom*," she says, her words garbled because her teeth still sit in a glass beside her pallet. "*Khanoom Bozorg* asks to see you."

"It is the middle of the night, Firoozeh."

"I know. She has ordered me to sit here with Dariush-*khan* while you are gone."

Mariam is annoyed. "Is she ill?"

"No, *khanoom*."

"All right. Wrap my *lahaf* around you. You are shivering."

"The shaking of the *zelzeleh* frightened me."

"Don't worry. I will be back soon."

Mariam steps quickly down the wide spiral staircase, using only a small candle for guidance. When the electricity is out, only the bedrooms can be kept warm with old braziers. Her feet are cold inside her slippers as she traverses the main hall past the salon and the dining room, then the sitting room, where she stops to peer out the arched windows to see if snow still falls onto the balcony, and finally she reaches her grandmother's door.

She is surprised to see the bed empty; only a deep, lopsided impression in the pillows flickers in the candlelight. "I am over here," says a tinny voice. She sits in one of the two Queen Anne chairs at the far side of the room; her feet rest on a stool needlepointed with an English hunting scene. A candelabra is perched on the round table between the two chairs; the strong and wavering light from it plays with the creases and shadows of the old woman's face, making her features look fluid. But Mariam knows that her grandmother is rigid as stone.

"Sit, daughter," she says, gesturing her chin at the other chair. "I want to talk to you."

Mariam does as she asks; she can remember the times when her knees quivered from the tone of such a disapproving voice, how her heart felt sore, how much she hated herself. She puts her candle on the table and folds her hands in her lap, leans her head against the back of the chair, and finds herself saying, "It is too bad the new houses don't have molded ceilings. I remember the intricate patterns in the old house. I miss them."

"Sit up. I did not ask you here to chat like schoolgirls."

Mariam looks at her grandmother. "You have not spoken to me in one month."

"I have been angry with you," she says, fiddling with her nightshift. "I hope by now you have realized your mistake. I knew it would take time for you to comprehend my point. So I allowed you to have it."

The implication that Mariam's intelligence or her ability to grasp ideas is inferior still bruises her. She has always known that she is not smart, that she has no aptitude for reciting poetry or reading the *Qoran* or managing money or manipulating people. These are the things her grandmother values, not to mention beauty, of which she never speaks. "Do you think I am attractive?" asks Mariam, surprising herself. The late hour and the candlelight has made her drunk, she thinks.

"What? Of course. What a stupid question."

"You never told me."

"I do not have to tell you. You should know it. Do I tell you I love you?"

"No, Maman Bozorg. You do not."

"Well . . . see?" The old woman clicks her tongue in frustration. "This is not what I wish to talk about, Mariam. The fate of your cousin is on my mind. I am thinking we must finally take him to a hospital, perhaps one that is still privately owned. We could change his name."

Mariam sits up. "Would it be that easy?"

"Nothing is easy; have you not learned that yet? Do you think it has been *easy* for me all these years trying to keep you two together? I have sacrificed more than any other grandmother. And now this. My grandson lost to me inside his own body and my granddaughter unable to think clearly. What kind of a wife will you be to him?"

Mariam blinks. "Wife?"

Maman Bozorg is leaning over and unraveling an Ace bandage from around her calf. "Daughter," she says, groaning. "Bring me another bandage from my commode; the thicker one. *Ai*, my joints."

Mariam does not move, and Maman Bozorg looks up at her. "What is it? Why is your face so pink?"

"You said wife," she stutters softly. "You want me to marry my cousin?"

"You frighten me, girl. Has your brain turned sticky like overcooked rice?" She sighs heavily. "It is my own fault. I forever overestimate you." She looks squarely at her granddaughter. "You have doted on Dariush all your life. What did you think such adoration meant?"

"I did not think about that. I love him like a brother; he is like my whole family."

"And what am I? Your *naneh*?" Mariam stares at her lap, says nothing. "Anyway," continues Maman Bozorg, "I do not care how you think of him. He is *not* your brother. He is *namahram*. You know this, child. Has all your religious education poured out of your ears? Only brothers and fathers and husbands and uncles and sons are *mahram*; cousins are not. If you want him to be *mahram*, you must make him your husband. You are both Moslem; the Law encourages your union. Did you think I planned all this merely so my grandchildren could live in my house as brother and sister? The line must continue; you must have children. *Allah* help you, Mariam, you must grow up!"

"Did Dasha know about this?"

"Of course not. Men are not as mature as women about these things. Does not the *Qoran* say a girl becomes a woman at nine years of age and a boy becomes a man at fourteen? Still, it takes men much longer to make reasonable decisions about marriage. That is why their parents—or grandparents—do it for them."

Mariam feels queasy. She swallows. "I do not think Dasha would like this idea."

"Why not? He has always loved you. He will recognize his destiny when he awakes and finds you with him."

Anxiety turns Mariam's skin cold. "But Dasha and I . . . we— he . . . loves me, but not . . . not the way he loves Layla."

Maman Bozorg narrows her eyes. "How dare you say that girl's name aloud. Understand this: Dariush lusted after Ebrahim's *kaufar* daughter. Lust is not the foundation for the trust and respect and loyalty that are necessary for a proper marriage. In fact, lust is impractical in a marriage." She shakes her head in disapproval and adjusts her scarf. "And Mariam, heed my words, I forbid you to bring her name to his ears when he wakes. If he asks you, merely say you do not know where she is. *I* will manage this issue. Do you understand? Answer me!"

"I will obey without question, Maman Bozorg," she says, her eyes still lowered, as is polite. For the first time since Dariush returned, she feels her old enemies creeping into her like *jenn*s of destruction. Fear, anger, and the loneliness.

"It is getting late," says Maman Bozorg. "Soon we will have to do the morning *namaz*. I need my rest if we are going to plan Dariush's move to a hospital. This terrible sleep must not go on. I will make inquiries about a brain specialist and you will prepare him for transport."

"*Chashm*, as you wish, Maman Bozorg," she says, rising on legs like rubber. "Good night, Maman Bozorg."

"Yes, good night." After Mariam is gone, she throws her unraveled bandage to the floor and sputters, with disgust, "*Ai!* Saint Ali! What will I do with that girl?"

Mariam collides with the wooden sofa arm as she races through the salon in the dark. She will not go back to her grandmother's room for the candle. She stumbles up the staircase on her hands and knees, sucking at the air as if she had been drowning. She bursts into Dariush's room, frightening Firoozeh, who yelps and raises her arms to heaven. "You can go back to the *haji-khanoom* now, Firoozeh."

The room is quiet, still, dim. Mariam puts her hand to her temple, tries to calm down, but her ears buzz, her eyes blink involuntarily, and her muscles quiver. She stands almost frozen a few steps from the bed. She cannot look at Dariush; she looks at the floor and tries to make out the fine crinkles in her leather slippers. Eventually, her breathing slows. She takes a step forward; the lacy dust ruffle comes into view, and she smells the apricot soap she had used to bathe her cousin earlier.

Her cousin.

She forces herself to look at him. In the candlelight his hair makes feathery shadows on the pillow. His lips are slightly open. She imagines kissing them, imagines that she is naked beneath the covers with him, rubbing against him, imagines his hot breath on her neck and the thrust of him inside her. She blinks and tears cascade down her cheeks. She wipes at the wetness with her fingers and gasps with revulsion and shame.

Roberto's face leaps into her mind. She has always successfully pushed these images away, but now she welcomes the memory of his touch. She closes her eyes. Sometimes he would kiss her violently, filling her mouth with his tongue, grunting, and lifting her buttocks off the mattress. Other times he teased her, fluttering his fingers over her breasts and streaming spider kisses along her inner thigh. She feels her nipples harden and the contraction of her vulva. Her eyes open. "No," she says aloud as if her grandmother can hear. She looks at her cousin's face again and whispers. "You are my whole family, Dasha."

And slowly, miraculously, like the moon rising on the desert horizon, his eyes open and he whispers, "Mimish?"

Forty-Two

Layla

When I was growing up, Banu would wake me in the mornings by cupping her tiny hand over my cheek and whispering, "What a beautiful face, like the moon." She would slide off the bed until her small feet touched the ground and shuffle over to open the window shades, flooding the room with sunlight. She stopped doing this after Dariush moved to Manhattan and I invited him to spend the night more often. It wasn't that he'd be in my bed in the morning—we pretended, out of respect for Banu, that Dariush slept in the guest room—but I guess she decided that since I was doing a very womanly thing, she would stop treating me as if I were an innocent child. It was, among others, a small gesture of disapproval that I was having premarital sex. I think if it hadn't been Dariush I was sleeping with, she would have had a mental breakdown—she felt much more responsible for my virginity than I ever did. But she loved Dariush, too.

When I returned from France to New York City, Banu resumed her wake-up ritual. I didn't object. I actually didn't object to much of anything.

At first, she cried almost every time she laid eyes on me. She followed me around—up to my bedroom, down to the library or the kitchen—she sat in the bedroom when I slept, hovered in the bathroom with a towel when I showered, and kept me from reaching the telephone before she did. The only thing she would not do was tend to my feet; she couldn't bear the sight. But I knew that came from guilt, not revulsion.

One evening, I went to her room, where she sat in her rocking chair and watched sitcoms and never missed *Dynasty* or *Dallas*. I stretched out on her small bed, snuggling into her lavender-scented pillow and running my palm over the soft, worn afghan blanket her sister had made. She was surprised to see me; I usually went to bed early. "What is it, *azizam*? Are you sick?"

"No, don't worry," I said in English.

"All right. I will not worry," she said in Farsi. She never spoke to me in English; she'd promised my grandmother to make sure I never forgot the language of my ancestors.

"Banu-*joon*," I said, "you must stop this crying and guilt."

She sniffed. "How was I unable to protect you? I had sworn to *Allah* that for the good *khanoom* Rachel's sake, I would protect her daughter."

"And you have." I reached over to touch her skinny arm. "You tried everything to keep me safe. Stop this guilt and this pity. You can't live like this."

She nodded, folded her hanky, and clicked off the little television. She sat for a moment quietly, then said, "When I saw this city, this Manhattan, for the first time—made up of spires and obelisks across the water—I knew it would take all of my strength to prevent your soul from getting lost in such a place. I was not frightened by the maze of streets nor by the rough crowds nor by the blaring horns. I had lived in a city most of my life, and I have had to get used to things being bigger than me."

I laughed and pulled gently at the tip of her sweater. "Remember when we used to go to the children's department at Bloomingdale's to buy shoes together?"

"Do not laugh, child," she said, laughing herself. "I still go there." And to be sure, she was wearing a pair of corduroy little boy's slippers on her feet. "Anyway," she continued, "I was not intimidated by Manhattan—at that time, when Kennedy, God give him peace, was president and Audrey Hepburn was still in the cinema, the city was not so busy as it is now. My fears were of the strange American ideas, the thoughts, the opinions that flew through the sooty air. I wanted to protect you from losing yourself in such things. I promised myself this. I had promised Mina-*khanoom*, your grandmother, that I would not allow you to forget where you came from. So year after year, I filled this home with all the Iranian rituals and traditions I knew—*Norooz* celebrations and Fire Jumping ceremonies and wild-rue incense burnings to keep away the evil eye, even some basic lessons of the *Qoran*. Do you still remember the prayers I taught you?"

"Some. I remember when we tried to fast during *Ramazan*."

"Yes. You did well until you discovered you were not allowed to smoke your cigarettes."

"I remember all the stories you told me of Iran, the old ones and the new ones of my mother. And I remember how you bought cantaloupe melons at Mr. Kim's fruit stand so that Baba-*joon* would be reminded of Iran."

"Yes. A Persian house smells like cantaloupe melons in the summertime. Your father needed to be reminded that his homeland had not died along with his wife, that we needed to visit Iran."

"See?" I said. "You did everything you promised to do. Nothing that has happened to me is your fault. My mother would be proud. *Khanoom-jahn* would be proud."

She frowned; her eyes seemed to look inward. "But how terribly wrong I was all this time." She held her palm to her forehead and shook her head. "I thought the danger to you would come from America, but it came from Iran."

"Banu-*joon*, you have to put these thoughts out of your mind now."

"Yes. You are right, *joonam*." She took a deep breath and came over to the bed to sit and embrace me. I buried my face in her neck and swallowed tears of grief that seemed always to be just behind my eyes. "We must look forward. No more sorrow."

Well, the next day, the solemn, guilty-eyed, despondent Banu was gone. Thank goodness she was again the bold little general, as my father used to call her, the devoted surrogate mother who often spoke before she thought and acted before she spoke. When I was small, even though I loved Banu, I often wished my father would meet a glamorous woman who could be my stepmother; someone who wouldn't wear drab polyester shifts, whose breath wouldn't smell of onions even before breakfast, someone who wouldn't call sweatpants and sweatshirts *peejameh* clothes, someone to whom I wouldn't have to fabricate an excuse to let me walk alone to school or to whom I wouldn't have to ask not to answer the telephone when friends called or to whom I wouldn't feel compelled to refer to as the maid and then feel like a traitor because I knew Banu preferred to be thought of as my governess: Miss Mayri Poppeens.

At the end of January, Banu decided my sadness and apathy were from the pregnancy, "a miserable but common thing" that would disappear when the baby was born. This was her way of keeping our thoughts in the present and future. "The past must become like an old yellowed and brittle storybook," she would say, kissing my forehead.

She was constantly rushing around putting loads of laundry on, dusting and vacuuming every day—even the barely used first-floor rooms—and dashing to Gristedes for ingredients to make my favorite foods.

"Your belly is not sufficiently big," she would say.

"The doctor says I'm just fine."

"Too skinny. Here, taste. The best raisin cookies I have ever baked."

"I'm still digesting the fish from lunch, Banu."

"Hours ago. Eat now. As a favor to me. If you eat my foods, the baby will resemble me."

The truth was, I didn't have much of a taste for Persian food. My cravings were for ham sandwiches on rye bread and bacon cheeseburgers brought in from a place on Seventieth and Third called Americana. I guess pork was a form of rebellion. Finally, Banu lost her temper. In that shrill, squeaky voice that can hardly ever be taken seriously, she yelled, "This food is poison! Too much salt. You will become swollen and fat like a Japanese wrestler. Dangerous for you, for the baby. I know these things. My mother was a midwife. No more food from outside."

I knew she was right. Besides, she was so cute standing there in her black polyester trousers and extra-small pink wool sweater, sleeves rolled up twice and hem almost reaching her knees. "You are mean," I mumbled to her.

"And you are grouchy, like a bear."

In the mornings, I'd come into the kitchen, my swelling breasts popping the buttons on my nightgown, and she would be sitting there, waiting, a full breakfast in the warming oven. It didn't matter if I wasn't hungry. "Is it a law that you must be hungry in order to eat? Here. Bread and cheese. Eat, my daughter, eat. Your pallor is gray like dryer lint. Taste my eggs and marmalade and you will love me again."

I'd rub my eyes, yawn, eat, and drink. Sometimes I'd look up and see her wiping her nose with her flowered hanky. "Stop crying," I'd say.

"I am crying from happiness. The Almighty has returned my precious girl to me and soon I will be an auntie."

I knew how her mind worked. She thinks God balances horrors with miracles. He gives everyone an equal share of good and bad. "Your destiny is written on your forehead, Layla," she had always said. So the baby was my miracle, the good that equalized the bad. I used to challenge her about this: what about So-and-So, who buried two children, has cancer, hates her husband, and lost all her money in the Revolution? And Banu would find something to explain it all. Like how beautiful So-and-So was with extraordinary violet eyes and a figure like Marilyn Monroe—even the shah had considered her for a wife—but she was too young at the time. And later, the suitors! Thousands! See? She had so much of a good thing, the Almighty had to balance it out with tragedy.

Well, I thought, I must be more attractive than I think.

She screened my telephone calls. Quick as a snake she'd grab the receiver. "Hallo," she'd bleat into the phone. "Ah, Hallo Laurrie. How are you? I no talk to you long time. How you parents? Good? . . . yes . . . no, she sleeping. She very pressed, you know."

"*De*pressed," I'd whisper.

"*Dee*pressed," Banu repeated. "I tell her call you. But maybe take few wiks, okay? . . . You say hallo to you parents. *Ciao*."

I lifted my eyebrow after she said that. "*Ciao?*"

"Everybody says this now. I like it. Italian *chic*."

My father called every day from France. We would speak only for a minute; long distance was expensive. I guess he just wanted to hear the sound of my voice. He asked me questions he didn't wait to hear the answers to: How are you feeling? Are you all right? Sleeping better? I reassured him, but in my mind I told him to come home. I knew what his response would have been; that the villa had to be sold, everything packed up or auctioned off. Partly that was true, but I knew that it was difficult for him to be around me, to see the bad memories haunting my eyes like watery ghosts.

When I came down dressed in a maternity jumper Katy had sent me from London, Banu clapped her hands. "Finally, you look six months along!" We were going to my second visit to the obstetrician. Banu wrapped my head in a newly knitted wool scarf, then ordered me to put on my fur coat, my boots, my gloves. I already felt the anxiety sweat in my armpits and under my eyes—leaving the apartment scared me—but I didn't say anything to her.

Out on the sidewalk, the frigid wind stung my cheeks and lips. Banu turned to Mario the doorman and said, "I see you get confetti off building. Very good." Mario looked at me. "Graffiti," I said. Then he nodded and smiled. "Yes, yes, Miss *Binoo*." I breathed deeply and my chest tingled. On the opposite sidewalk, an old Christmas tree lay on its side, strands of tinsel fluttering from dried-out branches. The holidays had come and gone. Banu said she missed putting up a tree and walking over to Saint Patrick's to sing carols with my friends on Christmas Eve. We'd always done that, unable to resist the coziness of Christmas. I took Banu's skinny arm, and we walked toward Madison Avenue; I recognized every crack in the pavement, but felt that my feet were not quite touching them.

There were differences in the neighborhood. Someone had hung bright yellow drapes in the second-floor window two buildings down from ours; there was a new brass knocker in the shape of an open lion's mouth on number 52A, and the wrought-iron railing around Dr. Marshall's basement office had been painted white. Madison loomed in the distance; yellow blurs of cabs rushing uptown. Two men passed us from the opposite direction; the steam from their mouths obscured their faces. Their milky eyes seemed to stare at me, looking for something. Did I know them? Did they know me? The scene of Dariush's arrest at the Tehran Hilton flashed in front of my eyes, making me squint. The man on the right had the same kind of wiry hair as the crazy general. My pulse beat in my neck, beat faster. I longed to run back to the apartment, but I walked forward, holding on to Banu, whispering the name of my baby over and over.

Later, in the doctor's office, Banu drove the nurse crazy with her questions about my condition and her sour, disapproving expression. During the sonogram, she insisted on having a close-up look at the baby's newly discovered penis; she outlined it with her finger, making smudges on the technician's screen. I lay there stunned and feeling foolish. What was the male equivalent of Rachel? Rachello? Rachard? Rach? Dare I name him Dariush?

The snow in February reminded me of the view from Feri's window seat. The cottony patch of Sixty-seventh Street that I could see from my bedroom window looked like any city street covered in snow. The world seemed smaller, and I felt just a little less like I'd been rocketed to another solar system, far away from everyone who mattered.

There had been no letters from Feri or from Asya. Uncle Hooshang had called me from London to warn me not to communicate with them for a while. The regime was really cracking down on the *Mojahedeen* and other opposition groups. For a while, it had seemed that the theocracy might fall, but not anymore. I knew that a mere letter postmarked from anywhere in the West, especially America, could give the *komiteh* an excuse to arrest Feri or Asya. So Banu decided if she couldn't thank Feri in words, she would donate something in her name. She gave all our old blankets and sheets and towels to a Russian church in *Boorookyleen*.

As for news from Amir? One letter. Not even a letter. A note. Scribbled on notepad paper from, of all places, the Istanbul Hilton, and hand delivered to the villa just two weeks after I'd gotten there: *Sorry. Will be delayed maybe some months. Don't worry—Amir*. What a horrible way to live, I thought. In secret. As someone else. As no one, really.

In early March, Baba-*joon* called and asked if I minded that he stay in Europe for *Norooz*. It would be the first time we wouldn't be together for the Persian New Year. He was sorry, but he had a meeting in Geneva with some bank people. I told him I didn't mind, I understood. The truth was, I hadn't realized it was almost spring and now that I did, I couldn't bear to celebrate it.

It reminded me of Dariush. Not that memories of him weren't always knocking around my head, unheedful of pleas to recede. But at *Norooz* I could sense his touch, his voice, his scent, his wit; I wore him like a piece of clothing. It had been the best time of year. Now it was the worst.

Banu got angry with me because I wouldn't let her lay the *Norooz* table with all its Zoroastrian fertility symbols and decorated eggs. "It is going to be a new year. You must begin a new life! Go out. Visit friends. Everyone wants to see you." She ignored me and laid out the arrangement on the credenza in the dining room where we'd always had it. Seven items that began with the Farsi letter *S*: an apple, some vinegar, a hyacinth flower, live herbs, sumac, garlic cloves, and old Persian coins. My father's heavy leather-bound *Qoran* was there too (even though the Zoroastrians who celebrated the arrival of spring came long before there ever was a *Qoran*) and two baby goldfish—I knew Banu thought that if I saw them darting about in their glass bowl I would remember how as a child it was my responsibility to feed them and change their water and hum to them so they would be healthy and happy for New Year's Day, bringing everyone good luck.

But I made her give them to eight-year-old Peter down the hall.

She pouted and took all the items to her bedroom, where she set up a little *Norooz* table. She borrowed my gold chains to grasp in her tiny wrinkled hands at the moment the New Year arrived so she would be sure not to fall into poverty for at least the next year.

The vernal equinox—the arrival of spring—was in the middle of the night that year, and I could hear Banu moving around in the kitchen, preparing tea and sweets for herself. I knew it was terrible of me to let her spend that moment alone, but the idea of smiling at the rebirth of the world soured my stomach.

So I closed my eyes, moved my hands under my nightgown, laid my palms on the bare skin of my swollen belly, and dreamed that my son's father was alive.

In mid-April, a breeze smelling like limes wafted off Central Park. I'd just had my eighth month checkup. Banu suggested we visit "The Big Museum" (she can't pronounce Metropolitan) and look at the costumes, especially the "old soldiers in steel shirts."

"No," I said. "Let's get a hot dog." *That* sent her into a whining fit: "You never like to go anywhere; you are always alone—reading while eating, eating while reading; you have gained too much weight. If you were not so tall, you would look like HumpeeDumbo."

"Humpty Dumpty," I said. She was right. I was fat. The doctor had said so herself. But I didn't really care.

Banu kept up this whining as we strolled down Fifth Avenue. The doormen smiled and gave me knowing looks as we passed— *Yeah, I've got a mother like that too.* Then a voice cut Banu short. "Layla?" the voice said, amazed and amused like an old classmate at a reunion. "It's me, Anahita. How *are* you?"

I stopped in my tracks, not sure what to say. Anahita's story was tragic; her father was one of the executed men Dariush and I'd seen in those pictures that got passed around. After the regime beat him and shot him for a reason they never revealed, they sent Anahita's mother a bill for the bullet they used to kill him, then emptied all her bank accounts and rented her house out from under her—to five families. She got on the first plane out and never looked back. Last I'd heard, she lived with Anahita and her brother in New Jersey.

I hadn't seen Anahita in almost two years. I'd run into her at brunch one Sunday in the Village at this German restaurant that made the best Belgian waffles. Our group was a mixture of Iranians and Americans. I don't know why she came; you could tell she was still suffering: greasy hair, no makeup, wrinkled clothing, puffy eyes from crying and insomnia. She'd turned inward and bitter. Who could blame her? Dariush made her sit next to us and kept a protective arm around her shoulder until she seemed comfortable; they'd been classmates since grammar school. Then suddenly, by about the middle of the meal, she began ranting and cursing about how the Revolution was the fault of the U.S. government and the ignoramus Jimmy Carter, whose criticisms of the shah's human-rights record had started everything. It was one of those unbearable social moments when being multicultural could make you everyone's enemy. I'd excused myself to the bathroom.

But now, on the sidewalk, Anahita looked like a different person. She walked toward me, leaned in and kissed my face, then glided her palm over my protruding belly, an intimate gesture that was purely Persian. "*Ach jahn*, Oh dear," she said with relish, like my baby was a gourmet meal I'd just put before her. "I'm so happy I ran into you. I just flew in this morning from Seattle—I'm living there now—and Helen here"—she pointed to a tall, chiseled-cheeked blond girl behind her—"Helen told me you were in New York."

Helen? Did I know this milky-skinned American girl who stared at me as if I were bleeding from somewhere? "I was two years behind you at Chapin," she said. "You probably don't remember me." She wouldn't make eye contact.

"I'm sorry," I said. "You're right. I don't remember."

Anahita laughed. "My mother says pregnancy makes a person absentminded."

Banu jumped in. "Your mother is knowledgeable," she said in Farsi.

I made the introductions and Anahita suggested we all go for tea, and before I could find an excuse to get out of it, Banu said yes.

Nobody ordered food except me. Butterscotch sundae. Whipped cream. Nuts. A fake cherry. Anahita touched my arm. "I heard what happened," she said gravely. "I'm sorry."

Banu cleared her throat loudly, like a crow.

Helen stared at me, unblinking. "I'm sorry too," she said.

"Well . . ." I faltered, looking down, finally plunging my spoon into the creamy mess.

Anahita babbled niceties to Banu in Farsi. How miraculously she'd seemed to have gotten over her troubles. Helen still stared; I could feel it. Magnet eyes. She wanted to say something; her unspoken words rumbled like a volcano about to blow. Finally, she said, "I just, like, want to tell you how, like, amazing it is that you, like, survived all that." Oh God, I thought, am I going to have to look up from this wonderful white-and-gold-syrup world? Unbelievably, painfully, Helen kept going. "I mean . . . I mean . . . you look so normal!"

Anahita gasped. "Helen!"

I looked up, and Helen was leaning in over the table as if I was going to tell her some beauty secret. "It's okay," I heard myself saying. "I think the same thing every morning when I look in the mirror."

After that, Banu stopped urging me to answer letters and phone calls and to go out. She realized I'd been right when I told her that my story had traveled in every direction, from friend to acquaintance, Iranian and American and European. I'd been turned into a great tragic Saint Joan who, by the way, would be terrific entertainment at any of the dinners or parties they sent invitations for.

"They will forget," Banu said to comfort me. "The next tragedy will make them forget. Besides, you are going to be a mother soon. *This* will be your life. We have much to do."

We bought baby furniture, tiny undershirts, layette gowns, pacifiers, stuffed animals, diapers, and booties. Banu was often stunned by the new baby paraphernalia that had been invented since I was an infant. "What this?" she asked a saleswoman. "Umbrella? How you open? . . . *Aivai!* Carriage for baby? Soon they make one fit in my pocket." Then another time: "Escuse

me, escuse me," she said, holding out a small package of ortho-
dontic nipples to the saleswoman. "These melted. Too much
warm in your store."

Then she wanted me to empty out the guest bathroom so we
would have a special clean place to wash up, to store items, and
to bathe the baby. After my father had gone to France two years
before, I'd set up a makeshift darkroom in that bathroom.
Dariush had urged me to do it, and my father wasn't around to
snicker. It wasn't that he disapproved of my "hobby," as he called
it. After all, most of my cameras had been gifts from him. It was
just that he didn't want me to take it seriously; he wanted me to
get married and have children. What else? He'd certainly gotten
his wish.

The last time I'd been in the darkroom was before I left
Manhattan—God, was that already almost nine months ago? I'd
been purposely avoiding it. After a deep breath, I turned on the
light. Photos I'd taken hung from clotheslines and were tacked
onto the walls. Stacks of eight-by-ten black-and-whites sat piled
on a small bookcase I'd fitted against one wall. The overhead
light seemed so bright; it flooded over the pictures like cello-
phane, hurting my eyes. There they all were. My pictures.
Flowers in Central Park, boats along the Hudson, smiling children at the Bronx Zoo, the sunrise over the ocean, friends splashing and diving in the waves in East Hampton. And Dariush.
Everywhere. In every pose and mood. Frowning and smiling,
pouting and squinting; wearing a baseball cap, a white T-shirt
that says I ♡ NY, an Armani suit and short, neat hair; sitting on
the wall at Central Park, on the steps at the Metropolitan shoo-
ing the pigeons, on a bench with Banu, squeezing her against
him, making her laugh and giggle.

I sat on the cold edge of the bathtub and let the tears come. I
felt the baby thumping against my insides, bruising my ribs,
leaning on my bladder, hiccuping. I wiped my cheeks, blew my
nose and began to gather up the pictures and chemicals and
equipment for storage in an old steamer trunk. When I lifted the
empty bookcase away from the wall, I found one last photograph. A tiny square Polaroid shot of three young friends that

was bent and creased down one portion. I dropped the photo into the garbage. "Fuck you, fortune catcher," I said out loud.

David was born in March. He had black eyes, the piercing stare of a deep thinker, as I'd once heard Baba-*joon* describe a picture he'd seen of my mother's father. He slid out of me, eager to be laid on my chest, soft in my arms, breathing warmly onto my neck. Banu said God gave me an easy labor to "even things out." I thought about how nothing would ever be even or fair for a boy who had no father.

Thousands of thoughts went through my mind between the second I saw my son and the second after, when everything changed. Just to touch his soft, dimpled skin with my fingers, to smell him and have his downy hair tickle my nose, to taste his salty tears on my lips, and to watch him over and over was enough to make me realize that joy was not lost to me forever.

Forty-Three

The Wrong Side of the World

Dariush is frustrated. Confused. He remembers the apartment of the old couple and the sound of Amir's voice, and he remembers the men smelling of wet wool who took him away from there. They had not been gentle. Pain had stabbed the inside of his head; explosions rose beneath his eyelids—flashes of yellow and orange that blinded him. Then he had fallen beneath the pain, become immersed in a healing pool of warm water. There was no sound or gravity, and he curled up like a baby in the womb. Floating. The faint pulse of a heartbeat. He stayed there for a long time. Then came the whirl of the water, twisting him, turning him, thrusting him, until he emerged from the tranquillity as through the mouth of a glass bottle into the dry wind of pain once again.

And here he is in the house of his grandmother.

Sometimes when he opens his eyes, Maman Bozorg is sitting beside him. She looks so small, not the way she appears to him in his dreams—as she looked when he was a boy, full-faced and strong-voiced, sitting cross-legged on a thick carpet, her back against a kilim pillow, on the patio of her old house, surrounded by trays of fruits and sweets and a massive samovar that looked like an armored knight.

Now her skin is pasty as rice cereal and her forehead marked with age spots. When she leans over him to feel his forehead, he smells the sickly sweet odor of tooth decay. She often rocks back and forth, fingering her prayer beads and whispering appreciation to her God for the recovery of her grandson.

Finally, he has enough strength to raise his arm and touch her hand. Tears spring from her eyes, and she kisses his knuckle. He says something, but she cannot understand. She leans in and hears the thin and questioning sound of his voice—"Layla?" he asks—and the word seems to buffet her away from him like a wind.

"Do not defy me, Mariam! Do not forget your place in the world." Maman Bozorg's eyes are oval, the lids stretching toward her eyebrows as they do when she is infuriated.

"Forgive me, Maman Bozorg, but what you want to do is not right."

"Right? What do you know of such a thing? You have not exactly led an exemplary life. On the Day of Judgment, what will *Allah* think of *you?* At least I have taken the gifts that he gave me and used them to take care of my grandchildren."

Mariam cringes, but tells herself not to allow the subject of their conversation to be changed. She gets up from the green sofa in her grandmother's sitting room and walks to the window that overlooks the front portion of the garden where the small *hoze* accommodates a dwindling population of goldfish. She talks with her back to Maman Bozorg, managing to keep her voice even. "Are you saying, my grandmother, that it is *Allah* who wants you to lie to my cousin about his wife?"

"I am saying that it is *Allah* who wants me to protect him. Tell me, girl, what will Dariush do if you tell him of Layla's ordeal in the prison? You know he will want to go to her. He will not think about the danger to himself. How many times must I remind you that he is still an enemy of this regime, that they will catch him and execute him? I am tired of your stupidity."

Mariam clenches her fists. "But they think he is dead. We buried him. No one is looking for him."

Maman Bozorg hesitates, and Mariam turns to look at her. "I have information," her grandmother says. "Information from the son of Khadijeh-*khanoom* who works in the government, that there is suspicion about Dariush's death. You know how our culture works, Mariam. Secrets are rare."

She is lying, thinks Mariam. Her hesitation and the way her words come out slow and methodical—she must be lying. Surely the officials would have come to search the house if it were true. Or maybe she has kept them at bay with her influence. *Khodayah*, Oh God, what shall I do? I could go against her and tell him the truth. But what if she is right? Dariush would be gone again. No. I will wait, she decides. He must get better, then he can know; then he will give me the strength to challenge Maman Bozorg's intentions.

"You are staring at me, child. Have you something to say?"

"I . . . I think your form of protection is harsh, Maman Bozorg-*joon*, but I . . . you . . . You know best."

The old woman grunts in approval. "Leave the telling to me. Do not talk with him about her. Understand?"

"Yes, *khanoom*."

"And Mariam: Do not ever again call her his wife. The marriage must be forgotten. Are you trying to sabotage your future?"

Mariam shudders. "No, *Khanoom* Maman Bozorg." She keeps her expression very still and prays that this time she is lying as well as her grandmother does.

"How are you this morning, my grandson?" she says, laboriously bending her joints to sit in the chair next to him. "Mariam tells me you drank some broth last night. Was it good?"

"Yes," he whispers. "Best." He smiles slightly.

"I remember when I had the typhoid and I ate nothing for many days. The broth tasted like a gift from the prophet. Are you hungry now? Shall I call for some juice?"

He lifts his hand and waves no, whispers, "Thank you."

She watches him for a few moments. He closes his eyes, then coughs. His eye sockets are sunken and brown like an old, dying man's. "So," the old woman finally says, "I have come to do a painful thing, my grandson." He looks at her and frowns. "In the name of God, the beneficent and merciful, I have come to tell you the truth." She sighs. "Your Layla has left you. She went on the very day you were arrested. She is in America. It was the Jew, your friend, who saved your life and brought you to me; it was he also who urged Hooshang to leave Iran so it would seem that you too had fled the country. We must keep you hidden." He tries to lift his neck and speak, then grabs her arm with a strength she did not think he had. "Layla," he says hoarsely.

She pulls away. "I told you. She is in America. The Jew told me she was angry that things had not worked out. She left you, Dariush. She has moved on. Everyone knew she would do it; her loyalties, her beliefs, are different from ours. Why do you look away from me? You must face the truth. I never wanted you to be hurt like this, but you had a stubborn mind of your own. Look at me, my boy." She wills her voice to become softer, as it once was when she sang him lullabies. "My Prince. Please. Is this the way to treat the grandmother who adores you?" She sniffs.

He does not turn, but finally reaches for her hand again and whispers, "I'm tired."

"Mimish," he says while she helps him sit up against the pillows. "I have strange dreams."

"Dreams of what, Dasha? Of Dracula? Like when we were children?"

He does not smile. "Of babies."

She frowns. The *naneh*s used to say that dreaming of babies was a premonition of death, just as dreaming of death was a premonition of birth. "What kind of babies, Dasha?"

"One baby, a boy baby, but I dream of him often."

"The same dream over and over?"

"No. Sometimes I am the baby." He winces in pain; his shoulder aches from the bullet wound. "I can't explain," he says.

"You'll tell me later, Dasha. Drink this tea with sugar now and I'll read to you from Ferdowsi."

"No," he says as she helps him sip the tea. "No more Persian history. Maybe later, read me something in French."

"Whatever you want," she says.

She spoon-feeds him some plain rice and yogurt. He chews slowly and without interest. "I have other dreams . . . about the war."

She bites her lower lip. "I'm sorry, Dasha. It must have been terrible."

"Yes. But the dreams are strange. They aren't nightmares. I hear the missiles whistling in the sky and the mines exploding, but then I am in Cannes watching fireworks shoot into the dark sky." He does not tell her that Layla is there beside him, her laughing face glowing red and blue and yellow and orange from the colored wheels of light.

"It sounds like a pretty dream," says his cousin.

"It means something. I don't know."

"Something good," she says, smiling. "Dasha, you're finishing the rice and yogurt. You're getting stronger. You'll be able to get out of bed soon."

"You've taken good care of me, Mimish. You're as good a nurse as my mother."

"Go on. Your mother knew everything about sickness; Layla's *naneh* Banu used to call her *Khanoom* Doctor Veeda." She looks away, realizing suddenly that she has brought Layla's name up. The silence between them is thick like *ahsh*, and he prolongs it by saying nothing, watching it flood her face like curdled milk, hoping she will raise her lids, look at him, and tell him something about Layla.

Mariam is holding her breath. Her vision of the room begins to turn gray. She used to do this years ago when her grandmother scolded her badly; she would lie on her bed and hold her breath until she swirled into a tunnel of blackness where there were no bad feelings of humiliation and abandonment, even if just for a few seconds. But now she cannot do this. She takes a deep breath. She must take care of Dariush, make him completely better. This is all she can manage at this point. Whether sheltering Dariush from the truth about Layla is righteousness or subterfuge, she cannot decide. She hates keeping things from him—lying—but she knows her grandmother is a smart and strong woman who has always known better. And she is frightened; she does not want him to leave her again. So, her heart burning with sorrow, she looks at Dariush's waiting eyes and says, "Here, have this last spoonful of rice, *azizam*."

"Praise God!" says Maman Bozorg, pruny eyes behind thick glasses, as she watches the big old black-and-white RCA. "The *Emam* has fooled the world!"

"You're quite right, *Haji-khanoom*," says Dariush, slumped in an easy chair, staring also at the television. "The third anniversary of the Islamic Republic has arrived." His voice is flat, his gaze dispassionate; he realizes he has been in Iran half a year now. "Look at them, marching in the street. Why are they still yelling 'Death to America'?"

"America is the Great Satan," mumbled Mariam, who sits cross-legged on the sofa, picking at her cuticles. "And it's probably the only slogan they know."

"Girl!" scolds Maman Bozorg.

"But Mariam's right *Haji-khanoom*. Those demonstrators are just a group of illiterate guys paid to raise their fists for the cameras."

She thrusts her chin up and clicks her tongue, but speaks softly and kindly to him. "No, my dear boy. You are mistaken. This is proof of the country's devotion to Islam and to the *Emam*. Look! Look! Millions went to Friday prayers to listen to our spiritual leaders. And the government has released one thousand political prisoners. God is Great."

"They'll arrest a thousand more next week," says Dariush, resting his chin against his fingers.

"And execute them as usual," says Mariam.

"Shut up, girl!" snaps Maman Bozorg. "What do you know?"

Without moving his head, Dariush looks to the right at his grandmother, then to the left at his cousin. "Mimish," he says, winking at her. "Thank you for setting up the shortwave for me."

"What is this?" clucks the old woman.

"I wanted to be able to listen to the BBC news," he says casually. Maman Bozorg looks furiously at her granddaughter, but Mariam continues to pick at her fingers, avoiding the stare she feels like a cold draft. "Did you know," continues Dariush, "that Iran is buying arms from the Soviet Union and North Korea and even Israel?"

Maman Bozorg gasps. "Impossible! Vile propaganda! The *ayatollah*s would never buy from Jews."

Dariush has promised himself that he will take a walk in the garden on *Norooz*.

The *ayatollah*s do not like *Norooz*. It is an un-Islamic celebration. Blasphemous. Pagan. Zoroastrian. It will remind people of the shahs. But it is the one thing from *before* that they cannot seem to eliminate. The people ignore the rhetoric. They jump over the fires and eat noodle *absh* and clean their houses and make new clothing and cook herb rice and white fish. Even Maman Bozorg allows Mariam to set a small *Norooz* table, but when the moment of celebration arrives and they kiss one another for congratulations and Maman Bozorg hands Firoozeh a small wad of new *touman*s, Dariush feels empty and cold. His grandmother's parchmentlike face is relaxed and content and his cousin's face supple with submission. The three of them sitting at the head of the long table, the clock ticking out the silence and hollowness of the house, a vacuum where his parents, sisters, and his beloved Layla should be, make him want to flee. But he must be patient; he must get well, then he will figure out what is going on here with these two women who have, by some means, gained control of his life.

Later, Dariush rests his hand heavily on Mariam's shoulder, taking small, slow steps along a gravel path between poplar trees. He wears a robe and pajamas that used to belong to his grandfather. It is from the time when American movie stars wore such things in black-and-white films about wealthy New Yorkers. Maman Bozorg has kept her dead husband's clothing perfectly preserved since his death nearly forty years ago.

"You know," says Dariush. "Our grandfather wasn't like Maman Bozorg. He was a modern guy. He went to school in London."

"I thought it was France, Dasha."

"Maybe. My memory isn't so great."

"It will come back. How is the pain? You're not dizzy right now, are you?"

"No. But the ache is always there."

"But it's much better than it used to be. I know you're going to be fine, Dasha."

He stops walking and closes his eyes for a moment. "I'll rest a second," he says.

She holds his other arm. "Lean against me, Dasha. I shouldn't have let you walk this far. Your body is too weak. Let's go back."

"No," he says, straightening up. "The *tob* is right behind those bushes. We can sit there for a while."

The old garden swing's flowered vinyl cushions are remarkably dry and just a little dusty. They sit there side by side as they had done so many times, shaded by the fringed umbrella above them and facing north where the mountains seem to rise straight up from behind the house.

"I miss mountain climbing," says Dariush.

"You and Jamsheed never took me." She pouts melodramatically.

He gently thumps his knee against her thigh. "*Ehh!* We would've taken you. You could never wake up early enough."

"But Dasha, four-thirty in the morning is torture. You could have gone a little later."

"That was the perfect time to leave, then by noon, when it was too hot for any sane person, we would be back. We had such a good time."

"It's good to see you smile, Dasha."

"Have you heard anything of Jamsheed? I would like to see him."

"Oh no, Maman Bozorg says it is dangerous for anyone to know you are here." Her eyes are wide with alarm.

"But Jamsheed is like a brother to me. I trust him with my life."

"Well, I don't know. You have to speak to Maman Bozorg." Her hands are clasped in her lap, knuckles white. They are silent for a while, swinging slowly.

Finally, he says, "You know, Mimish, when we were children, I sometimes found you annoying." He reaches up and pinches her cheek softly to show he does not mean this to hurt her, that perhaps even her annoying qualities were endearing to him. But she knows by the tone of his voice—as if he is beginning a bed-time story—that he is wanting to tell her something without actually saying it; that she will have to ponder his words for a while.

"Why did you find me annoying, Dasha?"

"You let life happen to you. You assumed everything was out of your hands. You had this idea that thinking for yourself was a sin. Whenever we did things that Maman Bozorg disapproved of, like playing backgammon or listening to rock and roll or going to the Ice Palace, you did it with a weight of guilt on your chest. I never understood it. Your mother wasn't like this at all; you didn't have to be."

"*I* am nothing like my mother," she says, chuckling with what sounds like regret to him. "None of Katayoon's rebellious and carefree confidence were passed on to me. She wanted me to rush around the world with her, to zip like a mosquito through life. And she expected me to make decisions on my own; she let me be totally free for as far back as I can remember. She didn't real-ize that I needed guidance."

"Sounds like Maman Bozorg talking, not you, Mimish."

She shrugs. "So? Maman Bozorg is smart. And she was there for me. While my mother was traveling in Europe or busy with all her projects, Maman Bozorg wanted me."

"You could've gone with your mother, Mimish. She wanted you to study in Europe; she always tried to include you in her projects. But you didn't want to; you always seemed content to stay at Maman Bozorg's dark and stuffy house, even when we were little. You wouldn't even go to birthday parties."

She slides a little away from him and folds her arms across her chest. "I was shy. I couldn't help it. I wasn't like you and Layla. And Maman Bozorg made me realize that there was nothing wrong with that—that I was meant to lead a different kind of life. I felt safe at her house."

"You were unhappy. She treated you badly. She still does."

Mariam stands up abruptly; the swing trembles and groans at the unevenly distributed weight. "I don't want to talk about this," she says, clenching her fists. "It's not right. You and I are the most important people in Maman Bozorg's life; she always did everything for us."

He stares at her and blinks his eyes slowly. She is agitated; he needs to back off. It is enough for now. So he says, "I know, Mimish. She is a devoted grandmother. Her pride and attention have always touched my heart." He lifts his head from its resting place against the swing back. "I think I've had enough fresh air; let's go in. It's chilly." He leans forward and puts his palms over his eyes.

"Are you all right, Dasha?" she asks.

"Just dizzy." And tired, he thinks. Will he ever be himself again? All that talking and walking, and now it is as if an arrow is stuck through his head; when he closes his eyes, he could swear he was tripping. Be patient, he tells himself over and over. Healing is a slow process, his father always said. How he misses his father.

The peach trees are blossoming when Dariush's vision improves enough so he can sketch. He asks Mariam if she can get him a drawing pad, and she sends the driver for one immediately. "This is wonderful!" she says. "Soon you will be able to read and your head will stop hurting you altogether. Dasha—you will not need me anymore." She says this teasingly, but her stomach knots with dread.

"I will always need you, Mimish." He stands at the glass patio door, hands on his hips, looking at the garden or maybe just thinking. She remembers a time when they were children, leaning over the wall of the water well, looking down into an abyss of darkness. Mariam had never seen the inside of the well; it had always been covered with a heavy wooden slab. But it had been the place where she and Dariush often played because he was so intrigued by how old it was, how the stones were so thin and tightly mortared together, how it must have taken years for the old masons to build it. That day when they peered into the hole, Mariam was shocked. She had always liked the feel of the stones on the well's outer wall; they had eroded over time and felt smooth against her back. She had thought the inside of the well was much the same as the outside; deeper, of course, but not so deep that she would not be able to see water at the bottom. She even thought the inside might be tiled in blue, like the fountain pools in Esfahan. But it was black, blacker than her grandmother's *chador*. "Where is the water?" she asked Dariush.

"It's probably dried up," he said. He handed her a stone and told her to drop it into the well so they could get an idea of how deep it was. "And if there's water," he said, "we'll hear the splash."

But they never heard anything. Dariush dropped in a bigger stone and they waited. Nothing. They yelled "Ho!" down the chute a few times, but the echoes they expected did not come back at them. Next they dropped in an empty Canada Dry orange soda bottle. Still nothing. Then a brass tray they stole from the pantry; it knocked against the stone wall with a loud, nasally clang, glimmered golden for a second, and fell out of sight without a sound. They shined a flashlight down the hole, but there was never an end to the blackness.

Finally, Dariush turned to his cousin and shrugged. "I guess it goes to the other side of the earth where everything is in reverse and upside down." Mariam was old enough to know he was teasing, and she shoved him playfully.

"I see," she said. "So everyone walks backwards on their hands?"

And he thought for a moment, then said, "No. It's where people say yes when they mean no, laugh when they're sad, and are beautiful when they're ugly."

Mariam had squealed with delight; she loved her cousin's inventiveness. "What else! What else do they do on the other side of the world?" she asked, jumping up and down.

He thought some more. "Okay," he said. "They go to the cinema when it's time to pray, go swimming when they have schoolwork, go to the *Fanfar* to ride the Ferris wheel when it is bedtime. Now you think of some, Mimish."

But her ideas were never as creative as Dariush's; she imagined people smiling when they were angry or speaking out when they were shy or having smart thoughts when they were actually dumb. The "opposite world" game had occupied them on many boring afternoons; they imagined hundreds of possibilities, each one more absurd than the other. They never opened the well again because the gardener had tattled on them and sent Maman Bozorg into a fury.

Over the years, Mariam had thought of the well often, perhaps because she had spent innocent and happy times there with Dariush and with Layla, whose theory on the bottomless well was far different from Dariush's (she suggested that it was a magic traveling machine that could take you anywhere in the world in a split second). But to Mariam, it was always a way she could imagine herself as the opposite of what she was, with an opposite kind of life, and an opposite kind of destiny.

Now, as Dariush turns around, his face silhouetted by the sunlight behind him, she feels as if she is looking into the well and seeing her cousin on the opposite side. As much as he is independent and confident, she is needy and insecure. As much as he can love her and still be away from her, she is lost without him. Silently, she curses the day she was born on the wrong side of the world.

She turns away from him and begins putting clean laundry in his dresser, blinking to hold back tears. She swallows and says, "Perhaps by the time the warm weather comes, you will be able to swim in the pool for exercise."

"Perhaps," he says, yawning. "Then again, I may not be—"

A rap on the door cuts him off. Firoozeh has the drawing book the *agha* wanted—and the *Khanoom* Bozorg wants to see her granddaughter right away.

"He will not stay, Maman Bozorg. I know this."

"Shut up, girl! You know nothing. He has everything he needs here. A beautiful home, properties on which he can make his buildings, the love of his family."

"His parents and sisters are in Europe. It's just us here."

"Just us? Are we rodents? We love him more than anyone else. We will take care of him better than anyone else. And you watch—the others will come back. They cannot stay in the West forever. They are Iranians."

"I know him. He wants to go."

"Where? To America? Impossible! That girl rejected him, betrayed him. He will not forgive her. Besides, he will have a true wife right here in time."

"No, Maman Bozorg."

"What, no?"

"I don't want that to happen."

"You don't want . . . You . . . You cannot go against *ghesmat*!"

"You mean, I cannot go against *you*. Destiny has nothing to do with this story."

"Do not raise your voice on me, Mariam. Insolent child!" For the first time since Mariam was small, Maman Bozorg strikes her across the face with the back of her hand. She is not as strong as she used to be, but the ruby ring on her gnarled finger cuts into Mariam's skin. Maman Bozorg waits for her granddaughter's tears, but they do not appear; she is disappointed. Mariam seems merely puzzled, like a person who has been woken from a deep sleep. "Feeble girl," says Maman Bozorg. "Wipe the blood from your face before it defiles my carpet." Mariam walks dazedly to the night table for a Kleenex. "What is the matter with you?" Maman Bozorg continues. "Do you want him to leave?"

"No! I don't know. I want him to be happy."

"Well, since you cannot think for yourself, I will think for you. Has it not always been so? And remember this, Mariam: His happiness, of which you are so concerned, is *here*, not anywhere else or with anyone else. If he has longings for other places, they will subside in time. And it is greatly *your* job to make him see this. An obedient and admiring wife, respectful sons and daughters, honest work—these are the things a man wants most. And we will provide him with those things. I will talk to him. You—go to your own room and rest; think about your duties."

Forty-Four

Maman Bozorg

In the year my Dariush was born, twenty-eight years ago, America rescued the pompous shah from his own people. I have heard that they admit this proudly in their history books.

There were demonstrations in the streets then too. It was about the *naft*. So valuable, this bad-smelling black liquid that came from the very bowels of our land. *Naft*. To whom did such a gift from God belong? The British who found it? The half-witted old shah who sold it to them? The Western companies who first sucked it from the ground? The modern shah who used it to finance his immoral extravagances? Or did it belong to the people?

Personally, I did not really care. My life had nothing to do with the *naft*; my wealth came from other places. Still, many people, including myself, understood that whoever controlled the *naft* controlled Iran. So they marched and they debated and they collected supporters in high places; broad-headed men. A man named Mossadegh led them. Yes, he was Western minded, but he was a true patriot. Of course, I always believed the *Qoran* should be the law, and not a document devised by mere men. In silence, however, I hoped for Mossadegh's victory over the son of the despot Reza Shah. I never dreamed Iran would see an Islamic Republic. *Allah* Akbar!

This young shah was not like his father; he was timid and weak and covered his insecurities with conceit. When the demonstrations began, he fled to Europe like a frightened boy. This is almost thirty years ago—thirty years in which the people had not wanted this king. Who wanted him? The Americans, of course. He was easy to manipulate. And they had delegated the world's preservation to themselves. In order to perform such a self-important task, they needed control. Of oil. Of Iran. Of the Soviet Union. Of the enemies of Israel.

It was very clever how the American secret infiltrators brought the young shah back. First they turned the demonstrations to their benefit—so clever, so unscrupulous, the Americans. They sent their disguised CIA men into the streets armed with sandwiches for the poor. Sandwiches? Yes. But not sandwiches made of cheese or watercress or scallions. Sandwiches made of paper money, money between two pieces of bread, money such as those people had never seen. They were asked to do just one simple thing in return: to march like the demonstrators, march and lift their voices in favor of their king, their shah, who would make them prosperous; where did they think such paper money had come from in the first place? So they did what was asked. And their hopeful voices overpowered the voices of the followers of Mossadegh. So you see, with sandwiches the shah was returned, a true puppet of the West.

But the pompous and self-satisfied Americans could not save the shah from the *Emam* Khomeini. Their evil tricks would not succeed over the Devout; they have always underestimated the power of Islam and of its True Believers. *Enshallah*, God willing, they are gone forever.

This is the story I told my Dariush yesterday. And I will tell him many other stories so he will not forget how the imperialist West squeezed the wealth and traditions out of us. I am sure he knows this, but Mariam's words have made me cautious; he must not think of leaving.

We sat outside on my balcony. The air is finally warm and fragrant with spring. I sat in my rocking chair, and Dariush lay on the carpet beside me, his head resting on a pillow that suddenly I remembered he had lain on as an infant. "You were once the size of that pillow," I said. And when he did not reply, I realized he was asleep behind his dark glasses. Poor boy, I thought, he still suffers from his wounds, is still weak. Or was it true what Firoozeh said about hearing Dariush moving around in his bedroom above her during the night, hearing the Western voices of the radio, and finding his candles in the morning burned down to nothing?

Though it was painful to my joints, I pressed my foot against Dariush's leg and stirred him awake. "You did not listen to my story," I scolded lightly. He stretched and said that he had heard the CIA sandwich story a thousand times; I should not worry that it is something he will ever forget. I praised him for this and reminded him that the stories must be remembered so they can be passed from generation to generation to keep such a thing from happening again. *Basheh*, he said, removing his glasses and rubbing his eyes. I told him we must fight against the baseness and arrogance of the West. *Basheh*, he said again, yawning this time. I told him we must be our own people; we must follow the ways of *Allah*, which are the ways of the True Believers. *Basheh, basheh*, he said, then he repeated those words in American— Okay, okay. He sat up, patted my knee, and told me to calm down.

"You mock me!" I said to him. "You think I am a silly old woman." He took my hands—his skin still feels as polished and warm as it did when he was a child—and he promised me that he would never think of me as a silly old woman, but respected me with all his heart. Teasing sparkles flashed from his amber eyes.

"And why are you speaking in that language?" I said. "I wish you would forget that language."

He threw his head back and laughed. It was difficult to remain angry with him; he does not like to be serious. Perhaps this is a good thing for me; I admit that I am sometimes too serious.

So then we sat for a while, enjoying the blue sky and the scent of roses. How wonderful it was to have him beside me. *Allah* has been good to me. I called Firoozeh to bring us honeydew melon-ball drinks, Dariush's favorite. Then I told him that this moment was the most pleasurable of my life because I knew that my grandchildren were taken care of and that I had fulfilled my obligation to leave with them all my knowledge of tradition and morality. Tears came easily to my eyes. I have never been the type to weep unless it is of some benefit, and this was one of those moments. I wanted Dariush to pay full attention now. He finds my weeping unbearable; it agitates him; he will do anything to make me stop. It has always been like this.

Why, why, why are you crying, Maman Bozorg-*jahn*? How like a young boy he sounded, using the same words he always had. He brought the Kleenex, a glass of water, a blanket for my legs. He hugged me, kissed the top of my head, begged me to tell him what was the matter and to stop weeping. Finally, after what I felt was an appropriate time, I told him I was weeping from both happiness and apprehension. He scolded me: Could I please not weep from happiness in his presence? He is cute as a mouse. He kneeled before me, held my arms, and demanded that I explain my apprehension to him, that whatever worried me he would fix, that a woman of my age should not have any troubles.

"It is your future, my boy," I said, running my finger over his dark, frowning eyebrows. "You must have a family, a full life. Your health has improved. You must begin thinking about this." He searched my face for a moment, then slid his hands off my arms and stood up. He walked to the edge of the balcony and leaned his hands on the railing, his back to me. I could have taken this gesture for reticence, but I chose to believe it was a reluctant willingness to hear the words of a wise old woman. So I inhaled deeply and continued. "There are several girls from good families who would, I'm sure, make excellent wives. But there is one in particular. . . . Perhaps you know who I mean . . . someone who cares for you a great deal—"

He interrupted me then. "I have already been married," he said.

The hairs stood up on my arms and I felt a familiar rawness on my tongue and I prayed quickly to Saint Abbas to help me control my fury. Calmly, I spread my arms and said, "Where is she, then?" He said nothing, raked his fingers through his hair, and turned around to face me. "I am still married to her," he said. I chuckled. "Well, it is no longer against the law to have more than one wife. You can have four, should you be able to afford them. It is the Prophet Mohammad's decree."

He thrust his hands into the pockets of my dead husband's trousers (their frames were remarkably similar) and he actually glared at me. I blew my nose and wiped my eyes, snuffling a few times. Looking away, I said quietly, "Layla deserted you. She did not have to leave. She was not in danger. It was you who the officials wanted. She should have stayed behind and awaited your return, but she could not stay away from her New York. I promise you, my beloved boy, she never loved you in the deep way that you deserve to be loved. You must—"

With this, he turned his face to the side and put his hand up to silence me. "Enough," he said. "Enough." He closed his eyes for a moment, then swiftly, before I could speak, he left me sitting alone on the balcony.

I am not a moron. I knew I had gone too far. But I am also never without hope where my grandson is concerned. No doubt, he was tormented by the memory of that girl much more than I had guessed. No matter. I would merely take a different course of persuasion; he was much more fragile than he seemed. I would win him with love and attention as is a grandmother's specialty. And I would be wise to soften my words about Layla for the time being.

I gave him some time alone. In the late afternoon, I decided to visit his room. I did not do this often, for the stairs are difficult for me, but it seemed a small obstacle at that point. I took my most sturdy cane with me.

He was asleep. Mariam sat in an armchair reading a Western book. She raised her eyebrows when I appeared, but did not rush to help me to a chair. I told her to go. I wanted to be alone with him.

I stood over him. He rested on his side, his face nestled in the pillow; the coverlet was tucked under his chin. I gently stroked his hair, which had grown too long, away from his cheek and forehead as I used to do when he was a child. Then, his hair had been much lighter, as golden as straw, as fine as the fringe of a silk carpet. His limbs were spread in various directions beneath the quilt. How large he is, I thought. Surely a man. Why am I always so surprised by this realization; it is the same shock I feel when I see my own reflection without first reminding myself that I am no longer a woman of forty.

I sighed and contemplated whether to sit and wait until he woke or return later. Seeing him sleeping so peacefully had eased my concerns. He was safe in my house, and he was my same Dariush who would forgive and forget. So I would see him later, I decided. And just as I was about to leave, I saw a fat drawing pad on his bedside table. *Vai!* How I wish *Allah* had saved me from that book. In my innocence, I was pleased to see it there. I thought: So he has begun drawing his buildings again; this will keep his mind free of her. I rested my swollen fingers on the pad. Why did I do this? I had no interest in, nor understanding of, his buildings. What evil *jenn*'s hand drove me to leaf through the pages and see that he had drawn the face of that girl over and over and over?

For the first time since my mother left this world, I truly wept.

Forty-Five

Layla

Banu called David Dovoud, the Persian equivalent. I asked her not to. He was David or Davy, an American boy. She wanted to know how Dovoud would feel when someday he would go to Iran and not know his own mother's language. I reminded her that he would probably never be able to go to Iran.

She shouted at me then, her voice like nails on a blackboard. "As soon as that Khomeini drops dead, everything will change!"

"Don't hold your breath," I said in English. "Longevity runs in his family."

"I know what I know. He . . . will . . . die . . . soon," she said while pounding a chicken breast with a mallet as if it were the *ayatollah*'s head on the butcher block.

My father came to see Davy, and it was the same with him. He called him Dovoud and whispered to him in Farsi baby talk. Not once did he question the name I'd chosen. He hides himself from the secret of my mother's religion as well as he thought he hid it from everyone else all those years.

When he talked to me about everything he'd had to do as a result of the Revolution—put the villa up for sale, curb our spending, stop working, even consider moving out of the duplex—all of these things he would call "temporary," using that word constantly, slipping it into sentences as if he were slipping an aspirin between his lips.

He stayed in New York only a week. Said he had to get back to Paris, where he'd rented a small flat. Said he was working on some export possibilities from Europe to the Middle East. The truth was, he couldn't stand to be in the States, where the loss of his business gnawed at his ego.

So he packed his suitcase to go back to Paris and told me I should start thinking about coming to live there, too. I hugged him tightly and said okay, but I knew that would never happen.

Banu made an appointment for Davy with an Iranian photographer. My father had ordered me to have pictures made and then handed me a list of people to send them to. I'd wanted to do the picture myself, but Banu made the appointment and then said it was impolite to cancel it. I told myself not to get ticked off; it was really not a big deal, just a picture. How bad could it be?

"At one time," Banu said just before we arrived at the address on Forty-seventh Street, "he was the most fashionable photographer in Tehran." At one time. The guy looked like he could have taken my grandmother's baby pictures. His "studio" was the back hallway of a camera store. Davy, though unable to lift his head yet, didn't like the place either. He wailed the whole time. I cursed myself for not walking out. But the man was trying so hard, cooing at the baby, dancing a combination of the waltz on tiptoes and the Persian arm-twirl. We made him sit down after a while; I thought he was going to have a heart attack. His son, who owned the camera store, came back and gave the man a pill to take. The son offered us tea and, lo and behold, behind some boxes, a samovar had been set up next to small tea glasses and a plate of his wife's homemade *zoolbia*.

It was an hour before we were finally able to get out of there. Luckily, Davy finally fell asleep in my arms. The pictures were taken that way. The old man, trying to make the best of a bad situation, explained that, in fact, babies at this small age look best with their eyes closed. Yes, I said, pretending I was very pleased, wondering how much I was going to have to pay for a roll of unusable negatives.

After, out on the sidewalk, I pushed Davy's stroller and walked at my own pace with Banu having to run after me in her flat slip-ons to catch up. "What are you doing, Layla. Layla?" she panted, sounding like a munchkin. "Wait. Why are you angry?"

I turned my head so she could hear me. "I can't believe we paid a hundred dollars for that! You didn't even bargain with him."

"But this is America!"

"That's *my* line. They were Iranians."

"But they are our countrymen. It is hard for them. You saw— he has no customers. He said he has to tell people he is Turkish or they won't come back. We could spare a little."

"A little! They robbed us."

I stopped to wait for a WALK sign. She stood next to me, her miniature hand patting her heaving chest. "All right. Maybe it was a little too high, the cost. I admit I was surprised myself."

"It's not like we're millionaires anymore," I said, calming myself down now that she was starting to agree with me. Besides, it was over. They could probably use the money more than I could.

"This is true," said Banu, squinting in the sun. "We are also struggling."

"Well, not quite."

She hadn't heard me. "You are right." She folded her arms across her chest. "They robbed us! I will go back and get the money."

"What? Banu. What are you doing?" I grabbed her sweater sleeve and pulled her toward me. "You can't go back and get the money."

"Yes I can. What do they think we are, the bank?"

"Come on, it's time to cross. Forget about the money. I'm tired and I'm hungry. Let's go home and have leftover *tahchin*."

She looked down at the pavement as we walked. "I'm truly sorry," she said.

"I know you are, and it's not a big thing." I squeezed her to me and kissed the top of her head just as a blaring fire truck passed and sent Davy into a howling fit.

* * *

The pictures *were* useless. Not because they were out of focus or too dark or too light. In fact, much of the shading was well done, in an Old World kind of way. The reason they were useless had to do with the angle of the shots; I couldn't tell how to hold the pictures. I kept turning each one around in my fingers, tilting my head this way and that, trying to figure out which way was up, how I might frame it so Davy wouldn't look like he was growing out of the left-hand bottom corner or sliding in from the top right-hand corner.

I showed the pictures to Banu. "Why are they like this?"

She peered at them and burst out laughing. "A fashionable way of taking pictures some years ago in Tehran." She held her stomach and giggled.

"What? What's fashionable about it?"

"You know, like movie stars. Marlene Dietrich, Marilyn Monroe, *Elzbit* Taylor. Very dramatic photographs, taken from the side of the face. Everyone liked this; the women wanted to look sexy and the men wanted to look sophisticated. Wait. I will show you." She brought me an old, small picture of herself, and sure enough, she looked like a long-necked dinosaur poking out from the left side. "It looks like you peeked your head in front of the camera at the last minute," I said.

"No, no. The pose took a long time to get right." She laughed again. "It was very popular back then, but now it looks very funny."

"Yeah. Funny. At least now I'll get to do Davy's picture myself."

During that time, motherhood saved me. Davy was so much work I didn't have to think about anything else. Not Dariush, not my father's precarious financial situation, not mine and Davy's and Banu's future. Motherhood was one cycle after another of feeding, changing, and holding. My thoughts and conversations with Banu were dominated by talk of how many ounces of formula the baby drank and then interpretations of the size, color, and frequency of his stools. Sleep was not on the agenda often enough, but Davy was a good baby. He didn't cry all that much; he just looked around as if he knew there was a lot to learn. My favorite time with him was in the middle of the night in the rocking chair when he drank from his bottle, gulping and sighing softly. Eyes closed and cheeks flushed with satisfaction, he sometimes tapped his tiny fingers gently against his bib as if he were already grown up and waiting impatiently for the world to catch up to him. *Can you see him, Dasha?* I whispered into the darkness.

"Okay," I said. "I've stuffed all the envelopes, the stamps are on, and they're sealed. Now Baba-*joon* can stop bugging me about these pictures."

"You ordered too many," said Banu, standing on a small stool, stirring her barley *absh*.

"I'll send the rest to friends here."

"Friends here should visit, not get pictures in the mail."

"I don't want visitors just yet. Danielle and Jean came over the other night. And Carol was here a few weeks ago. I don't want to see people who just come to stare at the poor scarred widow and her infant."

Banu kept stirring, but said nothing.

"Should I send a picture to Mariam?" She froze, kept her back to me. I was surprised myself. I didn't know I'd been thinking about Mariam. In fact, I avoided letting her into my thoughts. "Well?" I said. "What do you think?"

"Does it matter what I think?"

"What does *that* mean?"

"You never listened to me about her before. Why would you now?"

"When before? When we were kids?"

She looked at me over the tops of her glasses. "It was not too long ago that you were a kid, my daughter. I remember when you became tall enough to reach the latch on the wooden gate in the great stone wall between your grandmother's house and hers. I am sure that is the exact day I began to suffer from migraine headaches."

I shook my head and smiled. "What did you expect? We were the same age living right next door. Besides, we really had fun together."

"She was jealous of you," she said, setting the soup bowls on the table, then smoothing my head with her palm.

"She was jealous of my time with Dariush," I said, burning my tongue on the soup.

"Here. Water," she said, handing me a full glass.

"I understood her jealousy," I continued. "But we had good times together. I have good memories. And I feel sorry for her." Banu was shaking her head. "Her grandmother really messed her up," I said in English.

"A tower of snake poison, that old woman. So much hatred in her *del*. Still, there is a time when a person must take responsibility for what they do. Mariam was no longer a child. The letters full of lies she wrote to Dariush telling him to come back to Iran, that the Maman Bozorg was ill, that it would be safe for him—do you forgive her for this?"

"No. Not totally. But sometimes people lie because they really believe it's the best thing." I stared at Banu until she looked up from her dinner and saw on my face what I was talking about. "You and Baba-*joon* lied to me for years about my mother's real family because you didn't want me to be hurt. In the end, I got hurt anyway. Sometimes I wish you had explained it all earlier so I could have learned how to cope with it. But I forgive you now because you did what you thought was best. I think Mariam thought the same thing when she wrote those letters to Dariush. I don't think I blame her anymore. It's the old woman I hate."

"Yes, but in the end the punishment to her was also great. She lost the grandson she loved more than anything else."

"I promise you, Banu, she's more satisfied that Dariush was martyred in the *jihad* rather than married to me."

"It is my fault," she said, sitting back in her chair and rubbing her eyes. "I should never have allowed you to become so close to that family, to play with that Mariam. None of these terrible things would have happened to you."

"Nor the good things," I said. "Dariush . . . and Davy."

"You would have met Dariush another way. He was your *ghesmat*." She took a few spoonfuls of her soup, then yanked a tissue from the Kleenex box and handed it to me. "Wipe your eyes. No crying now, my daughter. You know it only makes you feel worse. Eat. Dovoud will wake up soon to be fed."

I did as she said because she was right; one memory of Dariush led to a thousand others, one tear led then to a million.

Later, after Davy was tended to and put back to sleep and Banu was in her bedroom watching *Dynasty* and the dishwasher in the kitchen whirred and rumbled, I sat in the living room with only the orange-yellow cast of the city lights streaming through the tall, thick-paned windows and the muffled sounds of Manhattan car horns to keep me company. I lit a cigarette and thought about how Mariam and I used to sit with our backs against the mosaics in her bathroom and smoke black-market Winstons. I thought about being a child with her. How we had to hide so many of the gifts I brought her from New York so she wouldn't get in trouble with her grandmother. Teen magazines with Bobby Sherman on the cover, tie-dyed T-shirts, a selection of Yardley pale-colored lipsticks, and so many others I couldn't recall. I remembered when, once every summer, Banu would take us to the Grand Bazaar downtown to shop for gold trinkets. There were no *matalak*s with Banu around; she filled her boxy purse with heavy pickle cans and walked in front of us, smashing any male who looked as if he might try to bother us. When the television show *Laugh-In* came along in the seventies, everyone who knew Banu said that Ruth Buzzi—the old woman who whacked dirty old men with her purse—must have known Banu too.

Mariam and Banu had never hit it off. Mariam didn't like it that Banu acted as if it was a top-secret mission to protect me. She said Banu was *foozool*—wanting to know everything that was going on. She insisted that it was her duty as a friend to teach me how to put such a bossy, nosy *naneh* in her place. I played along, to an extent, and I never openly told Mariam how much I truly loved Banu nor how much I knew Banu loved me. She wouldn't have understood. Her association with the servants was not like mine; to her, servants existed because someone paid them. She didn't trust them; she'd been taught not to. In fact, she believed that if she were to treat them nicely, they would take advantage of her. When she wanted something, she called for them. She didn't think of their existence beyond the realm of her own needs.

One day when we were about eleven, I rounded a corner behind Maman Bozorg's house and was horrified to see Mariam mercilessly kicking a soccer ball at the legs of an arthritic servant woman. When I asked Mariam what the hell she thought she was doing, she said the woman had agreed to this form of soccer playing, that Mariam was practicing goal shots. The woman didn't look at all like she'd been in agreement, grunting and grimacing in pain as she stepped up into the house. I'd snatched the ball, and my face was hot with anger. I started to scold Mariam, but before I could get out more than a few words, she laughed at me and said, "Oh, Layla. This isn't America," and my words were crushed by that mocking look she was so good at.

I know now that Mariam's occasional aggression was a response to the way her grandmother berated her and the way her mother neglected her. She looked for a sense of power and a release of anger. And the death of her father, which had created the sense of abandonment, had left her with only a few hopes: Dariush and me. Maybe if she'd been a different kind of person—less timid, more self-assured—she would have stood up to Maman Bozorg. I'd really thought she might manage that break when she went to Switzerland, but Maman Bozorg had carved her doctrine of sin too deeply in Mariam's heart. That was when we lost her. Maybe Dariush and I should have tried harder to help her, to get her out of Iran. But by then we were too wrapped up in our own flirtation and in the revelry of life in Manhattan.

I snuffed out my cigarette and reached for the picture of Davy on the coffee table. I'd surrounded him with white swaddling blankets on the floor and taken the shot from above. I'd used black-and-white film because I thought it made for a softer photograph. Davy seemed to be looking straight at the camera, but chances were he couldn't see clearly that far away; he was only a month old. Still, his black eyes were clear and the dark eyebrows above them were distinctly Dariush's. That was when I knew I would send the picture to Mariam. She was suffering Dariush's loss as much as I was; she had a right to see her little second cousin who was really like a nephew to her. So I grabbed pen and paper and wrote a short note to Davy's Auntie Mariam. I stuffed and sealed the envelope and scratched the Arabic letters of Maman Bozorg's address boldly across the front.

Forty-Six

The Water Well

Mariam does not usually fetch the mail; it is Firoozeh's job. But Firoozeh has come down with food poisoning from the black market chicken *Khanoom* Saadi sent as a gift to Maman Bozorg. Only Dariush and Firoozeh ate the chicken; poor Dariush, Mariam thinks, to be ill again is so unfair.

So Mariam fetches the mail and instantly knows that destiny is at work. She recognizes Layla's handwriting on an envelope bearing American stamps that has been clearly opened and inspected. She gasps aloud and instinctively looks about her to see if anyone is near. Of course there is no chance of that; the garden is empty, the driver is gone for the weekend. She stuffs Layla's envelope into her shift pocket and takes the rest of the mail to Maman Bozorg, who has fallen asleep in a chair in her bedroom, her feet immersed in a porcelain basin of cool water. The summer heat has become an invisible plague, and the electricity is never on long enough to allow the air-conditioning to cool the house.

Mariam leaves her grandmother's room quickly and quietly, worried that the sound of her own heart pounding will wake the old woman up. She goes to her bedroom and bolts the door. Before she opens the envelope, she looks up, closes her eyes, and prays to God that she is not about to be wounded. Her faith, however, is weak. She can already feel the pain leaking from the paper into her fingers, beginning a journey that she senses will break her heart.

Dariush wakes for the first time in five days without feeling nauseated. In fact, he is hungry. He sighs and closes his eyes again. The illness is over. He vows never to eat chicken again, to become a vegetarian. He looks to the chair where Mariam usually sits, but it is empty. He raises himself up on his elbows. His head reels, and purple amoeba-shaped images appear before his eyes. He falls back, sweating, and pounds the bed with his fist. Before this, he had regained much of his strength. The stabbing headaches and dizzy spells had abated to the point that he was able to leave the house secretly in the early mornings for walks. He was not afraid. He had decided long ago that Maman Bozorg was exaggerating the danger to him. He had taken some of his grandfather's old clothes—the baggy forties-style trousers, ill-fitting old button-down shirts, and thin-soled shoes—and wrinkled them beneath his mattress, soiled them with a little dust, spotted them sparingly with food stains. When he walked in the street, he blended in. Sometimes people would look twice at his light hair, but now that he had a beard, dark as his eyebrows, he looked unmistakably Persian.

The routes he took were fairly unpopulated and led to small villages that had not yet been overtaken by the city. At first he could not go far. His muscles had atrophied and he had the stamina of an old man. He told himself to be patient and set himself a goal. Just before he was struck with the food poisoning, he had reached that goal: He had walked more than two kilometers up the mountain to the *havang*.

It was an enormous boulder, ancient and smooth, eroded in a mysterious way so that it was hollowed out like a mortar, though lacking a pestle. Jamsheed had noticed this about the rock so they had named it that; the *havang*. It sat on the mountain at an angle so that if you climbed in and lay down, you could see the plateau of the city. Dariush crawled into the *havang* as he had done dozens of times and crouched to touch the cool, slanted stone. The sun was still low in the sky so the lip of the rock shaded him. He sat down and savored his accomplishment; *this* had been his goal, to reach this old place.

Memories echoed off the craggy walls; he closed his eyes and heard Jamsheed imitating Jagger—"I can't get no . . . Sat-is-fac-tion"—heard the clink of their beer bottles and the voices of the others who were like brothers, smelled their cigarette smoke and their hashish smoke, felt the kisses of the girls he had brought here to touch their breasts and press himself against them. He lay down, but could not see the dusty city, only pollution. He wondered if at night, when this place had always been the most beautiful, the twinkling carpet of lights was also concealed by the filth in the air. But he would never know. He turned and placed his cheek against the stone, wetting it with his tears. This is my country, he thought. This is where I come from. And I will miss it every day for the rest of my life.

When he had returned to the house, Mariam was awake and frantic. She had managed to keep Maman Bozorg from knowing that Dariush had left the house, but she was trembling with fear. He explained then that he had been going for walks to strengthen himself. But she could not calm down; she was frightened for his safety and of their grandmother. He held her shoulders and made her listen carefully. "I am not afraid. Not of the officials discovering me nor of our grandmother. I love you, Mimish, like a sister. And I trust you. I am leaving Iran and I want you to come with me."

She stiffened, and the confusion and panic in her darting eyes was disturbing. She clamped her hands over her face, said, "I don't know!" He told her there was time to think and decide, still much more time needed to choose a route and devise a plan. He shook her gently and told her to collect herself so that Maman Bozorg would not grow suspicious.

It was that night that he ate the chicken and fell ill.

And now. How long will it take for him to get his strength back this time? He opens his eyes and his vision is clear. He turns his head slowly to see what time it is on the bedside clock, but it is turned away from him. He frowns. Someone has moved things around on the table. His drawing pad is facedown—not the way he left it—and the jar of pencils is behind the radio, not in front of it. Then he sees the envelope leaning against his glass of water; Mariam has written his name on the front. Slowly, he reaches for it and lies very still while he reads it.

> *My dearest Dasha:*
>
> *Something has happened. Do not be concerned. It is not something terrible. I cannot explain it to you now, but maybe some day I will be able to. I am going away, but you must never worry about me because I will be safe and happy. Finally, I will reach for a goal of my own.*
>
> *Dasha joonam, I love you more than anyone else. I have never wanted to hurt you or betray you, but if you learn that I have, please know that I was manipulated. When you see our Layla (I am sure soon), tell her that I remember how much I love her and that I am sorry. Forgive me, but I have taken one of your sketches of her from your drawing book.*
>
>

You are always in my heart.
—Mimish

Maman Bozorg happily unties her scarf and slides it off her head; how she hates the hot summer. Her hair sticks to her scalp like gray seaweed. She steps up onto her needlepoint footstool and sits on her bed. She has always enjoyed her afternoon nap. As she removes her eyeglasses, she sees an envelope on her pillow.

> *Grandmother:*
>
> *You will not see me again. I no longer wish to be your granddaughter. I am indeed almost everything you have said I am: stupid, meek, uncontrolled, dependent. And I have no aptitude for lying or scheming or using the people I love. So, Grandmother, I am nothing like you. I have always been your great disappointment. Yet you held the promise of your love over my head if only I would do as you ordered. I lied for you, turned away from the world for you, gave up my mother, my friendships, my self-worth.*

You used me to inflate your own sense of power and now I know you have never loved anyone, especially not me. In the name of destiny, you justify all your desires. In the name of Allah, you justify all your evil. I leave you at the center of your own empty universe.

Maman Bozorg's crooked fingers hold the letter and shake it until the paper rips jaggedly down the middle. She crumples the sections, then tears at them like an infant ripping apart tissue. She grunts and gasps, and saliva sprays from her mouth like an aerosol. She lifts her cane from where it leans against her lace bedding and uses the strength from both arms to sweep everything off her bedside table: a wind-up alarm clock, a vase of yellow roses, a picture of her dead husband, several vials of pills, her prayer beads, and a crystal lamp painted with gold that shatters against the wood floor, now as insignificant as a pile of rock candy.

Firoozeh rushes in. "*Khanoom! Khanoom!* What has happened? What has happened?"

The old woman sits silently on the bed, her cane on the floor at her feet. She seems unaware of Firoozeh, but finally looks slowly toward the servant woman and says evenly, "Nothing terrible has happened. An accident only. Please clean it up now. I want to take my nap."

"She's coming," says Asya, watching surreptitiously from behind the drapes at the gravel pathway. "What does she want from us? Do you think the old woman knows we're here too?" She steps away from the window and says, "I'm afraid."

"She's harmless," says Jamsheed. "I promise you." He opens the door before she can knock and is struck by a face stained with a gray sadness. "*Salaam*, Jamsheed," Mariam says softly. "Thank you for letting me come."

"Please." He gestures her in. "You are always welcome to the house of your uncle. *We* are the *agha* doctor's guests here." Mariam looks over and spots Asya; at first she frowns, puzzled, then her brow relaxes and she says, "You are Fereshteh-*khanoom*'s daughter."

Jamsheed says, "Asya and I are married now."

"Congratulations," says Mariam. She stands awkwardly in the foyer clasping a soft black leather purse to her chest. Asya notices how gaunt she is, how opposite from when she visited Layla at the apartment. The *roopoosh* she wears appears to be the same one she wore then, but it swallows her now so that her head looks as if it is resting on top of a tent of black. Her shoes are dusty, and she stands stiffly as if she is cold, despite the sweltering heat.

Jamsheed takes Mariam's arm and leads her into the salon. He knows her well. She is almost over the edge. "Asya-*joon*, can you bring some cold water and maybe something sweet? Mariam, let me take your *roopoosh*; it's too hot."

"All right," she says softly, putting her purse on the sofa, then relieving herself of the trappings of her *hejab*. Her unruly hair fluffs about her face like a feather duster. Her forehead is spotted with pimples and her lips scabbed from her biting at them. The shift she wears is short-sleeved and brown; she looks as small as a child in it.

Asya brings the water and a bowl of raisins mixed with almonds. "Sit down, Mariam," she says, unafraid now, filled only with pity. "Drink some water. Are you all right?"

Mariam is gazing at a point on the carpet, preoccupied with her own thoughts. She looks at Asya. "Yes, I'm fine. Thank you for the water." She drinks and looks around the room. Asya and Jamsheed sit on the opposite sofa, leaning forward, waiting for her to tell them why she is here. Mariam says, "Everything looks the same. All of Auntie Veeda's things just as she left them. You have taken care of the house with such loyalty."

"It is nothing," says Jamsheed.

She licks her lips, swallows, and finally looks at them; her eyes seem lucid now. "I have come to tell you that Dariush is alive. And I have come to beg you to take him back to Layla."

Three hours later, after she leaves Jamsheed and Asya, Mariam walks on weak legs along the uneven sidewalk toward the post office. She smells rice in the air and knows her body needs nourishment, but the notion of eating nauseates her. She passes a *hejleh*, a wooden and paper shrine erected on the street corner as a tribute to a war martyr. She has never seen one before and stops to look. The shrine is decorated with pictures of a little boy who Mariam thinks should have been in the fifth grade rather than at the war front. Prayers are scratched on the walls of the shrine, and a small pair of soccer cleats hangs from a nail. She backs away, puts her head down, and walks on.

At the post office, the clerk narrows his eyes at her when he sees her letter is going to America; she raises her chin and looks him straight in the eye. "Give me the stamps or call the *komiteh*. Whatever you want. I am guilty of nothing. But hurry up, *agha*. You are wasting my time and this is none of your business." She knows the censors will delay the letter anyway, but it will get to Layla eventually.

After the letter is mailed, Mariam stands on the sidewalk and looks up at the sky. Not a cloud. Never a cloud in the summer. She hails a taxi and gives an address she has not spoken since she was a child.

The ride lasts an hour and a half. The never-ending traffic surprises no one anymore. There are government checkpoints every few kilometers. The taxi is air-conditioned, but eventually the radiator begins to steam and the driver turns the air off. As they make their way down the sloping avenues to the old part of the city, the heat becomes more intense. The driver picks up two other women for short trips. One is overweight and panting; she wipes the sweat from her face with her *chador* and says nothing to Mariam. The other is young and courageous; Mariam glimpses rolled-up jeans under her *chador*. Mariam smiles at her and the girl smiles back, but they say nothing, and when the girl hops out at her destination, she waves shyly and her long fingers remind Mariam of Layla. When they reach downtown, the odor of sheep dung wafts through the dry air and a *mullah* hails the cab. Mariam stiffens, but the driver does not stop, and she hears him curse under his breath. The *mullah*s never pay.

Mariam tips the driver well, tells him to enjoy a cool *sharbat* for his health. He bows his head many times, thanking her, wishing her the protection of *Allah*. He speeds off, and she stands before the tall, green wooden gate, her head shaded by pine trees. Down the street, she notices the Mercedes-Benzes and supply trucks moving in and out of the old Bahari driveway with its identical green wooden gates and small, round gatehouse. Her grandmother had told her that the house was a *komiteh* building, and Mariam cringes when she remembers how Maman Bozorg had giggled like a little girl when she said that *Allah's* sense of irony had imprisoned Layla in her own childhood house.

Mariam uses the rusted key she stole from her grandmother's closet to open the pedestrian gate, and she lets herself in. First thing she notices: There are no flowers. The beds along the driveway and in front of the house are filled with brown, brittle stalks. The house is as magnificent as she remembers from her childhood days, but she looks away from it. She has no good memories there. She walks along the south wall beneath the poplar trees, breathing in their spicy aroma, brushing her palm along the rough, hot wall until the old water well comes into view, then she stops.

The air near the stones ripples in the hot sun, and in this mirage Mariam sees herself and Layla as children serving teacups filled with sand to a circle of dolls. She hears them humming a Persian ballad and watches as they dance atop the well's wooden covering. She blinks and goes to stand by the well. She brushes dead leaves off the covering, then heaves the wooden slab off and bends far over the edge to smell the tart odor of cool, damp soil; she leans still farther in, trying to meet the velvety darkness, but it has always been too far away. She stands erect and removes her *maghnaeh*, which has become damp with perspiration. She holds it over the well, lets it hang like a limp animal, then opens her fingers and leans over to see blackness swallowed by blackness. She removes her *manteau* and drops this also into the hole.

She then sits on the dusty ground with her back against the smooth stones and cries, just as she had so many times as a child. Why had she cried so much? For the death of her father, for the neglect of her mother, for the disapproval of her grandmother, for the loss of Roberto and their child. The times she had not cried were the times when Layla and Dariush had been around her. They had given her love despite her meekness, her jealousies, or her anger. And now she cries because she has betrayed them. She had not loved them properly. She had loved them as Maman Bozorg loves: obsessively and manipulatively. Not as they had loved her: unconditionally and charitably.

She reaches into her shift pocket and removes the picture of Dariush and Layla's son. She holds it in her hands like she would a baby bird and peers at it through fresh tears. Aloud, she whispers, "I didn't know. I didn't know. I am not a very wise or strong person. But I have tried to make everything right finally. And you will grow up happy. I promise, little Dovoud. Auntie Mimish promises." She kisses the picture.

Her head falls back against the stone. She is dizzy and weak. Drunk. Eyes closed, she pulls herself up and lies down on the narrow lip of the well wall. She faces the sky and speaks silently to her God: Forgive me, but it seems I was born on the wrong side of the world. Tears glisten like shattered glass on her cheeks. She stretches her arms languidly above her head and sighs deeply. Then, imagining a soft black velvet mattress beneath her, she rolls over.

Forty-Seven

A Government Servant

The New York humidity strikes Amir like an affliction from inside his body. He sweats through all his clothing before the cab drops him at the flat he rented by phone from London. The old landlady does not seem to notice the heat or his mildewy state; in fact, she smells like cold porridge herself.

The flat is awful: a walk-up with bed and chair, roaches, bare lightbulb, no air-conditioning, and a stained bathtub. Amir accepts it. He is not one to dwell on past pleasures anymore. This is only temporary.

The job at NYU is not what he had hoped. It is rather embarrassing, in fact, to have the title of *associate* professor of history when he is a graduate of Oxford *and* a recent Israeli "government official." Americans are so very ignorant, but he is in no mood now to demand changes. His office at the university is adequate and quiet; his summer students will, no doubt, be either bored and boring or eager and stupid. No matter. He is here for only one thing.

It has been eight months since he saw Layla. Observing her now as she jogs up Park Avenue, he thinks she is more striking than ever. She wears baggy shorts and a tank top. Her sweat glimmers at him even from this distance. She looks much the same as when he last saw her: a bit of a stomach, some pounds to lose. But now, the child is born. Three months old. Her child. Layla's child. Perhaps one day, his child. He retreats quickly down a side street as she passes.

Suddenly, he thinks of his mother, dying of cancer in London where he left her two weeks ago. She would have liked a grandson to dote on; doting had been her specialty. How frustrated she had been that her illness had prevented her from caring for the wounds Jacob had given him. How thankful he was, however, that she was unable to touch him. He had grown sick of her touch long ago. And of her insistence on talking talking talking until his ears felt stuffed like cotton with her senseless words. Luckily, because of her ill health and the morphine, *his* convalescence had been quiet. He had spent quite a lot of time sleeping, drinking, smoking pot, and having doctors check on his appearance. At one point, he had dyed his hair blond and kept it that way until it grew out. When he was healed, he packed to leave, as planned. He remembers his mother lying in the four-poster with a floral bed jacket draped over her bony shoulders, gazing at him with uncomprehending eyes that strangely reminded him of Josephina.

The last time Amir saw Josephina was at a seedy hotel in Ankara days after Jacob had beaten his face. When he arrived, she was already fighting back tears. But not for his pain. "You took my dignity," she said. "Our relationship was a sadistic hoax. As soon as I started to love you, you started to hate me. You're a sick man, Amir Hakim. You used me and you broke the rules."

"So? What will you do? Tell Mossad that I used my position to help a friend? Where is the crime? I was not careless, did not blow my cover, and remained as devoted to my job as ever. Who of us can admit they've never done this for a mother or a cousin or a lover? They will laugh at you."

"So she was your lover?"

"Yes! She was my lover. She is my wife. She carries my child." The thrill of his lie electrified him, and he let loose. "Who have you been in my life, Josie? A good fuck? Not even that."

She slapped him where the bandage lay on his broken cheek. He sat on the bed, his elbows on his knees, breathing deeply to escape the pain.

"My brother was right about you, Amir Hakim," she rasped. "He told me you could never love anyone but yourself. I thought you would change. You are the same kind of monster your father was."

"A compliment," he managed to say while assaulting her with a backhanded slap, chipping her tooth on his knuckles. She cowered in the corner, mortified and seething. "I thought you might like to know that I'm leaving the organization," he said, relishing her wide-eyed shock. "I'm rather looking forward to a simple life."

She dabbed at her bloody lips with the back of her hand. "So unlike you to abandon your dreams," she said with a sarcastic grin.

He jutted out his chin. "I lost faith in Israel when Israel lost faith in me."

"Oh, Amir!" she sneered, mocking him with sparkling eyes. "You're still the same melodramatic arrogant narcissistic asshole you've always been." She paused. His eyes were wooden. She came close, weaving slightly on her heels. "The truth is that Amir Hakim was never important enough to Israel for Israelis to lose faith in him." She threw back her head, cackled. "You were a government *servant*, Amir—one of thousands. You're not unique, Amir. Maybe you could have been—so smart, so witty, so good-looking. But *not* unique. You know why? Because it is all you want, Amir, to be *unique*."

That had been eight months ago.

Now, he watches Layla push the sleeping child in a stroller. She walks from one end of the park to the other without tiring. The humidity does not seem to bother her, and this annoys Amir; is she so completely suited to this place? She sits on a bench sometimes and reads magazines like *The New Yorker* or *Photography*. She is always alone. He wants to sneak up behind her and cover her eyes with his hands until she screams with glee at his return. Most of all, he is delighted to see she no longer has the blank, red-eyed stare of a widow.

Perhaps it is time.

Forty-Eight

Layla

During a thunderstorm in June, the doorman called up and announced Amir Hakim. My voice shaking, I sent Banu upstairs to change Davy into his nicest jumper so he could meet the man who'd saved my life from the prayer-singers. Mouth open, eyes wide like an owl's, Banu obeyed.

I stood in the foyer, smelling like baby powder and Desitin and sour milk and realizing I hadn't dressed in anything but sweats since Davy had been born.

Amir stepped out of the elevator. Neither of us moved. He looked different; I'd grown used to his Islamic costume. Now he wore jeans, a black T-shirt, and a long black raincoat. He was clean-shaven and his eyes sparkled like oiled charcoal. His expression was deadpan. "Hello, Layla," he said. His voice sounded throaty, as if he were deeply sad or unsure of what to do next. I stepped forward and embraced him. He glided his hand over my back and pressed me against him; oddly, his hair smelled like Herbal Essence shampoo. It was comforting to be held by him; he knew my story, had gone through much of it with me, he understood. I suddenly became aware of my body—my still-swollen breasts, my puffy abdomen, my thighs—against Amir's solid bulk. I sensed he wouldn't let go of me until I let go of him. So I pulled back and told him to take off his coat.

We sat in the living room at opposite ends of the sofa. I noticed a fine scar on his right cheek and a slight bulge in his nose. They hadn't been there before. Or maybe they had. It didn't matter. I said, "I was worried about you. It's been almost eight months."

"Sorry. I got caught up in some dirty business."

"Really? Like what?"

"Nothing very interesting. I'd rather not talk about it. You look beautiful, Layla. Radiant, actually."

"It's not polite to give false compliments, Amir. You picked up some bad habits in Iran."

"I mean it." He didn't smile.

"Okay," I said. "Thank you, then. Maybe it's the joy of motherhood you see."

He looked away for a second, then back. "How are your feet?"

"Fine, if you don't count the way they look."

"Still scarred?"

"Yeah. But at least now I have toenails."

"Congratulations."

"How is Tehran? I heard things are calming down. Do you have news of Feri or Asya?"

"I left Iran a few days after you did, Layla. I've been in Israel."

"Oh," I said, disappointed. "All this time I kept thinking of you there." I tried to smile. "Funny. You were somewhere else the whole time."

Lightning flitted through the windowpanes. Thunder sounded and the brass clock on the mantel chimed the afternoon hour. Everything sounded low-volume. It was strange. I'd expected my reunion with Amir to be comforting, but this felt like an awkward first date.

Thankfully, I heard Banu's footfall on the stairs and soon she appeared, beaming, standing before Amir holding Davy in her little arms; she was dressed in her best shift with a faint gloss of pink lipstick on her mouth. Meeting the man who had saved her *dokhtar*'s life was a momentous occasion.

I introduced them and they bowed simultaneously, both of them saying "So happy to meet you" in Farsi. Amir approached Davy in that careful way childless people do, delicately stepping forward, peering over the blanket apprehensively, not sure they'll like what's there and concerned they might do something to harm it just by looking.

"Here, hold him," said Banu, pressing the bundle into Amir's arms. I laughed. Amir looked petrified.

"It's okay," I said hoarsely. "Pretend he's a football."

"I've never played American football."

I saw that he was very uneasy. "Banu, I don't think Amir has ever held a baby. Let's give him some time to get used to it. Here, give him to me."

Soon, after Banu brought tea, we had Amir holding Davy, feeding him his bottle, then actually burping him. Amir was smiling and cooing and making raspberry noises. Banu said, "You will make a great father, Amir." I almost snapped *No he won't*, but caught myself. Oh God, I thought, this is unbearable. I tried to shut my brain down, stare at Davy, only Davy, but I couldn't see Davy without seeing Amir and without wishing so hard that he was Dariush instead. For one shameful moment, I had this crazy idea that something had gone wrong in the soup of destiny and it was Amir who should have died instead of Dariush. My hands shook and I felt hot with guilt.

"He's beautiful, Layla," said Amir after Banu took Davy back upstairs.

"Thank you," I said, resuming my position on the sofa, hugging my knees, hoping to squeeze out the chill. "So, I hope you'll be staying in the States for a while."

"Actually, yes. I've moved to Manhattan; I'll be teaching history at NYU."

"Oh," I said, sounding like I'd been sprayed with cold water.

"Surprised?" he said, lighting a Winston.

"Uh, yes, actually."

"You don't approve?"

"No, I just never imagined you being anything other than a . . . well, a secret agent man." He didn't crack a smile. He watched the smoke rise from his cigarette, deliberately avoiding my gaze. He got up and walked to the window, putting his back to me.

"What's wrong?" I asked. "Are you upset about moving to New York?"

"No," he said, smoke curling above his head. "I'm upset because you told your housekeeper about my helping you escape Iran, because you use the word 'secret agent' as if it's a bloody joke, and because you talk to me about my job as if it is a regular job that in no way jeopardizes or *saves* lives." He spoke so softly I could hardly hear him, but I didn't miss the venom in his tone. He turned. His face looked hard like slate. We stared at one another for a moment. My cheeks felt hot with offense. Finally, I said, "I'm sorry I haven't handled myself in the way you would have wanted me to, but quite frankly, Amir, I'm not looking for your approval, and I resent it when you expect me to follow rules that you've never told me about." He bridled. I kept going. "Yes, I told Banu about you; she's like my mother. But I haven't told anyone else and I won't. But let's not forget that neither of us is perfect." Now *I* grabbed a cigarette and put it between my lips; he came and sat in a chair close to me and snapped open a gold lighter. I sat back and exhaled, looking away from him. I felt him watching me.

"I want us to be friends, Layla." His voice had completely softened.

"Friends don't lord it over one another."

"I'm sorry."

I looked at him; his heavy-lidded eyes were clear and unwavering. In a matter of moments, his expression had changed from harsh and patronizing to soft and amiable. It was discomfiting.

"Please, Layla," he said. "After what we've been through together, it would be a shame to go separate ways." He spread his arms, trying to make light of the situation. "Hell, I *need* you; I don't know my way around Manhattan. Where's the South Bronx, by the way?"

"You don't want to know. It's as dangerous as southern Lebanon." I remained solemn, but I knew I would agree to the friendship. I'd isolated myself from so many people because I didn't want to tell them my story; I didn't want to answer their questions or see the looks of pity and curiosity on their faces. Besides, I was a different kind of person now. I wasn't the same Layla whose life had been filled with people and events. Perhaps eventually I would go back to some of my old habits, but right now I was content to live peacefully, uneventfully, with my son. And Amir was right. We'd been through a lot together, and he'd been Dariush's friend too. Finally I smiled and said, "It might not be *too* hard to be friends with you, Amir."

"Good," he said, grasping my hands in his, strangely cold as raw beef. "Good, Layla."

There was an awkward silence after that. I stared at a tiny hole in my sweatpants and contemplated sticking my pinky into it. I had an itch to go up to bed and do a crossword puzzle or play solitaire. Anything but this. I couldn't understand it, but it was so easy to think of Amir as Dariush's friend and so difficult to think of him as my friend. For a moment, I felt I was in some weird parallel universe—which only made me want to laugh.

"So," I said, escaping my thoughts. "What will you be teaching at NYU?"

"Oh," he said. "Middle Eastern history, of course." He paused. "It's a temporary thing—between assignments." He paused again. I nodded and he continued in a suddenly low serious voice. "By the way, Layla, I really can't talk to you about my intelligence work. We cannot be friends unless you agree not to ask me any questions about it."

He must have seen the puzzled look on my face, but he didn't mention it. I searched his expression for some humor. None. "Amir," I said, staring right into his arrogant eyes, "I'm really not interested."

He smiled, nodded, and patted my knee. "That's the attitude, luv," he said, as if relieved we'd settled that one.

Before he left, he kissed my cheek. I smelled the Herbal Essence again, and the kiss was a little more lingering than usual. It made me hold my breath for a second, the way you hold your breath when you're a passenger in a car and the driver doesn't seem to be slowing down fast enough and you think he's going to hit the car in front of you.

Amir had an apartment in the Village near his work, but he came uptown several times a week to see us. It was nice of him, though I guessed the visits were as much for himself as for me. He never mentioned other friends, except for newfound "colleagues" at the university, and I could tell from his conversations with Banu about her food that he ate canned stuff at home when he wasn't with us. I sensed he didn't have anyone else, which was so odd considering he'd been this social stud when I first met him. He still had his charm, but it seemed muted. Maybe the years in Iran had done him some damage; how could they not have?

We went to the movies a lot that summer: *Star Trek II, The World According to Garp, An Officer and a Gentleman.* We watched World Cup Soccer and drank champagne when Italy beat Germany 3 to 1. We watched the reports about the Falklands War, and I felt a burning jealousy for those British wives whose husbands had come back from battle.

We took Davy to the park on Sunday afternoons. We would spread a blanket on the warm, sticky grass so Davy could lie on his stomach and gnaw on his teething ring. We stretched out and admired the glistening buildings beyond the trees along Central Park South. Banu would pack a basket with stuffed grape leaves and homemade yogurt and flat bread; we would eat and toast her in her absence with wine that made me light-headed. Davy would fall asleep with his cheek against my hip. I would lie back and look up at the hazy sky and find myself talking to Amir about the terrible fears that came over me sometimes: that the fanatics would send someone to kidnap me and take me back, that Davy would then never know me, as I had never known my own mother, that the fanatics might kidnap Davy or try to kill him. Amir wouldn't laugh at me or scold me for these irrational fears, but he didn't reassure me, either. He would reach over and take my hand and say nothing. He knew that I realized these fears would be with me forever, that nothing he said would make them go away. Just as nothing could bring Dariush back.

Amir invited me to spend Labor Day weekend in the Hamptons; a colleague at the university and his wife had rented a house. I said no; I didn't want to be around other people or away from Davy overnight, but it was really the thought of being near the cottage where Dariush and I spent that Fourth of July weekend, where Davy had been conceived, that prevented me from saying yes. It was Banu who convinced me otherwise; she must have remembered that weekend, too. "You cannot run away from your memories," she said. "They do not become tolerable that way. You must go to them, let them crawl into your heart so you can put them to rest there. Go, child, go to the seaside."

I'd forgotten how relaxing it was to lie in the sun, to fall asleep on a cushion of heat with the rhythm of the waves breaking in the background. I dug my feet deep into the sand, hiding the scars. I *did* cry, quietly, when no one could tell, but I also lay there and went over and over my memories of Dariush until it hurt less than it gave me comfort.

Amir's colleagues were Marc and Ruth, anthropologists who used their parents' money to travel to Central America and study obscure native tribes. Ruth liked to denounce the Reagan administration for its involvement in Nicaragua every chance she got; her frizzy dark hair and round cobalt eyes matched her zealous personality. Marc was her opposite: languid and droopy-eyed, an intellectual snob. The house they'd rented was spacious and modern; the furniture, the rugs, the sheets and drapes in my bedroom were all crisply white.

Marc cooked a huge bowl of linguine in clam sauce for dinner, and we all sat delicately on the stiff chair cushions so as not to chafe our sunburned legs. The odors of coconut oil and Solarcaine mingled with garlic. We talked about the schools we'd attended, our parents, Ronald Reagan's forgetfulness, and the fall in interest rates. I knew Amir had told them something about my background because Ruth had already mentioned it when we were on the beach that afternoon. "Amir tells me you're half Iranian," she'd said. And it had been easy to answer and talk about the terrible Revolution in impersonal political terms. But now, by dessert, Ruth suddenly felt comfortable enough to ask me about my ordeal in Iran. Amir had told them? I felt as if she'd asked me to take my clothes off. How much did they know? Damn him.

I threw Amir a disappointed look. He felt guilty, all right; I saw it in the way he bowed his head. He cleared his throat and said, "I don't think Layla likes to talk about that, Ruth." Ruth apologized immediately, embarrassed. That surprised me; maybe I'd been too harsh in judging her as a kibitzer. She tried quickly to steer the conversation to a more neutral area—tomorrow's weather, I think—but the damage was done; discomfort hovered in the air like smog.

Later, things got even worse. We sat on the terrace, catching glimpses of white water in the moonlight as waves curled onto the beach. Marc brought up "the Palestinian problem." Since the beginning of summer, Israel had been bombing Lebanon, going after PLO guerrilla bases hiding there. A lot of innocent Lebanese civilians had been killed by the shelling, hospitals and schools had been demolished, the Reagan administration and even the Israelis debated the issue. Marc said something about how he hoped Israel finished the job soon, blew those Palestinian terrorists into oblivion, taught them a lesson for trying to fight Israel from outside its borders.

Amir nodded. Ruth said something like "You bet," and the topic looked as if it would fade into nothingness as topics that everyone agrees on inevitably do.

But without my full permission, it seemed, my mouth moved and I said, "So you think it's all right to trap three hundred thousand people in the rubble of West Beirut just to kill six thousand guerrillas burrowed among them?" Amir winced as if he was tasting tamarind.

Silence. Then Marc said to Amir, "I thought you said Layla was Jewish," and he had this accusatory tone as if to say that Amir had fooled them. Ruth stared at me, her head cocked, as if I were a cluster of jigsaw puzzle pieces she hoped to put together somehow. Amir looked at me too, hoping I would answer Marc's question.

"Excuse me," I said, standing up; it seemed like my legs took forever to walk me off the terrace and to my room, where I spent the next hours thinking about my mother and remembering the last time I'd seen Mariam and she'd said my choices would give me the contentment I'd always searched for.

When it seemed as if everyone was asleep, I wrapped myself in a blanket and curled up in a lounge chair on the deck. There was a full moon, and the waves rolled onto the beach in coils of silver lamé. A humid breeze dampened my skin. I tried to imagine the sun rising, hoping such a vision would make me feel less marooned, less empty; when it was morning, I could go back to Davy and Banu.

I heard the door behind me slide open and I knew it was Amir. He turned a rattan armchair around so it faced me and sat down in it. His furrowed brows looked like black vinyl in the moonlight. "Look, Layla," he said. "Nothing I said would have made a difference to them. They're American Jews. They've been taught to believe whatever Israel does is right. For them, to disagree with Israeli policy would be a betrayal to their faith."

"Politics and faith are two separate things," I said, irritated and frustrated with him. "Israel is a nation, not a temple."

"This is not easy for them to understand."

"Bullshit," I said, slapping at a mosquito on my calf. "How can you generalize like that? That's like saying *all* Iranians think America is the Great Satan. I can't think of one American Jew among my friends who would have agreed with Marc's 'kill all the Arabs' attitude."

"Now, Layla. That's not what he said."

"That's what it sounded like to me. I know a zealot when I see one—and so should you."

He threw his head back and laughed quietly. He nudged my bare foot with his own. Our skin made contact, moist and slightly gritty with sea salt. "He's not a zealot, Layla. He's an anthropologist. Come on. Don't take it all so seriously."

"Why not?" I asked, pulling my foot away, curling it in under me. The deep shadows made by the moonlight didn't hide the expression on his face. I said, "I don't believe it—you agree with him, don't you?"

He leaned over and plucked a conch shell from the floor; we'd found it that afternoon in the wet sand. "Amazing, isn't it?" He polished it with his T-shirt while I waited for his answer, ignoring his attempt at distraction. Finally, he looked into my eyes and said, "If you're asking me, do I advocate the massacre of innocent people, the answer is no. Now, can we stop talking about politics? I'd rather you forgave me for wagging my tongue to Marc and Ruth about your ordeal."

I turned my gaze away and watched the waves. "Why do you tell people I'm Jewish?" I asked.

"Because you are."

"My mother was Jewish."

"That makes you Jewish." He paused. "What? Do you want me to say you're Moslem? After everything you went through in the name of Islam?"

"Of course not."

"Well?"

"Well . . . why do I have to be anything?"

He slid off of his chair and onto the end of my lounge chair: He moved in close until he could put his palms gently on either side of my head, weaving his fingers through my hair and caressing my cheeks with his thumbs. "Because," he said slowly, "if you accept who you are, you will find peace."

The hot breeze and the word *peace* fluttered over my skin like chiffon. Amir's hands were cool and smooth on my cheeks. That word *peace*—it seemed to have poured from his watery black pupils and rested on my lips like wine. I wanted the promise of it more than anything. I could have closed my eyes and let his mouth cover mine. Instead, a shiver rattled through me and I pushed him gently away.

Forty-Nine

Dirty Business

Dariush stares at his ceiling, at the mosquitoes swirling around his lamp light, at his watch: 11 P.M. He gets up and walks out on his balcony; the stone is still warm from the sunlight. Above the garden trees, he can see lights here and there. There is electricity tonight, though there is no explanation why. "Where are you, Mimish?" Dariush asks the moonless sky.

He tries to keep his optimism; she would never leave for good. Where would she go? He listens, as he has every night for a week, for sounds of the front gate opening or a footfall on the steps, a rustle in the garden. But there is nothing. If he had an idea of where she might be, he would go out and look for her. Maman Bozorg had nearly fallen to pieces when he suggested this. Wailing, she said, "I have lost one grandchild; I will not lose another!" But later, at dinner, she seemed only slightly solemn; she had even joked with him about how he, since child-hood, could eat only with his left hand even though he was right-handed in everything else. Either his grandmother was truly a wicked woman, Dariush thought, or she had become more unstable than ever before. When he again brought up what they should do about finding Mariam, she responded as if he were talking about a runaway servant. She waved her hand at him. "She will return. She has always been odd. Worry about yourself. She will return."

Dariush drops onto his bed again and promises himself that if his cousin does not return by morning, he will scour the city for her. Suddenly, he hears something. He sits up too quickly and squints at the pain in his head until it subsides. There! Again he hears it. It is the pedestrian gate squeaking open. Thank God, she is home! Leaving his shoes off, he creeps down the stairs so as not to wake Firoozeh. He reaches the side door just as she is turning the handle to open it. He pulls at it, forcing her in. He realizes his mistake immediately. This is not Mariam; this is a man who stands as tall as Dariush and is much stronger. Has he let a burglar in? Before he can reach for the light switch, the man grabs him from behind and clamps his palm hard over Dariush's mouth. "Don't bite me, you little sissy," the man whispers in Dariush's ear. Dariush stops struggling and the man releases him. Dariush turns in the dark and, with love in his throat, wraps his arms around his old friend Jamsheed.

Jamsheed and Asya have been awake all night. They pace the dark Namdar house, one following the other into different rooms, sitting in chairs or on sofas, their heads hung in thought, sometimes whispering with voices full of dread.

"You should have stopped him," Asya says.

"He didn't listen. I told you."

"You've known him since childhood; there must be a way to make him listen."

"Not always. Stop blaming me."

"Maybe we shouldn't have told him about Layla's ordeal."

"But Mariam said he should know."

"Why did she ask us not to tell him about the baby?"

"She said it would be too much. She said wait until we got out of the country. Anyway, she knows him best."

"Does he realize the danger of the old woman? She could feed us all to the *komiteh*."

"He says there won't be any danger after he finishes with her. We have to trust his judgment."

She snorts. "We have no choice at this point." She hugs her arms. "Where did you hide the exit documents?"

"I'm not telling you."

"Whether you tell me or not, if we're raided, they'll torture me anyway."

"Stop it. Don't talk like that. Maybe you should join your mother in Mazandaran until Dariush and I have arranged everything. The countryside is safer."

"No. I'm not leaving you. That's how people get separated forever."

They look into one another's eyes, seeing clearly despite the darkness. In one swift motion, they embrace, and it dawns on them both that the best remedy for their anxiety and fear is something they do very well together.

It is 5 A.M. The *Azan* leaks from the radio like syrup. Dariush struggles out of his grandfather's old, heavy bed, showers, and dresses unhurriedly in his street clothing. He craves a glass of tea and knows that Firoozeh has already gotten the samovar going downstairs, but he will wait until his grandmother is done with her *namaz*.

He looks around the room where, he knows now, he has been a prisoner. He will take nothing with him. Not even the sketch pad. He will leave that as a gift to his grandmother.

When Jamsheed and Asya told him that Layla had gotten lost in the city after he was arrested and that she was taken to prison, beaten, starved, and subjected to a mock execution, he vomited for twenty minutes in his parents' powder room before he took control of himself and spoke. He wanted to know the details: how had she recovered, who had taken care of her, how had she escaped. They told him everything: that Layla had found her way to Fereshteh's apartment, that his father had tended her wounds as well as broken the news of Dariush's death to her, and that Amir Hakim had arranged for her escape.

But there was much more to the story. Mariam had told Asya and Jamsheed shocking things. Dariush was not upset that she had explained everything to them and not to him. He knew his cousin; she was filled with shame. Still, he was relieved to know that she had finally seen their grandmother for what she was and had rebelled of her own accord. It was a good sign, he thought. Of course, he worried about her and could not imagine where she might have gone, but he allowed himself to trust her letter to him, that she had gone to a place where she could be happy. He resolutely believed he would see her again; to believe anything less would have hurt too much. He had forgiven her for the things she had done at their grandmother's direction even before he had known what they were. He had never been able to blame her for anything.

When he was a child, his mother would tell him that the best way to manage Maman Bozorg was to pretend to go along with her ideas and not to bother trying to change her. She said he must never feel guilty about such pretense, that he should live his life the way he wanted, the way he felt was right. She first told him this after the incident with the perverted *mullah* at the religious school; she had been proud that he had come to her immediately with the dirty business, that he had understood he was not the sinful one. She warned him that many people in his life would try to make him feel responsible for their sins or their woes or their inadequacies, and he must never give in to them.

How he missed his mother.

But he would see her soon. She, and all the others.

He looks at his watch. Five-twenty. He slips into his scuffed shoes, runs his fingers through his wet hair, and rests his elbows on his knees. So now he knows everything Maman Bozorg did in her frenzy of grandmotherly love. He knows about the lies she made Mariam write to him so he would come to Iran, about her part in having him drafted at the airport, about her offer to help Layla escape Iran so it would seem as if she had abandoned him when he returned, and about her repulsive idea that he and Mariam would marry. He has figured out the rest—unbelievable truths that he is ashamed to tell even Jamsheed. He remembers the sound of Amir's voice in the old couple's apartment; he knows it was Amir who brought him back from the front and had him taken to his grandmother's. And now that he knows

Amir also engineered Layla's escape, he realizes that Amir schemed with his grandmother to keep him and Layla apart.

That Amir betrayed him is not a surprise. He should never have allowed himself to trust Amir, no matter how desperate their situation. The waterskiing accident those four years ago had changed everything. For months after, he had fought a confusing feeling of dread and mistrust of Amir. He tried desperately and without success to believe what everyone was telling him: that Amir had saved his life. But he had flashes of memory, frightening flashes of Amir pulling him away from the surface and toward the green eddy of the deep. He did not tell anyone, not even Layla, about these images, but his intuition nagged at him to believe what he knew to be true: Amir had wanted to kill them both. His head feels heavy and he rubs his temples. An odd sensation flutters over him, a split-second image of something white approaching his face, of then being unable to move, in a deep but strangely conscious sleep. He sits up, shocked, blood rising to his face. So why hadn't Amir finished him off? It would have made Amir the winner. Was that what he had wanted? To win? One thing Dariush knows: Amir is playing this game with *him*, and Layla is merely a pawn. His chest tightens with guilt and fear. No, he tells himself, she will take care of herself; she would want him to believe that. He puts his hands on his knees and forces himself to stand up. Whatever Amir's motives, Dariush is perceptive enough to know that there are some things that go on in the minds of others that are unexplainable, unfathomable, unthinkable. His only regret is that he trusted Amir to help them escape when he knew in his gut that his old friend was unbalanced.

He takes one last look around the bedroom, notices the ashy sky beyond the balcony, and finally, with an expression of distaste, he turns his back and makes his way through the chilly, smothering house to his grandmother's quarters.

Maman Bozorg sits in her bedroom pouring tea into a saucer so it may cool. "Dariush!" she gasps, putting her hand to her chest. "You frightened me. What are you doing awake so early? And dressed in such . . . low-class clothing?"

"I've come to say good-bye," he says.

"Excuse me?"

"I'm leaving."

She ignores the seriousness on his face and forces a chuckle up from her lungs. "It is too early in the day to make jokes." He says nothing, stares at her as if she is covered with revolting sores of leprosy. He cannot remember what it felt like to care about her.

"Sit down, my darling. I will send Firoozeh for some tea."

"No," he says loudly so she will not call for the servant.

She sits as straight as her joints will allow, not taking her eyes away from his, as if she can subdue him with just this connection. He had lain in his bed all night thinking about what he would say to her at this moment. He had planned to confront her, to fill her with examples of the sins she had done, compelling her to see the terrible truth in the only way she would understand: as an affront to the rules of her religion and her precious God. But now he knows this will not work. Her fanaticism is as deep as the creases in her forehead and the disease in her joints.

"Good-bye, Grandmother," he says, turning his back to leave.

She snaps, "One step outside the gate and the *komiteh* will pick you up. You will not live without my protection."

He turns back slowly, trying to ignore the pounding in his head. "I have been walking the city every day for a month, *khanoom*, and no one has bothered me. I have had enough of your lies, Grandmother."

Sweetly, she says, "You are mistaken, my boy. Come here. I will explain everything." He does not move; he is mesmerized by the vacillation of her moods. Her lips curl. "It is that donkey cousin of yours; *she* has told you lies. I covered up for her and now she has tried to turn you against me." The room is silent except for the old woman's wet breathing. She begins to whine. "Have you forgotten, my boy, how I held you as a child? Have you forgotten that you are my favorite? Who has taught you such disobedience?" She wipes her eyes with trembling fingers. "You cannot leave! It will kill me! I will be alone. And sick. At the mercy of disloyal servants!" She cries now, and he feels nothing. Suddenly, she picks up the candelabra from the table and flings it toward him with all her might; it does not fly far, but he is stunned. "I forbid you to leave," she hisses. "I will erase you from my will!"

"I don't care about your will." She bridles and seems to hold her breath. "I don't care at all." And this time he turns and walks down the hall away from her room.

Despite her arthritis, she swiftly hobbles, with the help of her cane, and follows him, grunting and groaning and panting. "No! Wait! You cannot do this!" He is getting farther away. "I will call the *komiteh*!" she yells. "I will have you arrested!"

He turns but continues to walk slowly backward. "They would execute me. Is this how you claim to love me, Grandmother?"

She stumbles against the wall. "No!" She pounds her arm against the wood molding in frustration. "You are my boy! My boy!"

"No," he says, dryly. "I have never been your boy." And he stares into her watery eyes with unrestrained disgust. Then he is beyond the corridor and almost through her sitting room. "All right," she yells to his back. "Go! Go to your *kaufar* woman and your *kaufar* child! You deserve them. You are no longer my grandson. You are dead to me. Dead!"

He is frozen, but for just a second. He whirls around and goes back to where she stands in the doorway, bent as a water pipe. He grabs her jellylike upper arms. "What did you say?" he rasps. She gulps, frightened; yellowish saliva bubbles down her chin. He shakes her. "What did you say? What child!" She goes limp in his hands and slides to the floor, where her body quakes with heavy sobs. He stands above her for a moment. She clutches his shoe, and the skin on her hands turns almost translucent at the strength of her grip. He wrenches his foot away and, before she can look up, he is gone.

Fifty

The Fortune Catcher

October 1982

It is because of the Tylenol scare that Banu decides they should visit the fortune catcher. She is beside herself. Her little hands shake and grab like baby-bird talons as she snatches all the medicine containers in the cabinets and throws them in a black garbage bag. All the while she mumbles about their good luck and thanks God for bestowing it upon them, for keeping away the madman who is poisoning Tylenol capsules (and surely other medicines!) with deadly cyanide. Layla asks her what she is supposed to do if she has a headache or what they should give Davy if he has a fever or how Banu herself will manage a cold without her Dristan. Banu says she will wait until the police catch the demon poisoner and tell them it is safe to buy more. She is always sure the police can take care of everything. And until they do in this case, she insists they visit Emma, an Armenian fortune catcher who is also an herbalist and whom Banu has known since they were children living in the same Tehran neighborhood.

So Layla and Davy and Banu go to Queens, where Emma lives with her brother who left Iran years ago to make a good living selling mediocre Persian carpets to rich and naive New Yorkers. Any money he has painstakingly made, however, now goes to supporting all of his and his wife's exiled relatives.

The three take a cab (Ebrahim's Cadillac was sold months ago when he closed the office). Emma welcomes them to a rambling apartment on the third floor of an old brownstone. Banu had taken Layla to see Emma a few times in Iran when Layla was younger; she looks the same now, Layla thinks, swarthy "like a Hindi," Banu used to say; her most outstanding feature is a smattering of black oval freckles on the bridge of her bumpy nose. She is the only one home, but it is obvious that this is a rare occurrence. Rooms are overstuffed with furniture; wicker baskets are bursting with toys and sporting equipment, the living room clearly doubles as a bedroom (a bunk bed is wedged into the corner), and when Layla uses one of the two bathrooms, she counts six toothbrushes.

Exiles. Refugees. The diaspora.

The women sit in a spotless but cluttered kitchen at a table draped in a vinyl floral cloth. Emma answers the telephone and speaks in Armenian, then a smattering of Farsi, then Armenian again. She has already been an exile, Layla realizes, has been an exile her whole life. From Armenia to Iran. Now her children and grandchildren will speak in Armenian and in English. From Iran to America. She fiddles with the silver cross around her neck and leans over Davy in his baby seat, which Layla has placed on the table. He is fast asleep. "Face as beautiful as the moon," Emma says, kissing his forehead lightly, then placing the seat on the chair next to Layla.

Emma pours thick, bitter Turkish coffee into small china cups whose pink roses have faded almost to nothing. She sits across from Layla and Banu, tells them to drink, and begins mixing and laying out the playing cards in her indecipherable patterns.

The first fortune is for Banu, who sits forward as if she is about to receive a message from God. Layla fidgets. It used to be that she would be impatient for her turn, but the cards, like many things, have lost their magic for her. It is a beautiful autumn day—the air smells like warm, doughy pretzels—and she wishes she were pushing Davy along in his stroller on the sidewalk, checking out the Greek pastry shops and army/navy stores and old five-and-dimes that still have luncheonette counters guarded by a line of round, red stools.

Layla asks Emma for a glass of water and gulps it down. It is all she can do to keep herself from stomping her foot like a child and telling Banu she wants to leave right this minute. Banu, Layla sees, would not have noticed anyway; she is as engrossed in Emma's interpretations of the playing cards as she usually is in *Days of Our Lives*.

Layla had not expected that this little trip to Queens—to humor Banu—would annoy her so much. If, as Banu always reminds her, destiny is written on our foreheads, then why must we make any choices in life at all? Banu's credo about the way God has set up the world means Layla should believe that every raindrop falls in a predetermined place so every leaf and every flower lives or dies by a master design. But Banu does not think that far ahead, and Layla realizes why. Banu sits there jabbing her finger at Emma's cards, asking questions, making her own deductions, looking for answers as if this can give her some sense of control over her predestined life. But control is exactly what she has given up, is it not?

Banu finds what she wants in the cards: Money is coming her way, a whole lot of money, all at once, in a big brown envelope with foreign stamps on it, and the number twenty-four involved somehow. She relaxes in her chair and swigs her coffee until her lips touch the sludgy grains at the bottom of the cup; she places the saucer on top of the cup and turns the whole thing upside down so the thick remains can form patterns on the inside of the cup, patterns that will look like pictures to Emma, pictures in which she will find the future.

Now Emma begins arranging the cards in a wheellike design around the queen of hearts. "Here," she says, sliding a pile of cards across the vinyl cloth to Layla. "Touch and *nazr*," she demands, raising a bushy eyebrow and flashing a faint, tender smile. Layla touches the warm, slightly sticky cards and begins to *nazr*, which is like wishing, but more like silently asking the cards to tell you about the thing that is most important to you. She takes her hand off the cards and says "Ready," even though she has not asked for anything.

Emma finishes her wheel pattern; the playing cards are arranged in different places, facing different directions, looking a little haphazard but making sense and order to her. She sits back and surveys the cards. She begins to talk in a matter-of-fact voice, as if she is reading a lease document or a recipe: She speaks about money coming Layla's way—not too much, but enough to make her smile; she speaks about a letter someone mysterious from a faraway place will send her; she speaks about a boastful and jealous woman who is out to discredit Layla; she speaks about all those things that would fit quite well in anyone's fortune. Layla bites her tongue and endures for Banu's sake, and because she knows her Persian manners well. She keeps reminding herself it will soon be time to slide a few ten-dollar bills discreetly under Emma's coffee saucer and say good-bye. But Banu makes trouble. After so many years of having her fortune read, she understands just enough about the cards to be a playful annoyance. She points to a king of clubs. "Who is the dark man there?"

Emma looks at Layla and says, "An intellectual man with black eyes who loves you passionately."

"The man is Amir," says Banu, smiling at Layla like a teasing schoolgirl.

Layla ignores her and turns to fiddle with Davy's blanket. For once she wishes he would wake up and distract them from this foolishness. She takes a sip of her coffee even though she hates the taste. She does not turn the cup over.

Banu wrings her hands anxiously; she knows she is venturing into an area that is bound to upset Layla. Until now, Layla had managed to steer her away from bringing up the Amir issue. "Drink your coffee, Layla," she says. "Emma should read your grains. These cards do not see far enough."

"I don't want the coffee. It's too thick and strong. It makes me shaky."

Banu slides the cup in front of Layla. "Please, *joonam*. Take a few more sips; we'll empty the rest. This is important, this information about Amir."

"No. It's not. I don't want to know about it." Layla's words are clipped and her voice tight. But Banu cannot help herself. She points at the king of clubs. "He loves you! As if I didn't know. I think you should marry him."

"What?"

Banu puts her little hand—light as a piece of cloth—on Layla's back. "He could take care of you, Laylee. Someone must take care of you."

Layla shrugs her hand off. "And why must someone take care of me?"

"Why?" she repeats, looking at Emma in shock. "Well, because. Because that is the world; because that is the proper way. You have a child now."

"No," Layla says. "It's not the way for me."

"Listen to her, Emma," complains Banu. "What should I do about her?"

Emma sweeps the cards with her arms and collects them into a neat pile. "I would be proud of her, Banu-*jahn*."

Banu slaps her own forehead. "*Khodaya!* This is not the time to go against me just for the fun of it."

"Thank you, Emma *khanoom*," Layla says, her voice hoarse with frustration. "Banu, I don't love Amir Hakim. Sometimes I'm not even sure I like him. I can't imagine making love with him. A woman can live a decent life without a man. You yourself are an example."

"I am a different story, a sad story. Do not compare yourself with me; you will give yourself the evil eye. Do not laugh. You used to believe in such things. You must be practical. In the old days, no one married for love and a woman never expected to enjoy the lovemaking—am I right, Emma-*jahn*?"

Emma speaks slowly, carefully. "These are not the old days. And this is not the old country. You know this, Banu."

"What I know is that Americans live in a fantasy world!" hisses Banu, shaking her head. Tears form in her eyes and she blinks them back. Layla puts her arm around her, kisses her brittle cheek, and says, "You forget I was married once, Banu." Layla wants to say more, but the tears in her throat will not let her.

"And so you can be again," Banu says.

"No. I just don't trust him."

She bridles. "What? After everything he did for you and tried to do for Dariush?"

Layla cannot look at her. "I know. But I can't help it. I don't trust him." These last words come out as a whisper. Before Banu can come back with a nasty retort, Davy begins fidgeting. "It's time for his bottle," Layla says, pulling the can of Similac from her bag and emptying the liquid into a bottle. Emma coos at Davy and tickles his tummy. He puts on a sour face and pulls his knees up toward his chest. Emma says, "Poor gassy baby."

"Yes," says Banu. "Just like his mother was."

Emma pecks Davy's finger with her brown lips. "I have just the thing for you, my little liver."

Emma fills a small pot with water and puts it on the stove so Layla can warm the bottle in it. She reaches inside a cabinet filled with clear glass bottles and Mason jars labeled in Farsi script. She unscrews a jar and uses a long spoon to sift out some chocolate-colored powder, which she promptly empties into Davy's bottle. "Stir," she says to Layla.

"But what is it?" Layla asks, looking over at Banu.

Banu chuckles and picks up Davy, who has a fussy red face that says he is starving and ready to wail. "She will never tell you what it is, Laylee. Look. She is peeling the label off so she can give you the jar. Right, Emma-*jahn*?"

"You saw my mother do the same." Emma hands Layla the jar. "If I give my secrets away, I give my business away." She smiles and pinches Layla's cheek. "Stir," she says.

"But," Layla stammers, "is it okay for the baby?"

Banu *tsks* at Layla, then frowns, telling her she is insulting Emma. "Of course it is okay, Layla. Your own mother gave this very same powder to you when you were a baby in Tehran. I ordered it from Emma-*jahn* myself."

"Oh," Layla says, amazed and beginning to mix the formula. Emma can almost make Layla forget she is in America.

"Tell me, Emma-*jahn*," says Banu. "What do you have in that cabinet for headaches?"

"Headaches?" she repeats, setting out a plate of Pepperidge Farm Milanos. "The best thing for headaches is Tylenol, Banu-*jahn*."

"Tylenol!" Banu says, horror-stricken.

"Of course. None of my medicines compare with Tylenol for headaches."

"But what about the demon poisoner?"

Emma shrugs. "Avoid the capsules. That is all. Nothing to worry about."

"I trust your medicines more. Everyone knows the old remedies are better than the modern commercial ones."

"Well, then 'everyone' is stupid. Why stick to the old ways if the new ways work better? Sometimes they do, sometimes they do not. Pick and choose, I say. That is survival." She blows her nose into an embroidered hanky, unaware of the weight of her words. "Tylenol is best for headaches," she reiterates.

"All right, all right," says Banu, patting her hair. "I understand. No need to give a speech. Layla, stop staring into space. The milk is warm enough."

Fifty-One

Layla

It was a once-in-a-lifetime thing. Widows always say that, but it's true. Even if it wasn't, I wanted it to be. Maybe that was why I wasn't interested in a romantic relationship with Amir. The problem was, since our weekend in the Hamptons when he'd tried to kiss me, he clearly *was* interested. Since then, he'd begun throwing out corny clichés hinting at my unhealthy attachment to a dead husband. "Life must go on," he'd say, sounding like Alistair Cooke from *Masterpiece Theatre*. "Time heals all wounds, Layla. But not without hard work." At night, lying alone and missing Dariush so much my stomach hurt, I'd stare up at the shadows on my ceiling made by the streetlamps and think, *What if I don't want a cure? What if I want to love Dariush forever?* Sometimes I resented Amir, as if I blamed him for Dariush's death. Then I'd feel guilty and try even harder to make our friendship work. After all, he'd saved my life *and* had been a constant comfort throughout the summer. But it was becoming increasingly difficult for me to hide my irritation, annoyance, and discomfort. He just didn't get my "no" signals, and I remembered Dariush once telling me that Amir had been a socially challenged nerd in high school. Maybe once that would have surprised me—he looked as far from the part as a person could get—but now I saw he was just a little bit too ensconced in his own world—a world that obviously included me, but did not seem to require my consensual cooperation. I decided to see him less.

Anahita visited again from Seattle. It was unusually cold for mid-October. She called and invited herself for lunch. I didn't mind the way she forced her way into my life because she never showed a trace of pity or morbid curiosity for what I'd gone through. Besides, she'd endured some of the same kind of stuff; I was merely a few years behind her. I liked the way she thought. Her head was pointed toward the future. Always the future. She said she'd had enough of the past; she knew her father would have wanted her to move forward, not stagnate like so many exiles who still sat in front of CNN all day and night hoping for news of a coup that would restore their stolen futures.

"Good thing you decided not to move to Paris," she said, speaking English with a slighter accent than I remembered. "You'd be bored to death there. The French don't want to associate with anyone but the French, and the Americans are too busy trying to be the next Hemingway. That leaves the Iranians. Yuck. Revolution whining."

"So you like Seattle?" I asked.

"I love it. It rains all the time. It's green like pictures of Scotland. And people don't dress up too much."

"Sounds very different from what you're used to."

"Exactly."

"And your mother? Your brother?"

"In Los Angeles. People have started to call it Tehrangeles. I visit them often. For *Norooz* or weddings or just good Persian food."

The best of both worlds, I thought. "And your job?" I asked.

"Not very good pay, but I enjoy it. I work for a magazine that gives advice to parents on how to bring up their children. I'm a proofreader. But not for long." She chuckled and rubbed her palms on her jeans. "This is America, *naa*?"

I said something I hadn't said to anyone. "I've been thinking about getting a job, but . . ."

I didn't have to explain my doubts to her. So many people who were touched by the Revolution were thinking about getting jobs. Beyond the difficulties of getting a green card, the obstacles were huge—and mostly within ourselves. A lot of people couldn't manage their brittle and displaced egos, couldn't get beyond their pride: Either they'd had their own family businesses in Iran or they'd reached a certain level of importance in companies or government organizations in Iran and they couldn't come to terms with having to answer to a stranger or to start at the bottom. And these were problems only some people were fortunate enough to have; first they had to adjust to America, the culture, the food, the language, and, especially, to having given up the only life they'd known.

For me, the process was easier because I'd grown up in the States. Still, my father had brought me up with the notion that I would never have a job; I didn't have the confidence to think I could do much of anything that anyone would pay me for. Anahita and I talked about this. At one point, she said, "You know, Layla, in some way it was easier for me to change my ideas and my life; I was forced to do it because I had no money left. It was so hard in the beginning—I worked as a salesgirl in Saks, where I'd once bought thousand-dollar dresses. Anyway, it was hard for me to face the fact that there was no money and my old life was gone. But I've noticed that many people who still have even just a little bit of money, they have a harder time than I did believing that they have to change their lives; they still hold on as hard as they can to the old life. Some of us who were touched tragically by the Revolution . . ." She paused for a moment and stared directly into my eyes, reminding me, without a word, of the hardships we'd both endured. Then she continued. "*We* finally realize that the money isn't so important; that the money can come along again sometime. And *we* know the importance of moving ahead, of leaving things behind. Now, what kind of a job were you thinking about?"

The question embarrassed me. "I don't know."

"What was your major?"

I rolled my eyes. "Sociology."

She laughed. "Mine was child development. I wanted to do political science, but my parents didn't think it would be very useful to me."

I chuckled. "I'd thought about photography, but my father said that was only a hobby, not suitable for a degree."

"I'd love to see some of your pictures."

My face grew hot. "Oh no. They're just amateur prints."

She pleaded and pushed until I gave in and brought out a small portfolio I'd compiled for a class at NYU before Dariush and I had left for Tehran. They were varied shots, some of Central Park, a few of Banu's pruny face in different moods, and several of what I thought were pseudo-artistic shots of building gargoyles. "These are very good," she said sincerely, though a Persian woman would never tell me if she thought they were bad or even needed work. "I'd like to take them to Seattle, to show them to someone at the magazine." I was stunned. I thought she was joking. But in fact she knew of an entry-level opening in the photography department. I would probably just be answering phones at first. "But remember, Layla, the first most important post-revolutionary lesson that hardly anyone learns is humility. Without it, you can go nowhere in this country."

So I gave her the portfolio, sure nothing would come of it, unsure what I would do if something did. I'd never even visited the West Coast.

Baba-*joon*'s voice cracked across the phone line with shame when he told me we couldn't afford the duplex anymore. He wanted to use the money from the sale to buy a smaller place in Paris and had calculated that we could live adequately for many years on what remained as long as we didn't spend recklessly. He kept apologizing to me, his voice on the edge of tears. I told him that I didn't care about the money we'd lost, but I knew he didn't believe me. He still hadn't realized that the past year had changed me. I actually felt relieved about selling the duplex; it didn't feel like home anymore, not without my father in it, not without my old self in it. Besides, I told him, a smaller place (not necessarily in Paris, I put in quickly) for Banu and me and the baby was a better idea anyway. That was when he told me about sending Banu back to Iran.

Banu and I cleaned and tidied the duplex so real estate agents could lead people through the rooms, so they could finger the silk bedspreads brought from Tehran and leave mud from their shoes on the carpets sent from Tabriz, so they could talk about how they would remodel the kitchen or have shelves built for the living room.

The wrinkles that curled around Banu's mouth looked like question marks. But she said nothing, talked mostly to Dovoud, teaching him Farsi. Finally, I arranged the words on my tongue, went to her room, and told her what was happening.

Her face was stricken. She wailed. "But I cannot go back to Tehran. I cannot leave you alone. I cannot bear to be separated from Dovoud!" She slapped her forehead with the palm of her hand. "What have I done to deserve this dismissal? Have I not always been a good *naneh* to you and an honest employee to your father?"

We sat side by side on her little bed; I had my arm around her, and she let her head rest on my shoulder. I felt her tears like hot liquid bleeding through my blouse. I told her she was jumping to conclusions. I told her we respected her, loved her. And finally, I told her we couldn't afford to pay her anymore.

She suddenly became quiet, holding her breath, it seemed. She sat up and looked at me. Minuscule bubbles erupted at the corners of her stiff mouth. In a shrill burst, she laughed. It was not the laugh of someone who'd just been told their income was about to disappear. It sounded like a laugh of relief and pleasure. Maybe, I worried, it was a hysterical laugh. Quickly, I told her my father had set up a modest bank account for her in Tehran— at least the *touman*s we had in Iran that were illegal to transfer out of the country could be put to some use. Banu ordered me to stop babbling, and she pulled me in and hugged me to her fragile chest. "I will never leave you," she said. "Never. What would I do? Who would I scold? Who would I worry over?" She pulled back and shook a bony finger at me. "And what makes you think

I stay for the salary? It has *always* been too little. Your father is so stingy, like a fat man with his dinner."

In late October, Amir invited me to attend a bar mitzvah—for the son of an old friend of his mother's. It had been some weeks since we'd done anything together. I told him I'd think about it. That didn't last long. Banu squinted her eyes at me and launched into one of her tirades: "What are you doing, child? This is not proper. All right. So you do not want him as a husband, but you cannot put him aside after everything he has done for you."

So I agreed to go.

Amir was actually surprised to learn that the bar mitzvah would not be my first. I told him he was naive to think that a person could grow up on Manhattan's Upper East Side and not ever attend a bar mitzvah. I didn't tell him how, as a child, I'd wished I could have had a bas mitzvah of my own.

At the temple, Amir didn't know anyone besides his mother's friend, to whom he never formally said hello. I couldn't figure out whether he was shy or merely unsociable. We sat toward the back. To me, many faces looked familiar. I saw several women I'd gone to Chapin with; they waved tentatively from faraway seats. I couldn't remember any of their names, and I was glad we wouldn't be attending the party afterwards.

When the young boy who was becoming a man began reading from the Torah in his high voice, a rush of warmth flowed through me. He looked so small, the boy, standing up at the lectern flanked by the cantor and the rabbi, desperately trying to follow the Hebrew in front of him and intone properly; he was so nervous and excited in the way little boys can get, with droplets of perspiration on his upturned nose and cheeks blotchy red as if he'd been skating on an icy pond for hours. He had a good voice, a resounding voice that reminded me suddenly of a Vienna choirboy.

The cantor began to chant, and the warmth inside me turned hot and uncomfortable. My underarms became slick with perspiration. I felt nauseated suddenly. Amir's hand, resting on his knee next to me, blurred and I wondered if I was going to faint.

The hairs on the back of my neck stiffened like dry pine needles. The cantor's baritone whine floated through the temple like an oily fog, and it settled on my skin like a *chador*.

Judaism and Islam twisted and twined through my veins. The intonations and incantations of the clergy—calling believers to prayer, reciting the sanguinary histories of the prophets, sermonizing on the laws of the Torah and of the *Qoran*. How alike my two religions were, how disappointingly and frighteningly alike.

When the ceremony was done, Amir turned to me. I was sure he misinterpreted what he saw in my face; he couldn't have known that the tears in my eyes were squeezed out of terrifying memories and lingering scars. With a smile, he said, "Think how rewarding it will feel to you when it is Davy's turn, Layla."

In that moment, I wondered, Who is this guy? How could he have the unmitigated audacity to presume to know my future hopes for my son? He scared me suddenly—I wondered exactly how rational he would be if I challenged his assumptions.

I wanted to go home, but he'd made reservations at Tavern on the Green, and he looked so eager about going to that tacky tourist trap that I couldn't say no. When we arrived at the table, he was still talking about Davy and the bar mitzvah. We sat down. I waited until after we ordered, then I said, "Amir, why do you assume I want to raise Davy as a Jew?"

He tilted his head. "Don't you want to do the right thing, Layla?"

"Yes," I said. "But you can't know what's right for me. *I'm* not even sure."

"But I *do* know what's best for you." He took two rolls from the bread basket and put one on his plate, one on mine. "I know you better than you know yourself," he continued in a sickeningly good-natured voice. I put my roll back into the basket and tried to listen without cringing. "All your life, you've had to hide some part of yourself, whether it was the Persian side or the Jewish side or the American side. Now you have an opportunity to belong to something completely. You flit from culture to culture like a chameleon changes the color of its skin. Being a Jew isn't just about faith, it's about history and values and culture. I don't understand why you wouldn't want to just rest from all this turmoil."

I was biting the inside of my cheek. "I don't feel *turmoil* anymore," I said, but he didn't seem to catch the flippancy in my tone. "And I don't mind being a chameleon; my father used to call me that as a compliment. Look, Amir, you had a childhood where everything was just so, everyone learning the same things, believing the same things, even celebrating the same things; a childhood like a dish of white fluffy rice. But my childhood was like *ahsh*, like soup with beans and noodles and spices and yogurt and lemon juice—contrasting tastes and smells and hopes and ideas. It may be true what you say about the peacefulness of belonging to one culture completely, but you forget that I've never *completely* been one thing or another. I was brought up in this country; I'm a lot of things. America is a lot of things." My throat tightened as he shook his head, disagreeing with every word. Suddenly he looked ridiculous in his perfectly ensembled suit and tie; I yearned for Dariush's relaxed way of dressing. Amir looked like a swarthy Ken doll.

"Think about David, Layla. A child needs to grow up knowing where he belongs, who his ancestors are. *You* are the one who is being naive, because even an American needs to know where he fits in society."

He was beginning to sound like a Vanderbilt of Old New York, and I was determined not to lose my cool. "When I was a child growing up here, it was hard," I said. "Kids thought I was born in a tent or that my father drove a camel. One time I dressed up in an antique Persian wedding costume for Halloween and the children laughed me out of the classroom. They called me the Queen of Sheba." He shook his head and laughed. "It's true. People didn't know very much about the world beyond Europe, except what they saw in Hollywood movies. They'd never even heard of Iran; I had to call it Persia so people would understand and then they'd ask me to tell them about the harems."

"So why put David through the same thing, Layla? Do you want him to lead such a difficult life?" He was chomping on his filet mignon by now, oblivious to the offense I was taking.

"But that's what I'm saying," I said, growing nauseated from just the cheesy aroma of my fettucini Alfredo. "It's *not* like that anymore. It will be much easier for Davy. And he has me—not a father whose view of the world never matured beyond the moment his wife died, and not a small immigrant woman whose best understanding of America came from *Petticoat Junction* and *All in the Family*. It will only be difficult for Davy if I don't teach him to stand up to other people's ignorance and if he tries to fit into what he thinks other people want him to be." I paused heavily and stared at his angular face so he would know I was talking about him, but he merely smiled and said, "Dessert? You'll love the apple crisp. Waiter?"

"No," I said, my voice firm. The waiter stood poised with pen. "The check, please." The waiter gone, I looked at Amir, but he didn't seem fazed at all by my overruling assertiveness. I took the opportunity to really drive my point home. "You know what, Amir?"

"What, beautiful Layla?"

"Come December I'm going to buy a huge spruce tree and decorate it with white lights and red porcelain apples and popcorn strings. Then I'm going to put a brass menorah in the window and frame it with blue lights. Come spring, I'll build a tiny fire on the roof and jump over it; I'll set a Persian New Year's table and decorate it with Easter eggs. And when it's time, I'll send Davy to a school where some of his classmates will be Iranian, maybe some Israeli or Mexican or Nigerian. Maybe he'll go to a few bar mitzvahs when he turns thirteen just like I did, maybe he'll be invited to a Christmas Mass, maybe he'll visit a mosque. He'll make his choices, one by one, on his own. *That's* my idea of the right thing."

He smiled oddly, as if I were some pleasant museum piece tacked to the wall. I expected a philosophical tirade, but he said nothing. I shivered and watched him sign the bill.

In the elevator up to the duplex (Amir insisted on kissing Davy good night), I suddenly experienced a metallic, bitter kind of taste in my mouth—intuition, but too late. I stood at Davy's bedroom door while Amir leaned into the crib; I looked away. Banu was asleep across the hall. We went back downstairs, and Amir suggested we have some tea. "No," I said, not even pretending to be regretful. "I'm really bushed. I've got to go to bed. We'll talk tomorrow."

"*Basheh*, all right," he said, the Farsi sounding like an insult to me. We were standing in the foyer, waiting for the elevator. I looked at my shoe, running the tip of it along the grout between tiles. The metallic taste in my mouth persisted, and I wanted water, but I wanted him gone first. Without warning, he reached over and cupped my chin. I pulled back, but he came forward. Oh shit, I thought, looking at him, trying to assess the situation. His pupils were large and very black, his lips parted. Passion. Oh no. I could see the outline of his erection straining against his trousers. I crossed my arms over my chest, but he didn't or wouldn't understand the body language. "Please, Amir," I said in a firm voice.

"Please what?" he replied, still approaching. My back was against the wall now; I could feel the knotty surface of the wall fabric. Gigantic fronds from Banu's favorite potted palm tree pointed at me like mocking fingers. "Amir," I said again. "This is not okay."

He slid his palms beneath my now shoulder-length hair and caressed my neck and shoulders. "Of course it's okay, Layla. Relax."

"No." I grabbed his wrists and tried to pull his hands away. "It's not okay *with me*." But I never got those last two words out because he was in his own sexual trance, and he swooped in and pressed his lips against mine, exhaling and moaning at the same time. I tried to push him away, but he conveniently misjudged that too and kissed me with such severe and smeary emotion—his whole body shuddering and undulating like a near-dead fish—that I felt his saliva dripping down my chin. Just then, the elevator arrived, and he kissed the tip of my nose in a nauseatingly possessive way, smiled as if everything had been settled between us, and disappeared into the elevator. His rank, musky odor stuck to me like crude oil, and I locked the elevator door and the kitchen door—checked them both twice—before rushing upstairs to shower him off me.

I spent a stunned and sleepless night alternately staring at my ceiling, watching Davy asleep like an angel in his crib, and standing at my heavy-paned windows to gaze jealously at the slumbering neighborhood. *Okay, Dasha,* I whispered. *What am I supposed to do now? He's* your *friend. I know, I know. I should have been up front with him as soon as he made that first pass. Well, I didn't want to embarrass him. He's got so fucking much pride. He's worse than Mimish.* I imagined how, if Mariam were here, she'd say it was my own fault for leading Amir on, for naively thinking friendship with a man was possible. And Banu's old words about boys wanting to do only *that thing* rang in my ears. I rubbed my temples. *Well hell, Dasha. That's just crap. Amir's had plenty of red-light signals from me, but he's refused to acknowledge them. And frankly, that's not very nice of him. And how long am I going to let him fill my gas tank with guilt about saving my life, trying to save yours, et cetera? I've got to settle this once and for all. And Dasha, I don't forgive you for keeping your doubts about Amir to yourself. He is one strange secret-agent man.* I fell asleep with Dariush's soft laughter tickling through the vessels of my imagination.

I called Amir the next morning and asked him to meet me near Gracie Mansion, in a small park there that overlooks the East River. It was a sunny fall day, windy but not too cold. He arrived smiling broadly, the space between his two front teeth lending him a boyish look. He wore a tweed jacket with faded elbow patches, flannel trousers, a button-down shirt, and a cardigan—very professorial. It was almost impossible to imagine such an affable-looking person forcing himself on me as he had the night before—almost impossible, that is, until he embraced me and clamped his lips on mine before I could turn away. "This is very romantic, Layla," he said.

My hand itched to slap him. "Romantic?" I managed to say as he handed me a small box of Godiva chocolates and took my wrist to lead me to a wooden bench. He was nauseatingly animated and perky. "What a splendid idea, Layla, to meet here in the outdoors. What a wonderful day. I'm very fond of autumn. I've always wanted to be married in the autumn."

I yanked my wrist from his grip. "What are you talking about?" I got up from the bench and faced him, leaning my back against the railing above the water. A seagull swooped over his head; strands of his hair stuck up from the cold breeze. "Amir," I said, swallowing. "I want us to stop seeing one another."

"Stop seeing each other?" he repeated.

"Yes. Our friendship has turned into something else."

"Of course it has. It was inevitable. Destiny."

"No," I said. "I don't believe in destiny."

He threw his head back and laughed. "Then you are no Persian girl, Layla."

I swallowed down a retort; I would *not* be goaded into a discussion. "Amir," I said, staring straight into his onyx eyes. "Please pay attention. I don't want to see you anymore." I didn't look away, but he did, finally. His face turned pale and he squinted against the autumn sun flickering off the water. He opened his palms to the sky in a helpless kind of motion, then looked at me. "I love you," he said, in a voice that sounded like it really meant *How could you do this to me?*

Well, I thought, here comes that guilt arrow straight through my heart. I looked over my shoulder into the swirling black water. He stood up and came to me, grabbed me by the shoulders with quivering hands. A vein in his neck pulsed against his shirt collar. I could think of only one thing to say. "I'm sorry." I imagined him lifting me up and throwing me over the side into the river.

"You're making a mistake, Layla. You are not the best judge of what's right for you."

"It's time I learned to take care of myself."

"You can't. You never have."

I hated him for saying that. For the first time since before the Revolution, I realized how much I'd changed; what Amir had said wouldn't have fazed me then. Now it enraged me, but still I refused to get dragged into a discussion; it was what he wanted, to distract me from what was really going on.

"You're confused, Layla." Something in his expression made me nervous. It was as if some layer of his personality had peeled away, but I couldn't quite make out what was underneath. All I knew was that my intuition told me to placate him, even while I disconnected myself from him. "You can be happy with me, Layla. David will be secure."

I swallowed and said, "I know you mean well, Amir, but everything you want for me is not everything I want. Maybe it's my fault that you feel so certain about what's best for me; maybe my being silent all these months gave you the idea that you were responsible for me. I'm sorry."

"You're confused," he said again.

I shook my head. "No," I said. "I know what I want." I paused. "And what I *don't* want."

His frown was so deep I thought his brows might melt into his eyes. He finally said, "You may not love me the way you loved Dariush, but you *do* love me, Layla. And you need me. We need each other. Give us a chance. You know you want to. We're so good together." It was the first time he'd mentioned Dariush's name in months; somehow it gave me strength. I firmly pushed against his chest so his hands would disengage from my shoulders. My palms were sweating. I turned and looked at the metallic bridges across the river; the wind stung my eyes. Could I rationalize with him? I spoke without looking at him. "You don't understand, Amir, how much space my memories of Dariush take up; there isn't enough room for anyone else yet."

His body stiffened. Abruptly, he turned and walked away from me, staying next to the railing, hands in his pockets, shoulders high and tight. I took this gesture for sadness, but if I'd been honest with myself, I would have known that it was sheer anger that made him walk away like that. He stopped, twisted his head to relax his neck muscles, inhaled deeply, and turned around. His expression was unreadable. He leaned his elbows on the railing next to me, then turned, face close to mine. Desperate eyes. "Marry me, Layla." I was stunned. Hadn't he heard anything I'd said? Quietly, he spoke again. "You know, there are a lot of people in the world who would give their right arms to have someone who cares about them as much as I care about you. And you know something else? Your Dariush—he was not so special. Really very mediocre, actually. And he was unfaithful to you, you know."

"That's a lie!" I snapped.

"Even his own grandmother was more important to him than you were. How blind you were to his faults. You've deified him. Didn't you ever date anyone else but Dariush? Were you a bloody virgin when you married him?"

"Of course not," I snapped, immediately regretful for taking his bait. Before he could respond, I said, "I only ever wanted Dariush for my husband and no one else, Amir. Nothing has changed that, not even his death, and certainly not you."

His face turned red with rage. "If he'd loved you the way he should have, he would have taken better care of you."

"Fuck you," I said, trying to wrench free from his grip on my arms that was so tight my skin burned under my sweater. I could feel the heat of anger seep through his hands. He was crazy. I tried to be calm. I kept my voice even and said, "So does that mean you saved my life for some sick reason of your own? When did you start betraying your friendship to Dariush, Amir? Before he died or after? Now take your hands away. You're hurting me, you bastard."

He did, then studied them as if they belonged to someone else. His face was dripping with sweat. He looked out over the water; it seemed he knew he'd used up every strategy. He looked at me and narrowed his eyes. His voice was hoarse. "You're not worth it," he said. And in one swift movement, he turned and ran from the park, his jacket flapping behind him like a little cape.

I stood there and bowed my head, relieved that he was gone, relieved that I wasn't worth it and hoping I would never be worth it again. I looked up toward where he'd been, glad to see there was no trace of him. My hands were shaking; I put them on the cold stone wall. A seagull swooped down and gulped a fish from beneath the surface, then flew over me and pooped on the railing next to my hand. I started to laugh and I couldn't stop. A white-haired woman on a bench nearby looked at me, gathered her various shopping bags, and moved on.

As I walked home, taking the wide sidewalks of Park Avenue, I felt at once tremendously unburdened and deeply lonely. I stood at the corner of Park and Sixty-seventh Street, looking all the way downtown to the Helmsley Building; it never looked as far away as it really was if you tried to walk it. Was that how the future was? How destiny was? In the distance, glowing, unfocused, but familiar as your own silhouette? Was it just a matter of wiping my forehead clean and walking toward what I wanted? And catching it?

Fifty-Two

Islam and Dust

Mariam asked us not to tell you about the child," says Jamsheed, sitting across the dining table from Dariush, who drinks tea with trembling hands.

"Has it been born?"

"Yes," says Jamsheed. "You have a son, seven months old."

Dariush drops his forehead into his palms, then lets his hands fall to the table and looks up. "I want to call Layla." He rises quickly and strides toward the telephone in the study.

"Wait!" says Jamsheed, rushing after him. "You can't. It's too dangerous. The phones may be tapped."

"So? I won't say anything to identify myself. She knows my voice. At least I can tell her I'm alive, that our son has a father."

"It's too big a risk; one of you could say something inappropriate. And then what?" He takes Dariush's arm and firmly turns him around. "Will you have her go through the hell of your death all over again? Believe me, I was with her. If you love her, save her at least from that. We cannot contact anyone outside until we are safely in Turkey."

"Enshallah," says Asya, coming over and touching Dariush's arm softly. He looks at both of them, then closes his eyes for a few seconds. Finally, he echoes Asya's prayer and whispers,

"*Enshallah.*" He returns to his chair at the table, blinking lids over glassy eyes. "What about Mariam? When will she join us?"

Asya and Jamsheed exchange a look; who will speak first? "She won't be joining us," says Jamsheed, almost in a whisper. Dariush snaps his head up; his pupils are sharp now. "What?" he says. "Why not? What has happened to her?"

"She asked us to let her be," says Jamsheed. "She said she was going to a place where she can be at peace."

"What place?" says Dariush, his voice louder. "There's no place like that. She doesn't have anywhere to go but our grandmother's house. We have to find her."

Asya steps forward tentatively. "She begged me to keep you from looking for her. She seemed to know exactly what she wanted to do. She said she couldn't face you after everything she'd done to hurt you. She said she wanted to be alone and that we shouldn't worry about her because she would be safe and far away."

Dariush is breathing fast; his eyes dart. Jamsheed sits next to him and touches his arm. "Dasha," he says. "She is a grown woman. You cannot take responsibility for her anymore. She promised me she would be all right. She said she knew you would want to look for her, but she asked me to tell you that if you truly wanted to make her happy, you would go back to Layla and your son."

Dariush stares at the glow of the chandelier on the mahogany table and finally brings his forehead to rest wearily on the cool wood. He is dizzy again, and the dull pain behind his head wound has returned. Jamsheed places his hand on the back of his friend's head and keeps it there, lightly, for a few moments. Finally, he urges Dariush to go up to bed. "You are still weak, Dasha. You must heal or your symptoms will come back." Dariush stands without protest. Taking each slow step up the wide staircase, he realizes now that, for the sake of his wife and child, he must accept his limitations.

They need money. *Touman*s to buy dollars on the black market. The man, a German truck driver, who will take them across the border, wants twenty-five thousand dollars. It is why Jamsheed and Asya have been unable to go before this. They could have gone with the Kurds, who take less money, but who also take more risks through mountain passes on horseback, often just a snow drift away from the *pasdaran*. Or they could have gone to Pakistan, over the border with a shepherd, sheepskins strapped to their backs, crawling like lambs until nightfall. They had chosen to wait for a miracle.

Dariush tells Jamsheed to find buyers for the furniture in the house; if that does not bring enough money, they will sell the house itself. Jamsheed turns white. "Your mother will kill us for selling her antiques." And Dariush says, "I'd rather die by Veeda's hands than the *komiteh*s, wouldn't you?" They work into the night—or for as long as Dariush can manage, for sometimes his head pounds and his vision blurs and he must go to bed— and they work like engineers, mapping out their route to the north, testing one another for holes in the plan, dreaming up alternatives in case of this or in case of that.

In the end, they rent the house to the Italian embassy. Dariush says, "You have an oily tongue, Jamsheed. Those Italians think this is the best-built, most elegant house in Tehran. And to receive rent for one whole year in advance! You should have been a rug seller." With the money, they buy identification papers of dead soldiers, a used Paykan (they have already sold the Mercedes, the BMW, and the Range Rover), religious clothing for Dariush, and heavy boots made to order for the three of them. They pack one duffel bag with three winter coats, gloves, hats, thick socks, two changes of underwear each, a bar of soap, toothbrushes, toothpaste, Tampax, pain medication, and three prayer mats that they find in the guest rooms where Veeda had put them as a kindness to visitors inclined to say their *namaz*; the mats were very dusty. They pack a small cardboard box with bottles of water, bags of pistachio nuts and dried cherries and tamarind, two jars of fruit compote, and a box of Asya's homemade *halva*.

Now they wait for the German to call.

Dariush looks through old pictures, high school yearbooks, silent films of childhood weekends at their *bagh*. And he feels the shame again, the shame he told Layla about even before they returned to Iran. It was the Revolution that had made him see his country as it really was. He had been born into a class that cared only about money and social position, and certainly not about exposing their children to the truth. A thousand families in the whole country made themselves feel big by keeping the rest of the population down—poor, malnourished, illiterate, always subservient—while they (no, *we*, he corrects himself), while we all passed our days admiring ourselves, doting on our successes, and preening for one another—with the help and loyalty of our programmed servants. No wonder the people spat into the dust when they thought of us. No wonder the whole country shat on our snooty heads!

He distracts himself by making drawings of what he thinks his son looks like. Once, he calls his grandmother's house from a pay phone on the street. Firoozeh tells him that Maman Bozorg is in good spirits. "She is waiting for your return, Dariush-*khan*. She makes me keep your room clean and ready, and I prepare your favorite foods every day. I am tired. What shall I do?" First he wants to know if Mariam has called or come to the house. Firoozeh tells him no. Then he gives her advice about his grandmother, tells her there is only one way to live with a madwoman: agree and forget. All Firoozeh must do, he says, is bathe, feed, and dress his grandmother; keep her immediate surroundings clean and do not try to argue with her. As long as Firoozeh is paid, this is all she is required to do. Dariush is never returning, but if his grandmother imagines he will, that is her problem. No? The servant woman agrees and breathes a sigh of relief. "May God be at your back, Dariush-*khan*," she says.

Asya reads Veeda-*khanoom*'s books on feminism and thinks about a time when she truly believed she would become a professor, free to teach others without worrying about the shah's secret police whisking her away for saying something unacceptable. That was a time when she was strong and tenacious, when the fight for political freedom filled her with purpose. But the new government had torn the idealism and hope from her heart. She could never have imagined such a thing as the Morality Police. Not only had she and her compatriots failed to gain political freedom, they had lost their cultural freedom as well. And now they have no choice but to flee their home. Finally, she calls Fereshteh in Mazandaran to tell her, in a code they have devised, that she will be leaving soon. They sob to one another. What can they say? One of them could die before they can embrace again.

Jamsheed studies Dr. Namdar's medical books. Dariush is pale and thin, his energy lasts only for a short time, exertion and stress wear him down quickly. Though he has been walking, his muscles are atrophied. Jamsheed suspects he may have a stomach parasite, and the dizzy spells he experiences could mean there is something in his skull that has not healed. He knows it would be best to immobilize Dariush for a time, but this is not an option. He wishes they could postpone their escape a few months, especially now that the *Haji-Khanoom* Bozorg does not seem to be a threat, but this is impossible. It is already autumn; the German will come and go one more time, then the winter storms will arrive in the Zagros Mountains, and who knows what will happen between now and the next summer, when the German may decide not to return at all?

The German calls on a breezy morning that, to Dariush, smells like the terrible mixture of dust and gunpowder that he remembers from the front. Jamsheed speaks to him in the language he knows so well from his studies in Munich where he and Gunther had lived in the same building. The conversation is clipped and short. Jamsheed hangs up and says, "We must go today."

The drive to Tabriz will take them much longer than the usual ten or so hours. They will go slowly to avoid suspicion. Besides, there will be many other cars on the road north and many checkpoints as well; they will sometimes have to travel through small towns and villages along the way.

Dariush takes one last look around. The week before, they had stowed all of the family's personal items in trunks and taken them to the cellar. His room had never looked so clean or so sparse. Well, he thinks, the Italians will fill it up; maybe the ambassador has a young son who will appreciate the armoire with a false bottom where he used to hide his *Playboy* magazines and occasional Baggies of hashish. Downstairs, he stares for some moments at the place between his mother's Louis XV chairs where he and Layla had been married, then he goes out to the swimming pool. He walks around it once just to feel the flutter of memories on his skin and smell the faint sweetness of his passed innocence. As he is leaving for the carport where Jamsheed and Asya wait, he spots something small and round behind a fat bush. It is a soccer ball, once white, now faded to gray, its skin peeling from the effects of the weather. He picks it up and squeezes it gently as if it were an orange. He and Layla were kids, he remembers, before the house was built and this was their summer garden; his father had ordered a field of grass planted just for playing soccer. How old had she been? Eight? Nine? She was trying to tell him something about how Mariam had burned herself on the samovar; words poured out of her mouth. But her meaning did not register; he only smelled her— jasmine and vanilla cake. He bounced the soccer ball expertly from his knee to his foot to his knee to his head. She became angry and tried to kick the ball away, but then it was a game to him, and he was amazed at how adept she was, how difficult he had to work to keep the ball. Finally, they were both giggling and panting and sweating and they fell onto their backs where the sprigs of grass tickled their ears and she looked up at the blue sky and he looked over at her red cheeks and glistening lips and knew for the hundredth time that he was in love with her.

Three Iranians travel north toward Azarbaijan in a dirty white Paykan—one of so many. A husband and wife sit in the front; he picks at his mustache and she lights cigarette after cigarette. A young *mullah* sits in the backseat, his white turban neatly wound around his head, hiding the lightness of his hair and a nasty scar above his temple; his beard is dark and poorly clipped. He rests his hand on a small *Qoran* on the seat beside him.

When they reach Karadj, the road splits and they go straight, not to the right toward Chalus where so many of Dariush's memories lie, where they would have passed the Karadj Dam and the walls of the Namdar *bagh* and the turn off to the Shemshak ski area, where they would have entered the dark, suffocating tube of the Kandavan Tunnel, then climbed into the clouds of the Alborz Range where the two-lane road twists up and down and around the mountains, a dangerous ledge off which many vehicles had rolled into oblivion. He had traveled that road hundreds of times north through the lushness of Mazandaran Province to the Caspian Sea. He tries not to think about these places because in all his memories are the faces of the people he loves, and he does not want to think about how much they have suffered because of him or of the possibility that he will never see them again.

Just beyond Karadj, they become trapped in a checkpoint queue. This was expected, so they each inhale deeply and try not to look at one another. Dariush removes the water bottles from the box and they drink. Jamsheed inches the car forward. "Stop picking at your mustache, Jamsheed," says Asya. "It makes you look guilty."

Dariush chuckles. "Everyone looks guilty, or is it petrified?"

They reach the checkpoint, and Dariush suddenly remembers driving along this road wearing only his bathing trunks, his mother in a halter top next to him, his father napping in the backseat. Now the road is like a war zone with these teen-aged *pasdaran* with high testosterone levels, holding their guns and wearing their sneers like licenses of power, though they are barely old enough to judge themselves, let alone others. "Papers," says the *pasdar*, poking his head through the window, eyes gliding over their belongings, taking in Dariush's religious clothing, bowing his head slightly. "*Agha*," he says politely. Dariush nods. Jamsheed hands him their identification papers and his and Asya's proof of marriage. "Where are you going?" the boy asks.

"To Tabriz. My cousin"—Jamsheed cocks his head toward Dariush—"we are taking him to the *madraseh* where he will be teaching."

To their surprise, the boy smiles, showing a mouthful of crowded gray teeth. "I am from Tabriz. Which *madraseh* are you going to?"

There is stunned silence. Jamsheed begins to mutter something. Asya feels sweat break out above her lip, and she looks out her window only to see two *pasdaran* pushing an old man into their jeep and throwing his empty vodka bottle in after him; she knows the man will get eighty lashes and she wonders how many lashes one gets for impersonating a *mullah*. "It is a new *madraseh*," pipes up Dariush, exaggerating the baritone in his voice to sound more scholarly. "It is to be named after the *Emam*, with his exalted blessing."

"*Enshallah*," says Jamsheed.

"*Enshallah*," says the *pasdar*, who then gestures with his arms like a magician showing off an illusion. "Please, go ahead. And go with God."

They hold their breaths until Jamsheed gets them around the bend and out of sight, then they burst out laughing like children who have successfully stolen a treasure chest of candy. They talk all at once. "Did you see the look on his face?" "He didn't even ask to look in our trunk!" "He barely glanced at our identification papers." "Dariush, you were destined to become a *mullah*!" And finally they settle down, each remembering silently that they have only just started a long and treacherous journey where *pasdaran* are not likely to be as credulous as this last one. They know that eventually the checkpoints will become more frequent and the soldiers more edgy. There has been much dissent in Tabriz, not only from the *Mojahedeen*, but also from the more moderate clergy, and from the independent-minded Azarbaijani people. Once they reach the city, it will be best for them to veer off the main roads and move stealthily through unfamiliar alleyways to avoid checkpoints. They have only a map and their intuition to guide them.

They stop every so often at roadside teahouses, sitting for a while in the shade of a lone tree or inside a cool *kahgel* hut. Dariush notices how other travelers avoid his eyes and check their clothing, how they stop laughing and restrain their conversation when he appears, how a radio is quickly turned off or children sent away to play.

In the car, he says, "They hate the *mullah*s. Why don't they rebel against them?"

"The people are tired," says Jamsheed. "One revolution is enough. And now a war bleeds them of their zealotry."

"Anyway, these people," says Asya, gesturing to the expanse around them, which has turned flatter, the asphalt road straight and rippling with shiny black mirages in the distance, "the poor, the illiterate, the villagers—they are not affected by this regime the way we are; they go on with their lives and hope that perhaps a new government will give them running water and electricity. For them, life is very much the same kind of struggle as before."

Dariush sighs and chases two pills down with a swig of water. Outside the car window is a beige blanket of scorched dirt that spreads until it undulates and slopes up into mountains of the same color, peaks dusted with new snow.

Jamsheed pops a cassette into the tape player—Barbra Streisand singing "I Am a Woman in Love"—and Dariush thinks of Cannes last summer, on the beach with Layla, searching for a grain of sand in her eye; he can smell her honey breath as he dozes off.

They spend the night in the town of Zanjan, in a *kahgel* inn whose courtyard is lit by Chinese lanterns hanging from trees. The dusty smell of the desert is gone; the air has a fresh ozone odor as it does when the first rain comes to Tehran after the dry summer months. Jamsheed notices how pale Dariush looks and he helps his friend up the worn-down adobe steps to his room and a lumpy bed. The wound on Dariush's head, having never been stitched properly, looks discolored, gritty, and glazed with scar tissue. He redresses it and covers his friend. "Sleep, Dariush," he says, but Dariush is already dreaming about the sensation of his son's smooth cheek against his lips.

Tabriz, once the capital of Armenia, ancient city of the Silk Road, sprawls before them like a clay metropolis. They follow a winding route marked in red pencil on a map the German had sent Jamsheed. It is nerve-racking. The streets twist and turn, some without name plaques, others making sudden appearances, forcing them to backtrack. The map seesaws between Dariush and Asya; sometimes Jamsheed stops the car in frustration and snatches the map from his wife as if he can make better sense of it than she. Asya curses him: "You dog sperm! I'm the one who received an award in geography. Stick to your doctoring; I'm managing this." Dariush clutches his stomach in laughter. "She is definitely a good match for you, Jamsheed."

At one point, when it seems they are hopelessly lost, Dariush suggests that he ask for directions; he speaks the Azarbaijani dialect. This is where all of his mother's family came from. But Jamsheed will not agree; he thinks it is too dangerous, that it could make someone suspicious. Why would a *mullah* want to know how to get to a textile warehouse anyway? So they struggle on.

It takes them three hours to find the place, and when they arrive, the German is waiting, sitting behind the wheel of an enormous cargo truck, scratching out figures on a pad of wrinkled paper while his trailer is being loaded with bales of raw wool. He points to a small teahouse down the street, motioning for Jamsheed to meet him there. Asya and Dariush wait in the car. Jamsheed returns with a sour face. "The wait to cross the border is one week."

"What? What do you mean?" asks Dariush.

"Because of the war, the road to Turkey is the only way for the truckers to get out, not to mention everyone else who's trying to leave. The *pasdaran* give out numbers and you have to wait in line while they check every vehicle and give a lot of people trouble. Then from the other side, there are diplomatic problems with Turkey; apparently they keep raising the transport taxes."

"What do we do?" asked Asya.

"Gunther wants us to go with another guy who's already two days away from crossing."

"Does he trust him?" asks Dariush.

"He didn't exactly use the word *trust*, that's what worries me. But Gunther says the guy's done this sort of thing before. Naturally, he wants more money."

"How much more?" asks Asya.

"Double."

"Fifty thousand dollars!"

They all look at one another. Finally, Dariush says, "Let's do it. It leaves us with very little for the rest of the journey, but I don't want to stay in Tabriz for a week; we could get into trouble here. I want to go now. And so do you guys."

A hesitation, then both Asya and Jamsheed nod and say together, "Let's go."

It is the following night when they reach the other cargo truck, shining like silver in the moonlight, parked just ahead of the jagged ruin of a *kahgel* wall. They have had to drive through villages, skirt the great salt Lake Urumiyeh, sleep the night on the hard ground, wrapped in Veeda's down comforters, huddled together against the autumn frost. They have had to use wooded areas to relieve themselves and spring water to quench their thirsts. They have come upon tribal women dressed in layers of colorful fabric who have offered them tea and tried to sell them handspun kilims. And finally, at nightfall, they have had to dump the car, Dariush's religious clothing and Veeda's comforters in the trunk, beneath an ancient abandoned cliff dwelling. Wearing most of what they had packed in the duffel, they hike stealthily through the brush to the highway.

Gunther's "colleague" is gruff and toothless—not like Jamsheed's sympathetic friend at all. The man's name is Heinz, and he makes them stand behind the truck, in the shadow of the jagged wall so others waiting to cross the border will not see them. He will not open the trailer until he sees their dollars. Jamsheed gives him half of the agreed amount, tells him he will get the rest when they reach Turkey safely. In response, Heinz spits into the dirt next to Jamsheed's shoe and opens the trailer.

The truck is filled with bales of raw lamb's wool. The bales are about three feet square and wrapped in wire mesh. Heinz tells them they must climb over the cargo until they reach a hollowed-out area where they will be able to squeeze between the bales. Suddenly, headlights streak through the night; Dariush has no trouble discerning that they belong to a jeep coming from the direction of the border. *Pasdaran.* Quickly, hearts racing, they move toward the wall and crouch down against its rough crevices that smell like cave rock until the lights pass and diminish.

They climb into the truck with difficulty, and with little help from Heinz. The bales are stacked high and tightly, so they crawl over them until they find a small hole, hardly large enough for the three of them. They slide in, snagging their winter coats on the wire mesh, then sit with their knees against their chests, staring in disbelief at one another in the semi darkness. Heinz shuts the trailer door with a clatter, and they are buried in the pungent scent of sheep.

It is dark and already warm. "At least the wool will keep the cold out," says Jamsheed. "As we go up into the mountains, there will be snow." They spread their coats beneath them to keep the wire mesh from cutting into their bottoms. Their hands are sticky with lanolin. The wool has not been cleaned well; Jamsheed smells the dried dung in it and Dariush feels the stone and dirt between the soft hair. Asya is trembling with disgust. She knows there are lice and other bugs; she already feels them crawling along her scalp and burrowing beneath her clothing. None of them sleep. Dawn is in three hours. Jamsheed and Asya wrap their arms around one another, and Dariush builds an old mosque in his mind, pressing each and every turquoise tile into the dome with his own hands.

In the morning, the border closes. They hear the *pasdaran* alerting everyone with their loudspeakers. Asya whispers, "God help us." Heinz opens the trailer and the three are blinded by the indirect sunlight. Suddenly, a plastic bag comes flying over the bales and into their hole. Bread and cheese and water. And later, near sundown, more of the same.

Their clothing is drenched in their own sweat; dust has gotten into their lungs and they cough quietly into their palms. Their legs are numb. In embarrassed silence, they relieve themselves into the wool. Then they finally sleep, from exhaustion, in a kind of delirium. Dariush dreams of being in the mountains, breathing fresh air, wildflowers all around him. He wakes with a start, hardly able to bear the dust in his nose and his throat. He is reminded of something Layla said to him just before they were married, something about Islam and dust. What was it? He tries to picture her sitting in an old chaise lounge on Katayoon's patio, upset because of the obstacles in their way, because of what had happened to Iran, because she could not understand it at all. Her cheeks were flushed from the cool breeze, and she burrowed down into one of Katy's mink coats. He sees her now as if she is close enough to touch. "Religion is like the desert dust," she had said, angrily pressing her lips together. "It has this subtle way of getting into everything. Have you seen how it suddenly appears in a thin film on the furniture, how it hides in between the threads of the carpets, how suddenly you feel this graininess under your fingernails? The servants sweep it up or wash it off, but it always reappears even if you close all the windows and all the doors and cover yourself from head to foot. And it's so small and so light and so quiet that you think it can never harm you, but if you don't pay attention, it'll pile up and suffocate you."

The sound of the motor, loud and grating, wakes them. It is hard to believe they are moving. The truck crawls along, never shifting beyond second gear. Often they stop, hear rough voices, but cannot discern what is being said. Suddenly, the trailer door rattles open; Asya is so startled she gasps, and Jamsheed instinctively clamps his hand over her mouth. The beam of a high-powered flashlight floods the trailer, jerking this way and that above their heads, then glowing faintly between the bales. A surly young voice says in Farsi, "What company are you bringing this wool from?" Heinz says, *"Pashm,"* the Farsi word for wool. His accent is terrible, and the customs inspector chuckles. "Hey, you German donkey, I can see that it's wool, but where did you get it from?" There is silence. The inspector exhales, shuffles some papers, and says, "Okay. Here it is. All right. You can go." Silence. "Go!" he iterates and Heinz, finally understanding, sputters a few *Danke schön*s, then the door clatters shut and the three passengers close their eyes with relief.

The loaded truck struggles up the Zagros Mountains, its engine straining, tires beaten by potholes and rocks and uneven asphalt. They smell snow and hear the crunch of ice beneath them. Asya wonders about the bandits Fereshteh had always told her about, how they have robbed travelers on this route since the beginning of the Persian Empire. Dariush yearns for water until it is the only thing he wants in the world. And Jamsheed tries to control his bowels. After what seems like many hours, the truck begins to descend at a sharp angle; it twists and brakes heavily around sharp turns, shoving and pressing and battering the passengers against one another. At the moment when it seems they will not be able to stand the jostling any longer without breaking bones and tearing muscles, the road flattens. Now, Heinz shifts from one gear to the next easily, over and over, until they are moving quickly. The trailer rocks methodically, and the three fall asleep until the truck comes to a stop.

They look like beggars on the side of the road. Their clothing is covered with tufts of wool, and their hair is oily with lanolin and perspiration. They sit on a short stone wall watching the town of Van in the distance. It beckons to them, but they are exhausted. Heinz and the truck are gone. The deal was that he would drive them to Istanbul—nearly sixteen hundred kilometers away—but he refused to let them sit up in the cab with him. Asya said she would not spend another moment amid dead sheep hair, and Jamsheed and Dariush were glad she refused. Heinz wanted all his money, but Jamsheed gave him only half of the rest and if Dariush had not stood between them, despite his vertigo, they would have had a fistfight. Heinz left them with some choice German curses that Jamsheed had never heard before, and here they are, sitting on this wall, hunched over, filthy, dazed. Dariush, staring ahead as if in a trance, suddenly, softly, says, "We are free." Sluggishly, Asya looks at him. "Yes," she whispers incredulously. "We are free." She then turns to her husband, who meets her gaze with watery eyes. He reaches under her chin, undoes the knot of her scarf, and slides it off her head. She smiles, shakes her shoulder-length, curly hair, scratches her head, then grabs the scarf from him and shreds it in half. They are laughing out loud now, embracing, kissing. Dariush feels the laughter in his chest bubbling up and as he opens his mouth to roar with bliss and relief, he also tastes the salt from his tears. He looks up toward the peaks from where they came, but he doesn't see the majesty of their height and vastness; he sees to the other side, beyond the fields and the desert, somewhere—a safe place, he hopes—where Mariam rests peacefully.

Fifty-Three

Dust Devils

After Amir leaves Layla in the park uptown, he roams the city and finally arrives at his bare apartment without any memory of where he has been. He stumbles in the dark to his bed and crawls between the dirty sheets, shivering, unable to close his eyes. His legs ache from walking and running; his stomach is empty, burning.

How can he have lost her? He knows there is a solution to this new problem, but his brain cannot work diligently on it; his rational thoughts are interrupted by visions of her face—smiling, laughing, pouting, then saying, "I don't want to see you anymore." And her body—the promise of it writhing beneath him, breathing heavily with the same passion Dariush had once known but will never know again. He squeezes his eyelids together. *I will not let her go* rings in his head, then he opens his mouth and releases a long, low wail of anguish that bounces off the peeling walls and reenters him through every pore. Abruptly, he is asleep, his muscles stiff as those of a corpse.

In the morning, the sunlight infuriates him. He dresses for his class, walks to the university, and stands before his students, hating them, imagining himself strafing them with bullets from his Uzi, splattering their insignificant lives onto the walls. Later, he walks over to a deli and orders a pastrami sandwich but lets it sit before him untouched. The waitress asks him if he is all right and he slowly raises his eyes to her, but says nothing. She backs away, quickly drops his check on the table, and does not approach him again.

Amir has never given up on anything in his life. He pushes his sandwich plate away roughly, nauseated by the smell. He orders coffee and lets it burn his tongue. He knows Layla will eventually regret her mistake. What she said to him yesterday was out of fear; she has already lost one husband. She is trying to protect herself. So there is no reason for him to feel humiliated and betrayed. He must merely be patient. He never imagined a relationship could be so difficult, require so much attention and sacrifice. Now he understands why his father had so often been forced to manipulate his mother in order to save her from her own bad decisions.

He rubs the back of his neck and lights a cigarette. He is more relaxed now. He knows what he must do. It had been a mistake for him to quit Mossad and come to New York. Surely Layla was more captivated by him when he was a man of political secrets and power. A lowly associate professor deserves little respect, and respect is what will make Layla want him again. So he will finish out the semester then contact the Office and offer his services. They can use him. He has ears in the organization; he knows the Americans are thinking about selling arms to Iran in exchange for hostages kidnapped in Beirut. Why else had that Robert McFarlane character from the State Department met with Begin last summer? It is a stupid move, Amir thinks. The Americans are inept when it comes to dealing with the Iranians; they will end up putting some G.I. Joe megalomaniac on the project, and in the end the whole deal will blow up in their faces.

He smiles slightly and orders an apple pie à la mode, which he eats to the last crumb.

It is Banu who discovers the envelope from Mariam in the mail. Wrinkled, torn, and smudged with various imprints, it feels strangely warm against her fingers. She hates the stamps bearing

Khomeini's face and covers them with her thumb. She recognizes Mariam's handwriting and worries. Mariam has only ever caused her *dokhtar* pain.

"What is it?" asks Layla, seeing concern in Banu's face as she steps from the elevator.

"A letter. From Mariam. Mailed two months ago."

Layla takes the envelope eagerly and tears it open. Banu stands facing the counter pretending to pour tea; when Layla gasps, the sound shoots through Banu's back like a bullet, and she curses herself for not throwing the letter into the garbage.

Layla stares at the sheet of thick drawing paper, at her own face as she used to be—with long hair and a smile she does not wear anymore, an innocent, expectant smile. Behind this face, seeming to go on forever, is a dark tunnel. She knows Dariush's pencil stroke as well as she knows the scent of his skin. At the bottom of the page, Mariam has written the line from an old French love song,

Et si tu n'existe pas, moi pourquoi j'existerai?

And in Farsi, beneath this line, she has written,

Forgive me. He is yours.

Layla is shocked and crying, holding her palm over her mouth.

"What is it? What does it mean?" asks Banu, standing behind Layla, holding her shoulders.

"I don't know. Dariush drew this."

"What? Are you sure?"

She nods, swallows. Banu quickly gets her a glass of water. She gulps it down. "The writing is from Mariam. This French part is from a song we used to listen to. It means, 'If you didn't exist, then why should I exist?' Then you see what she writes in Farsi. I don't know, Banu. Does this mean there were belongings of Dariush's that they found with his body that they never showed me? Does it mean something different happened to him than what I was told? I don't know."

Layla peers closely at the sketch. She lays it on the table and flattens it with her palms, then brings her face close to it. She inspects his pencil strokes, searching for a hidden message. She remembers how they had always raced one another to find the hidden "Nina"s in the Hirschfeld drawings of the Sunday *Times*'s Arts and Leisure Page. She looks for her name in various places: a "Layla" hidden in her eyebrow, a "Layla" draped from her earlobe. Nothing. She wonders if he had tried something more daring: an "I love you" in her hair up near the crown or down where the strands rested on her chest. She asks Banu for her magnifying glass, then scrutinizes the sketch until her eyes and neck ache. Banu sits at the table beside her, saying nothing, bursting with questions—one in particular: Could this mean the boy is alive?

Layla rubs her eyes and her fingers come away wet with tears. She does not want to think about the possibilities. She wants the truth and can think of only one person who can find it for her.

Amir cannot believe Layla is sitting on the stairs in the dark hallway outside his apartment door. His first thought is to praise himself for knowing in his heart that she would return to him. Still, he had not expected it to happen so soon, only a few weeks after their meeting in the park. A strip of light from the dirty fixture falls across her eyes, but the rest of her is in shadow. Her green irises are ringed in black, and the arch of her eyebrows seems more pronounced. He catches himself and does not move to embrace her; something is wrong.

"Hello, Amir." Her voice is low and grating. "I'm sorry to bother you, but I need your help." She looks down, her eyelids seeming like liquid, like cream, in the tarnished light. So she is feeling guilty, he realizes. She has come for a favor, not to confess her love. All right, he thinks. This will do. At least she will come to see how much she *needs* him. "No bother," he says, and he uses his key to open the apartment door.

The place smells like mold and rotten fruit. Dust devils skitter across the wood floor like sagebrush in a ghost town. It is dark; the overhead bulbs have burned out, so Amir turns on the bedside lamp. It is cold and bare; Layla crosses her arms and

stands in the middle of the floor. Amir fiddles with the thermo-
stat and says, "Sorry I can't offer you something to drink or eat.
Just some teabag tea, if you'd like."

"No, thank you. I can't stay long. Banu must be frantic."

"How long have you been waiting for me, then?"

"Since two."

"You've been sitting out there in that filthy dark hallway for
three hours? Why didn't you come over to the university? I've
been in my office."

"I wanted to see you alone."

He comes close, peers at her. "What's happened? Is something
wrong with David?"

"No. David's fine." She reaches into her purse and brings out
an envelope and holds it out to him. "I got this today. Can you
help me find out what it means?" He sees the Iranian stamps and
his chest tightens, but he keeps his face neutral. "It's from my
friend Mariam, Dariush's cousin."

He slides the letter out, opens it up, and raises his eyebrows.
"She's quite an artist. Did she draw this from memory?"

"Dariush drew it."

"Really?" He makes his voice sound forcibly calm and unbe-
lieving, as if she's confessed to being abducting by aliens. Inside,
his heart hammers against his chest like a hard little ball.
"What's this down here? Who wrote this?"

"Mariam did. I'm not sure what she means. I guess she didn't
feel free to write anything straightforward. And look, the envelope's been tampered with and the postage date is more than two
months ago."

"That's the censors."

"I know. Well, what do you think?"

He shrugs. "I think she found a drawing of you that Dariush
had done some time ago and thought you should have it."

"But what about the lyrics she wrote and then she says, 'He is
yours.' What could she mean by that?"

Amir shakes his head and hands the paper back to Layla. "I
really have no idea, Layla. She's *your* friend. I can't begin to analyze what she's thinking. Unfortunately, being a spy doesn't

qualify me as a psychotherapist. Didn't you say she was a little unstable?" He walks to the window and lights a cigarette, leans against the wall. Even in jeans, Layla's long, thin legs strike him with lust; she wears a jacket over her button-down shirt, but when she crosses her arms, the collar gapes and he can see the bamboo color of her skin and he imagines standing behind her and sliding his hands down underneath her bra, rubbing himself against her ass until he comes into his trousers.

Layla stutters, "I, well, I think it's strange, this drawing. I mean, when did he do it? At the war front? In the training camp? He would have shown it to me. I was thinking that maybe he left some things behind or that . . . he might be . . . might have . . . died in a different way or at a different time than we were led to believe."

He is silent, watching her, his cigarette hanging loosely between his fingers. She bites her lip and blinks several times. Finally Amir says, "You're grasping at straws, Layla. This is so unlike you, so irrational. I see hope in your eyes and I dare not say for what. Dariush is dead. His own father buried him. I think you should go home, Layla. Put some soft music on, take a hot bath, and watch an old comedy on the telly. Put the drawing away; look at it when you're a little stronger. For all we know, he could have sketched it years ago and left it in a drawer."

Layla sniffs and wipes at her cheeks swiftly. She folds the drawing, puts it in the envelope, and stuffs it into her purse. She thrusts her chin up and shakes her hair out of her face. "You're right. I feel so stupid. I'm sorry to bother you."

"I said before—no bother." He looks at his watch. "Shall we have dinner together?"

She frowns. He has caught her off guard. "I . . . um," she stammers. He snuffs his cigarette out in the ashtray, grinding it with his thumb until the tobacco bursts from its paper skin; this is the only outward sign of his fury, and she does not see it. "Maybe another time," he says before she can come up with an excuse.

"Okay." She buttons her jacket and moves to the door. Her head is down, hair hiding her face. She forces herself to look at him. "Thank you, Amir."

He manages a smile. "Anytime." He listens to her steps on the wooden stairs, fading to nothing. He peers out the window as she emerges from the building beneath him and hails a cab. When she is gone, when he can no longer see the back of her chestnut-colored head in the rear window of the cab, he raises his fist and pounds it straight through the plaster wall.

Fifty-Four

Ghestmat

Dariush and Jamsheed and Asya rent rooms in a motel in Van that is filled with stranded Iranian refugees. Many of them have been there for months, either because they have no money to get to Istanbul or they are injured from their perilous journeys through the mountains on horseback with only the help of the Kurds, some of whom had cheated them and stolen from them and lied to them. They all have their own horror stories, and this is what occupies their days and, often, their nights. When new people come, the stories are told again. Most of them have no passports and, more important, no entry visas for European countries or America. Jamsheed and Asya and Dariush are no different. The challenge now is to find a country that will take them.

The first thing Dariush wants to do is call Layla, but no matter how many times he tries, the circuits are busy. He tries to reach his parents in London, Layla's father in Cannes, but he cannot get through. Van is not exactly a cosmopolitan city. He is frustrated to the point that his head spins and aches, and the pills do not help. "We have to get to Istanbul," he tells Jamsheed.

"I inquired. The bus comes in three days."

"Damn!" he says in English, pacing the small lobby floor.

Jamsheed grabs his friend's shoulders. "You cannot lose your composure. Not yet. We may be out of Iran, but you know the journey is not over. It's only a few days more. You have already waited months. Even if you could reach Layla, she would have to worry about you until you reached Istanbul."

Dariush speaks softly to Jamsheed's face, but the pain of his yearning cuts through every consonant. "I want her to know that I'm alive. I want to hear her voice, to know about my son!"

"It's only a few days more. You have already waited months. Rest. Recuperate. Please, do this for me. You forget you are not completely healed. If I deliver you to your parents in bad shape, your mother will kill me." He flashes a tentative smile, and Dariush's jaw muscles finally stop spasming. He exhales and says, "*Basheh*, okay. You're right." He rubs his eyes. "I'll go take a nap."

"Good, good. We'll wake you for dinner."

The bus will not come until one week later. They sleep a lot. Jamsheed and Asya tell everyone they are on their honeymoon so no one bothers them to come down for tea and the constant sessions of commiseration. Sometimes the three of them eat in one of the few restaurants in the small town. The food is good—mutton and rice and fruits, especially pomegranates. The wine tastes extra fine because they can drink it freely. They have their clothing washed and dried and ironed; Dariush dreams about the comfort of his Levi's and Nikes, stowed in a box at Ebrahim's villa in Cannes.

The bus ride will take about three days. A nervous young woman with a small child sits next to Dariush. Several of the woman's fingers are tinged black with frostbite from her escape on horseback through the Zagros. The child, a two-year-old girl, leans against her mother's breast staring at Dariush's gauze dressing on his forehead with unblinking, expressionless eyes. After the usual small talk, the woman warms up to Dariush's sincere smile and tells him how her husband, now in Tehran trying to sell their property, had paid the Kurds to transport her and their daughter over the border. Once the child falls asleep and the bus is dark except for a few dim overhead lights, the woman begins to cry quietly. "I am afraid my husband will not be able to get out. What will I do without him? How will I get to my sister in Oklahoma?" He hands her a tissue from his pocket and says, "My wife and boy are waiting for me too. I am not in the best shape, but look, I am on my way to them. And so will your husband be soon."

She peers at him more closely. "Where are they, your wife and boy?"

"In America."

She blows her nose. "Thank you, *agha*. You have given me hope."

Some moments later, she asks him if he would be so kind as to hold her sleeping daughter so she can use the toilet. Once the child is nestled in his lap, her soft, plump cheeks snug against his chest and her child-breaths subtle as a bird's, this is when Dariush feels a swirl of emotion fill his chest and throat. He is so eager to hold his son that his spirit wants to break out of his skin. But that is not all he feels. There is his anxiety for Layla and his stinging disgust for his grandmother. But most of all, there is his fury at Amir. His teeth chatter and the muscles in his legs quiver with the strain to stay still. While the crisp autumn air forces its way through the seams in the old bus, Dariush feels too warm. He shuts his eyes tightly and throws his head back onto the headrest, but he cannot erase the image in his mind of Amir holding his boy in the way he now holds this little child in his arms. What had Jamsheed said just yesterday when the subject of Amir had come up? "That was a boy who could not accept his *ghesmat*, a boy whose desire to be your equal—*to be you*—led us all into a coiling wind of misfortune. It is a sad thing, to despise oneself so much." But Dariush does not feel pity. Not this time.

Amir is jet-lagged. The rain bothers him. The magnificent sight of Topkapi Palace across the Bosporus irritates him. Even the idea of the Turkish bazaar does not cheer him. He gives a false name at the Istanbul Hilton registration desk and slides a wad of *lira* notes across the counter. The clerk, looking over his shoulder first, hands him a copy of the guest roster, a ragged, brown paper package tied with dirty string, and a master guest-room key. When he gets to his room, he checks the roster, finds the room number he wants, memorizes it, then opens the parcel with his Swiss army knife, and smiles. A small, square metal box. He uses a combination to open it and tenderly takes the nine-millimeter Beretta into his hand. The sensation of power, like an injection of adrenaline, shudders through his body. He packs the gun under his heavy jacket and slips the silencer into his pocket.

He lies across the bed on his stomach and falls asleep immediately. He dreams that his body has been punctured by bullet holes and the blind fortune catcher is rushing to collect his blood in a huge iron rice pot. He startles awake, looks at his watch. Still plenty of time until the bus arrives, until Dariush arrives. He has not slept more than a few hours a night since he learned that Dariush was out of Iran. That stupid old crone; she had promised him Dariush would never leave, never *want* to leave. Minutes after Layla had left his apartment a week ago, he placed a call to the old fanatic woman but had gotten only the blithering, toothless maidservant wailing that her mistress had turned to stone since her grandchildren had left her. So he knew they had fled. Then another phone call, to Turkey, to Van where, Amir knew, most refugees ended up. If Dariush had escaped southeast through Pakistan, Amir may not have found him at all, but he had taken the most available escape route, one Amir had often plotted for others. And the hotel operator in Van was happy to offer Amir information about a certain guest and the bus schedule for Istanbul. Then he had booked his flight.

He washes his face in cold water and rakes his fingers through his thick, straight hair; his reflection in the mirror satisfies him. He imagines how Dariush must look now: disfigured, perhaps even mentally disturbed from such a long coma, maybe paralyzed. Layla would surely not want him even if she were ever to see him again. Still, he cannot take that chance. He looks out the window at the distant, crowded city, a mosque on every street corner. He picks absentmindedly at his rough, raw cuticles and decides he cannot stay in this boxy room another moment. He

looks at his watch: an hour until the bus is scheduled to arrive—
enough time for a breather.

In a discreet corner of the large hotel lobby, Amir sits deep in a
plush chair with his back to the registration desk. He wears an
old-style captain's hat that he found in London a year ago; the
hat is all that appears above the back of the chair. He does not
want to risk being identified later, even though there are barely
any people around; it is definitely not the tourist season. Two
women sit at a table in the far opposite corner, drinking coffee,
gossiping, oblivious. He knows it would have been best to stay
in his room, but he does not have the patience he used to. He
orders coffee and an *International Herald Tribune*. Suddenly a
familiar scent of jasmine perfume wafts toward him; sweat
breaks out above his lip immediately, and he feels Josephina
standing at his elbow. He does not look up at her but knows she
is aware he has seen her. She plants herself in the plush chair
opposite him and lights a cigarette. Her hair is collected into a
neat, low bun and she wears a flowing, midnight blue coat.

"You are not as good as you used to be, Amir," she says in
English. "Using an old cover identity on the flight manifesto?
Tsk, tsk. And forgetting to keep your tail clean? Staying at the
Hilton, of all wide-open places? Very sloppy work."

He tries not to clench his teeth. "I am a civilian now, darling
Josephina. My movements are not of your concern." He looks at
his watch. The bus from Van is due to arrive in half an hour, and
the lobby is not where he intends to meet Dariush.

"Am I keeping you from an appointment?" Josephina asks.

He does not answer.

She leans back in the chair, composes her expression, and
crosses her lean legs slowly so he can hear the subtle swooshing
sound of nylon on nylon. "What are you doing here, Amir?" He
had forgotten how she could say menacing things in a sweet,
silky French–Middle Eastern tone.

"I'm here on a personal matter."

She purses her lips to take a sip of Amir's espresso, then grabs
another cigarette from her Dunhill pack, lights it, and says,
"You look pale, Amir. And thin. In fact, you look terrible. I sup-

pose married life does not suit you; you look like you've been living in a camp. Are you sick?"

Amir is confused. Married life? What is she yakking about now? Suddenly, he remembers their last meeting when he told her that Layla was his wife. "I'm quite happy," he says, smiling at the thought, and at the hostility in Josephina's eyes. "Never felt better." He looks at his watch. Fifteen minutes. He calms himself by remembering that this is Turkey; buses are never on time. "Look, Josie. I'd love to chat, but I'm expecting a phone call in my room." He begins to get up, feels the slight tremble in his legs. Josephina puts her hand on his arm; long, perfectly manicured fingers, slick red polish. "Sit down," she says.

Dariush is exhausted. His head aches from the jostling bus ride and also from the steady stream of cigarette smoke over the last forty hours. He has never been to Istanbul. In the old days before the Revolution, it seemed more important to see Europe. Visiting Istanbul had been rather like slumming it. It is drizzling now and a fog hovers over the Bosporus, hiding the spires and domes of the city once called Constantinople—*Ghostantaniyeh*—seat of the powerful Ottoman Empire.

"Ho! Dariush," says Jamsheed, tapping his friend's arm. "Your head feels okay?"

"Yeah, okay."

"Can you believe it? We'll be arriving early. The driver says it's a first."

"May he live forever," says Asya sarcastically. "I want a hot bath more than I want a visa for the U.S."

Amir snatches his arm from Josephina's grasp. As he lowers himself back into the chair, he catches a glimpse through the window of a tour bus lumbering up the drive; he feels as if his bowels are about to move. Quickly, he says, "What do you want from me, Josephina?"

"The truth about why you are here."

He puts his hands up in a gesture of surrender. "All right. I'm here as a consultant for the university, to verify some artifacts. Satisfied?"

Josephina raises an eyebrow. "I don't believe you."

Amir hears the squeak of the air brakes as the bus stops outside. He taps his fingers impatiently on the wide arm of the chair and tells himself to *Think, think!* At least he was smart enough to have chosen a seat with its back to the reception area. He puts his hands in his lap and slinks down a bit more in the wide armchair. Josephina lights another cigarette from the stub of her previous one just as Amir hears the muffled and tired footsteps of refugees approaching the registration desk. He has no choice now; he must sit here until Dariush is checked in and gone to his room. Josephina has ruined his whole plan.

"Well," she says. "I have all day if you're going to play games with me." She calls to the waiter for more coffee, glances over at the registration desk, and frowns. "How interesting," she says.

"What?"

"Looks like there's a foreigner among the Iranian refugees from Van—a tall, blond one. Must be a crazy journalist."

Amir's heart races and he tries to speak slowly. "What does he look like?"

"Like I said. Tall, blond."

It is torture for Amir to keep from turning around.

"Looks like he's been wounded," she continues, eyeing him. "Head wound. Bandages on his forehead. Maybe a limp. Very gaunt. Well, serves him right. Only an idiot goes to the Islamic Republic for a story."

The refugees descend unsurely from the bus, and the doormen watch them with contempt as they walk beneath a wide and long awning into the hotel. Dariush has an uneasy feeling as they approach the registration desk, but chalks it up to fatigue.

Their rooms are ready for them; a roster was sent ahead. "Probably the worst rooms in the whole place," says Jamsheed.

"Probably," Dariush agrees.

"Why?" Asya asks. "And why are they looking at us as if we're criminals?"

"Penniless refugees? Criminals? What's the difference?" says Jamsheed. "What is it, Dariush? Something wrong?"

Dariush hesitates, looks around the large reception area. "No," he finally says. "Nothing. Leftover paranoia. I'm just tired. Do you have our room keys?" Jamsheed drops one into Dariush's palm. "Let's go. I want to call Layla."

Amir catches himself tapping his fingers on his thighs and wriggling in his seat. He takes a deep breath, trying to stave off a powerful eagerness to set eyes on his old friend. He pushes his back against the seat and feels the sweat creeping down his spine toward the Beretta. He closes his eyes briefly in relief; the Beretta is all that matters right now. The sensation of the weapon cutting into his back gives him the strength to squeeze the anxiety out of his thoughts. He must not worry; it is not the first time he has had to modify a plan. He looks over at Josephina, who sits like Jackie Onassis with her straight spine and unreadable expression. Finally, she returns her gaze to him. "Well, the miserable souls have all gone to their moldy rooms. So, shall we go for something to eat?"

"I have no intention of going anywhere with you." He tries not to think about Dariush's hand picking up the telephone in his hotel room and of Layla's lithe fingers bringing the receiver to her ear in Manhattan. He has to get to Dariush before the call is made. Quickly, he sits up. "I told you, I'm here on a personal matter. If you don't believe me, it's because you don't *wish* to. Look, Josie. I have a new life now. I don't give a goddamn about what the Office is up to, so you can forget the notion that I'm here to mess up your operation. I've got a good job as a professor in New York. So leave me alone, would you?"

She falls back in the chair and gives him a crooked smile. His patience spent, Amir suddenly bounces to the edge of his seat, stares at her with his chin tucked in, eyes piercing, breath like a bull's in the ring. She sputters with laughter. He leans forward and covers her hand with his; she tries to pull back but is not fast enough. He squeezes her smaller fingers into a fist, cracking her knuckles, threatening to break every bone. The two gossiping middle-aged housewives, dressed in conservative black, look concerned, but Amir knows they will do nothing. This is the Middle East; what goes on between a man and a woman is up to the man. He pulls Josephina closer to him, close enough to see her small acne craters and the scar he gave her above her left eyebrow, close enough to smell her lipstick and close enough to realize that she is dragging him into a game. He cannot help being impressed by her composure. Her lips are clamped shut and trembling, but that is the only sign of her discomfort. She speaks in a raspy slow voice: "If you hurt me, you will never make it out of this country alive. Are you a fool?"

He releases her and immediately turns away. "I'm going," he says. "If you have any self-respect, you'll leave me be." He begins to turn away and she quickly clutches the sleeve of his jacket.

"All right," she says softly in Hebrew. "Go. I won't bother you anymore." Her tone is oddly crestfallen, and she lowers her eyes from his stare. He is stunned. Finally, he has broken her. He yanks his arm from her grasp and weaves his way swiftly through the lobby and toward the guest rooms.

Dariush has placed his call to New York through the hotel operator. Now, he sits on the gaudy maroon bedspread, his hands clasped between his knees, and waits for the phone to ring. Outside, it is a rainy November afternoon—one year since he lay in a minefield, expecting death, seeing in his mind the strange vision of an unborn child. He smiles. His son is now eight months old. And Layla. Soon, Layla.

The corridor is eerily silent and dim. Out of habit, Amir waits a moment to make sure Josephina has not followed, but he is sure she will not. He pulls out the Beretta, attaches the silencer, and slips it into his jacket pocket, his hand around the butt. His mouth is sticky with dried saliva, and he smells his own nervous fart. If everything had gone as planned, he would have been waiting in the room for Dariush. No matter. *He*, Amir, is the man with the gun.

He begins to walk down the corridor and only when he reaches the door to Dariush's room does he pull the Beretta from his pocket and unhook the gun's safety. The adrenaline is rushing now, but Amir moves slowly and silently as a ghost. He holds the gun with one hand, turns his shoulder to the door, and fits his master key quietly into the knob.

Dariush sits on the bed, back to the door; he feels it open—the slight decompression in the room, a change in air flow. He does not get up from the bed; he is too tired and thinks it must be the maid with extra towels. He half turns and before he can stand up, Amir is in the room, door closed behind him, and pointing the weapon at Dariush's face. The gun, however, is not what Dariush sees. And it is not fear that makes his pulse beat behind his eyes or fills his throat with bile. He does not care if Amir shoots; he wants to break his knuckles on the bastard's skin.

Amir hesitates, knowing that hesitation is failure. But he has never seen this look on Dariush's face. It lures him, enchants him, even consoles him. A look of pure hatred—so irresistible compared to one of indifference. And now his finger does not want to pull the trigger. "My old friend," Amir's oddly quivering voice says. "Your face has changed. You've lost your breeziness. Life is difficult, isn't it? You once had everything, now you have nothing. And you are quite nobody—far from the perfect specimen a certain lovely green-eyed woman thought you were."

Dariush takes one step back and prepares to lunge over the bed and onto Amir, which is just what Amir wants—to kill him when he is thinking only of Amir. But the telephone rings. Two pairs of eyes, one amber, the other ebony, dart toward the sound, then back to watch one another. Both men think of Layla. The ringing phone slices through their nerve endings. Dariush thinks, *I can't let him kill me now*. And Amir thinks, *I must kill him now*. All at once, Dariush reaches for the phone receiver and falls to the floor behind the bed. He calls "Layla!" but it is too late; the dial tone drones. He hears a thump against the edge of the mattress above his arm, and a small burst of feathers and bits of cotton batting rains down on him. The bullet then passes through him, he does not know where exactly—near his shoulder, his chest, his neck? Warm blood soaks his shirt and he waits for unconsciousness or Amir's next bullet, but neither comes. *You cannot kill me twice, bastard.*

Amir's head jerks to the left for a split second as he realizes that the door behind him is opening. There is no time to do anything, certainly not to turn and shoot. Josephina's foot kicks the gun from his hand, then kicks his groin, purposely driving the point of her spiked heel into the soft wrinkles of his left testicle. He writhes on the floor. She retrieves the gun and kicks Amir several times, breaking a rib, bruising a kidney, gashing his brow. Then she moves away. He can vaguely make her out, standing with her gun pointed at the floor behind the bed where Dariush had fallen. Above his own rapid breathing, he hears her trying to speak in very poor Farsi to Dariush.

"Who are you?" she says. It comes out *Who were you?*

Amir listens for a response. Nothing.

"Who are you?" she tries again. This time, it comes out *You are who me?*

Nothing. Amir holds his breath.

Then "Who the hell are you?" says Dariush in English, his voice raspy and weak.

Nonononono rings in Amir's ears. Tears of pain sting his eyes, and he feels as if he is spiraling down a cold tunnel. He pictures Dariush's face, not filled with hatred, but sanguine and mischievous and eager, beckoning to Amir the way he did when they were boys. His chest twists with loss and he looks across what seems like a sea of brown carpet and focuses on a pair of faded cloth slippers that he soon realizes belong to the blind fortune catcher, sitting on the floor, his back comfortably against the bed. Amir groans and the soothsayer smiles with pity. He says, "This is not your *ghesmat, aghayeh aziz.* You are meant to have what you want." He leans in until Amir can see a reflection of blue lights on his black lenses and the spittle at the corners of his mouth. He lowers his voice to a rattling whisper that reminds Amir of his father's voice. "You can take him with you, *agha,*" he says. "Take him with you."

A current of strength spirits through Amir's broken body. The fortune catcher is gone and Josephina kneels next to him; he can see up her skirt to her white, lacy crotch. Gunmetal touches his temple. He begins to talk, tastes salty blood from his own tongue.

"I never loved you, Josie. Never." Even in his pain, he is delighted by her stricken look. He wants to chuckle, but instead he begins to cough and realizes suddenly that maybe his lung is punctured.

Josephina's face is marked with anguish. "You are deep in the pit of your tortured life, Amir Hakim," she chokes out. "Tell me, how can I have ever wanted you?" She presses the point of the gun deeper into his skin and begins to cry. Without warning Amir reaches up and clamps his hand around her delicate throat; she startles and drops the gun behind him. She cannot make a sound, he knows. He feels expertly for the arteries in her neck and knows when he has blinded her by cutting off blood flow to her optic nerve. Her hands are clasped around his arm, but his muscle is locked like stone. Soon he will have his gun back and, even if he must crawl, he will go and finish what he was meant to do: *He will take Dariush with him.*

Moments ago, when the woman stood over him with the gun, Dariush was sure it was the end, that his son would one day know that his father had been found dead on a dirty floor in the corner of a Turkish hotel room.

He had not been afraid, only enraged—at Amir, at Maman Bozorg, at himself, at his destiny, at God. He had only vaguely heard the woman trying to talk to him; maybe he had been in a death trance. Then his own voice had spoken, weak, distant, almost gone. And the woman was bending over him, asking his name, checking the bullet wound, smiling in a bittersweet way. She had shredded the pillowcase and tied a piece of it around his left arm. "Lie still," she told him in a tone that reminded him of Mariam.

He had slept, perhaps for a moment, though it feels like it could have been a whole day. His stomach hurts, cramping like a fist is trying to come through his skin from the inside. Instinctively and despite the pain in his damaged arm, his head reeling from blood loss, he struggles upright and grips his middle. The pain suddenly flies away. There, beyond the rumpled surface of the bed, he sees what at first looks like a stone sculpture of the woman on her knees, hands at her throat, eyes with that certain creamy void of a Renaissance sculpture. His mind is sluggish.

What is she doing? Why is she so silent? And so pale? And where is Amir? He blinks twice, rubs his eyes with his good arm, and finally comprehends the scene, finally sees that Amir, though injured on the floor, has still enough insanity and viciousness and strength in him to murder.

Dariush throws his right arm across the bed and grips the quilted spread. He hoists himself up onto his knees; his muscles feel like liquid and he cannot stand. The woman's lips are tinged with blue. His heart pumps hard with urgency and exertion as he painstakingly drags himself onto and across the bed; his other arm is useless and leaks blood like a punctured water hose. As he gets closer, he hears Amir's labored breathing and grunting. Vomit rises into his mouth, spilling onto the bed. He closes his eyes for a second. *No thinking, no thinking. Just doing. Move!* With one last froglike push of his legs, he reaches the edge of the bed and looks down on Amir's back, his curled-up body, the straining veins in his taut arm, trembling with the effort to end the woman's life. Dariush reaches down and picks up the Beretta, searching for the strength to keep the heavy weapon steady, on target. "Let her go," he rasps. Amir twists his head toward Dariush as quickly as a crocodile snaps. His face is contorted, his bottom lip swollen and bleeding from his own teeth marks; Dariush remembers how Amir had always bitten his bottom lip when something required his full concentration—when they were boys, so long ago. He thinks, Could this animal have been my friend? "Let her go," Dariush says again.

And he does. She drops like a marionette, unconscious.

"You will never shoot," says Amir in Farsi. "You are not brave like me, Dasha."

Slowly, tiredly, Dariush says, "I don't care to be like you."

Amir's eyes go dull with defeat. He swallows his twisted smile and in one swift motion, he rolls over, clamps his hands over the Beretta as Dariush holds it, and shoves the barrel into his own mouth. Before Dariush can wrench himself free, Amir slides his thumb over his old friend's trigger finger and squeezes.

For an instant, Amir is pleased.

Then, nothing.

Fifty-Five

Layla

The phone rang differently that day; it sounded like laughter. I know it's silly, but that's how I remember it. When I heard his voice, I just cried. We both did. He told me where he was and I said I was coming. He said no; he didn't want me on that side of the world and away from our son. What I could do was get them U.S. visas.

Of course, I tried to reach Amir immediately. The phone was disconnected. I went to his apartment, despite how our last meeting there had turned out, and the landlady said she was looking for him too, that he was a month late on his rent. I found his office at the university, but it was being used by someone else, another professor of Persian poetry, an Iranian who knew only that the previous professor had missed so many classes that he was asked to leave several weeks before. It was all so strange and I had this feeling Dariush knew something about it when I called him the next day to say that I couldn't find Amir to help with the visas. There was silence. "Are you there?" I'd said nervously—overreacting—visualizing some evil *mullah* snatching him away even as we spoke. "I'm here, *azizam*," he said, his voice strangely despondent. "Don't count on being able to find Amir."

I was on my own. I'd have to get the visas like everyone else. Legally.

It was not easy. I couldn't prove that Dariush was my husband or that Davy was his child. The people at Immigration wouldn't even consider Asya and Jamsheed. They told me to forget it; there was a long list of Iranians wanting visas, and nobody could be bumped up. I went back several times, hoping a different agent would be more accommodating. None were. All I had to do was mention Iran and they began to shake their heads. My father and Dariush's parents were having the same trouble in Europe. No one wanted them, could care less about them.

I was beginning to panic. We'd wired Dariush money, but how long could we keep that up? I tried not to think of the stories about it taking years to get visas in Istanbul because there were so many Iranians there. Finally, I went to Immigration again. This time I took off my shoes and my socks. The agent was a plump guy who smelled like bananas. "Excuse me," he said. "What're you doing there, young lady?"

I stuck out my legs and felt a twinge of embarrassment when he winced and looked away. "Iranian government officials did that to me," I said. "They've done a lot worse to my husband. And the people who are traveling with him saved both our lives and got us out of that country." He said nothing, but his expression was thoughtful, penetrating. I continued. "Please. Grant them visas; they need political asylum. I promise they'll make good Americans." He rubbed his face with a pudgy hand, leaned heavily over his cluttered desk, then inserted a piece of paper into his typewriter. "You can put your shoes back on, young lady. You got me in the heart. Call them. Tell them to go to the American embassy in Istanbul day after tomorrow and pick up their entry permits."

At the airport, Banu continued to insist that she hold Davy in her arms. He was clearly happier there than in the stroller; bumping him up and down against her hip gave Banu a way of expending nervous energy. Davy, all of nine months old now and oblivious to almost anything but infant reality, was mesmerized by the huge flags hanging above us, flags that had hung from the railing in the International Arrivals Building at Kennedy for as long as I could remember.

As usual, it was crowded. It was mid-December, and Christmas travelers were already trickling in. People were dressed in all kinds of costumes and babbling in foreign tongues—all craning their necks to catch the first glimpse of their loved ones emerging from Customs and Immigration. We were no different.

Where was he? His flight had landed an hour and a half ago. I knew he might have to answer some questions because of his political asylum papers. I wished he wasn't alone; Jamsheed and Asya could only get tickets for next week's flight. And Jamsheed had said Dariush's head had been injured. They'd X-rayed it in Istanbul and found a small fracture; the doctors said it would heal with time and rest, but Jamsheed wanted Dariush to be seen by the doctors here as soon as possible.

Was that him? Oh God. That blond hair, it was the right color. But no. A man in a suit with a mustache and a huge nose. Not him at all. How different would he look? Would I recognize him? Of course I would. Would he recognize me? With my short hair and still some weight from the pregnancy and these dark smudges under my eyes from Davy's night bottles?

He would be different, I knew. We'd spoken on the phone as much as possible during the past weeks, and I was a little worried. Could a year apart change the shape of two people enough to make them like worn puzzle pieces that don't quite fit together as snugly as when they were just out of the box? We would have to learn about one another again. Well, I thought, we would see. No use worrying now. He was alive and coming home and there was no chance in hell that some insane military general or filthy *pasdar* or fanatic *mullah* would grab him from me now.

Banu's bird voice behind me talked softly to Davy, calling him her American boy; unbelievably, she'd come to think of this phrase as an endearment. She was changing, but not in every way. The night before, in her excitement over Dariush's arrival, she'd said, "You do not know how comforting it is for me to know that you are not abandoned and that Dariush is coming back to take care of you."

Suddenly, I saw him step out from the swinging doors, a bag in one hand, his other arm in a sling, and I knew what Banu had said the night before had been way off the mark. I think she knew it too, because I heard her voice stop in midsentence and she held her breath, as I did, while he walked down the path from Immigration. He didn't see us right away. He seemed to be looking, but *not* looking at the same time, as if he couldn't really concentrate. His hair was long, to his shoulders. Messy. Dull, like his eyes. He was incredibly skinny; the jeans he wore sagged everywhere. I couldn't wait to hold him in my arms. I stepped forward on quivering legs. When he saw me, he hesitated and closed his eyes for a second as if saying a prayer. I saw the terrible scar above his temple, and something in my chest twisted painfully. Now we both had wounds and scars that would be a part of us forever, that would be a part of whatever we made of our lives. I saw myself in him, saw myself as I'd been a whole year before, suffering and hurting and confused. He would heal, I told myself. I would help him.

He dropped his bag and embraced me, leaned against me for support. He said my name over and over and squeezed me tighter and tighter and it felt like he was siphoning my dreams back into me. It was like falling off a cliff onto a cloud. I kissed and kissed his neck, his damp cheeks, his mouth. Finally, he looked over at Davy and his lip trembled. He quickly gave Banu a kiss on the cheek, then carefully raised his hand and caressed Davy's soft face with shaky fingers. Davy frowned, undecided. He was definitely not into strangers. Then, in an instant, he smiled, gripped his father's finger, and held on.